TENDER THE STORM

ELIZABETH THORNTON

ZEBRA BOOKS
Kensington Publishing Corp.
http://www.kensingtonbooks.com

ZEBRA BOOKS are published by

Kensington Publishing Corp.
850 Third Avenue
New York, NY 10022

All Kensington titles, imprints and distributed lines are available at special quantity discounts for bulk purchases for sales promotion, premiums, fund-raising, educational or institutional use.

Special book excerpts or customized printings can also be created to fit specific needs. For details, write or phone the office of the Kensington Special Sales Manager: Kensington Publishing Corp., 850 Third Avenue, New York, NY 10022. Attn. Special Sales Department. Phone: 1-800-221-2647.

Zebra and the Z logo Reg. U.S. Pat. & TM Off.

First Zebra Printing: August 2002
First Pinnacle Printing: June 1991
10 9 8 7 6 5 4 3 2

Printed in the United States of America

Books by Elizabeth Thornton

TENDER THE STORM

THE PERFECT PRINCESS

PRINCESS CHARMING

STRANGERS AT DAWN

WHISPER HIS NAME

YOU ONLY LOVE TWICE

THE BRIDE'S BODYGUARD

DANGEROUS TO HOLD

DANGEROUS TO KISS

DANGEROUS TO LOVE

Chapter One

Carte blanche. The shock of the words left Zoë speech-less. It was not so with the other girls. Mademoiselle had taken a lover, and the whole school buzzed with the scandal of it. The babble in the dormitory had faded to whispers when Madame's maid called for silence as she doused the candles on her rounds. But schoolgirls be-ing schoolgirls, they pursued the topic of conversation beneath the bedclothes in hushed tones and intermit-tent bursts of suppressed girlish giggles.

Zoë pulled the bedcovers up to her chin and let the words revolve in her mind. *Carte blanche.* She could not, would not believe that Mademoiselle would sink to such a level. Mademoiselle was everything that was good. Her virtue was unquestionable. And she, Zoë, had the best reason in the world for her convictions. Though none of the girls knew it, Mademoiselle was her sister. Claire would no more accept *carte blanche* from any man than she would betray her family to the commissioners who had set up the guillotine in Rouen's market square. They were Devereux, and though be-reft of their parents' guiding hand for the moment, to shake off the tenets by which they had been raised was unthinkable.

"Fleur? Are you awake?"

It took a moment for Zoë to realize that the question was addressed to her. Fleur was the name she went by now, and had been for the last several weeks, since she had been placed in Madame Lambert's Boarding School for Girls. Fleur Guéry, her papers said, an orphan of fourteen years. *Maman* had told her that she must forget the name Zoë Devereux. She must forget that she was a young lady who had just celebrated her seventeenth birthday. She must dress and act the part of a silly schoolgirl until they could escape from France. One day, when the madness was over, they would return. But for the present, the name of Devereux was anathema to *enragés* such as Robespierre and St. Just.

"Are you awake?"

"Mmm," murmured Zoë discouragingly.

The girl in the next cot raised on one elbow. "Fleur," she whispered, "what does *carte blanche* mean?"

Zoë rolled to her side, facing the shadowy form of the girl in the next bed. The question was a serious one and deserved a serious answer. Softly, deliberately, she said, "*Carte blanche* is what a man offers a woman when he wants all the pleasures of marriage but none of the responsibilities."

There was a pause. "I don't think I understand."

Zoë sighed inaudibly. The exchange was extraordinarily reminiscent of the one she had had with her own mother when she, too, had heard the words *carte blanche* for the first time. Her thoughts drifted to that day, three years before, in the early days of the Revolution, when there was still a semblance of order in the world.

The Devereux house in the Faubourg, St. Germain was a happy place. Happy, carefree, and, most of all, cloistered behind its monumental iron gates and walled courtyard. Leon Devereux had removed his family to this more secluded setting on the other side of the Seine to protect the innocence of his daughters from the

6

growing depravity which was evident everywhere in the streets of Paris. He was to learn that depravity, like an insidious fog, could not be kept out by locked doors and stone walls.

"*Maman?* What does *carte blanche* mean?" Zoë could hear the sound of her own voice, as if she had just uttered the words.

She'd heard them first on the lips of her younger brother, Leon, named for his father, when he had been in conversation with his tutor. There was something about the way Leon had smiled, something about the way the tutor had frowned when they had caught sight of her which had instantly aroused her curiosity. And that Leon, later, refused to explain the words to her when they were in private was not to be borne. She was older than he by a good twelve months.

"*Maman?* What does *carte blanche* mean?"

The ladies were in the morning room which overlooked the sweep of lawns and the river. Madame Devereux was planning the week's menus. Her daughters were occupied with mending sheets and table linen. Though there were maids who could just as easily have done this menial task, Madame Devereux firmly believed that there was no aspect of household management to which her daughters should not be able to turn their hand. In this she was following her own mother's precepts.

After Zoë voiced her question, there was a protracted silence. Claire paused in mid-stitch and looked up questioningly. When their mother's cheeks began to glow with color, both girls became alert.

As a mother, Madame Devereux was out of step with her generation. Her daughters knew it. Unlike their friends' mothers, Elise Devereux never shrank from answering her daughters' questions, however delicate or improper others might judge them. Claire and Zoë had no misapprehensions about what awaited them on their respective wedding nights. They knew how babies were conceived and how they were born. Through hints and innuendo they understood that their mother wished to spare them some of the anguish she had suffered, through ignorance, when she had first become a bride. Marital relations were not something a wife was to endure, Madame Devereux had carefully pointed out. The act of love was the supreme expression of everything a husband and wife felt for each other.

Leon was never present when these conversations took place. Sometimes the girls surmised that their father must be the source of information for his son as their mother was for her daughters. At other times, they deduced that the male of the species was born knowing everything there was to know about relations between the sexes. It had never occurred to Claire and Zoë that this act of intimacy could take place between a man and woman who were not husband and wife. Their mother had never hinted at such a thing until Zoë had asked her bald question. Leon, the youngest of the Devereux children, had known it long before.

Zoë's thoughts came back to the present. She sighed again and looked over at her companion. She judged Marie Roussillon to be about fourteen years. Certainly old enough to begin to learn something of the ways of a man with a woman. Drawing on what she remembered from her mother's conversation, she embarked on an explanation.

"Some women sell their beauty and bodies for money. Not respectable women, you understand. Not the kind of women gentlemen marry, but the other sort."

"Oh," said Marie, and lapsed into a reflective silence. After a moment, she said, "Do you think any gentleman will ever offer us *carte blanche* when we

8

are grown up?"

"No," answered Zoë emphatically. "We are good girls. We have been raised and educated to be wives and mothers."

There was no immediate response to this gem of wisdom. But Marie had by no means exhausted the subject of conversation as her next question was to prove. "Do . . . do ladies ever offer *carte blanche* to gentlemen? What I mean to say is—do gentlemen ever sell themselves to women for money?"

"Not to my knowledge," answered Zoë truthfully, and she wondered why she had never thought to ask her mother that question.

"Fleur?"

"Mmm?"

"Mademoiselle is beautiful, isn't she?"

"Yes." It was a circumstance which had been of grave concern to their parents, particularly Madame Devereux. Manners and mores had been changing so rapidly in Revolutionary France that it was no longer possible for a father to examine too closely the background and credentials of the gentlemen who came to his house and who must be introduced to his daughters, especially to his beautiful elder daughter.

"And . . . and do you think Mademoiselle is a good woman or the other sort?"

Zoë did not have to deliberate before answering, "Mademoiselle is a good woman, naturally."

"But if she has accepted a gentleman's *carte blanche* . . ."

Zoë snorted. "I won't believe it unless I hear the words from her own lips."

"Then where is she? Why did Madame Lambert send Clothilde and not Mademoiselle to douse the candles?"

Zoë was troubled by the selfsame question. No answer came to her. "Go to sleep, Marie," she said quietly. "I'm sure everything will be explained at assembly tomorrow morning."

But her own advice was easier to offer than to follow. Sleep evaded her. It seemed that every small sound in that Spartan dormitory became magnified to a disturbing pitch. Anxious and restless, Zoë groped in her mind for answers. As time passed, her thoughts lost focus. Memories crept up on her and she gave up the struggle to suppress them.

They had come for their parents on a wet and blustery night at the end of October — was it only two months ago? Her father's only crime was that he was a rich man and formerly a friend of the aristocrats. Leon Devereux was a banker and financier with international influence. It was enough to doom him and his whole family.

Zoë would never forget the scene. They were in the *salle,* a room she could never remember without thinking of sunshine. It had been done over in her mother's favorite color, from pale primrose yellow to deep tones of gold. As she did every evening, Zoë seated herself at the piano, at her father's request, and played a selection from Mozart, his favorite composer. She knew the pieces by memory, and could let her thoughts wander as her fingers moved effortlessly over the keyboard.

This was to be their last night together in the house in St. Germain. Leon Devereux had come to see, more and more, that his days were numbered. Of the gravest concern to him was the fate of his family if ever anything should happen to him. It was a familiar tale. Executions of whole families, except for very young children, followed quickly upon one another. He had determined it would not happen to his. Under assumed names and identities, with forged papers, they were to hide out in Rouen.

The family was to be scattered, but not for long. Leon Devereux had friends. He had put things in motion. When everything was in place, they would sail for America or England. He had no preference. It was enough to escape the terrors of France.

Meanwhile, the two younger children, Zoë and Leon, were to take up residence in separate boarding schools in Rouen. Claire, too old to pass herself off as a schoolgirl, was to join Zoë at Madame Lambert's, but, as an added precaution, her relationship to Zoë was to be concealed. Only Madame Lambert, the head mistress and proprietress of the school, was to be taken into their confidence. Madame Lambert and Madame Devereux had been, in their youth, on the friendliest terms. Over the years, they had kept up a correspondence. For friendship's sake, Madame Lambert had agreed to employ Claire as a teacher of piano and voice. The parents were to go into hiding with a local locksmith, who, for a considerable sum of money, had agreed to conceal them in a tiny, windowless room above his workshop.

Their last night together was to be spent as normally as possible. Only one servant knew of their circumstances. Salome was Madame Devereux's personal maid and had been with Madame Devereux since before her marriage. She was from the island of San Domingo. Her skin was as brown as coffee. In these circumstances, concealment was impossible. Salome understood this. When it was safe to do so, she would rejoin the family in the country of their adoption.

It was Salome who went to answer the sudden pounding at the front door. Over the preceding months, Leon Devereux had unobtrusively reduced his staff of servants, especially the ones whose loyalty was questionable. Many people of his class had been betrayed to the Tribunal on the word of a less-than-honest retainer. It was better by far to do for themselves and to rest easy in their beds at night than to be waited on hand and foot by servants who were not to be trusted.

The pounding came again, and Zoë started to her feet only to be told by her father to continue playing. His quiet, reassuring manner brought a modicum of calm to them all. Leon, who was very much in his father's image, was the first to collect himself. Though he was a year younger than Zoë , she envied him his poise. As if nothing of any moment were taking place, he returned to the game of chess in which he and Claire were engaged.

But something of fearful, awful moment was taking place as they were to discover almost immediately. Deputies from the Commune burst through the doors of the *salle*. The domestic scene which met their eyes halted them in their tracks. But the respite was only momentary. They had come to arrest Leon Devereux and his wife on charges of conspiracy to treason. Resistance was useless, as the warning glance which Leon Devereux shot at his young son was meant to convey. Leon's threatening stance relaxed somewhat when, in answer to his father's question, the chief deputy reported that he was to convey Leon Devereux and his wife to the Abbaye prison. It did not seem as if the authorities were in a hurry to bring the Devereux's to trial, else they would have been lodged in the Conciergerie which adjoined the Palais de Justice. There were no warrants for the arrest of the younger members of the Devereux family. But no one was deceived into thinking that that would not soon follow.

Leon Devereux conducted himself with remarkable restraint. Madame Devereux took her cue from her husband. She was the daughter of a general. There would be no sign of cowardice from her.

They embraced their children in turn. "You must

proceed with your lives as normally as possible," was their father's parting advice. "Our arrest must not interfere with your progress." His words were weighted with meaning.

Zoë did not know what was to be done. Her brother was all for brazening it out in Paris and organizing an escape attempt. It was Claire's will which prevailed. Nothing would sway her from the course her father had set for them. She was the eldest. Leon Devereux had impressed upon her what must be done should they be overtaken by events. They were to set out for Rouen in the morning as arranged. She had promised their father that she would follow his instructions to the letter.

From the moment of their parents' arrest, Claire had become a different person. Zoë had never remarked such resolution, such clear-eyed determination in her sister. Both Devereux girls had been educated for nothing more taxing than their future roles as wives and mothers. Their accomplishments in the feminine arts were unquestionable. They had not expected that they would have to make their own way in the world. In their social circles, there was always some male in the background, a father, a husband, a brother, who would direct their affairs. Leon was not yet sixteen and too young to assume the responsibilities of a man. Claire was the eldest. She assumed the mantle of guardianship for her younger siblings as if she had been bred for the task.

Carte blanche. The words drummed inside Zoë's head. Under the bed clothes, she stirred restlessly. Mademoiselle had accepted *carte blanche* from one of Robespierre's commissioners to Rouen. No. It was impossible. She would not believe it until she heard it from Claire's own lips.

* * *

When Mademoiselle did not appear for breakfast the following morning, Zoë's habitual serenity suffered a fracture. Her thoughts lacked coherence. Her conversation became disjointed. The girls scarcely spared her a glance until Zoë herself became the focus of attention.

Without warning, during morning assembly, and before Madame had the opportunity of explaining Mademoiselle's absence, a deputy arrived at the school demanding to see the papers of one Fleur Guéry. With an unquiet heart, Zoë filed past silent girls and went to the dormitory to fetch her documents.

When she returned, the deputy was ensconced with Madame in her study. Zoë's legs seemed to have turned to water as she handed over her forged papers.

As the deputy studied them, Zoë's eyes wandered over him. She judged him to be in his late twenties. Though his dress was meticulous, it was restrained, and of the sort gentlemen once reserved for the country. His long, cut away coat embraced broad shoulders and flared at the back over tight-fitting, white duck pantaloons. His spurred boots, *à la hussarde,* were spotless. His knotted cravat, beneath his white waistcoat, boasted no lace, nor even a frill. The hilt of his shortsword gleamed brightly at the loop on his waistband.

His turnout was immaculate. There was only one incongruous note. On top of his crop of dark blond hair, he was wearing the red cap of the Revolution, originally the badge of the *sans-culottes,* and now worn by those who were fanatically loyal to Robespierre and Jacobin principles. That one article of clothing changed the young man's pleasantly handsome appearance into something more sinister.

"You are Fleur Guéry?"

Gray eyes, cold and indifferent, gazed dispassionately at Zoë. She nodded in affirmation.

"You're to come with me. Fetch your belongings."

The words froze Zoë's blood in her veins. She looked helplessly at Madame.

If Madame was frightened, she did not show it. Her manner was everything that was gracious, as she interposed her own considerable bulk between Zoë and the young deputy.

"There must be some mistake, surely," she began pleasantly. "I have known Fleur's family these many years past. I can vouch for the girl's identity."

"Her identity is not in question," said the deputy. Zoë found his voice as cold as his eyes. "Fetch your belongings," he instructed curtly, his gaze resting on Zoë's bowed head. His voice warmed slightly when he added, "Child, the Revolution does not make war on schoolgirls."

It was far from the truth as Zoë well knew, but somehow she found the words comforting. She chanced a quick look at the deputy and thought she detected a softening in him. Without the red cap, he might even appear human, she decided. The thought emboldened her to appeal to his better nature.

"Monsieur," she began, and got no farther.

The deputy's hand slammed on the flat of Madame's desk. Zoë fell back. "There are no ladies and gentlemen in modern France," he yelled. "You will address me as *'citoyen,'* do you understand, *citoyenne?"*

Zoë did. These new forms of address were adopted to promote equality among all France's citizens. In public, everyone paid lip service to this latest directive. In private, and among friends, people adhered to the old ways. She had made a blunder and quaked at her folly.

'Where are you taking her?" asked Madame, diverting the deputy's attention to herself.

"Commissioner Duhet wishes to question her," was the short answer.

At the mention of Duhet's name, Madame seemed to

15

regain some of her composure. "I'll help you pack," she said, and without waiting for permission, swept Zoë from the room.

In point of fact, there was very little to pack, only a change of clothes and nothing of any value or anything which could betray Zoë's real identity. It took only a moment or two to place everything that Zoë owned in the world into a worn grip.

"Everything will be fine, you'll see," said Madame as she personally tied the strings of Zoë's bonnet under her chin. She patted Zoë consolingly on the shoulder. "I had hoped to have a few words with you in private to explain . . ."

The door opened, and Madame's voice faded as the young deputy entered the dormitory. He lounged against the door, saying nothing, but his very presence was intimidating. Zoë had not realized the man was so tall. She was conscious of his scrutiny, and her heartbeat accelerated in alarm.

"W-won't I be returning?" asked Zoë, appealing to Madame.

It was the deputy who answered. "That depends on the commissioner. It's more than likely."

"There, there, child. Don't fret," said Madame. She darted Zoë a significant look. "I'll be sure to let Citoyonne Michelet know what has become of you." Michelet was the name by which Claire was passing herself off.

There was nothing more to say. Squaring her shoulders, and with a last glance around the drab interior where she had found refuge for the last number of weeks, Zoë allowed the deputy to conduct her from the premises.

Madame Lambert's School for Girls was situated close to Rouen's Vieux Marché. Zoë shivered involuntarily as the deputy directed her, with a touch on the elbow, towards the market district. It was here, in the fifteenth century, where Jeanne D'Arc had been burned at the stake. And it was here that the guillotine had been set up when Commissioner Duhet had arrived the month before with orders from the Convention to purge the city of anti-Revolutionary elements.

When they came into the square, Zoë averted her gaze from the bloody instrument of execution. For the moment, it lay idle. By the middle of the afternoon, tumbrils with their human cargo would arrive from the Palais de Justice, and the slaughter would begin. Zoë had never seen an execution nor ever wanted to. But she had heard the roll of drums which preceded the fall of each head. The sound carried for miles around, and a deathly stillness seemed to envelope the city while the executions were in progress.

In a curt undertone, the deputy admonished, "Do you wish to be thought unpatriotic? Lift your head, child. Do not call attention to yourself."

Zoë obeyed automatically. Under cover of drawing her short mantle more closely about her, she glanced sideways at her companion.

Unsmiling, the deputy urged her forward.

They made their way downhill through Rouen's busy, cobbled streets towards the docks. The inhabitants were going about their business with as much confidence as they could summon. Though arrest and summary execution were commonplace for the most paltry reasons, a man had to earn a living to provide for his family. Already, the bread queues were forming so that citizens could procure their meagre ration of black bread for the day.

When they came to the Hotel Crosne, where Commissioner Duhet had set up his headquarters, they halted.

"Stay close," said the deputy as he ushered Zoë into the foyer. She felt the sure touch of his hand at her back

17

as he drew her closer to the broad shield of his body. Startled, she lifted her head to slant him a curious glance, but the deputy was looking straight ahead.

He led her past groups of raucous soldiers interspersed with cowering supplicants who had come to plead for relatives who had been arrested during the night. At the sight of the tall, stony-faced young deputy with his red cap, the throng parted to let him pass.

Up one flight of stairs, the deputy slowed his steps. He rapped brusquely on a door. A feminine voice bade him enter. He opened the door and pushed Zoë through before closing it soundlessly at her back.

Zoë stood transfixed, staring at the young woman who came to greet her. "M-Mademoiselle," she stammered, even in that moment of intense relief and emotion, remembering not to betray her sister by voicing her real name.

Inexplicably, Claire's cheeks went hot with color. Before Zoë could do more than register this interesting fact, she was swept up in a tearful embrace. It was to be some minutes before the sisters drew apart.

No one who did not know them would have taken the two girls for sisters. Claire's long flame-colored hair framed a perfectly oval face. Her eyes were blue, her skin translucently pale. Leon Devereux avowed that his beautiful, elder daughter was in the image of his maternal grandmother, and he had in his possession a miniature to prove it. Zoë, like the rest of the Devereux's, was of a darker cast. Her expressive brown eyes, huge, arresting, and fringed with long, sooty lashes were her best feature. Her abundance of thick hair, which fell to her waist in the manner of a young girl, was too straight for her taste. She was impatient with it, and had looked forward to the day when it might be swept up or sheared into one of the shorter, classical styles which were coming into vogue. Circumstances had de-

18

creed, however, that she preserve the mode of a school-girl.

It was not only in looks that Claire and Zoë were opposites. Of the two, Claire was the more gregarious and impulsive. It was not precisely that Zoë was shy. But she was more reserved. Claire had a way with people. Zoë was uncomfortable with strangers, especially if those strangers happened to be gentlemen. Claire was never stuck for a subject of conversation. Zoë had no small talk. They were as different as night and day. But they were sisters and they were devoted to each other.

When she could find her voice, Zoë exclaimed, "Claire! Have we . . . are we under arrest?"

"No, dearest. Far from it," answered Claire, smiling and laughing. With a swish of skirts, she propelled Zoë to a small table which had been set for two. "At long last, Papa's friends have found us. Oh, darling, just think, within the hour, you will be on the first lap of your journey to England! Now, come and eat, and I'll tell you all about it."

Speechless, Zoë set her grip aside and allowed her sister to remove her bonnet and cloak before accepting the chair which Claire indicated. Another odd note registered. While the rest of Rouen battled with starvation, Claire's table was lavishly set with mouth-watering savory pastries, delectably soft bread, and a selection of preserved fruits.

"Eat," instructed Claire softly, and took the seat opposite. She leaned her elbows on the table, and rested her chin on her folded hands. It was evident that she was not to share in the repast. Her pleasure was to be in watching her sister consume the sort of delicacies they had not enjoyed in years.

Zoë obediently selected a pastry and cut into it. The aroma of braised chicken tickled her nostrils. She brought her fork to her mouth and nibbled delicately at the morsel she had speared, tasting nothing. Her reflections became more involved as she began to take stock of her surroundings. On another level, she absorbed her sister's words as Claire began to speak.

It was evident that Claire occupied a suite of rooms. The furnishings were not elegant, but far superior to the normal run of hotel furniture. A fire blazed in the grate, and two commodious armchairs had been placed close to the hearth for comfort. Zoë's eyes shifted to take in Claire.

Her sister was dressed in the mode she had adopted since they had arrived at Madame Lambert's. A girls' school was no place for the flimsy, high-waisted muslins which were becoming fashionable in Paris. Not that their mother had ever permitted them to adopt the current mode.

Claire's long-sleeved chemise gown was in gray taffeta and tied at the waist with a long sash. The full skirt brushed the floor. Though the neckline was low and laced in front, it was artfully filled in with a white lacy fichu. Claire's decorous aspect should have been reassuring. Zoë felt her alarm growing. Her sister had given her not one word of explanation for her changed circumstances.

"Did you hear what I said?" asked Claire when she came to the end of her recitation.

Carefully, Zoë set down her cutlery. "I heard you," she answered quietly. "I am to be conveyed to Coutances and from there I shall be taken to Jersey and thence on to England."

"The story is that you are to be questioned by Commissioner Duhet respecting the identity of Jean Guéry, our father's cousin. He has been accused of treason."

"I understand," replied Zoë. Her memory was phenomenal. She rarely needed to be told something twice. "And what about you and Leon? Do we go together?"

Claire shook her head. "No. It's not possible for the moment. As soon as may be, Leon and I shall join you in England."

"Why is it impossible?"

Claire brushed back an errant strand of hair from her cheek. "There is only one passport. It's made out in the name of Fleur Guéry. Philippe . . . that is, Papa's friend, says that these things take time. Just be patient, Zoë, and we'll all be together soon, I promise you."

Disregarding her sister's advice, Zoë demanded, "Why is the passport in my name? Leon is the youngest. If only one can go, it should be he."

"You know our brother. He wouldn't accept it," said Claire flatly.

Zoë considered Claire's words. Leon, as they both well knew, had never been susceptible to petticoat government. Though he was only fifteen, he considered himself a man. A mother's wishes must count for something. Sisters were a different matter. He accepted Claire's authority only because his father, before his arrest, had told him that he must.

"He's being rebellious?" mused Zoë absently. It was more of a statement than a question.

"Need you ask?"

A look of amused comprehension passed between them.

"Shall I see him before I go?"

"It's not possible," answered Claire. Her attention was taken with the preserved fruits which were artfully arranged in a pedestal dish on the center of the table. Selecting a plum, which she scrutinized carefully, she went on, "You must leave within the hour. Leon could not leave the school without occasioning comment."

Zoë swallowed the lump which had become lodged in

21

her throat. She felt that she was living through a nightmare. She wished she could waken from it and find herself in her own chamber, in the house in St. Germain, and with her family restored to her.

When she could find her voice, she asked, "What news of Mama and Papa?"

"They are well," answered Claire quickly. Too quickly.

"And?" prompted Zoë.

Claire shrugged helplessly. "They've been moved from the Abbaye." At Zoë's stricken look she added quickly, "Don't look like that, darling! It's not the Conciergerie. They're in the prison of Les Carmes."

"Oh God! What does it mean?"

"Nothing," interposed Claire. "Nothing at all. I shouldn't have told you. You're not to worry about it, do you understand? We have friends who are working on their behalf. Things are not quite hopeless yet, Zoë."

"You're right, of course," said Zoë, trying to wipe the despair from her voice.

"That's better, darling. Now eat, if you please. There's not much time, and you have a long journey ahead of you."

Zoë did not return Claire's smile. The unasked questions which teemed inside her head were being answered in ways she could not like. For two months, they had kicked their heels in Rouen. If their father had friends who were supposed to help them, they would never have known it. No one approached them. They were coming to accept that they would have to remain as they were until the storm in France had passed. Now, suddenly, there seemed to be no end to the help they could call on. Why?

Scraping back her chair, Zoë burst out, "Why are you here, Claire? Where did this food come from? Is it true what they are saying?"

"Dearest! Don't upset yourself like this! What should I be doing here? Papa has powerful friends. Didn't he tell us so? I'm here as a guest of those friends, nothing more."

For a moment, it seemed as if Zoë would pursue that subject. But there was something in her sister's stare which made her own eyes fall away. In a more subdued tone, she said, "This Philippe of whom you speak. Is he Philippe Duhet?"

"He is," admitted Claire. "What of it?"

Zoë's eyes flew to Claire's. "He's one of Robespierre's commissioners. Surely he can never be a friend to us?"

"He's been bribed," answered Claire. "That's all you need to know."

"And you trust him?"

"I trust him for the simple reason that he has yet to be paid in full. Now eat while I tell you what you may expect."

Zoë toyed with her food. She felt miserable. "I'm not a child, Claire," she said, interrupting her sister's flow of conversation. "I am seventeen years old. I have a right to know exactly what is going on."

For a moment, Claire hesitated. Her expression became grave. Her eyes touched on Zoë and slid away. Suddenly, she laughed. "I've told you as much as I dare in the circumstances," she said lightly. "The less you know, the less you can betray to the authorities if you are ever questioned. And as for you not being a child, what makes you say so?" Her eyes were alight with cajolery as they swept over Zoë's slight form.

Zoë shifted uncomfortably. She could not deny that she looked the part of a schoolgirl. Under the short, frilled frock with its high neckline, her small breasts were flattened with a binder. Black stockinged calves and ankles peeped from beneath the frilled hem of her gown. Her long hair was swept back with a ribbon. No one looking at her would take her for more than the child she purported to be.

Her gaze shifted to Claire. Her sister's beauty, her femininity, were indisputable. Even if they were to change roles and clothes, every man's eyes would still be drawn to Claire.

Their mother had been highly sensitive of this unpalatable fact. It was for that reason she had chosen to hide her daughters in a girls' school under the watchful eye of Madame Lambert. And still the ruse had not succeeded.

Philippe Duhet, Robespierre's commissioner, had offered Claire *carte blanche*. And it had been accepted. In her heart of hearts, Zoë knew the rumor was no idle tale. And the price of her sister's sexual favors was not jewels or fine clothes for herself, but refuge for the people she loved best in the world.

Blinking back tears, Zoë managed a tremulous smile. Matching Claire's light tone, she essayed, "I may not be as beautiful as you, Claire, but thank God I don't have your red hair."

Zoë could almost hear the hiss of Claire's relief as she slowly exhaled. The awkward moment passed. Both girls chuckled at this long-standing family joke.

"I'm ready to listen," said Zoë, picking up her knife and fork. "Tell me what I may expect as I eat." The food almost choked her as she forced it down. She ate for only one reason — to gratify Claire. It seemed a small recompense for everything her sister had lost.

Chapter Two

As he pushed through the doors of the Hotel Crosne, Rolfe deliberately schooled his features into a cold, dispassionate mask, as befitted one of the commissioner's deputies. Outside, on the quay, a detachment of citizen soldiers, undisciplined, newly pressed into service, stood around awkwardly, waiting for his order to mount up. They were a motley crew and, for that very reason, suited his purposes admirably. His own man, the one he had been assigned to conduct to a safe house in Coutances, would melt into their ranks without occasioning suspicion. Fleetingly, he allowed his eyes to touch on the gentleman in question.

Housard was in his mid-thirties, stocky of build, and he held the reins of the calèche, which had been seized from some absentee aristocrat's coachhouse, as if he were born to it. Rolfe had been given to understand that the man had once followed the profession of law. It was fortunate, Rolfe was thinking, that he seemed to have some experience with horses. On this jaunt, he would have need of it. Because of the girl, it would take them three days instead of the anticipated two to reach the coast.

Impatiently, his gaze searched the interior of the closed carriage. "Where's the girl?" he asked abruptly,

25

addressing his question to one of the young conscripts.

The boy shrugged his shoulders in a telling gesture.

Annoyance rippled through Rolfe. He uttered a low expletive. This was one assignment he had tried to beg off. He had no wish to play nursemaid to a whimpering child. But his contact, Tinténiac, had persuaded him to accept it when he had pointed out that the child would very likely become a victim of the guillotine if she remained in France. Rolfe could not hold out against that argument. Nevertheless, he was not pleased with this turn in events.

He had almost made up his mind to go and search for the dilatory wretch when she descended the front steps. She was alone, which surprised him. Rolfe had half-expected Duhet's mistress to take a tearful farewell of the girl. There must be some connection between them. Duhet, himself, had set the child's escape in motion. It was Duhet who had arranged for the girl to meet with his mistress for this final leavetaking. And it was Duhet who had provided the letters of authority which would take them all the way to Coutances.

The child halted only a step away from him. The top of her head was level with his chin. One quick upward glance from beneath the brim of her bonnet was all that she chanced before staring submissively at the toes of her wooden clogs. Something stirred deep inside Rolfe. With her huge, expressive eyes, the child had the look of a wild thing cornered by hunters.

"Mount up," bellowed Rolfe, before he betrayed himself by some rash act. A show of compassion from one of the commissioner's deputies would only invite comment. "You, inside," he barked out, gesturing to the girl.

At the rough tone, her eyes widened fractionally before she hastened to obey him. He followed her into the carriage and settled himself on the opposite banquette. A moment later, the coach rolled into motion.

The child was terrified of him. That much was obvious from the way her eyes stared resolutely at the gloved hands clasped tightly in her lap. The small leather grip, which had seen better days, was set to one side of her, whether consciously or unconsciously, as an obstacle to anyone who thought to sit next to her.

God, he hated the role he must play. He wanted to reassure the child that the red cap on his head was as hateful to him as it was to all right thinking people. He wore it as a badge of intimidation, nothing more. He maintained a reluctant silence. Between Rouen and Coutances there were many check points. It was essential that the girl keep to an attitude of distrust until detection was no longer a possibility.

His eyes lingered on her bent head. Damn! He could not simply let her sit there in abject misery. Moderating his tone, he said, "Were you told that I am to escort you to Coutances?"

Her head bobbed an affirmative.

"Were you told why?" he asked patiently.

Her eyes lifted and became fixed on his cravat. "Yes."

Rolfe was aware that the child did not know whether he was friend or foe. He decided that, private as they were, there could be no harm in testing her powers of deception. "Why are we going to Coutances?" he asked.

Finally, she gave him a direct look. "I am to identify a man who is in custody, my father's cousin, Jean Guéry. He is an enemy of the Revolution."

She had given the official reason, the one which was inscribed in his letters of authority. Rolfe nodded his approval. "Quite so. And once you have done this, you will be returned to Rouen." Her small white teeth bit down on her bottom lip. "Child, you have nothing to fear," he said in a calm, reassuring tone.

"I'm not afraid," she countered, but her eyes darted away from him, affecting an interest in the passing scenery.

With an audible sigh, Rolfe closed his eyes. What more could he say to relieve her of her fears? He knew what he wanted to say. He wanted to tell her that he was an English gentleman — an aristocrat, for God's sake — who had been raised from the cradle to treat the gentler sex with the utmost respect. He wanted to tell her that he liked children, as his own nieces in England could vouchsafe. He spoiled them outrageously. If it was in his power, he would spoil this child too. He was fond of children. He'd been told more times than he cared to hear that he would make a wonderful father. But that was his mother speaking, the dowager Marchioness of Rivard.

Rolfe's eyes swept over the girl in a comprehensive glance. He was almost old enough to be her father, he decided. He was nine and twenty, after all, and his first sexual experience had occurred when he was sixteen. A sudden, vivid impression of the curvacious Cyprian who had relieved him of his tiresome virginity filled his mind. She had been an older, experienced woman with the patience of Job. She'd had need of it, for his ignorance had been abysmal. He hadn't thought of Fifi — or was it Mimi? — in years, and wondered what had jogged his memory.

28

The girl, of course! Rolfe was conscious of the hot tide of color rising in his neck. It didn't matter that the child could not read his thoughts. He felt as if he had defiled her merely by thinking them in her presence.

She was an innocent, pure and unsullied, on the threshold of womanhood. Anyone with any intelligence could see at a glance that she was gently bred. When such a girl married, even then, she would not be subjected to a man's baser, sensual nature, not unless her husband were a brute. The marital bed was not where a gentleman played out his carnal lusts. It was a man's duty to beget heirs. It was no part of his duty to debauch his innocent wife.

Deciding, belatedly, that it was time to change the direction of his thoughts, he addressed a question to the child. "Who was the woman at the hotel?"

She gazed at him somberly before replying, "She is one of my teachers."

"What's her name?"

"M . . . Citoyonne Michelet."

"You are not related?"

"No."

Rolfe grunted, but decided not to press the matter. The woman was not significant. Nor was there any profit in trying to determine who was foe and who was friend. As far as possible, Tinténiac preferred his agents to work independently. There was safety in anonymity. For all he knew, Duhet himself might be a member of his own network.

La Correspondance. He'd been recruited to the network two years before, when an assassin's bullet had cut down his elder brother. Edward's transgression had been that he was too closely associated with the French Royalists in England. The family seat in

Kent, Rivard Abbey, had opened its doors to aristocrats seeking sanctuary from the Terror.

It was Edward's death which had shaken Rolfe from his natural indolence. "I'm apolitical," was the excuse he was used to employing laughingly when Edward tried to persuade him to take a more active role in events. He wondered what Edward would have to say about the role he had assumed.

No. There was no point in wondering. He knew exactly what Edward would say if he were alive. He would be aghast. That the Marquess of Rivard should court danger when the succession had yet to be secured was unthinkable. And yet, by some strange irony, it was Edward who had made himself the target of assassins.

Rolfe sighed and turned his head to stare unseeingly out the coach window. He had no real excuse for evading his duty to beget heirs except that it was an unpalatable one. And what duty wasn't? But more and more of late, the obligation which fell to his lot had begun to weigh heavily on his conscience. His mother, who knew nothing of his involvement in British Intelligence or of his frequent jaunts to the Continent, was vocal in her objections to his single state. He did not see how he could withstand her determined onslaught much longer.

Only one more assignment after this, he promised himself. One more "letter" to post and his field of operations would switch to England. Time enough, then, to consider leg-shackling himself to some eligible girl. He wondered idly what the future had in store for the child who was huddled so pathetically in the corner of the coach.

* * *

They stopped to water the horses on the banks of the River Risle, just outside Le Bec. It was here, by and large, that the conscripts parted company with them. They were bound for Toulon, in the south, where combined Royalist and English forces were successfully holding the port against French besiegers. Their party was now reduced to two coachmen and three conscripts, not counting the deputy.

Zoë was not permitted to leave the confines of the coach until a meager repast was prepared. Though she was not hungry, she was glad of the opportunity to stretch her legs and warm herself at the blaze which someone had kindled in a circle of stones. A pot of stew was suspended over the flames. One man was on guard duty. The others were huddled around or involved at various tasks.

A tin cup of something hot was thrust at her.

"Thank you," she murmured, and cupped her frozen fingers around the hot utensil, savoring its warming properties.

"Sit," said the deputy.

He was a man of few words as Zoë had discovered, and those few were mostly commands. She settled herself on the rock he indicated and studied him with veiled glances.

To her knowledge, he was exactly as he appeared — an agent of the commissioners. Claire had told her that the deputy was under orders to conduct her to Coutances. When she was safely delivered, transportation would be arranged to take her to the coast and thence to Jersey and England. Meantime, she was to trust no one, and the pretense that she was Fleur Guéry must be maintained until she reached England.

Apart from the deputy, only one other held any interest for her. He was older than his companions. Zoë judged him to be on the wrong side of thirty or thereabouts. Her eyes followed him as he tended to the horses, leading them down in pairs to the ford to slake their thirst. He knew his way around horses. He knew how to gentle them with soft words and smooth touches. Such a man could not be all bad, Zoë was thinking, and took comfort from that thought.

"Eat." The deputy thrust a spoon under Zoë's nose. A moment later, she was given a hunk of black bread. She ate in silence.

Before continuing on their journey, the deputy indicated that Zoë was to attend to her personal needs. He gestured to a clump of bushes which lay hard by their camp. Zoë was aghast, though she dared not argue the point with him. With every appearance of docility, she walked straight into the bushes and passed through to the opposite side. Some few yards farther on, she spied a more secluded spot which served her sense of what was fitting.

She had scarcely finished adjusting her garments, when the deputy swooped down on her. Like a naughty child, she was hauled back to camp by the scruff of her neck. Men laughed at her predicament as the deputy railed at her and administered several stinging swats to her posterior. Her cheeks burned scarlet. Tears trembled on her lashes and spilled over. It was too much for her.

She hauled herself out of his arms. "I'm not a child," she choked out, her eyes shooting sparks at him.

Coarse laughter greeted this childish display of temper as men stood about, waiting to see how the young deputy would take his revenge.

In a move calculated to demonstrate her immaturity, Rolfe tousled her tumbled locks. "Settle down, duchess," he said, joining in the general hilarity. "Obedient children don't get spanked. Remember that in future."

His words had a sobering effect. Zoë's eyes went stark with fear. If she was caught out in her deceit, the penalty she would suffer would be far graver than a few swats to her backside.

With a muffled curse, the deputy swept her up in his arms and deposited her inside the coach. She shrank from him, averting her head. His hand caught her chin, turning her tear-streaked face up for his inspection.

"I . . . I want my mother," said Zoë. She was merely trying to throw him off the scent, she told herself. Such words, coming from a child, were only to be expected. But the truth of her statement twisted like a knife in her heart. More tears welled in her eyes. Impatient with herself, she blinked them away.

As the coach lurched and began to move off, Rolfe removed a handkerchief from his coat pocket. "Dry your tears," he said quietly.

Zoë obeyed and stole a sideways look at him. There was a suspicious twinkle lurking at the back of those grave eyes. She sniffed, deciding with a kind of determined defiance that she would rather be the object of his fury than his scorn. Pointedly, she lifted her chin.

Rolfe removed his handkerchief from her clenched hands and studied the girl's profile. "You must never disobey me again," he said seriously. "Do you understand?"

Her lip trembled.

He bit back a smile. "You put yourself at risk when you did not tell me where you were going. Anything might have happened to you. I'm responsible for your safety. I won't tolerate disobedience, kitten. You'd better make your mind up to it."

The tilt of her chin dropped by several notches. Now that he had explained himself, she saw the sense of obeying him. "I beg your pardon," she managed in a small voice.

"That's better. Now see if you can catch some sleep. You look half hagged to death."

She was too keyed up for sleep, and too craven to voice her opinion. Without argument, she closed her eyes. It was only a matter of minutes before the sham became reality.

When the girl beside him was breathing softly and evenly, Rolfe removed a blanket from beneath the opposite banquette. He shook it out, and draped it around her small form. Having done this, he gathered her in his arms, pillowing her head against his chest.

Zoë would have been thunderstruck if she had glimpsed the deputy's bemused expression as he gazed down at her. It was a curious blend of tenderness and apology.

Rolfe closed his eyes and gradually drifted into a light sleep.

They made Lisieux by nightfall. Zoë had to be shaken awake. Disoriented, she stumbled from the coach. She would have fallen over her clumsy wooden clogs if the young deputy had not caught her. Eyes downcast, she mumbled an apology and turned away as he made to enter a stone building.

Zoë huddled close to the coach and looked about her. Relief shivered through her. They had stopped at a hostelry. It had occurred to her that she might be forced to spend the night in the cells of the Law Courts. She'd been plagued with the terrible foreboding that she would disgrace the family name by breaking down like a terrified schoolgirl.

A thousand times over since they had gone into hiding, Zoë had reminded herself that, twice over, she was the granddaughter of a general. The blood of heroes ran in her veins. It was inconceivable that a Devereux should conduct himself with anything less than fortitude, whatever the circumstances. The other members of her family, her parents, her sister, her younger brother, were an example she should be striving to emulate. Of them all, she was the one who had the least to endure and the most to which to look forward. The thought braced her faltering courage until the deputy returned. When he towered over her, Zoë sagged weakly against the coach.

Her gaze made a slow appraisal of his taut features. His lips moved. She heard the grate of his voice. Evidently, the deputy was far from satisfied with the only available hostelry of which the town of Lisieux could boast. He seemed to be undecided. She felt the heat of his eyes as they traveled over her.

"You're frozen," was all he said.

In the next instant, he had made his decision. His small troop of men were ordered off to find their own pallets.

Zoë, much to her relief, was to go with the deputy.

He led the way into the inn and found a place for her beside the hearth. A welcoming warmth enveloped her.

"Stay," he ordered, as if she were his pet dog.

Irritation moved through Zoë, but she merely nodded her acquiescence. Should the inn come under cannon fire, she resolved that she would not move a muscle. She had learned a humiliating lesson she had no wish to repeat.

Satisfied by her response, Rolfe stalked off to find the landlord to make arrangements for their sleeping quarters.

Only then did Zoë lift her eyes to examine what manner of place and people she was among. *Crude* was the word which sprang to her mind. The stench of unwashed bodies, fried fish, and tobacco smoke permeated to every corner. The din rose and fell with the rhythm of breakers beating against the shore. Words she had never before heard, but which she knew intuitively were obscene, were bandied about without raising an eyebrow. And the lewd, suggestive remarks and gestures which were addressed by the male patrons to the few females who were present were accepted as if they were the highest tribute. Zoë had occasion, in happier days, to put up at various inns when traveling with her family. Those exalted hostelries bore no resemblance to the madhouse which the deputy had chosen for their night's lodging.

From the corner of her eye, through the haze of smoke, she remarked that she had become an object of interest to two disreputable-looking gentlemen, one of whom was old enough to be her father. The younger man winked at her and Zoë immediately averted her head.

Claire had been very explicit in her advice before they had parted company. Until she was among friends, Zoë's whole demeanor was to be one of submission. On no account must she gaze directly into the eyes of any male past the age of thirteen summers. To do so was to invite liberties which she must find distressing, to say the least.

At the time, Zoë had accepted her sister's advice without demur, though she deemed it superfluous. In the first place, she was, quite genuinely, terrified into

36

submission and feared to look her own reflection in the eye let alone look directly at some predatory male. In the second place, Claire had spoken from personal experience. In Zoë's whole life, no gentleman had ever exceeded the bounds of propriety. Dressed as she was, she was sure she must repel any advances. She was coming to recognize the error of her logic.

With studied naturalness, trembling, she untied the strings of her bonnet. It was in her mind that one glimpse of her long, little girl's tresses would correct any misapprehensions which may have arisen respecting her age and station. With eyes downcast, she set her bonnet on her lap and lifted the weight of her hair to lie forward, concealing her bound bosom. For something to do, she stretched her hands out to the blaze and pretended an involvement in this simple act which she was far from feeling.

There was no way she could have heard the men approaching. The level of noise was rising steadily as the consumption of the local brew increased. But Zoë *did* hear them. And the soft tread of their boots, to her ears, was the most sinister threat she had suffered in many a long day. Her first instinct was to take to her heels. "Stay!" he had ordered, and only some act of Providence dare take precedence over what the deputy commanded.

She turned slightly, presenting her back to the men who stalked her. Quelling her rapid breathing by sheer force of will, she flexed her fingers and rubbed her hands together to conceal their shaking. When a man's hand stole around her ankle and caressed her calf, she let out a scream.

"There, there, little girl. Don't be afraid. We won't hurt you. Me and my mate just want to make sure

37

that you're warm. Ain't that right, Lou?" A grotesque smile accompanied the suggestive remarks, as the hand on her calf slipped higher.

The younger man kneeled at Zoë's feet, ostensibly to stir up the fire with the poker. The other was bent over her, pressing a cup of some foul-smelling liquid to her lips. Zoë's heart began to gallop, forcing blood to thunder at every pulse point in her body. She looked around wildly, seeking help from some sympathetic spectator. Her plight, though not unnoticed, caused little comment save of the unsavory kind. And then she saw it—the red cap atop the blond hair, and moving in her direction. Her heart gave a great leap of gladness.

She scarcely recognized the deputy's voice when he spoke. She was used to hearing more strident tones. A whisper of sound, low and infinitely menacing, hissed from between his clenched teeth. Child molestors, he called them, and a few other choice epithets. Though the words were new to Zoë, she had no trouble catching his drift. Neither did her accosters. They straightened slowly and turned to face the deputy, surveying him impassively. Apparently, the red cap held no intimidation for these rough men.

The younger man moved like lightning. Rolfe was faster. He darted away from the descending poker. It sliced into a long trestle table. In one deft move, Rolfe grabbed his attacker's arm, twisted it behind his back and hurled him against the wall. He sank to the floor like a scuttled warship. His friend let out a roar, but before he could charge, Rolfe had unsheathed his short sword, and the point of it was pressed to the man's throat.

"Out!" said Rolfe, gesturing with his head to Zoë. "Wait for me at the door."

Zoë did not delay for a second telling. Head downcast, she elbowed her way through the silent crush of people. Nor did she turn to survey the scene when an unholy yell split the air, followed by the sound of splintering furniture. There was a moment's unbroken silence and then conversation and catcalls resumed in every quarter as if there had been no interruption.

Moments later, when the deputy strode through the taproom door, her elbow was taken in a bruising grasp. Zoë had to run to keep up with him.

"Where are you taking me?" she panted, her gratitude for his timely rescue instantly replaced by a fresh wave of panic.

He stopped in his tracks and gave her a rough shake. "Don't you have enough sense to run for cover when you are being hunted? God, even a dumb animal has more brains than you."

His grasp on her arm did not slacken as he dragged her up the narrow stairs and along a lighted hallway. For the first time since she'd entered the inn, her fear abated to be replaced by a more violent emotion.

Taking umbrage more at the slight to her intelligence than his rough tone and manhandling, she pointed out tersely, "You told me to stay where I was."

Cool gray eyes raked over her. "You removed your bonnet," answered the deputy cryptically.

"My bonnet?"

They came to a door. Rolfe pushed through, dragging Zoë behind him. A lantern was lit and set on a small table beside the bed. When he released her to lock and bar the door, Zoë took a few steps into the room and whirled to face him. Her emotions were too involved to give more than a passing thought to the peril of her situation.

"Why am I to blame when others attack me?" she demanded. "You are the one who is to blame for leaving me alone in that den of iniquity in the first place. And as for my bonnet . . ." Her voice trailed to a halt as she became aware of the deputy's lingering appraisal.

Rolfe's eyes slowly roved over the challenging posture of the child before him. Her figure was childish, as yet undeveloped, though, when he had administered the spanking she had deserved, he had detected the suggestion of womanly softness beneath her garments. She was small boned and dainty. Her profile was sculpted in delicate lines; her mouth was full, with the promise of something — the word *sensuality* came to mind and was instantly rejected. Her chin was square. Far from detracting from the oval perfection of her face, this irregularity merely added piquancy. But it was those huge eyes of hers, dark, veiled, and hinting of feminine secrets which, he was persuaded, made men make fools of themselves. Or perhaps it was that dark skein of shimmering hair which tempted a man to test the feel of it between his fingers.

Shaking his head, frowning, he asked, "How old are you?"

"Fourteen," she answered at once. Guilty color swept across her cheekbones, riveting the deputy's alert gaze. "More or less," she added in a husky, self-conscious undertone.

Wearily, Rolfe covered his eyes with one hand. "Thirteen! Good God! You're just a babe!" He raised his head and surveyed her through half-closed lids. This time, he observed the short, frilled frock beneath the opening of her threadbare cloak. He noted the wilted ribbon on her mane of hair. She was all legs and arms, he decided then, like a skittish colt. He could not say why, but he was suddenly swept by a feeling of self-disgust mingled with unbridled rage at his own sex in general.

"You look older," he said, his voice verging on the accusatory.

"Thank you," said Zoë, and dropped her eyes.

Rolfe laughed and pinched her cheek in an avuncular fashion. "You won't always thank a gentleman for saying that you look older. Why is it, I wonder, that children are always wishing their lives away?" The question was rhetorical and Zoë made no attempt to answer it. Releasing her, he moved to the grate and used the bellows to fan the embers of the fire. A moment later, it blazed to life.

Zoë watched him in considering silence. She scarcely knew what to make of his playful manner. When a knock came at the door, it barely registered.

"I ordered food," said Rolfe. "Are you hungry?"

Was she hungry? She did not think so. "Ravenous," she answered, hoping to please him, and was rewarded with a smile of such singular sweetness that she was instantly overcome with confusion. Happily, the deputy did not remark on her bemused state.

What they dined on, Zoë could never afterwards remember. Her thoughts, already chaotic because of the deputy's softened manner, jostled each other even more frantically when he removed the red cap and combed his fingers through his hair.

Throughout their meal, she was aware that in a veiled fashion, he was giving her a list of safeguards she must employ if she wished to avoid attracting unnecessary, masculine attention. There was nothing new in this. *Maman* or her sister Claire had already voiced some of the same advice. Zoë nodded her agreement from time to time as if hanging on his every word, but behind her carefully bored expression, she studied her companion as if she had discovered a new and interesting specimen of fauna.

He was younger than she had at first surmised, and just the right age for a lady of her years. Devoid of the odious red cap, he looked less menacing. His hair was blond, but not without color. It was rich and warm looking, reminding her of her mother's yellow *salle* in the house in St. Germain when the sun came streaming through the west windows. His eyes were gray, with a trace of blue, not the expected green. And that crooked, half smile which he doled out as if it had been as scarce as black bread did something decidedly odd to the regularity of her breathing.

Apropos of nothing, she asked, "Do you play the piano?"

"What?"

"You have the hands for it—long fingers, like mine," and she flexed her fingers as she always did before embarking on a difficult piece of music.

He shook his head. "The thought processes of children were ever beyond my ken. Fleur?" His eyes held a glint of steel. "Did you hear what I said?"

She felt like laughing, but managed to look shamefaced. "I heard you."

"And?"

"I'm to keep my hair covered and my eyes on my shoes. I must never, never smile at strange gentlemen or permit them to address me if you are not present."

"Good girl. You *have* been listening to my words."

"Yes, but . . ."

"What?"

42

She was playing with him and was rather taken with her own temerity. "Why must I keep my hair covered? *Maman* never once forbade me to take off my bonnet."

The question seemed to discompose him. "Just take my word for it. Hair like yours is more than most men—" He broke off and stared at her wide-eyed look with something like suspicion. "Just do as I say and don't ask questions."

It was an answer she had heard often enough in her young life. She shrugged philosophically and ate the last morsel on her plate.

"I thought you were an orphan," said the deputy conversationally.

Startled brown eyes flew to his face.

"You mentioned your mother. Twice, as I recall," he pointed out.

Zoë's expression became guarded. "I . . . I am an orphan. It's just that . . . sometimes . . . I remember happier days."

Rolfe drained the tankard of ale he held in his hand. "I understand. Just be careful of what you say before others. All right?" There was a smile in his eyes.

Zoë nodded, and silently questioned the young man's concern. Any deputy worth his salt ought to pursue the blunder she had stumbled into. He was like no deputy she had ever heard of. She stared at him wonderingly.

"Time for bed, little one," he said, scraping back his chair. "We have an early start in the morning."

"Are we . . . are we going to sleep here? Together?" She looked around the confines of the small room with growing alarm. Apart from a table, two upright chairs, and the bed, there was no other furniture.

Between exasperation and cajolery, he explained patiently, "Not together. You shall have the bed, and I shall curl up on the floor like your faithful hound. No one will attack you as long as I'm with you. Does that satisfy your sense of propriety, your ladyship?"

She recognized that he was employing the tone of voice he would reserve for a favorite niece. For a moment, fleetingly, Zoë wished that he could see her as she really was, or as she would like to be—a young lady of fashion who was worthy of his attention. Her eyes came to rest on the bed and she wisely banished that rash thought.

He left her, then, with a stern admonition, and a very telling look, to see to her ablutions. Zoë lost no time in following his instructions to the letter. When he returned, she was in her shift, under the covers.

"Good night, *ma petite fleur*," he said and doused the lantern.

She listened to his movements in the dark as he stripped out of his clothing. "I don't know your name," she said after a lengthy interval. Her voice was heavy with drowsiness.

Rolfe stilled with his shirt half over his head. He shook off the thought that the child had the voice of a temptress, low and sweetly seductive. "It's Rolfe," he answered more harshly than he intended, and struggled out of his shirt.

Zoë smiled to herself. Between wakefulness and sleep she murmured, "That's a good name for a hound."

The darkness enveloped her like a warm blanket. She felt safe and strangely protected, as if the night had not held terrors for her these several months past. She yawned and turned over to her side. Words whispered inside her head —"kitten," "little one," *"ma*

44

petite fleur," "your ladyship"—lovelier, more romantic by far than any endearments she had ever heard. She wondered how her name, her *real* name, Zoë, would sound on his lips. "Good night my faithful hound, Rolfe," were the last words she said before she succumbed to sleep.

Rolfe merely grunted in answer and adjusted his long length to the hard floor.

Chapter Three

Zoë awoke the following morning to find her nose pressed against a pillow of something soft and, at the same time, scratchy. Her nose twitched. By slow degrees, she lifted her lashes. She blinked rapidly, trying to drag herself from the last vestiges of her dream.

She was cuddled up to her faithful hound, she was thinking. She smiled softly and combed her fingers through Rolfe's thick mat of hair.

Her hound growled deep in his throat. The sound did not deceive Zoë for an instant. It was a pleasure sound, much like the purr of a lazy, replete lion. She stroked her faithful hound again.

"Fifi," said Rolfe, and tightened his arms around the soft, feminine form in his embrace. He did not waken.

Fifi! Zoë's sleepy smile instantly departed. She raised her head and tried to make sense of the mat of dark gold hair which seemed to have sprouted on her pillow overnight. The pillow rose and fell in a regular rhythm. Gradually, she became conscious that her pillow was a man's hairy chest. She went as stiff as a poker.

Rolfe groaned a protest at the implied rejection and dragged her closer. Fifi —or was it Mimi?—had

46

never seemed more desirable than she did at that moment. By some trick of the light, her guinea gold curls had converted to a rich mahogany, darker than the strongest brew of coffee. Her coarse features were sculpted in finer lines. Her eyes were huge, with the look of a faun, dark and hinting of feminine secrets. And the pout of those full lips promised a ripe sensuality. The pressure of his arms tightened, bringing her warmth closer.

Zoë did not panic. To do so could prove disastrous. Though every instinct urged her to force the man to release her, a deeper fear prevailed. To waken him might provoke those distressing masculine attentions of which Claire had spoken.

"Fifi," muttered Rolfe, and nestled closer.

Zoë took stock of her position. The deputy was insensate with sleep, that and the jug or two of ale he had consumed over supper. It did not take much imagination to recognize that his slumber was not without its dreams. Her fear left her. "Fifi," she mouthed soundlessly, her brow knit in a mulish frown. She glared at his sleep-softened features.

Gently, so as not to wake him, she wedged her hands against his hard, muscled chest, trying to gain herself some breathing space. At her touch, the deputy emitted another soft sound of pleasure. Zoë held her breath. Rolfe dreamed on.

It took a moment or two before it registered with Zoë that Rolfe was in his pantaloons and was lying on top of the covers whilst she was trapped beneath them. She deduced, correctly, that, finding the floor too hard for comfort during the night, he had risen without really wakening and had sought a more agreeable pallet. Hers. Or Fifi's.

Slowly, carefully, Zoë inched away from the powerful masculine frame. When she had gained a space of several inches, she took her first deep breath. It was a mistake. The covers slipped to her waist. A faint recollection of having removed her shift during the night was confirmed by the sight of her naked torso. She jerked. Rolfe, feeling the provocative feminine movement, rolled on top of her. Bare skin met bare skin.

Zoë's eyes went as round as saucers. Her most pressing fear was that the deputy would waken and discover that the little girl who he had put to bed had developed breasts during the night. She damned herself for a fool for removing the binder which flattened her shape, and she promised the fates, if they would give her another chance, that she would never do anything so rash again.

Several minutes were to pass before Zoë's confidence returned. The deputy was a dead weight, but he had made no threatening moves. She decided it was safe to breathe. Soft feminine contours grazed hard masculine muscles. Zoë stopped breathing. The sensation had not been unpleasant, she decided. With slow deliberation, experimentally, she inhaled and exhaled. Her heart started to pound against her ribs. The sensation was more than pleasant. It was . . . delectable.

She'd never felt the press of a man's weight before. She had no notion how her senses would be stirred by the fit of his hard planes to her soft curves. His warm breath on her shoulder heated her skin all the way to her toes. And the scent of him, like a forest after a fresh fall of summer rain, was the headiest, most alluring perfume she had ever inhaled. She'd never smelled a man this close to her before.

Rolfe's dream was beginning to fade. "Mimi," he said plaintively, trying to lure the girl of his dreams back into his orbit.

"Mimi!" mouthed Zoë, thunderstruck. So now there were two of them, were there? Fifi? Mimi? She gritted her teeth. Libertine, she was thinking, and she brought her knee up smartly.

Rolfe let out a howl of pain. He jerked to his side. Zoë rolled to her stomach and feigned sleep.

"What the hell?" Disoriented, holding his groin, Rolfe looked about him, trying to get his bearings. The woman in the bad was snoring softly. Fifi? Mimi? Oh God no! It was the child, Fleur. What the hell had he done to her?

He leapt from the bed as if he had been scalded by boiling oil. Reaching for his shirt, he shrugged into it, and slowly, reluctantly, turned to face the bed. He took several, deep shuddering breaths as his eyes anxiously scanned the inert form beneath the covers. The girl in the bed turned over. The snoring resumed but, this time, more stridently.

Relief washed over Rolfe in waves. He sank onto the nearest chair. It was all a dream. The child was beneath the covers. He knew—oh God, he hoped—that he had been lying on top of them. Nothing could have happened, could it? He combed his fingers through his hair.

He'd never had a dream like that before. The reality of it was stunning. Even the smell of the woman still filled his nostrils—vaguely reminiscent of field lilies after a spring rain. Oh God, he hoped it wasn't the girl's scent. Damn him to hell for all eternity if he had so much as laid a finger on the child!

He dressed quickly and quit the room.

Zoë heard the grate of the key in the lock. She pulled herself to a sitting position, clutching the bed-clothes under her chin. She'd had a lucky escape and thanked God for it.

Gratitude to the Deity slowly dissipated. Mimi and Fifi indeed! She felt insulted. Her eyes began to snap. The man was a scoundrel! He had almost taken advantage of her! Rogue! Libertine! Villain!

Further reflection tempered her outrage. Honesty compelled her to confess that she had contributed significantly to her near ruin. There was no explaining it but, for a time there, she had not been in her right mind. She'd been curious. She'd wanted to experiment. There was no saying where it all might have ended if the deputy had not breathed another woman's name. She ought to thank him for it.

Scowling unbecomingly, she dragged herself from the bed.

When Rolfe returned to their chamber, the child was fully dressed and sitting demurely at the table, hands neatly folded in her lap. Their eyes brushed and held.

"Did . . . did you sleep well, kitten?" He set down a breakfast tray in front of Zoë.

"No," she said without elaboration, and noted the jug of milk and solitary cup of coffee on the tray.

"No?" He said the word carefully.

"You snore like a horse," she answered sullenly.

He angled her a relieved grin. "Do I? No one has ever told me that before. Here, drink your milk."

"I don't like milk," said Zoë, and eyed the cup of steaming coffee with covert longing.

"Nonsense. It's good for you."

"Why is it good for me?"

"Well . . . I don't know. Just look at the animal kingdom. All infants drink milk. Did you . . . did you dream last night, kitten?"

"I had a nightmare," said Zoë nastily.

"Oh?" In the act of handing Zoë the jug of fresh milk, Rolfe went very still. His eyelashes swept down. His voice was not quite steady when he asked, "What . . . what did you dream?"

Zoë absorbed Rolfe's extremity in one quick, comprehensive glance. Suddenly, she felt like the veriest she-devil, to tease him so. She could not understand such churlish behavior. It was quite out of character for her. And quite unjustified.

She had suffered no insult, except inadvertently. And to have developed a proprietary interest in the deputy after such a short acquaintance was positively ludicrous. Moreover, he was the innocent party. It was she who had involved them both in an experiment.

Hastening to put him out of his misery, she said, "I dreamed that a nasty-smelling hound was in my bed. Big, and shaggy, and quite dead." She said the last word with emphasis.

"A dead dog," repeated Rolfe blankly.

"Dead," averred Zoë, and reached for the jug of milk in Rolfe's hands. He did not resist as she took it from him. "I tried pinching him, but it was no use. I could not budge him."

"Were you . . . afraid?" He seemed to be hanging on her words.

She dismissed the notion with all the wounded dignity of a child who has been mistaken for something younger than her years. "I'm not afraid of dogs! Especially not dogs in dreams."

51

"How did you know it was a dream?"

"Because when I kicked him, he disappeared."

The hiss of his breath was barely audible as he slowly exhaled. "Drink your milk," he said, and flashed Zoë one of his rare smiles.

Zoë hated milk with a passion, but when she set her mind to make amends, she did not spare herself. She raised the mug to her lips and forced the oily liquid over her gullet.

In companionable silence, they ate their breakfast which comprised nothing more savory than black bread and honey.

When Zoë had readied herself for the next leg of their journey, the deputy intimated that there was a present waiting for her in the carriage.

She followed him out of the inn with her heart beating rapidly. With the exception of her male relatives, no gentleman had ever been permitted to give her a gift. Sweets, a book, flowers — all these she knew to be perfectly acceptable. She hoped that he had not chosen anything more intimate, else she must refuse him.

Rolfe halted when they came to the carriage. "Close your eyes," he said.

It was absurd, but anticipation and excitement were stealing her breath, as if she had been, in very truth, a young child waiting to open her birthday presents. Smiling shyly, she closed her eyes.

Rolfe reached into the carriage and pulled something from one of the banquettes. "Open your eyes," he said.

Wordlessly, Zoë stared at the object in Rolfe's hands.

"Take it," he said, pushing it into her arms.

"A doll!" It was the last thing she had expected to see. She had given up dolls when she was ten. Didn't the deputy know that at thirteen or fourteen a girl considered herself too grown-up for such trifles? Evidently not. "Th—thank you," she stammered.

The child's confusion gratified Rolfe immensely. He knew enough about children to know that any little girl would count herself fortunate to be the recipient of such a gift. He had come by it in Rouen and had intended it for one of his nieces. Not for a moment did he regret giving it to this child. His nieces were spoiled. They lacked for nothing. One doll more or less would not be missed in their household.

"It's a *china* doll," said Rolfe knowledgeably. He had been given to understand by his young nieces that no other kind counted for anything.

Zoë lifted her eyes and looked about her. The deputy's men were watching the little scene with keen interest.

"A *china* doll!" exclaimed Zoë, trying to inject some enthusiasm into her voice. "I've always wanted a *china* doll." She did a little jig on the spot. "Ooh," she crooned, "and she's a bride!"

She held out the doll for everyone's inspection. At the pretty picture she made, hard masculine eyes softened. Dutiful words of admiration fell from lips which habitually engaged in an uncouth, vulgar converse.

"The coachman shall have to drive very carefully," said Zoë seriously, beginning to warm to her part. "*China* dolls are easily broken." She was talking from sad experience. On her seventh birthday, she had been given such a doll. During the night it had fallen from her bed to the floor and had smashed into smithereens. She'd been inconsolable as she remembered.

"He'll be careful," said Rolfe, handing Zoë into the carriage. He winked at the coachman and followed her in.

Men grinned at each other as they swung into the saddle. The pleasure of this one child for the familiar things of childhood seemed, in some unspecified way, to imbue the future with a sure foundation for hope.

Inside the coach, Zoë was conscious of the deputy's interest. What could she do? She must continue with the role or stand to be discovered. With feigned absorption, she played with her new toy.

From that moment on, Zoë and her doll became inseparable. At every checkpoint, she held it to the coach window and pointed out objects of various interest. When they stopped to break their fast, the doll was fed too. She was lavish in her praise when the doll was good and she scolded furiously when her doll was naughty.

Her charade was not entirely without purpose. The doll became the badge of her tender years. Seeing it, men softened, remembering a younger sister, a daughter, some female child to whom they owed their protection. The doll was a shield. Zoë used it with consummate skill.

Rolfe, more often than not, was reminded of his young nieces. "You never spank your doll, I see," he remarked. He rather liked the soft crooning sounds the child made when she was singing her "baby" to sleep.

It was their second night out of Rouen. They had

reached Caen and found lodgings at an inn which was a considerable improvement on the one in Lisieux. The sleeping arrangements were also different. Rolfe had bespoken a private parlor with a tiny bedchamber adjoining. The bedchamber was for the child. Rolfe was more than happy to bed down on a pallet in front of the parlor fire.

"I beg your pardon. I wasn't listening," said Zoë, coming to herself. She'd been thinking of the members of her family, wondering where they were and what the future might hold for each of them. She blinked back incipient tears.

"Your doll," said Rolfe. "You never spank her." On many occasions, he had observed his nieces laying into their respective "babies" with excessive zeal. He'd been appalled. His sister-in-law had given him to understand there was no harm in it. They were merely letting off steam.

Zoë pinned him with a fierce glare. "I don't believe in spanking children," she said. They both knew that she was referring to the time when the deputy had spanked her.

Unrepentant, Rolfe grinned. "What's your doll's name?" he asked, adroitly turning the subject.

She had never thought to give the silly doll a name. "Zoë," she said, because it was the only name that came to her on the spur of the moment.

"Zoë? That's Greek, isn't it?"

"Is it?" He had said her name. Her real name. And the sound of it was something wondrous and oddly different from the way anyone had ever said it before.

"Definitely Greek. It means . . . 'life', if I'm not mistaken. It's a good name. I like it."

Her eyes widened. Frankly curious, she asked,

55

"What did you do before you were a deputy?"

His expression became shuttered. "This and that," he said, and yawned. "Isn't it time for Zoë's bed?" And he looked pointedly at her doll.

Thoughtfully, Zoë rose to her feet. She really knew very little about the deputy. "Are you married?" she asked, and could not think why she had asked such a thing.

"No. Why do you ask?"

To cover her confusion, she said the first thing that came into her head. "I thought you might have a little girl like me at home." Inwardly, she groaned. With every word she uttered, she made him more aware of the paucity of her years. It was the last thing she wanted.

For a moment, he looked to be struck dumb. Then he laughed and reached out to ruffle her hair. "No, I'm not married. And I don't have a little girl like you at home. I only wish . . ."

"What?" she prompted.

"That I could adopt you. Well, we shall see."

Rolfe meant it as a compliment. The child's blank stare was unrevealing. A moment later, when she swept from the room with her doll clutched to her bosom, he could have sworn that he had ruffled her feathers. He sank back in his chair and considered the exchange.

Adoption. He had said the word on impulse with no clear thought of what he was saying. He considered it now and decided that the idea was not without merit. If the child was alone in the world, there was no telling what might happen to her. He frowned, not best pleased by the drift of his thoughts.

* * *

Everywhere there were refugees—people who had abandoned their property and means of livelihood in the hopes of finding some quiet corner of France where they might live without interference. Brittany and Normandy, for the moment, seemed to offer the only haven, relatively speaking.

Without passports, however, movement from city to city was almost impossible. But forgeries were easily come by. And for those who had both money and connections, commissioners could sometimes be bribed to provide the proper documents of authority. The possession of a passport was not, in itself, a guarantee of immunity. There were checkpoints at the exits to every city. And it was here that men saw the ruin of all their hopes.

On the outskirts of Coutances, a roadblock had been set up. It was a familiar sight, but lost none of its menace for all that. Zoë could scarcely contain the sharp rise of terror which threatened to overcome her at such moments. It was not aristocrats who were hunted now. Most of those had long since perished or made their escape from France. It was survivors of the defeated Grand Army of the Vendeé, or members of the wealthy mercantile class, or refractory priests who practised the old, proscribed religion, who had become the new enemies of the Revolution. The authorities were determined to purge the young republic of all subversive elements. Some of those in authority were assiduous in following their orders. Others were selective. And some few were lax. Zoë looked into the impassive face of the young captain who was on duty and wondered what she might expect.

"Everybody out." His voice was clipped and held

the hard edge of authority. "You there, old man, get down off the box."

Inside the coach, Zoë's eyes flew to Rolfe. Without haste, he removed his letters of authority from the inside of his coat. The red cap, which he had taken to leaving off when they were on the road, was already on his head. He eased his way out of the carriage. Unsmiling, he held out his hand, and Zoë allowed him to help her down. One of the coachmen, the elder of the two, whom Zoë recalled went by the name of Housard, was climbing down from his perch. The younger man held the reins in his hands, keeping his team steady.

There was a slight drizzle falling, threatening to turn into sleet. People were huddled about miserably in groups while their papers were inspected. One man was arguing volubly as his wife and two young children looked on in unremitting despair. Their case did not look hopeful. In the fading light, shadows lengthened, casting a grotesque, unearthly appearance on the proceedings. The smell of fear seemed to pollute the atmosphere. Zoë tried to swallow, but her throat was too dry.

Having scrutinized Rolfe's papers, the captain gave him the most negligent of salutes. In Zoë's eyes the omission was sinister. She was used to seeing the deputy treated with the utmost respect.

"Captain, a moment please." The bored, faintly drawling voice belonged to Rolfe. "You're a newcomer, here, if I'm not mistaken?"

The captain stiffened perceptibly at the challenging tone. In the act of reaching for the coachman's papers, he hesitated.

Zoë could not be sure but she sensed that, in that

58

moment, an unspoken message passed between Rolfe and his coachman. Her heart skipped several beats when the captain spun on his heel and took the two strides which brought him level with the deputy.

An uneasy quiet descended as bystanders became conscious that something of some moment was taking place. And though no man in that sad crush wished his neighbor ill, no one was sorry that the spotlight had moved to the deputy and his party.

The two men who stood toe to toe were of an age. Both were meticulous in their dress, though one wore the uniform of the revolutionary army and the other was in civilian garb. The captain's bearing proclaimed that he was no untrained conscript, but was used to military discipline. The deputy's posture was deceptively indolent, and for that very reason commanded respect.

What the captain was to say in answer to Rolfe's question was never to be discovered. The young deputy put another question to him; this time, in accents that deceived no one. It was evident that the deputy considered himself the captain's superior.

"What's going on here?" he asked. "And I mean *precisely*, Captain. Has there been an attempt to storm the prison where they are holding Guéry?"

"Guéry?" repeated the captain. He knew of no Guéry, though he did not reveal his ignorance. He was not quite sure where the deputy's authority ended and his own began. In the regular army, he knew the chain of command. The deputy was right about one thing. This was a new detail for him. And working with civilians, he had yet to determine his place in the hierarchy.

"Guéry," bellowed the deputy, and began to pace

impatiently. His jaw tightened as he took in the miserable huddle of people and the long line of vehicles which blocked the road to Coutances. He spun to face the captain. "By God, if your chaps have allowed Guéry to escape in Commissioner Duhet's absence—"

"Sir! There has been no escape attempt. The town is quiet."

Rolfe pulled the gauntlets from his fingers and ran them through his hands, regarding the captain in simmering silence. At length, he said softly, "Then if it's not Guéry, what the devil is going on? Why the long line-ups? Why the delays?"

The captain, if anything, adopted a more rigid posture. "Sir, we have information that an English spy is making for the coast."

"An English spy?"

"A Frenchman, sir, a traitor who must not be allowed to fall into enemy hands. Robespierre, himself, wishes to question him."

The name of Robespierre evidently evoked the deputy's respect. *"Nom de Dieu!"* he exclaimed. "Has France not enough to contend with? Civil war scarcely diverted! The whole of Europe against us! Spies! Is no one to be trusted? You did right, Captain, to stop my coach. Pray continue."

Far from being reassured by the deputy's sudden about-face, the Captain seemed uncertain of what he should do next. His eyes made a slow sweep of the groups of civilians and vehicles which blocked the road. He had it in his mind to allow the deputy and his party to take precedence over the others. A moment's reflection stayed the impulse. Commissioners and their deputies were sometimes fanatical in their subscription to the principle of equality. And the red cap on the deputy's head persuaded him that he was dealing with a fanatic. No, the deputy would not thank him for special favors. On the other hand, to delay him unnecessarily could prove most unpleasant.

Coming to a decision, the captain barked out an order, and the soldiers made hast to return passports to travelers before ordering them to proceed.

Zoë, at a curt nod from Rolfe, made to enter the coach. On an impulse, she turned and ran swiftly to the man who had been arguing his case so volubly as their own coach had drawn to a halt. At Zoë's approach, the daughter of the family, a child of no more than eight or nine summers, looked up. Like the rest of her family, she was painfully thin and dressed in pitiful summer garments.

"For you," said Zoë, and thrust her doll into the child's arms.

Joy fleetingly warmed those unrevealing eyes before their expression became guarded.

"I'm too old for dolls," said Zoë as the child flashed a questioning look at her father.

"Fleur!" Rolfe's hand closed around Zoë's arm like a vise.

"I have nothing for the boy," she said miserably, and threw him a look of shameless appeal.

His answering look spoke volumes, but he dug into his pocket just the same and pressed something into the boy's hand before hoisting him into his father's arms. The man was effusive in his gratitude.

"And now, *ma petite fleur!*" Rolfe's hand grasped Zoë's elbow with a fair force. She stole a sideways glance at him, wondering if she had provoked him to anger by her impulsive act. She thought she must have done so. His jaw was set like granite.

He walked her back to the calèche in tight-lipped silence. When he addressed the captain, however, his mode was everything that was conciliatory.

"Your chaps are very sharply turned out, Captain. I'll give you that."

"Thank you, sir."

"They are on their toes, and no mistaking."

The captain's stance relaxed somewhat.

"Not much would get past them, I make no doubt."

"Thank you, sir."

"I know what you are thinking."

"Sir?"

With a flourish of one hand, the deputy indicated his own motley crew who, among the lot of them, could not have provided a complete uniform for one man, and that not belonging to any single regiment.

"Don't deny it, Captain." Amusement coated Rolfe's voice. "You professional soldiers look down your noses at these conscripts. I'm not finding fault with you. It's only natural. But may I say, Captain . . . what is your name, by the bye?"

"Mercier, sir."

"Well, may I say this, Captain Mercier? One of these days, these young men will be a force to be reckoned with throughout the world. And do you know why? I'll tell you why." The deputy had begun on a harangue that was evidently dear to his heart. No one dared answer his rhetorical questions. "Europe has never before seen their like. In the future, our French republican armies will prove invincible, and for a very simple reason. The rank and file, like these men here, have made France's cause *their* cause. They are not professional soldiers. They are patriots, Captain Mercier. *Patriots*, I say! Not merely the paid agents of corrupt governments."

The young men to whom the deputy referred sat straighter in the saddle, their shoulders squared, their expressions set in more heroic lines. Zoë was appalled to discover that, through sheer nerves, she was on the point of giving in to a fit of the giggles.

The captain's slow, assessing glance hid nothing of his scepticism.

"But I'm digressing," said the deputy. "You have your orders to follow, as I have mine. Well, get on with it, man!"

"Sir?"

"Our passports. I believe you were on the point of examining them."

Self-consciously, the captain called over two of his lieutenants. Their examination of the proffered papers was of the most cursory kind. Zoë was more than a little relieved when she was returned to the carriage. To her dismay, the deputy still dallied with the captain.

"Commissioner Duhet, he's gone to Paris, I've been given to understand?"

"Angers," corrected the captain.

"So far south? Ah well, when one has only the benefit of an itinerant commissioner, one must make do as best one may. Pity! I shall no doubt meet up with you in an hour or so once I've executed my errand in Coutances. Angers you say? That's a devil of a long ride for my taste. Well, well! Duty is a hard taskmaster." And with a friendly wave from the coach window, Rolfe called to his coachman to get underway.

The cordial manner was not in evidence when Rolfe turned his stormy gray eyes upon Zoë.

In an attempt to forestall him, she blurted, "I'm

63

not sorry that I gave away your doll. That little girl? She was so . . . pathetic. I . . . I wanted to do something for her, 'tis all."

The gale in his eyes moderated a little, but there was still enough ice in his voice to freeze live coals. "I warned you once before never to disobey me."

"Oh!" So that was it.

"Have you no sense, little girl? Didn't it occur to you that the last thing I wanted was for you to call attention to yourself?"

"No," said Zoë. "I thought . . ." She glanced down at her clasped hands then looked up quickly before her courage completely deserted her. "I thought you were trying to divert attention from the coachman."

"You thought!" In stunned silence, he stared at her for a full minute, then threw back his head and emitted a low laugh. "Children!" he exclaimed. "They're more acute than we grownups give them credit for! 'Out of the mouths of babes!' " He shook his head and regarded her with a softer, more endearing aspect. His eyes, she noted, were more blue than gray.

'You did a fine thing, a very fine thing, when you parted with your doll. It was a most generous gesture."

"No, really, it was nothing," answered Zoë, with more honesty than the deputy could possibly have imagined. She was thinking that if he wished to turn the conversation, she had no objection. For a moment there she had feared that she was about to be subjected to another humiliating spanking.

"I promise I'll make it up to you."

"I wish you would not." She did not wish the deputy to be always thinking of her in such terms.

"I know how much the doll meant to you."

"I doubt it." At the look of patent surprise which crossed his face, she hurriedly added, "No other doll could possibly replace Zoë in my affections."

"We shall see."

Zoë absorbed Rolfe's words in unsmiling silence. It was evident to her that the deputy supposed that they would meet up with each other again. She knew better. Once he delivered her to her destination, others would come for her and give her escort to the island of Jersey. She would never set eyes on him again.

Her eyes burned. Her throat hurt. Misery settled in the pit of her stomach with all the weight of a marble tombstone. In the space of an hour, he would be out of her life forever.

As the coach rattled its way slowly uphill, over cobbled streets, towards the Law Courts, Zoë stared blindly at the unwitting object of her bewilderment. The man was an agent of the Convention. He was a bigot. He must be. Commissioners and their deputies were hardened *enragés,* purveyors of the new fanatical religion. It was they who carried the Reign of Terror from the floor of the Convention to the provinces. Sensible folk would shake in their shoes whenever their paths chanced to cross these *représentants en mission,* as evidenced by her own alarm when she'd first set eyes on the deputy. She'd been terrified out of her wits then.

But that was all of three days ago. In that short space of time, there had been a material conversion in her feelings towards the young man. From the moment he had ushered her out of the school and onto the streets of Rouen, she had been vaguely aware of his protection. Subsequent events had confirmed that first impression. She was persuaded that it was more,

65

on his part, than mere devotion to duty. There was a kindness there which she had not mistaken. It was no act. He really cared about her well-being. He'd looked out for her comfort. And with the best will in the world, he had given her a doll to occupy the long hours of tedium when she was confined to the coach. Even the spanking he had administered was one more evidence of his concern. And she could not remember without smiling, his droll dismay when he had suspected that he might have taken advantage of her in his sleep.

He was a strange man, this deputy who cared about people. She could not reconcile his office with what she had observed of him.

In Coutances, at the Law Courts, they parted company with the conscripts. If they wondered why the deputy made no move to join them, they gave no sign of it. The parting, on all sides, was effected with nothing but friendliness. They had been in close quarters for three days. For the most part they had rubbed along together tolerably well.

The coach made several sharp turns. Zoë lost her bearings. With a suddenness which surprised her, it drove through the open doors of a livery stable. The doors closed behind them. She was helped to alight. She had barely stepped down from the carriage when the coachmen on the box jumped down and others took their places. A set of doors opposite the ones they had driven through were flung open. The carriage rolled out into the dusk. The doors were swiftly closed behind it.

The deputy guided her through a door and down a dimly lit corridor. They passed through another door and entered a room where there were two men and a woman seated around a table. At sight of the deputy and his companions, the men shouted a greeting and came forward. Zoë was taken in charge by the round-faced, motherly woman and pushed onto a stool close to the hearth. Within minutes, a bowl of hot pea soup was warming her cold hands and nourishing the ache of hunger she had scarcely remarked until that moment.

Snatches of conversation registered in Zoë's brain. She and Housard were to be conveyed to a safe house on the coast within the hour. The deputy was bound for Paris and one more run. They spoke of letters and packages as if they were couriers delivering the post. There were jests and back slapping and the occasional glance in the direction of the coachman. The mood was one of jubilation and self-congratulation. The deputy had smuggled their "package" through the roadblock, right under the noses of Robespierre's agents, Zoë heard them say. And then the deputy, with a meaningful look at Zoë, said something to make his companions guard their tongues.

Zoë pretended an interest in the soup she was spooning into her mouth, but behind her carefully blank expression she calculated that the deputy's coachman could be no other than the spy the soldiers were hunting. It wasn't until the deputy tore the red cap from his head and threw it in the grate, however, that everything became clear to her.

When the flames licked round it, a cheer went up. And then the deputy went down on his haunches before her and smiled into her somber eyes.

As from a great distance, Zoë heard those deep, resonant tones as he made his adieux. Her eyes huge in her face, she drank in the sight of him, taking his impression as if she were afraid that, in time, he would fade from her memory. But she would only have to close her eyes, she decided, and she would see Deputy Rolfe's gray eyes darken to blue as they crinkled with mirth, and his slow smile, just so, half-tilted at the corners. Her gaze carefully traced over each feature, from the gilded cap of disheveled hair to the laughter lines slashing deeply into his face.

He kissed her on both hands and then, with one last lingering look, he was gone.

No. She would never forget him. Not till her dying day. And in that moment, she realized with shattering clarity that her heart had been given irrevocably to a man whose identity she did not even know.

Chapter Four

In various quarters in the city of London, grand houses, some rented, some purchased outright, had been made ready as a temporary shelter for those French refugees who were arriving in England, friendless and without a sou to their names. In the Gloucester Road area, in the district of Marylebone, a whole row of Georgian houses was turned over for this purpose. It was to one of these residences that Zoë came on the first day of her arrival in London. She was taken in hand by a member of the reception committee whose purpose it was to interview these new émigrés and help them get settled.

Madame Bertaut was not herself French, but the widow of a French diplomat. She was an affable lady in late middle age. Her friendly manner and unfailing tact inspired confidence. With many encouraging smiles and long, patient silences, she gradually jogged Zoë into revealing the salient details of her background and circumstances.

"Leon Devereux? That name rings a bell."

"My father was a banker."

"Good heavens! Those Devereux?" exclaimed Madame Bertaut. She looked at Zoë more closely. "My late husband mentioned your father quite frequently.

Before the war, his financial empire spanned the English Channel, I was given to understand."

Zoë remained silent. She knew nothing about her father's business.

After a moment, Madame Bertaut continued, "Your parents were arrested, you said?"

Zoë had to search to find her voice. Without elaboration she told of her parents' arrest and subsequent removal to Carmes.

Madame Bertaut made notations on a piece of paper as Zoë gave her explanation.

"And your brother and sister? What happened to them?"

"We became separated," answered Zoë. To reveal the assumed names and identities of her siblings was to place them in jeopardy. Claire had been very firm on that point before Zoë left Rouen. Until they were all safely together in England, she must employ the greatest circumspection. It was no secret in France that her parents were awaiting trial. It was perfectly safe to reveal as much as she knew about their circumstances. With respect to her brother and sister, she must remain obstinately vague.

"How old are you?" asked Madame Bertaut.

"Seventeen."

The pencil stopped scratching. Madame Bertaut's head tilted inquiringly. "Seventeen?"

Warm color heated Zoë's cheeks. "This is merely a disguise."

"You don't have to explain to me, my dear. I understand perfectly. I've seen young women dressed as boys, men dressed as old women, and . . . well, you know what I mean. Best to keep these things to ourselves. A loose tongue might very easily prove disastrous for those who are risking their lives to bring others out of France. Do you take my meaning?"

Zoë signified that she did. She had been enjoined to secrecy in the livery stable at Coutances. Wild horses could not drag from her either the name of her savior or the means he had employed to get her safely to England.

A moment or two later, Madame Bertaut set down her pencil and surveyed her companion. Smiling, she observed "Zoë. That's an unusual name. I like it."

She could not have known the effect of those few words on the grave-faced girl who stared at her unblinkingly. At the sound of her name, something inside Zoë, a tangled skein of suppressed emotion, seemed to unravel. Only then did she begin to feel a shadow of the old Zoë stir in her. It would be an exaggeration to say that she smiled. But her features softened with a becoming animation. She was Zoë again.

"We try to find everyone employment as soon as may be," explained Madame Bertaut, and thereupon launched into an account of opportunities which were available for a girl of Zoë's education and aptitude. "Fortunately, your English is impeccable," she confided.

Zoë was assigned to a small box room in the attic which she was to share with another unattached young female. Francoise had been in England for a number of months, and was older than Zoë by several years. Her poise, her quick intelligence was something to be envied, in Zoë's opinion, as was her sleek good looks. *Soignée* was the word that came to Zoë's mind. Soignée and very French, with her modish cap of dark curls and deeply set, chocolate brown eyes.

71

Over the next little while, Francoise became something of a mentor to Zoë. She found Zoë suitable clothes to wear and showed her how to adapt them to the current mode. She offered a hail of advice on how Zoë should conduct herself in society. And she introduced Zoë to the other residents of the house.

The house was crowded to the rafters. Whole families were domiciled in a single room. Few of the residents had any pretension to blue blood. They were journalists and professional men, with a sprinkling of officers of the old guard. Some of them were ardent Royalists. Most of them were moderates, idealists who were appalled when they found themselves the scapegoats of extremists on either side of the political spectrum. They gathered in the front parlor at all hours of the day and night. As the womenfolk bent over their embroidery or knitting, the gentlemen would hotly debate French politics, and relive the old quarrels in France. These were safe topics. There were few among them who did not show some reticence in revealing their personal histories, and Zoë divined that, like herself, they had family and friends in France they wished to protect.

From time to time, a courier would arrive at the house with reports of what was happening at home. As one day followed another, the news became more disquieting. The terror was growing in momentum and there seemed to be no end in sight to its excesses. Of her own family, Zoë heard nothing.

"The English have a saying: 'No news is good news.'"

The comment came from one of the newer residents. Charles Lagrange, a journalist, and one-time editor of the Paris *Liberté,* had arrived in England al-

72

most at the same time as Zoë. She judged him to be something under fifty. He was thin almost to the point of emaciation. The rumor was that he had been hiding for months in a friend's cellar before he found safe passage to England.

"What does it mean, 'No news is good news'?" asked Zoë.

He put his hand on Zoë's shoulder in a consoling gesture and withdrew it almost immediately. "What it means, *ma petite,* is that there is still hope."

Zoë's eyes traveled to the young couple who were on the point of leaving the room. Madame Bertaut was with them. Her expression was grave. No one doubted that she was the bearer of bad tidings.

No news is good news. In the days that followed, Zoë was to cling tenaciously to that worn, English proverb. And though there were few occasions for rejoicing in the house in Gloucester Road, she, like the others, maintained a cheerful facade from the moment she stepped outside her chamber until the candles were doused every evening.

In the close confines of the small room which she shared with Francoise, it was inevitable that the girls would begin to confide in each other. Even so, there was a certain circumspection which was impossible to overcome. By tacit consent, each girl permitted the other the privacy she wished for herself.

It soon became evident to Zoë that their reasons for drawing a veil over the past were far different. Zoë's one wish was to protect her family. Francoise was alone in the world. It was her sanity she wished to protect. She could not recall the last weeks of her life in France without falling into a deep despondency.

Happily, there was no dearth of amusements in London to distract those of a melancholy turn of mind. The members of the more established French community had taken it upon themselves to arrange outings and parties, duly chaperoned, for their more recently arrived compatriots.

London was far different from the Paris Zoë remembered. And though she did not consider the English capital the equal of its French counterpart in grandeur or beauty, in all other respects she much preferred it. To walk through its streets without fear of molestation was an experience to which she felt she would never become accustomed. The shops on Bond Street, no less than the fashionables who crowded its pavements, quite bowled her over. There were trips to Ranleagh Gardens in Chelsea and to Vauxhall across the river, and not even the chill December weather could dispel one iota of her pleasure. Hyde Park was within walking distance and scarcely a day went by that Zoë and Francoise did not persuade one of the gentlemen to act as their escort. More often than not, it was Charles Lagrange who accompanied them. With Zoë his manner was avuncular. With Francoise he was invariably scrupulously correct.

"Hyde Park again?" he asked, mildly teasing. "That's the third time this week. What's the attraction?"

"Nothing . . . nothing," answered Zoë at once, avoiding Francoise's eyes. "Merely a walk to work up an appetite for dinner."

She missed the amused glance her two companions exchanged. It was five o'clock in the afternoon, the moment when the fashionable houses of nearby Mayfair disgorged their blue-blooded occupants for their

74

daily rendezvous in the park. The stylish carriages, the thoroughbred horses with their equally thoroughbred riders, the celebrated beauties—Zoë had never witnessed so much refinement in one place or such a display of elegance. Not that she would have admitted as much to her companions. Her extravagant admiration she deemed childish, and the last thing Zoë wanted was to be regarded in that light.

Her conviction that Hyde Park at five o'clock in the afternoon was the acme of elegance was dispelled on her first visit to the opera in the Hay Market's King's Theatre. The gorgeously bejeweled ladies in their opera boxes had her gaping. Surely Versailles at its zenith could not have boasted such splendor or ladies of such irrefutable breeding and grace.

It was Francoise who disabused her of such foolish notions.

"Fashionable impures?" repeated Zoë.

"That's what the English call them. Look at them—like merchandise in a shop window! They rent these boxes at astronomical prices to sell their wares to the highest bidder."

"Are you saying they are common prostitutes?"

"There's nothing common about them," Francoise snorted. "They're at the top of their profession. Some of them are mistresses to the wealthiest titled gentlemen in all England."

"Mistresses," said Zoë, and shuddered. She felt as if someone had just walked over her grave. "What are you wearing to the party at Devonshire House?"

The subject of mistresses was dropped, as Zoë hoped it would be. But she could not shut her mind to the distasteful thoughts which the word had evoked.

The Christmas party at Devonshire House was an event which Zoë anticipated with mixed feelings. The do was in the nature of a charitable gesture towards the French community in London. And though Zoë deemed the duchess of Devonshire's motives as the highest, she did not care to think of herself as the object of anyone's charity.

She voiced that thought to Francoise and was reproached with the older girl's irrefutable logic. "We *are* charity cases," said Francoise. "The bread we eat, the garments we wear, the roof over our heads, even our pin money — where do you think it all comes from?"

Zoë had no answer. "Where?" she asked.

"From the fat purses of people like the Devonshires, that's where. We should be grateful to them, Zoë."

Zoë hastened to assure her friend that her gratitude was bottomless. Nevertheless, it was borne in upon her that she must give serious consideration to her future. She could not forever depend on the charity of others. If her parents did not come for her soon, she must strike out on her own. Madame Bertaut had intimated that there was time enough to find suitable employment in the new year, when the members of the *ton* returned to town from their great houses in the country.

"Madame has every confidence that she can place me as a companion or a children's governess," Zoë informed Francoise one evening as they undressed for bed.

"You know my feelings on that subject," answered Francoise flatly.

Since Zoë's first day in town, Francoise had dropped some elaborate hints about her one and only experience as a governess. As Zoë understood, she had been forced to hand in her notice or else be hounded into accepting *carte blanche* from the master of the house.

"Wedlock, Zoë. It's the only solution for girls like us. Find yourself a young man before you are whisked off to some godforsaken place in the country. You'll never find a husband there. Englishmen are not like to offer for dowerless French girls, whatever their pedigree."

"I have no wish to marry," demurred Zoë. At her friend's words, her thoughts had taken flight. She was thinking of a young man with blond hair, whose eyes changed color with his moods. Her *chevalier*. "Rolfe." She mouthed the word silently, over and over, as if it were a benediction, and wondered if it were his real name and where he was and what he was doing.

Rolfe eased back on the large fourposter bed, savoring the release of sexual tension which left him pleasantly replete. The warm, naked woman at his side moved restlessly and Rolfe stilled her with one arm flung carelessly around her waist.

"Rolfe?"

"Mmm?"

"You mustn't fall asleep! Not here! Not unless you're prepared for some very unpleasant consequences. I thought I told you. George is due to arrive within the hour."

Roberta Ashton raised on one elbow and with the pads of her fingers lightly traced the slumberous features of the man who had just made love to her.

"George?" muttered Rolfe, and batted her hand away.

"My husband," retorted his companion.

Rolfe opened one eye. "I thought you were separated."

"He wants a reconciliation." Amusement coated her voice.

"Damnation!"

In one smooth movement, Rolfe threw back the bedclothes and rolled to his feet. Unashamedly naked, he stalked the room, retrieving the garments he had practically torn from his person a scant hour before. The woman watched the play of candlelight on Rolfe's sleek, muscular torso, and a soft purr caught in her throat.

"Don't worry, darling," she crooned, "George was never known for his punctuality."

"I'm not worried." The response was muffled. Rolfe was pulling his shirt over his head.

The lady dragged herself to a sitting position and artfully arranged the covers so that her up-tilted breasts peaked over the edge of the sheet. Her green eyes widened. Her lips pouted. She ran her fingers through her short titian ringlets, arranging them into a reasonable semblance of order. If Rolfe cared to glance in her direction, he must surely be struck by the picture she presented.

Rolfe looked straight at her. "Where are my boots?" he demanded.

"Try under the bed, darling." Her tone was dulcet. It was through sheer force of will that she managed to restrain herself from gnashing her teeth.

The Honorable Mrs. Roberta Ashton prided herself on her strength of will. In her short liaison with Rolfe Brockford, the marquess of Rivard, she'd had more need of it than she'd had in the previous thirty years of her life. Not that the lady looked her age. With her high-breasted girlish figure and translucent complexion, she could easily pass for a woman a good five years younger, if she had a mind to. It so happened that she had a mind to.

"You have only to say the word, Rolfe, and I'll send George packing."

In the act of pulling on his boots, Rolfe stilled. He half-turned in his chair, and gave her a long level look. "Now why should you wish to do that?"

An angry flush spread from her throat to her hairline. This was not the answer she wanted. Her little ploy was meant to bring the marquess to heel. She knew, of course, that she was not the only woman in his life. He had never pretended otherwise. But she was the only woman of any significance. To her knowledge, Rolfe had never remained as constant in his attentions to any woman as he had to her. It was this thought which had given her the confidence to force his hand. She was coming to perceive that she had acted prematurely.

"I see," she said carefully, and reached for a silk negligee which was spread on a chair beside the bed. She slipped her arms into it, and came to stand beside Rolfe. He was shrugging into his coat.

'You are jumping to conclusions, Rolfe. I didn't say that I was returning to my husband. Nothing could be farther from my mind." She touched a hand to the lapel of his coat and smoothed an imaginary wrinkle.

"You should give it some thought," he answered seriously.

She stiffened. "So that's it!" she exclaimed.

His eyebrows lifted.

"Off with the old love and on with the new?"

"What does that mean?"

"The opera dancer? The little brunette in the chorus? Your eyes never wavered from her all evening! Is that why you were as hot as coals for me tonight? You must think I'm a veritable innocent if I don't know when a man is making love to me but thinking of another woman!" She could scarcely believe that she had betrayed herself by voicing the ugly suspicion. If she didn't find her control, she knew she would lose him. "Forgive me, please? It's . . . it's been a wretched month without you." She gave him a tremulous smile. "I'm jealous of any woman you look at. Can you blame me? Not only are you the most eligible bachelor in the whole of England, but the women who are eager to share your bed are legion."

"Oh, legion!" he drawled.

"Darling," she wheedled, "don't you love me a little?"

"About as much as you love me, I should say," he answered softly.

The snap of her teeth almost gave her away. Recovering quickly, she soothed, "If you only feel a fraction of what I feel for you, I shall be well satisfied."

"Look, I do have to go. Do you mind?" Rolfe took a step backwards and her hands fell away from his shoulders.

"Shall . . . shall I see you tomorrow at the Devonshires' do?"

"What about your husband?" He was scanning the room to see if he had left anything.

"Darling, I've already forgotten him."

Before she could think of a way to detain him, he was striding out of the room. She ran to catch up with him and halted with one small hand on the balustrade. "*Will* you be at the Devonshires' party?" Her eyes followed him as he descended the stairs two at a time.

When he reached the marble foyer, he glanced in her direction. After a slight hesitation, he answered, "I'll be there."

As he made his exit a frigid draft fanned the flames of the candles in the silver candelabrum which was set on an elaborately inlaid commode. The front door latched gently at his back. The lady turned aside and entered her chamber. The slam of her door reverberated ominously throughout the house.

Cursing the driving sleet, Rolfe turned up the collar of his greatcoat and struck out towards Piccadilly and his club in St. James. He was too keyed up, too restless, he decided, to go back to the big empty house in St. James Square. In a day or so, he would go down to Rivard Abbey. The thought should have filled him with pleasure. He cursed again, and wondered why the release of sexual tension left him strangely dissatisfied of late.

He must be tiring of his mistress, he decided. The thought amused him. It hardly seemed possible. Roberta Ashton was everything a man could possibly want in a mistress. Beneath her ethereal beauty beat the heart of a voraciously passionate woman. She was experienced and knew how to appease a man's desire as well as rouse it. And if she occasionally showed symptoms of a jealous nature, he had no real quarrel with that. What woman didn't? It was an annoyance men learned to tolerate.

That she was a married lady and moved in his own circles did not weigh with Rolfe. To his knowledge, the marriage was virtually over. It wasn't only that

81

George Ashton was a complacent husband. He was almost in his dotage. His grown children by his first marriage were older than his wife. The poor clod had mistaken the character of the dowerless young beauty who had latched onto the wealthy widower in her first season. He'd soon wakened to his mistake when his wife had taken a string of young lovers. Ever the gentleman, George had retired to the country, permitting his wife to go her own way.

Damn! He hated these games women played! She'd thought to make him jealous! Jealous! Her ploy was so patent that a callow youth could have seen through it. It was she who was the jealous one, as she'd proved by her reference to the little opera dancer.

She could not have been more mistaken in her assumptions. His attention had been fixed on the girl simply because she reminded him so forcibly of the child he had conveyed from Rouen to Coutances. Fleur Guéry. He'd promised himself that he would look her up once he was back in England. He'd been back for over a week, but there had been little enough time to find her direction. There had been a succession of interminable meetings with Titéniac as Rolfe related some of what he'd observed in France. He'd never undergone such a thorough interrogation and had wondered what it might mean.

One thought led to another. He was almost at King Street before he realized he'd been so lost in reverie that he'd gone the length of St. James Street without turning into his club. Shrugging philosophically, he allowed his long strides to carry him forward.

The house in St. James Square was as fine as any to be found in the whole of London. Nevertheless, Rolfe was toying with the idea of putting it up for sale. There was no doubt that in the last number of years, the square had lost caste. Most of the nobility and gentry had moved westwards to Mayfair. Their places were being taken by rich cits, or worse, gaming dens and select bawdy houses. Behind those imposing facades, God only knew what depravities were being committed. Even to walk the length of King Street was an undertaking in itself. Ladies of the painted frailty with their retinue of liveried servants were very much in evidence. Not that Rolfe minded for himself. But his mother was scandalized by the incessant comings and goings in the square at all hours of the day and night. She was angling for a move to Mayfair. The most persuasive argument that she had put forward to date was that should her son marry in the near future, his bride's innocence must be corrupted by the iniquities which were so blatantly perpetuated in and around St. James.

Wedlock. As he nursed a glass of fine French brandy before the blazing grate in his bookroom, Rolfe let the thought revolve in his mind. Again a feeling of restlessness swept over him. That he could not put his finger on the source of his dissatisfaction irked him excessively. Until less than a month before, he had not been plagued by such vague feelings of discontent. He had a full life. He wanted for nothing. He was seldom bored. How could he be in his line of work? Danger and boredom were, in essence, irreconcilable. On the other hand, wedlock and boredom were bedmates, if *ton* marriages were anything to go by. Perhaps it was boredom he craved?

From contemplating wedlock, Rolfe's thoughts turned to his nieces. Spoiled little brats, he thought affectionately. The unspoken words immediately brought to mind the picture of another little girl, Fleur Guéry, with her huge doe eyes and solemn little face. Something about the child must have captivated him. Scarcely a day went by but his thoughts were drawn to her.

Stretching out his long legs, he crossed one booted foot over the other, wondering why it was he could not seem to put her out of his mind. His mistress, he knew, would be mortified if she knew that his thoughts dwelled more on this one slip of a girl than on any other female of his acquaintance. Frowning, he set down his glass sharply. A moment later, he took himself off to bed.

Chapter Five

Behind their high, stone walls, some of the great
Georgian mansions on Piccadilly gave every indica-
tion of being fortresses, or jails. Devonshire House,
in particular, had the most forbidding appearance of
them all. That it possessed one of the finest views in
the whole of England counted for nothing to the
Devonshires' guests. Only the servants who were
domiciled in the attics had an unobstructed view
across the walled screen to the pleasant aspect of
Green Park, on the other side of Piccadilly.

The interior of the house, however, soon dispelled
its first, gloomy impression. Zoë and Francoise,
with Charles Lagrange acting as their escort,
climbed the outer staircase and passed through to
the grand entrance hall, two stories high, and with
two cantilevered staircases at one end, which rose
gracefully to the next floor. The contents of the
house Zoë knew to be splendid. The plates, the
linen, the fine porcelain and furniture were thought
to be worth a king's ransom. And the duke's picture
collection was widely held to be without par in all
Europe. Thoughts of plates, porcelain, pictures and
such like were soon banished, however, when the
girls' beheld the elegance of the fashionables, espe-

cially the ladies, who waited in line to pay their respects to their hostess.

The padded bustles and hoops of a few years before had given way to a more classical silhouette. Skirts fell in graceful folds from just below the bosom. Trains were longer and swept the floor, a cause for peril for those gentlemen who had yet to accustom themselves to the latest in feminine fashions. And though, at first glance, the sea of pale muslins and silks was uniformly colorless, the precious gems and metals which adorned the bare throats and arms of some of the most beautiful women in London added a brilliance which could not be eclipsed.

Zoë fingered the pearl gray muslin which she had altered to the current mode at Francoise's behest, and she decided that she was very glad she had taken the older girl's advice. True, had she worn the green velvet she would not now be frozen to the marrow. But Zoë counted comfort as next to nothing when making her curtsies to the crème de la crème of English society. She was French. She was female. To be considered *démodé* was to lose face twice over.

"I told you so," murmured Francoise in a soft undertone, and arranged the folds of her pale primrose muslin in a pointed reference to the gowns she and Zoë had spent hours unpicking and putting together for tonight's party.

Zoë flashed her friend an amused look and behind her painted fan remarked that though the ladies were alert on all suits, the gentlemen, from all appearances, could not make up their minds whether they were fish or fowl.

It was a fair comment in the opinion of Charles Lagrange. Some of the older gentlemen sported powdered wigs with queues. The younger generation, and the French who were present, to a man, eschewed this outdated fashion. Their locks were natural, in a variety of styles, from a short crop, to shoulder-length hair tied in back with a ribbon. Some gentlemen wore elaborately embroidered velvet or silk coats and waistcoats with a fall of lace at the throat and wrists. Others had adopted the more austere French fashion, and sported a simple knotted cravat or stock in pristine white silk or muslin, set off to perfection with a plain dark frock coat.

Snuffboxes were very much in vogue as were quizzing glasses, the latter an affectation which embarrassed Zoë excessively. If a lady caught a gentleman's fancy, he did not hesitate to raise the glass which was suspended from his neck on a ribbon. Bold eyes would thereupon make a thorough appraisal until some other lady chanced to come into the gentleman's line of vision.

At the entrance to the Grand Drawing Room, Zoë made herself known to her hostess. Georgina Devonshire, at something under forty, was the reigning queen of society and still justly accredited as an incomparable. Her hair was of that hue which Zoë. esteemed above all others — more fair than titian — and her Junoesque stature filled Zoë with nothing but admiration. But it was the duchess's manners, unstudied and generous, which completely won her over. And though Zoë spent only a moment or two exchanging idle words on the difficulties meeting

French émigrés in London, by the time she passed on down the reception line, she felt as if the duchess was one of her most devoted friends.

The stars of the Devonshire House galaxy were out in force — among them Lady Melbourne, Sheridan the playwright, and Charles James Fox, the Whig orator of some distinction. It was rumored that the Prince of Wales was to put in an appearance later in the evening. But with eight hundred guests congregating in several saloons, Zoë felt sure that in the squeeze she was bound to miss the foremost *chevalier* in the whole of Europe.

There was no music, no cards, no entertainment of any description. People wandered about, from one great room to another, sipping champagne and striking up conversations with total strangers, as the fancy took them. In the space of an hour, Zoë had conversed with no less than three duchesses, five marchionesses, and a sprinkling of the lesser nobility, and those were of the English fraternity. On the French side, it seemed that every other guest lay claim to a title. Some of the faces, Zoë recognized. She had been introduced to them at various functions since arriving in London.

They were in the supper room, exclaiming over the plethora of delicacies which the duchess had laid out for her guests, when Zoë caught sight of a face she recognized but could not put a name to. Over the brim of her crystal glass, she studied the gentleman in question.

He was, by her reckoning, in his mid-thirties, distinguished looking, but far from handsome. His nose was too big, his chin was too square, and his bushy, black eyebrows met in the middle. Though he had adopted the newer fashion of simplicity, he wore a powdered wig tied in back in a queue with a black ribbon.

He turned to the side, revealing the presence of two gentlemen with whom he had been conversing. Zoë gave only a cursory glance to his fair-haired companion. But it jogged her memory as nothing else could. Deputy Rolfe had blond hair. And then she recognized the older gentleman. It was Housard, the man who had acted as their coachman from Rouen to Coutances. The last she had seen of him was on the island of Jersey.

Her eyes swiveled back to his blond-haired companion. She gave a little cry and set down her glass, spilling droplets of wine over the white linen tablecloth.

"Zoë? You look as though you'd seen a ghost." Francoise touched a finger to Zoë's ashen cheeks. "Are you all right, dear?"

"Excuse me," said Zoë. Her voice trembled in agitation. The gentlemen had their backs to her as they idled their way to the marble foyer. A whole roomful of people obstructed her path to the man whom she was almost certain was Deputy Rolfe.

"Zoë, what . . . ?"

She used her elbows to clear a way to the door. In the foyer, the crush of people was formidable. She looked around wildly, refusing to accept that she had lost her quarry. But Deputy Rolfe and Housard were nowhere to be seen. Drawing several, steadying breaths, she took stock of her surroundings. A number of people were already calling for their coaches to convey them to the next soirée in their round of parties. Others were ascending the stairs to take in the famous picture gallery. She sagged against a table, not knowing where to begin to look for them.

It was Tinténiac who led the way as they ascended the marble staircase. Rolfe and Housard fell into step behind him. They lingered in the gallery, ostensibly to admire their host's picture collection, then, unobserved, slipped into a small anteroom.

"Her Grace is most generous," observed Tinténiac, indicating a silver salver set with three crystal glasses and a decanter of amber liquid. Not one of the gentlemen doubted that it was the finest contraband cognac that France had to offer.

For a time, conversation was desultory and touched on the war and recent events in France. The gentlemen were ready to replenish their glasses before the reason for their clandestine meeting was finally broached.

Rolfe had heard some of it before from Tinténiac. It was known that a secret society with its origins in France was behind a series of assassination attempts in England.

"We suspect that your own brother may have been one of the first casualties," observed Tinténiac.

"Have you proof of this?" asked Rolfe sharply.

"None whatsoever. But all things considered, it's not an unreasonable supposition."

"What Monsieur Tinténiac means to say," interposed Housard, "is that the victims of these plots were not chosen at random. Your late brother, in common with three other victims, was known to be backing a Royalist landing in France."

"Backing? Do you mean with money? It's the first I've heard of it!"

"Nevertheless, it's the truth," retorted Housard. "To the tune of ten thousand pounds, to be exact."

Rolfe's expression was arrested. "Ten thousand pounds?" he murmured. He was remembering that when he had taken over the estates on his brother's demise, that very sum of money had shown up in the account books as having been dispersed to a certain charity for French émigrés, *Les Amis du Soleil*. He'd been curious about the group. Investigation had proved fruitless. No trace of any group by that name could be found, and he had come to the conclusion that the whole thing was a fabrication.

"I presume your brother did not take you into his confidence," commented Housard.

"You presume correctly. In those days, France seemed like the end of the world. Quite frankly, I wasn't interested, and Edward knew it." Rolfe gazed speculatively at his two companions. "What exactly is to be my assignment?" he asked.

Tinténiac rose to his feet. "I'll leave Housard to put you in the picture," he said and bolted his drink. "No sense taking any chances. I'll patrol the gallery. Better lock the door behind me."

When the door was locked behind Tinténiac, Rolfe turned his attention to his companion. "Well, Monsieur Housard, I'm listening. How do you fit into Tinténiac's network, precisely?"

Housard brought his glass to his lips and imbibed

slowly. After a moment's considering silence, he said, "Tinténiac's network has nothing to do with me except insofar as Tinténiac and I collaborate from time to time."

"Such as at the present moment," interposed Rolfe.

"As you say," Housard readily agreed. "In normal circumstances, France is my field of operations, not England."

"Then why the change?"

"This secret society, which goes by the name of *La Compagnie,* by the bye, has spread to England."

"I see." Rolfe knew he would not get a straight answer, but he asked the question just the same. "Who are you, Monsieur Housard?"

He had known, of course, that his coachman was no ordinary fugitive from the French authorities. His instructions had been to deliver him to the safe house in Coutances whatever the cost to life or limb. The child, Fleur, was small fry in comparison.

Housard carefully adjusted his stocky frame in the commodious Queen Anne chair. "Who I am is not important. For the moment, I am passing myself off as an émigré, a former lawyer of moderate persuasions, whose name went on the prescribed lists last spring."

"A moderate," mused Rolfe. "Are you really a moderate, Monsieur Housard, or is that persuasion assumed like the role you are playing?"

Housard permitted himself a small smile. "I really am a moderate," he said.

"And how do you come to know so much of this secret society?"

"That's easily answered, my lord. One of my agents, who infiltrated the Paris ring, was able to pass on invaluable information before she was discovered."

"Discovered, you say? What happened to her?"

"She was silenced. Permanently."

Rolfe's eyes flared, but he made no other comment. After a moment, Housard went on in the same conversational tone, "Before she died, Marie was able to give us, among other things, the names of *La Compagnie*'s agents who were either sent to, or recruited in, England. Unfortunately, those names were assumed, as you may understand, and have since been discarded."

As he considered his companion's words, Rolfe absently toyed with his glass. Finally, he observed, "The task of discovering their identities would seem monumental, Monsieur Housard."

"True, but for one thing. Most of those agents have been set in place in the last month or so. Their scent is still warm and ought to be easily picked up. And should we run only one of two of them to earth, they will lead us to the rest of the pack." Housard leaned forward in his chair as if to give due emphasis to his words. "It is imperative that we discover them soon, my lord. It is not only French lives which are threatened, but English lives also. It is my considered opinion that before long there will be a rash of murder attempts against some very highly placed people in England."

Surprise etched Rolfe's features. "Are you saying that this society is a tool of Robespierre, himself?"

"By no means, my lord. At least, not as far as we

can determine."

Rolfe murmured encouragement, and before long, Housard embarked on his tale. *La Compagnie,* so he told Rolfe, was founded before the Revolution swept France, and on the loftiest principles. As is the way of things, in time, corruption set in, so much so that those who founded the society, most of whom had died heroically for their convictions, would no longer have recognized it in its present form. By degrees, idealism had shifted to fanaticism, and assassination became *La Compagnie's* tool of persuasion or of eliminating those who opposed its creed.

"It is at this point in *La Compagnie's* history, that we believe your brother was singled out for assassination," averred Housard. "But very soon after, there seemed to be no thread, neither rhyme nor reason is what I mean, to the selection of their victims, or at least, none that I was able to detect for some time."

When Housard fell silent for a moment, Rolfe interposed, "Yes, but what you have yet to explain is this, Monsieur Housard: what *is* the creed of the society?"

"Respecting the rank and file of its members, I should say that they are fanatically committed to the principles on which the Revolution was founded— you know, equality, liberty, fraternity. But more and more I am forced to the conclusion . . ."

"Yes?"

Housard shook his head. "It seems preposterous, I know, but everything leads me to believe that *La Compagnie* is now in the business of murdering people for profit, and its members have become the dupes of *Le Patron* or his cohorts."

"Le Patron? I presume you are referring to the top man in the organization?"

"You presume correctly. It's the name he goes by within the society. I've been on his trail for some time past. Much good it has done me! He's careful. I'm no nearer to unmasking him than I ever was. Perhaps you shall have better luck in England." At the look of surprise which crossed Rolfe's face, Housard answered, "We know that *Le Patron* has come in person to oversee things here. But that's all we know."

At the end of ten minutes' conversation, Rolfe found himself beginning to subscribe to Housard's theory. *La Compagnie* had become the unwitting tool of some powerful figure or group bent on making a fortune by hiring out its assassins.

"And your assignment is to break their ring," said Housard at one point, "and with all speed."

Rolfe gazed at his companion curiously. "And what is to be your part in all this?" he asked.

Smiling, Housard answered, "You forget, my field of operations is France. It is to be hoped that by working together we shall smash *La Compagnie* on both sides of the Channel." He glanced at the clock on the mantel. "If you have no other questions, my lord?"

"Just one. Who in England will vouch for your character, Monsieur Housard, and I mean besides our mutual friend, Tinténiac?"

Housard's bushy eyebrows lifted. "Will your prime minister's recommendation satisfy you, my lord?"

Rolfe grinned. "In our line of business one can't be too careful. No offense meant, Monsieur

Housard."

"None taken, my lord."

"Please. Call me Rivard."

It was Housard who had the last word. "I have no use for careless agents, Rivard. Be sure you do check out my credentials," and so saying, he rose to his feet, indicating that the interview was at an end.

Rolfe's expression was deliberately bland. What he was thinking was that his companion must be a very big fish in British Intelligence. A word came to him—*Delta*. It was the code name of the most elusive spy in France. *Delta*. He wondered if *Delta* and Housard were one and the same person.

Chapter Six

On quitting the room, Rolfe practically ran down
a young woman who stepped into his path. He said
a few words of apology, flashed one of his engaging
grins, and made to brush past her.

Zoë could scarcely take in that the man of her
dreams was there in the flesh. Like a fish out of
water, she stood panting, staring up at him. Her
gaze lingered on every dear and well-remembered
feature and slid over the broad shoulders molded to
perfection in a dark frock coat. It registered in some
corner of her mind that the deputy's taste ran to the
simple and unadorned, and then she realized that
he was turning away without recognizing her. He
had given her his back before she had the presence
of mind to call out his name.

It was Housard whose face first registered a comi-
cally surprised recognition. "The little flower!" he exclaimed. "And all grown up too!"

Rolfe's smile faded as his eyes came to rest on the
young woman before him. His brows drew into a
straight line. "Fleur?"

Zoë could sense his disappointment, and her confidence wavered. Inwardly, she chastised herself for
expecting too much. It was foolish to have harbored

the secret hope that if ever the deputy saw her as she really was, he would be completely bowled over. One quick, comprehensive glance told her that, as a woman, she had made not the slightest impression upon him.

Before she could gather her wits, Housard smoothly interposed, "Child, what are you thinking of? Make your curtsies to the marquess of Rivard."

The lowered voice, the significant glances, were not lost on Zoë. She flushed, knowing that Deputy Rolfe's identity must never be revealed, and wondered at her colossal imprudence in voicing the name he had assumed in France. And then the full significance of the title Housard had given him struck her with full force. *The marquess of Rivard.* The man of her dreams was no deputy. Nor was he French. He was an English aristocrat.

"Rolfe is the name I prefer," said Rolfe quickly to cover the girl's acute embarrassment. "It's the name with which I was christened."

In a split second, everything became clear to Zoë. "Zoë is the name I prefer," she responded. "Zoë Devereux, my lord," and she bobbed him a curtsey.

"Zoë! Ah, that explains the doll's name!"

Inwardly, Zoë groaned. The last thing she wanted was for the man of her dreams to be always thinking of her in connection with dolls. But the damage was done. To her great disappointment, Rolfe's ready smile and the manner which he soon adopted verged on the avuncular. It was pride which fixed a smile to Zoë's lips and kept her voice steady as she related the particulars of her present situation in reply to his polite spate of questions.

"And by the new year, I hope to find a position as a companion or governess with an English family." She had painted as optimistic a picture of her circumstances as was humanly possible. Anyone listening to her would never guess at the homesickness she suffered or the ache of longing for the family she had left behind.

"A governess? A companion?" Rolfe did not trouble to hide his incredulity. "Child, you should be in the schoolroom, learning your catechism and sewing samplers, and such like." His eyes roamed the mill of people who were standing about, admiring the Rembrandt and Titian paintings on the walls. "Where is your chaperone?" he asked abruptly.

Zoë's spine straightened. "I left my *escort* in the Great Drawing Room. Monsieur Lagrange is his name. Perhaps you know of him?" This last was addressed to Housard who had been watching the interesting byplay between his two companions.

"I know of him," admitted Housard politely. "An unexceptionable fellow."

The blue in Rolfe's eyes faded to a telling gray. Zoë observed the phenomenon with an uneasiness which was born of experience.

"I should like to make the acquaintance of this unexceptionable fellow." Rolfe's eyes lingered on the girl's faintly belligerent expression and he chuckled. In a lowered voice he said, "Halfling, this is England. It doesn't do for even very young girls to forget the proprieties."

"I'm seventeen," she offered hopefully.

For a moment, he was confounded into silence. At length he murmured, "Seventeen? You're not

99

hoaxing me?"

"I'll be eighteen on my birthday." That the anniversary of her birthday was nine months away she conveniently did not mention.

She straightened, trying to appear taller, as his eyes made a slow perusal of her person. He shook his head. "Some girls are young for their years," was his only comment.

And with that damning, unwitting setdown, Zoë saw all her hopes come to ruin. It was too painful, too mortifying, to continue in this vein. She was groping in her mind for a way of detaching herself from her companions, when they were joined by a lady.

"Rolfe, darling, so this is where you have been hiding yourself?" A pair of startling green eyes made a quick and thorough assessment of Zoë before returning to the marquess. "I've been looking everywhere for you."

Rolfe's gaze swept the slender figure of the titian-haired beauty at his side. Their eyes met and held, and the smiling glances they exchanged, exclusive, intimate, spoke volumes.

"Roberta," drawled Rolfe, and in the next moment had drawn the lady away, as if he had quite forgotten present company.

His manners, thought Zoë, were deplorable. She should have been angry. She was crestfallen, and wished that the floor would open and she could sink into oblivion.

Almost as an afterthought, Rolfe called over his shoulder, "Monsieur Housard, would you be so kind as to convey the child to her chaperone?"

Zoë could not tear her eyes away from the couple as they strolled the length of the gallery. In comparison to the beautiful sophisticate who partnered the marquess, she felt dowdy and childish. And foolish beyond permission.

It was inconceivable that a gentleman who moved in the marquess's select circles, surrounded by beautiful and worldly women, would spare a second glance at an impoverished French émigré, and one, moreover, whom he regarded as a mere schoolgirl. But then, if she had known that her savior was an English nobleman, she would have accepted that her case was hopeless, and would never have allowed herself to weave such girlish fancies. She resolved, in that moment, to rout the handsome marquess from her heart and mind.

At that point in her reveries, Rolfe made a half turn and captured Zoë's unwary stare. The smile which he flashed her was one of his rare ones, without art, and as sweet as warm honey. Zoë stopped breathing. And when he winked, just so, and her heart skipped several beats before racing out of control, her newfound resolve shattered into a thousand shards.

"At least she's not Mimi or Fifi." Unthinkingly, she had spoken the words aloud. Her cheeks went pink. From under her lashes, she chanced a quick look at her companion.

Monsieur Housard's expression was everything that was kind. And in that moment, Zoë knew she had completely betrayed her *tendre* for the marquess. Making a supreme effort to recover herself, she offered, "Ladies are always losing their hearts to

101

knights in shining armor. It doesn't signify." The arch and amusing tone she had tried to adopt fell flat.

"Hero worship," intoned Housard softly. "It was only to be expected after what you've been through together."

"Was it?" asked Zoë doubtfully, and obediently placed her fingers on Housard's proffered arm. In the marquess's wake, they strolled to the marble staircase.

"Are you anxious to return to Lagrange?"

"Not particularly. Why?"

"There are a number of young gentlemen present this evening who, I am persuaded, would be more than happy to make the acquaintance of the young lovely who is hanging on my sleeve. May I make them known to you, Mademoiselle Devereux?"

A laugh was startled out of Zoë. "Schoolboys?" This time, she hit just the right note.

"Not all gentlemen are as blind as the marquess," observed Housard suavely, and he had the pleasure of knowing that his gallantry had hit the mark. A sparkle crept into the girl's eyes.

She smiled shyly up at him. "In my experience," she remarked, not quite truthfully, "young men are dead bores. I've always been partial to older gentlemen." This last was no dissimulation. She was devoted to her father.

"Such as the marquess?"

She pivoted to face him. "*Is* he too old for me?" she asked baldly.

Covering her small hand with his own broad one, Housard directed her steps forward. In a gentle

102

tone, he said, "My dear, there are none so blind as those who will not see. To Rivard, you are still the child you pretended to be when we set out from Rouen. When he observes that others accord you the respect which your advanced years merit, he'll soon see the error of his ways."

Zoë's eyes danced at the picture which flashed into her brain. "When I'm in my dotage?" she quizzed.

"True! With the English, one learns the virtue of patience. Who are Mimi and Fifi?"

She chewed on her bottom lip. Her expression carefully innocent, she replied, "Two of my dearest friends." She sighed soulfully. "I wonder if I shall ever meet up with them again?" And before Housard could question her further, she embarked on a spate of anecdotes on all the interesting places she had visited since arriving in England.

Housard had no objection to this turn in the conversation. But behind his bland expression and desultory comments, he made a study of the girl.

Zoë Devereux, he decided, was like one of those rare vintage burgundies which he vastly preferred to any other libation. Champagne, port, even French cognac came a poor second best. It required a connoisseur's palette to appreciate the less obvious and infinitely more intriguing nuances of a fine, full-bodied burgundy.

That the marquess of Rivard had shown himself wanting in this respect surprised him a little. On that hazardous coach ride from Rouen to Coutances, Rivard, as he remembered, had positively doted on the child. They had both remarked the child's intrinsic merits. Far from being the burden they had expected, the girl had turned that grim journey into something to be recalled with a certain pleasure. Just thinking of her, as brave as Achilles, enduring unspeakable terrors without a word of complaint brought a softening to his eye.

Seeing her now, as a young girl on the threshold of womanhood, he was struck with the thought that, given a few years, Zoë Devereux's vintage would come into its own. On the other hand, the lady who hung so tenaciously on the marquess's arm, he was persuaded, had no hidden depths, no unexpected nuances with which she might surprise a gentleman of discriminating tastes. It was regrettable that the marquess was a philistine with respect to his preference in women, and doubly regrettable that the girl hero-worshipped the marquess.

Thus, Housard, who was generally too preoccupied to be deflected from present business, found himself conjecturing how he might bring a smile to the girl's forlorn little face. Zoë, he decided, was sorely in need of a little masculine attention. And though he considered himself, in the normal course of events, committed to a graver purpose, he set himself to while away the next hour or so in pleasant dalliance.

It would have surprised Housard to know that this innocent game of dalliance was observed by the marquess and judged to be highly objectionable. And the only thing that kept Rolfe from putting a stop to it was the presence of his mistress. Roberta Ashton was sticking to him like a limpet. He had been appalled when she had cornered him in the gallery when he was in conversation with the child. The thought of introducing Zoë to his mistress had made him uncomfortable — guilty almost. It was evident that the child adored him. Her admiring glances were an embarrassment. And yet, inexplicably, he had no wish to disabuse Zoë of her childish fancies. Nor yet subject her to the sometimes salacious conversation which passed for flirting in his circles, and which Roberta Ashton had honed to a fine art. That he, himself, frequently indulged in this harmless form of address with ladies of a certain class, he counted as of no moment. He was a male, and far from innocent.

It was the word *divorce* which finally distracted Rolfe from pursuing Zoë with his eyes. "Who is thinking of getting a divorce?" he asked, suddenly conscious that he was expected to make some comment.

"I've been toying with the idea."

In a mildly amused voice, Rolfe droned, "Yesterday, if memory serves, you were toying with the idea of becoming reconciled to your husband."

"That was yesterday."

Roberta Ashton had finally hit upon a subject to divert the gentleman's attention to herself. Her eyes scanned the crush as she tried to divine which beauty had caught the marquess's interest. Her eyes came to rest on the little French girl whom she'd surprised in conversation with him in the gallery. A small frown pleated her brow. After a moment, the frown lifted and her eyes moved on.

"Divorce is not unheard of in our circles," she said, flashing him an arch look. She wondered if she

105

had gone too far. And yet, she reasoned, marriage to the marquess was not entirely outside the realms of possibility. From time to time, gentlemen were known to risk everything for the women they loved. She had the feeling that Rolfe Brockford would dare everything for the woman of his choice. It was a heady thought. Her hopes were dashed by his next observation.

"Then we must move in different circles," he said with a certain dryness.

He was beginning to wish that he had never taken up with Roberta Ashton. She was playing games, and they both knew it. No married woman in her right mind flirted with the idea of divorce, especially not a woman involved in an adulterous relationship. Such a woman stood to lose everything — her place in society, her means of support, her very children could be kept from her if her husband had a mind to. And for a gentleman to be named as a wife's lover in a divorce action could prove a very expensive business. Punitive husbands were known to have been awarded astronomical sums. There was worse. A man of honor was expected to marry the lady whose virtue he had compromised, or face social ostracism.

Rolfe's eyes narrowed to silver slits, and an ironic smile played about his lips. "How odd," he drawled, "that the estate of matrimony should be so little to your liking. By anyone's lights, Ashton is a most . . . complacent husband."

She pouted prettily, and peeped up at him through the sweep of her lashes. Half laughing, half sulky, she responded. "And so old and utterly boring. But you needn't worry, Rolfe. I know that matrimony holds no allure for you."

There was just enough inflection in her voice to turn the statement into a question. Rolfe saw a way out of his dilemma, and he grasped it.

"You misjudge me, my dear. My own nuptials are not so very far distant."

There was a shocked silence. "Your n—nuptials?" she stammered. " 'Tis the first I've heard of it, Rolfe." With his cruel words, she saw not only her hope of position and wealth fading, but also her claim on what had proved to be, throughout their short liaison, a very liberal purse.

He made a show of removing his gold filigree snuffbox from his coat pocket. With finger and thumb, he dipped into it. "Naturally, you are the first to be taken into my confidence."

"But who . . . ?" Her eyes flashed, then cooled to ice-cold emeralds. "The little French girl, I presume?" she said, her voice etched with venom.

"The little . . . ?" Humor warmed Rolfe's eyes. His gaze shifted and came to rest on Zoë. "She is a mere child," he demurred, and unthinkingly tightened his lips as a young fop whose reputation was notorious even by *ton* standards bent over Zoë's extended hand. He shut his snuffbox with a snap. "She needs a keeper, that one," he said indistinctly.

For the first time, it was borne in on the lady that she had suffered an insult in the Devonshires' gallery when Rolfe had whisked her away before she could be introduced to his betrothed. At the time, she had been flattered by what she had supposed was his loverlike eagerness to have her to himself.

That eagerness she now saw in a new light, and the heedless, bitter words slipped out before she could guard her tongue. "The most noble marquess of Rivard shackled to that little drab? You're hoaxing me, Rolfe! The girl is no beauty! She has no address! In short, she has nothing to recommend her!"

Cool gray eyes lifted to meet hers. "Innocence is its own recommendation," he said, a curious inflection that was not quite anger in his voice.

She caught a glimpse of steel in one who habitually gave the appearance of being as soft as satin. Forcing a small smile, she said, rather helplessly, "Forgive me. It's just that I had no notion that you were thinking of getting married. Naturally, you took me by surprise." A teasing lilt crept into her voice. "May I be permitted to say that you don't have the look of a man who is madly in love, Rolfe?"

"Love? What has that to say to anything? I'm talking about duty."

For a fleeting moment triumph flashed in her eyes. Laughingly she offered, "Then may I be the first to wish you happy?"

"That would be premature. Nothing is settled."

"Oh?" When he did not respond to her hopeful look she went on, "In any event, it makes no difference to our arrangement. We ladies know when to turn a blind eye to a husband's little . . . intrigues."

He assumed a mock melancholy air. "My dear Roberta," he observed, "as the law stands, a wife would be a fool to do anything less. A single lady, on the other hand, is not constrained to fall in with her betrothed's wishes, nor tolerate his follies, for that matter."

"I don't think I follow you."

"Don't you?" One eyebrow quirked. "You never used to want for sense. What I mean is this—until I get my ring on the girl's finger, it behooves me to conduct myself with all the circumspection of a novitiate in holy orders. And my advice to you is to emulate my example."

"What?"

"Divorce is a distasteful business."

The smile on her lips slipped as the full significance of his blandly offered words registered. "Are you suggesting that we should stop seeing each other?"

He shrugged, the gesture adroitly avoiding the necessity of a verbal reply. In the next moment, he returned the salute of some gentleman who had just entered, and making the lady a courtly bow, he sauntered off.

Beneath his charming and gracious exterior, Rolfe was seething. Roberta Ashton, he reflected, was a designing woman, and he was just beginning to see where those designs led. The night before, she had babbled about reconciling with her husband. This evening, the talk was all of divorce. Damn if she was not angling to land him in her net! He could scarcely credit it. The lady was no innocent. She must know that the scion of a great and noble house might not marry where the lady's virtue was in question, not even if he had a mind to, which Rolfe certainly did not.

Divorce. The very word repelled him, but not half as much as the thought of marriage to Roberta

Ashton. It was well known that the lady changed lovers as often as she changed her gloves. He was only one in a long string of swains. Neither of them had demanded fidelity of the other.

She was fishing. That thought steadied him. Nevertheless, in the unlikely event that George Ashton was serious in his intent to procure a divorce, Rolfe was resolved that it was not he who would be cited in the divorce action.

His eyes scanned the crush and fell on Zoë. The little French girl, he decided, would do very well as a diversionary tactic. His lips quivered in amusement as he reflected that it was Roberta herself who had put the notion into his head.

As he approached the knot of young fribbles who surrounded Zoë, her eyes lifted to meet his. She gave a start, then blushed furiously, and lowered her lashes. She really was a charming child, he thought, and adroitly cut her out of the herd.

Having spent a good half-hour promenading through the spacious public rooms under the avidly interested gaze of the *ton,* and the affronted stare of his erstwhile mistress (who had lost no time in acquiring a new beau), Rolfe returned Zoë to her gaping companions. Introductions were made, and some commonplaces were exchanged. Soon after, Rolfe quit Devonshire House.

But he was restless. The thought of the cold, empty house in St. James held no attraction. He put in an appearance at Covent Garden and after the performance slipped into the Green Room where well-breeched lordlings and performers hovered about sipping champagne from long-stemmed glasses. The girl who had attracted his notice the week before, and who had been the source of his mistress's jealous temper tantrum, was present, and to all appearances, unattached. Rolfe lost no time in attaching the pretty little thing to himself.

The following morning, he penned a note, couched in the friendliest terms, to his former mistress. The message, however, was unmistakable. Their arrangement was at an end. To sweeten the parting, he gave into his footman's hand a velvet box containing an expensive, diamond trinket. When his lackey returned from Mrs. Ashton's house with the intelligence that both box and letter had been accepted, Rolfe congratulated himself on extricating himself from the woman's clutches quite painlessly.

Further reflection tempered his exuberance. There was still the problem of the lady's husband. George Ashton must be brought to realize that his errant wife held no interest for the marquess of Rivard. Hard on that thought came a picture of the little French girl, Zoë.

Within half an hour, Rolfe's team was hitched to his curricle, and he was on his way to Gloucester Road.

Chapter Seven

As the old year slipped into the new, the residents of Gloucester Road were highly diverted by the spectacle of Lord Rivard's handsome curricle and four coming and going at all hours of the afternoon. And that the passenger in this enviable rig was invariably the same pretty young female, and she a member of the French community, occasioned more than a little tongue wagging.

The housekeeper at number 53 summed up the speculation when she observed darkly to the august butler of that residence, "That pretty little thing? For all that she's French, she looks respectable. Summat should tell her that yon lordling is like to offer her no more than a slip on the shoulder."

Mr. Teviot, the butler, glanced out the window and caught a glimpse of Zoë in a green velvet pelisse with a large-brimmed bonnet tied under the chin with matching ribbons. "She's one of Madame Bertaut's houseguests," he intoned with the air of one who has superior knowledge.

"So?"

"Madame Bertaut knows her duty." To the housekeeper's questioning look he answered in the same infuriating drone, "Unless I'm much mistaken, yon lordling's character must be beyond reproach, else Madame Bertaut would have sent him packing."

The butler at number 53 was wiser than he knew. Madame Bertaut permitted the marquess of Rivard's innocuous attentions to her charge for only one reason. She had discerned in his lordship's expression, in unguarded moments, a certain something, a tenderness towards Zoë which augured well for her future. The hope that the marquess would offer for the girl, she confided to no one, not wishing to betray a turn of mind which she knew would be ridiculed. Madame Bertaut was an incurable romantic.

On the other hand, Francoise was not a romantic. She viewed Lord Rivard's attentions to her friend with marked suspicion.

"Does he overstep the bounds of propriety?" she demanded as Zoë returned from one of her drives with the marquess.

"No," said Zoë, swallowing her disappointment.

"Has he taken liberties, or made suggestive remarks?"

"He's a pattern card of rectitude," replied Zoë, studying to inject some enthusiasm into her voice.

Francoise was far from satisfied with these assurances. "What do you talk about?"

Zoë removed her wide-brimmed bonnet and toyed with the ribbons. It had taken her hours to unpick the green velvet gown and fashion the cloth into the pelisse she was wearing with its saucy bonnet. Her efforts to appear modish were wasted on the marquess. He never seemed to notice what she was wearing.

"We talk of France, sometimes, and . . . and my

113

family." Lord Rivard had been kindness itself. By dint of careful questioning, he had gradually encouraged Zoë to talk about the past, particularly her early life, when her family was together, and Paris was an enviable place to pass one's days. He thought her parents' case was hopeless. Not that he had said as much to her. But there was something which crept into his voice, a way he had of diverting her when her recollections became melancholy, that warned her to expect the worst. She longed to unburden herself about Claire and Leon, too, but could not bring herself to go against Claire's express wishes.

"Where does he take you?" persisted Francoise.

"Today, he took me to Gunters."

"Gunters?"

"In Berkeley Square. Number 7, to be precise. It's a pastry shop and teahouse and sells the most delectably flavored ices. The marquess bought me one."

"You ate an ice in the middle of winter?"

Zoë dimpled. "I assure you, Francoise, the English set no store by the vagaries of their climate. The place was packed to the gunnels. The marquess ordered two ices for himself."

A small frown pleated Francoise's brow. "What is he up to?"

Zoë made no response to this moot question. From his lordship's conversation and manner, she very much feared that, if it were possible, he would adopt her and send her to the country to live with his nieces. But she had no wish to confide this mortifying intelligence to her friend, or to anyone, for that matter.

In point of fact, Rolfe's reasons for taking up Zoë were by no means clear, even to himself. Roberta Ashton, with her show of jealousy for the girl, had first given him the notion. He would confound the designs of his erstwhile mistress, and those of the husband he had cuckolded, by demonstrating an interest in another lady. Within days, he knew that his ploy had succeeded, either that or Roberta Ashton's veiled threats had been empty ones. Already there was an on dit circulating that he had been supplanted in the lady's affections, if not her bed, and the imperturbable husband gave no evidence of being shaken from his habitual indifference to his wife's peccadilloes.

But in spite of escaping Roberta Ashton's coils, Rolfe continued in his attentions to Zoë. That others saw the girl as something more than a child at first amused him, but very soon after became a cause for concern. The girl was a mere fledgling and far from conversant with the ways of the world. Moreover, to all intents and purposes, she was alone, without male relatives to protect her. From the most disinterested of motives, Rolfe decided that since he was the one who had rescued the child from France, it fell to him to stand in the role of guardian to her.

"How many others have you brought out of France?"

The question came from Housard as both gentlemen took a rest from their labors. They were in Tinténiac's office in Whitehall, and had spent the morning, as had become their custom in the last little while, painstakingly sifting through a plethora of reports on recent émigrés from France.

"What?" asked Rolfe. "Oh! Scores of them. Why do you ask?"

"Are you in the habit of finding the direction of those you've rescued?"

"Certainly not." There was a twinkle in the Frenchman's eye Rolfe found mildly annoying.

"Why is Zoë different? Why do you bother with her?" asked Housard.

Having no clear idea of why, indeed, he persisted in his attentions to the chit, Rolfe said something vague about feeling responsible and adroitly changed the subject.

They had one lead on *La Compagnie* — a printer who they hoped would not prove too difficult to track down. Not only had they come up with a comprehensive description of the man, but he had a red rose tatooed on the back of one hand.

"It shouldn't be too difficult to locate him," said Rolfe.

"We should get Tinténiac on to this with the list of his known contacts."

"Then what?"

"We wait. We observe. We move in for the kill, but only when he's led us to the others."

"That may take months."

"True. And time is something I cannot spare at the moment. I must return to France soon." When Rolfe said nothing in reply, his companion grinned and went on, "I leave you in charge of this operation, Rivard. It shouldn't be too strenuous for the next week or so. However, I hope you will keep me informed. Tinténiac knows how to reach me."

"Thank you," said Rolfe and tried to look as if he meant it.

Housard was right about one thing. There was nothing for Rolfe to do in the next week or two except read through reports. It was inevitable that his mind would turn to Zoë and the problem she presented.

He hit upon the happy solution of placing her with his own family, as governess to his young nieces. The girls had a nurse, but had yet to begin their education proper. When he broached the subject with Zoë, however, he found her chary of the suggestion.

"You're too kind," said Zoë. "But please don't put yourself about on my account. Madame Bertaut is hopeful that I may be comfortably settled as soon as may be."

Frowning faintly, Rolfe said, "I wish you would tell me why you would be more comfortable with strangers."

Zoë faltered and said a few incoherent words before she tactfully changed the subject.

Her reasons for refusing the marquess's offer of employment were her own, and were confided to no one. Zoë was setting a strong guard over her wayward heart. The marquess, for reasons known only to himself, was pleased, for the moment, to single her out. He took her up in his carriage. She was invited to parties where she strongly suspected that his lordship had inveigled an invitation for her. He was kindness itself. But he did not love her. His whole manner, his address, was demonstrably unloverlike. Nothing but misery could attend her accept-

117

ing a position in his household where she must be thrown continually in his way. She loved him, but she was far too sensible a girl to hope for the impossible. And since her love was unrequited, Zoë had determined that her best course was to put some distance between herself and the object of her love.

"You won't reconsider . . . ?"

"I can't go against Madame Bertaut's wishes. Please, try to understand." Zoë tried to soften the refusal with a smile.

When Rolfe set her down at Gloucester Road, his manner was chilly.

"Shall . . . shall I see you soon?" asked Zoë, her resolve to put some distance between herself and the marquess faltering at the first test.

"My good girl, I am not the gentleman of leisure you seem to think me. I have business which will take me to Kent for some few days." And having delivered this setdown, Rolfe inclined his head gravely and instructed his groom to give his wheel horses their heads.

Later that same evening, as he played a few indifferent rubbers of piquet at his club in St. James, Rolfe was joined by a distant relation on his mother's side with whom he was on the friendliest terms.

The duke of Crewe was something under forty and had a brood of growing hopefuls which, to his friends' disgust, had become almost his sole topic of conversation. The seed of an idea germinated in Rolfe's brain, and by the time he and His Grace settled themselves in a quiet alcove to crack a bottle of claret, it had grown to maturity.

After patiently attending His Grace as he de-

118

scribed the latest hair-raising pranks of his hellion sons—a circumstance which seemed to occasion their sire, surprisingly, no little pride—Rolfe steered the conversation to a subject which was of more interest to him. The duke heard him out in silence, and seemed quite taken by what Rolfe proposed until a name was mentioned.

"Zoë Devereux," repeated the duke carefully. "You want me to find employment in my household for Miss Devereux?"

"I do," said Rolfe.

"I hope you are hoaxing me!"

"I beg your pardon?"

"Zoë Devereux? Isn't she the lady whom you have been squiring about town this fortnight and more?"

"Scarcely that," answered Rolfe with a new reserve creeping into his voice. "The girl's circumstances, as I have explained, are not happy. My intention was merely to divert her."

"Is she your convenient?" asked the duke baldly. At the look of sudden fury which crossed the younger man's face, he quickly interjected in a placating tone, "No! No! It is not I who says so, but—"

"But?" intoned Rolfe in a voice so soft, so menacing, that the duke began at once to cast around in his mind for words which would find favor.

Finding none, he said rather helplessly, "I collect that no one has told you that Miss Devereux's name figures in this establishment's betting book." He inhaled sharply and went on, "The odds are two to one that the offer you make her will be honorable rather than . . . that is . . . er . . . rather than . . . the other sort. You must see that if there is any

119

scandal attaching to this chit, it would be quite improper to take her on as my children's governess."

"There isn't any scandal," snarled Rolfe.

"If you say so, Rolfe," agreed the duke, and excused himself on the next breath to answer the signal of some crony who had, at that very moment, entered White's portals. Soon after, the duke observed that his young relative had quit the premises. Only then did he feel free to approach the gentleman who kept close tabs on White's infamous betting book.

"The Devereux chit," he said, and he placed his bet. From that moment on, the odds changed to three to one in favor of Rivard's taking the girl in holy matrimony.

Rolfe's frame of mind when he posted down to his estate in Kent was far from calm. He could not believe that his peers would misjudge him so—to cast him in the role of a debaucher of innocents! And the ill-bred speculation about little Zoë had him gnashing his teeth in impotent rage. That he had only himself to blame for this sad state of affairs was soon borne in upon him. Further reflection convinced him that if he wished to protect Zoë's reputation from malicious tongues it were best to sever the connection altogether.

Rivard Abbey, on this occasion, brought no ease to Rolfe's restlessness. His mother, the dowager marchioness, was more assiduous than ever in her entreaties that he should settle down to do his duty. He answered her suitably, though very vaguely, and immersed himself in estate business with his steward. Even his nieces seemed to have lost their power

120

to charm him. For the first time he saw their scapegrace manners as a sad reflection on their management by their elders. His own neglect of his young wards he freely admitted.

Rolfe was not back in town a day but he began to have second thoughts about his conduct toward Zoë. Though he was fully sensible of the fact that he must not, on any account, compromise the girl's good name, on the other hand, in all conscience, he could not simply cut her from his acquaintance without offering some explanation. He might have written her a note. He chose not to do so, persuading himself that the written word was open to misinterpretation. No. He must see her in person and make her understand that it was for *her* sake he was forced to keep her at a distance.

He let another week go by before presenting himself at Gloucester Road. On the doorstep, he met Madame Bertaut. From her, he had the intelligence that Zoë had taken a position as companion to Lady Kilburn. To say that he was astonished would be to put the matter mildly.

"Companion! Lady Kilburn! Without so much as a by-your-leave? Who the devil is this Lady Kilburn? I've never heard of her!"

With the greatest circumspection, Madame Bertaut smothered a small smile. It had been brought to her notice that both Zoë's name and Rivard's figured in an ill-bred wager in one of the gentlemen's clubs in St. James. And though she knew that as a lady she must deplore such dubious goings-on, she wished, rather whimsically, that, just this once, she might place a bet of her own. She would stand to make a fortune.

Calmly, reasonably, she faced down the storm in those turbulent gray eyes and embarked on an explanation of Zoë's changed circumstances. For reasons known only to herself, she became mischievous. She painted a picture of Zoë's situation which was not quite accurate, and, at the same time, not quite total fabrication.

Lady Kilburn had her residence, Kilburn House, in the village of Twickenham, by Richmond. This elderly widow was afflicted with an arthritic condition. She rarely went out in society. Nevertheless, she did not pine or lack for company. Her son and his wife doted on her, and her two schoolboy grandsons, who attended Eton, on the other side of the river, were frequent visitors. This was far from remarkable since Lady Kilburn made light of her own troubles and was deeply interested in the welfare of others.

Zoë came to her notice through the kind offices of the countess of Jersey, a near neighbor. The countess was a close friend of the duchess of Devonshire. Zoë had made an impression on Georgiana Devonshire, and where Her Grace bestowed her favor, she was generous to a fault. She canvassed her friends and in very short order had an offer of employment for Zoë.

The position of companion to Lady Kilburn was not onerous. There was a nurse in residence, and also an unmarried cousin who served her kinswoman in the capacity of friend and confidante. Zoë was instructed to make herself useful, in some vague and unspecified manner, and more particularly, to be on hand of an evening for the quiet entertainments which the ladies enjoyed in the green drawing room.

Zoë considered her situation a fortunate one, for not only was she within easy distance of London (and therefore in a position to be reached if and when Madame Bertaut had any report of her family) but she also found the society of the elderly ladies at Kilburn House pleasant to a degree. What Zoë had not divined was the Lady Kilburn was something of a philanthropist. She was a Christian lady, a daughter of the manse, and highly sensible of the duty one of her exalted position and fortune owed to those in less happy circumstances. It was a testament to the lady's character and upbringing that not one of the beneficiaries of her charity ever suspected themselves to be in that unenviable position, least of all the latest addition to her household.

Three weeks to the day of having removed to Twickenham, Zoë was surprised in her daily constitutional around the environs of the house by the spectacle of Rolfe's splendid curricle and four driving through the stone gates of the park at a dangerous pace. It swept out of sight round a turn in the drive before Zoë had time to collect her wits. A moment later, she quickened her step. It was a good ten minutes before she reached the house, and another five minutes after that before she had divested herself of her outer garments and answered Lady Kilburn's summons to wait on her directly.

A little breathless, Zoë entered the morning

room. Rolfe was seated in the comfortable, stuffed armchair closest to the blazing grate. It registered that the conversation revolved around Lady Kilburn's grandsons when Rolfe rose to make his bows.

That his eyes were as gray as Zoë had ever seen them relieved her most pressing anxiety. The marquess was not the bearer of bad news respecting her parents. Not a trace of sympathy warmed the chill in those wintry orbs. Then what, she wondered, had ruffled his feathers? And why, when he had snubbed her so patently at their last meeting was he now seeking her out? Containing her patience as best she might, at Lady Kilburn's behest, Zoë accepted a chair close to the warmth of the fire.

On one level, she was conscious that her employer had returned to the topic of her grandsons. On another level, Zoë contemplated the object of her most persistent and most unwanted dreams. Lord Rivard's resemblance to her deputy was, she decided, only superficial. This man was more urbane, more polished, and far more elegantly turned out. From his form-fitting tobacco brown cut away coat, to his supple leather topboots he was the epitome of the man of fashion. His hair, too, was arranged differently, giving him a more severe aspect. Zoë swallowed a sigh. If it was highly improbable that she could attach the likes of a Deputy Rolfe with this unsmiling stranger the task was beyond contemplating. And if only her dreams would accept the inevitable she would be a far happier girl.

She was jogged from her reveries when her employer made to get up. The operation was always a difficult one, but Lady Kilburn never allowed anyone to assist her, averring that to do so would be to encourage a dependence which would serve her ill. On this occasion, she surprised her nurse and kinswoman by declaring with an uncharacteristic tartness, "If you would be so kind, ladies, I should like to retire. Well? Don't just sit there! Give me your arm." Miss Peabody and Mrs. Stonewell exchanged a questioning look but did as they were told. Zoë made to help them. "No, no, Zoë. No need to trouble yourself. I'm quite certain that you and Lord Rivard will wish to catch up on mutual acquaintances and so on. You'll have another sherry, Lord Rivard? Zoë, see to it, there's a good girl. My physician, you know—he has promised to look in on me." At this point in Lady Kilburn's monologue, her nurse attempted to remonstrate but was shushed into silence. "It's been a pleasure, Lord Rivard, a pleasure. Don't hasten away on my account. We'd be delighted if you would sit down to dinner with us, but I won't he offended if you're promised elsewhere. I know how it is with you young people." And with many other such inanities, Lady Kilburn carefully steered her companions through the door.

Zoë and Rolfe faced each other across the room.

"Sherry?" asked Zoë.

"Thank you, no."

Silence.

"As you wish." Zoë seated herself and Rolfe followed suit.

"Lord Rivard," began Zoë, and stopped for he had spoken at exactly the same moment. She inclined her head, indicting that he should speak first.

With marked formality Rolfe observed, "Madame Bertaut asked me to present her compliments."

"Thank you. How does she go on?"

No more than half a minute was taken up in satisfying Zoë on that point. Rolfe cleared his throat and continued, "Madame Bertaut seems to think that felicitations are in order."

"Felicitations?" repeated Zoë blankly.

"On your nuptials to Lord Robert."

"Lord Robert!" Zoë was thunderstruck. Lord Robert was Lady Kilburn's elder grandson, an engaging scamp of thirteen summers or so. "I collect Madame Bertaut has mistaken my meaning," said Zoë. She chuckled. "You may tell her that there is no hope of an offer of marriage from that quarter." Her lashes swept down to conceal the smile in her eyes. Madame Bertaut, unless she was mistaken, was set on fanning the flame of jealousy in his lordship's breast—a ridiculous notion!

"No hope, Zoë?"

"None!" answered Zoë emphatically.

Rolfe's smile came into play. His eyes were more blue than gray. "I'm glad to hear it."

"I beg your pardon?"

"Now don't frown at me, kitten. I make no apology for telling you that virtue holds no appeal for men of that kidney. You're well out of it! And quite frankly, it's women of a different . . . well . . . in any event, you shouldn't wish to acquire that kind of polish." Observing Zoë's unsmiling face, Rolfe amended in a placating tone, "You are just as you should be, kitten, and very nice too, if I may say so."

126

Zoë regarded his lordship with a smoldering eye. She knew, of course, that he was laboring under a misapprehension. She suspected that Lady Kilburn's references to her scapegrace grandsons had confirmed the totally erroneous picture which Madame Bertaut had painted of the elder boy. Zoë's conscience constrained her to correct that misconception. It was feminine pique which propelled her on a different course.

That the marquess had paid her the indirect compliment of calling her "virtuous" was no compliment at all by her lights. And though she had only the vaguest notions respecting the "polish" to which he alluded, she knew, without a doubt, that it was something all women must covet. She did not possess it. The marquess had said so, and he should know. But, oh! that he should think so was more than she could bear.

Carefully arranging the folds of her skirts, she said, "You are quite right when you say that Lord Robert is not like to offer me marriage." She sighed. Her lips trembled. Her lashes swept down, veiling her expression.

"What's this?" Rolfe's eyes narrowed.

Zoë gestured helplessly. "I am a stranger here with no family. I have no dowry." She paused, casting around in her mind as she tried to recall some of what Francoise had said on the subject. "That makes me fair game, you see." As Rolfe's expression turned hard, Zoë faltered.

"Don't stop there, kitten. I would know the whole," he encouraged.

Far from reassuring Zoë, this rigidly imposed con-

127

trol awakened every instinct for caution. It was too late to turn back, however. In a voice that was barely audible she said, "I regret to say that the offers which I have received made no mention of marriage." This was no lie. The only offer which had been made to her was of her present position as Lady Kilburn's companion. Rather defiantly she determined that wild horses would not drag that admission from her.

"No mention of marriage?" Rolfe's voice was as smooth as satin.

Zoë's bravado suddenly deserted her. She was beginning to see that she was spinning a web that might very easily entrap her. She smiled shyly. "May I know the purpose of this visit, Lord Rivard?"

But Rolfe was not to be so easily distracted. His calm tone at odds with the chill in his eyes, he said, "Lord Robert will answer to me for this insult."

Zoë's hand fluttered nervously to her throat. "You can't! You mustn't!"

"Why mustn't I?"

"He . . . he's just a boy," she confessed.

"All the more reason that the young coxcomb be taught a lesson before he becomes a hardened rakehell."

A vision of Lord Rivard's face — somewhere between shock and laughter — when he caught up with her pretended suitor appeared before her eyes. Shuddering, swallowing painfully at this mortifying picture, she lost no time in exculpating her innocent victim. "Lord Robert is everything that is respectful. I never meant to imply . . . what I mean to say is . . . Lord Robert has no interest whatsoever in females."

Rolfe's eyebrows rose. He regarded her steadily for a long moment. He noted the flush that lay across her cheekbones and the eyes which could not quite meet his. "Then who . . . ? Oh! Now I comprehend! Those fribbles who danced attendance on you at the Devonshires' party! So that's what Madame Bertaut was hinting at! What is it, Zoë? Do they ride out here and pester the life out of you? Give me the names of these rackety ne'er-do-wells and I promise you I shall make short shrift of them."

Zoë wrung her hands. She was on the point of confessing the whole when a flash of inspiration came to her. "But how will that look?" she cried out. "You are no relation to me. If you pursue this matter you will occasion the kind of gossip that must bring infamy to my name! No! No! You must do nothing!" After an interval, she said in a more normal tone, "You still haven't told me the reason for this visit."

Rolfe gazed at Zoë in simmering silence. That this little innocent should suffer the particular attentions of gentlemen of a predatory nature offended every feeling of decency. Was it not this very thing he feared would come to pass? Had he not known that no dependence could be placed on the scruples of his own sex? The girl had no male relatives, no one of any consequence to look out for her interests. More than anything, he wished that he might assume that role. But he also recalled the conversation in White's with his kinsman, Crewe. Zoë was right. To involve himself in her affairs would be the worst possible service he could do her. Unless . . .

Into Rolfe's mind flashed fragments and impressions which resolved themselves into a comprehensive whole. It was more than time that he was wed. And when that day arrived, the designs of Roberta Ashton, and all women like her, would be forever frustrated. Neither did the threats of the wronged husband, in these circumstances, trouble him greatly. George Ashton (if he ever did have any intention of naming him in a divorce action, which Rolfe very much doubted) would make himself a laughing stock if he pursued that course.

But beyond all that, and of far more significance to Rolfe, was the happy estate of the lady he would take to wife. The woman of his choice would have the protection of his name. His marchioness would not he subject to the sort of insult Zoë had endured since she had left her father's house.

The solution was simple. Zoë must become his wife. No sooner had the thought occurred to him, than every muscle in his body seemed to release a tension he had not known possessed him. Air rushed into his lungs. His chest expanded. He felt lightheaded. Zoë must become his wife. It was the perfect solution.

Little Zoë. She was scarcely more than a child. He must impress that fact on his mind. Even so, his little kitten had the heart of a lion. On that harrowing coach ride from Rouen to Coutances, she had displayed more pluck than most men of his acquaintance. Her manners, her deportment, her quiet air of gravity — everything about the child had captivated him. She was a Devereux, of the great

Devereux banking family. She might well be a penniless orphan. He did not care. From this day forward, Zoë and her happiness would be in his safekeeping.

One day, in the future, when she was older, it would be necessary to consummate their marriage. He must beget heirs. He resolved that he would be the most restrained and gentle of husbands, scrupulous to a degree of the girl's finer feelings. He would never give his little Zoë cause to fear him. In the meantime, his life would go on as before. Zoë would make no appreciable difference to the way he ordered his days.

He noted that Zoë's little boot was tapping a tattoo on the carpeted floor, and he remembered that he had once or twice surprised in her the fire of an incipient temper. He smiled.

"What should I be doing here, kitten? I've come to take you away."

Zoë's delicate eyebrows winged upwards.

"As my bride."

Her jaw dropped. He was perfectly serious. She could read it in his eyes.

"Miss Devereux, will you do me the honor of accepting my hand in marriage?"

She must refuse him. It was the only honorable thing to do. All inadvertently, with her unruly, capricious tongue, she had brought him to this pass. He was the flower of English manhood, the chivalric knight of a former era set on rescuing a damsel in distress. She was not worthy of him. She could not be so base as to entrap him into marriage under false pretenses. The words of refusal trembled on

131

her lips.

"Well, kitten? What answer am I to receive?"

Surely, this could not be her speaking? "Oh Rolfe! Yes! If you really wish it!" And, conscience-stricken, she promptly burst into tears.

Chapter Eight

Within weeks of their quietly arranged nuptials, Zoë began to perceive that it was not a husband she had acquired but something in the nature of a guardian. And though that guardian was possibly the most benevolent of autocrats who had ever walked God's earth, it made no appreciable difference to the acute misery from which she suffered. Rolfe was as unattainable as he ever was.

In other surroundings, Zoë's unhappiness might have been mitigated to some degree. At Rivard Abbey, in the society in which she found herself, and with Rolfe scarcely ever there, there was no alleviation of her distress.

Zoë's introduction to her mother-in-law was not auspicious. Rolfe's mother, the dowager marchioness, was a slight, rather delicate-looking lady. Her health, as she would have it, was very indifferent. She tired easily. Upsets of any description were known to bring on that tiresome affliction which she called "spasms." Over the years, she'd had a succession of doctors, none of them lasting for very long. She regarded the whole tribe of medical men as quacks and charlatans. Not one of them had ever diagnosed any of the vague complaints from which she habitually suffered. Nor were they, after the first flush of acquaintance, very ready with their sympathy.

On being informed by her son of his marriage, the lady was immediately overcome with palpitations. She half-swooned in her chair, and neither the application of burnt feathers under her nose nor the tot of medicinal brandy which her maid forced past her lips could restore her completely to her senses. But where the maid failed, the son had more success.

"Tears of joy I had expected, Mama," said Rolfe with amused tolerance. "Come now, congratulate me on being a dutiful son and say how-do-you-do to your daughter-in-law."

When this cajolery failed in its objective, Rolfe made to lead Zoë from his mother's sitting room. Only then did Lady Rivard regain a modicum of her composure.

"But Rolfe . . . what of . . . what of Lady Jane?"

"Lady Jane?"

The dowager straightened in her chair and threw off her maid's hand with its burnt feathers. "Lady Jane Hudson! You've been promised to her since you were both in the cradle."

Rolfe was startled into laughter. "Lady Jane Hudson was no more eager to have me as her suitor than I was to take her to wife. Mama, the girl is positively terrified of men. She is a confirmed spinster."

"What has that to say to anything?" wailed the dowager. "Her father is a duke. Her connections are unexceptionable. The girl is an heiress. And . . . . and His Grace was expecting you to pay your addresses."

As the spate of words continued unabated, Rolfe's

face turned stern. When his mother paused for breath, he said in a controlled tone, "The thing is done, Mama! When you are more yourself, I shall bring Zoë to you."

Zoë obediently allowed Rolfe to lead her from the room, reflecting that her mother-in-law had yet to address two words to her. Nor was she blind to the full significance of the exchange between mother and son. Rolfe had entered into a wholly unsuitable alliance. In France, the name Devereux stood for something. In England, Zoë Devereux was a nonentity and far beneath the touch of a marquess. Rolfe flashed her a reassuring smile, and Zoë tried to take comfort from the strength of her husband's arm beneath her fingers.

Zoë's introduction to the rest of the members of Rolfe's family was only marginally more promising. His nieces, Ladies Emily and Sara, on first acquaintance, were exactly as Zoë had anticipated. They stared at her solemnly with their uncle's intelligent gray eyes, and obediently made their curtsies at their nurse's prompting. Zoë noted the faintly anxious smile on Miss Miekle's face and wondered at it. It was only later, on further acquaintance of her nieces, that Zoë came to understand the lady's anxiety. By that time, she wondered that Miss Miekle could smile at all.

The girls' mother, Charlotte, was some few years older than Zoë. She was no beauty, but she was not precisely plain either. She had a fine pair of eyes. Within minutes of making her acquaintance, Zoë recognized that Charlotte had a *tendre* for Rolfe. Her pity was stirred. For all the notice Rolfe took of his sister-in-law, she might have been a piece of furni-

135

ture.

At dinner, that first evening, it looked as if the girl and she might be friends. But under the dowager's chilly stare, Charlotte's overtures faltered. She was polite, but reserved, and after some few attempts to converse with her, Zoë also lapsed into silence. It was Rolfe and his mother who carried the burden of conversation. If they were aware of the unnatural muteness of the dowager's two daughters-in-law, they gave no sign of it.

Throughout the meal, Zoë's thoughts drifted to the dining room in the house in St. Germain. The room would have been ringing with laughter, or the sound of young, querulous voices as she and her siblings argued ferociously with each other. A lump formed in her throat. Shortly after, she asked to be excused, pleading a headache.

Her apartments adjoined those of her husband. This was not significant. Rolfe had been at some pains to explain to Zoë on her wedding night that she had nothing to fear from him. They had entered upon a marriage of convenience. Her protests had merely amused him. Into the palm of her hand, he had pressed the key of the adjoining door to their chambers and had advised her, with a very direct look, to make sure that the door was locked at all times.

She had toyed with the idea of disobeying him. But the certain knowledge that her entrance into his chamber in some filmy garment would occasion nothing but chuckles or remonstrances checked the impulse. She was a wife, and she was no wife at all.

Over the next few weeks, Rolfe was very infrequently at the Abbey. In his absence, Zoë formed the notion of playing some part in the management of her husband's household. She was her mother's daughter. Her education fitted her for her role as chatelaine of a great house. Her accomplishments in the kitchen, no less than the drawing room, were indisputable. And how pleased and proud Rolfe would be when he returned to find his house improved beyond all recognition.

Rolfe returned to find his house in an uproar. Zoë's efforts were regarded by the dowager as the height of impertinence. The servants were at a loss to know which lady was mistress of the domestic domain, and Charlotte was so unnerved by the hostile atmosphere which prevailed that she had taken to her room. Rolfe made haste to pour oil on the troubled waters.

"Look, kitten, my mother is an old woman, and accustomed to ruling the roost. So what harm is there in letting her feel useful?"

"She's not old, and don't call me that," said Zoë.

The smile on Rolfe's face gradually faded. "I had not known I had married a fractious infant," he said coldly.

Color heated Zoë's cheekbones. This was not the homecoming she had planned for her husband. She knew herself to be at fault for precipitating the present crisis. She had been too eager, too hasty in the execution of her design. But if she was at fault, the dowager was no less so. The woman was a tyrant. And it was unjust that she, Zoë, should bear the brunt of Rolfe's censure. Angry, hurt tears sprang to her eyes.

She made some excuse to leave the room, but Rolfe caught her by the wrists and laughingly reproved, "No, no, kitten! I can't be angry with you. But I wish you would tell me why you would rather burden yourself with household chores when you could be out riding, or walking, or amusing yourself in more pleasant diversions?"

Zoë's chin came up. "And I wish you would tell me what my role is to be."

Rolfe dropped her wrists. "Charlotte, to my knowledge, had no difficulty in finding a place for herself."

"Thank you," said Zoë, and left him.

Charlotte's role was not one that Zoë envied, nor had she the least inclination to emulate it. Her sister-in-law was completely under the dowager's thumb. Even the management of Charlotte's two little daughters was taken out of her hands. It was to the dowager that the children's nurse made her reports.

Rolfe's nieces, no less than his mother and sister-in-law, were a sad disappointment to Zoë. Whenever Rolfe had spoken of his nieces in London, his words were always couched in the most affectionate terms. Nothing could have prepared Zoë for the reality of these undisciplined, angelic-looking hellions who were indulged beyond redemption.

She could not smile at their misdemeanors. Nor did she reproach Rolfe with her misgivings. There was no point. Whenever he was present, the children's conduct improved immeasurably. They were cunning if not shameless manipulators of the adults who had the ordering of their young lives.

Fearing that she would give in to the almost overpowering urge to box the ears of these obnoxious miscreants, Zoë took to avoiding them as far as was humanly possible. Perversely, though her husband denied her the role of wife and chatelaine, he wished her to become a second mother—or perhaps it was playmate—to his nieces. Zoë, wisely, in the interests of self-preservation, demurred.

There came a day, however, when Zoë felt impelled to enter the children's domain. Such were the shrieks which emanated from the nursery that she was sure that poor Miss Miekle had finally yielded to the very natural temptation to throttle the life out of her nurselings.

When she pushed through the door, it was evident that she had entered a battle zone. Dismembered dolls, far beyond the powers of resuscitation, lay about in odd corners. Picture books with the pictures torn out and the pages defaced were scattered at random. There were ink-splotches on the walls and dried stains on the carpet. To Zoë's surprise, however, it was Miss Miekle who was cowering in the corner, and the children who held her at bay with a series of earsplitting howls, each one more hysterical than the last.

Zoë slammed the door, and order was instantly restored. She regarded her nieces with a hostile eye.

Lady Emily, at five, was a year older than her sister, and the leader of the two. Her coolly assessing gaze met Zoë's without flinching.

"You daren't thpank uth," lisped Lady Sara, and flashed a questioning look at her elder sister for confirmation.

"Uncle Rolfe doesn't permit anyone to spank us," advised Lady Emily with a sage little smile.

"Leave us, Miss Miekle," purred Zoë.

"Oh, but your ladyship—"

139

Zoë silenced her with the wave of one hand. "Come back in five minutes. I'll look after your charges till you return."

Miss Miekle hesitated, then reluctantly slipped out of the room. Zoë's eyes narrowed on the diminutive forms before her. Lady Sara, as was her wont when alarmed for any reason, was sucking on her thumb as if her little life depended on it. Zoë crushed the faint stirrings of pity which this sad spectacle provoked. Her gaze fell on Lady Emily, and the incipient rush of pity instantly subsided.

There came into her mind a recollection of her own mulatto nurse, Salome, who had been her mother's nurse before that, and who had come to France as a young girl from the island of San Domingo. Salome's methods of maintaining order in the nursery had been, to say the least, highly unorthodox. She had kept her young charges, quite literally, spellbound. An unholy smile turned up Zoë's lips.

Closing her eyes, as in a trance, she raised her hands and waved them in front of her face. She began to hum.

Lady Sara edged closer to her big sister. She grasped her hand. "She's casting a thpell," she breathed.

Zoë's eyes flew open. In the way of a witch with an incantation she began to drone.

"Wizards and warlocks and witches with black cats,

Sorcerers and demons and magicians with blind bats,

The magic of Zoë is no empty boast,

Touch Emily and Sara and I'll call out my . . . "

140

she floundered momentarily and came up with a weak "hosts." By degrees, she came out of her trance. She smiled down at her round-eyed audience. "There now, children, that should do it."

"Do what?" demanded Lady Emily.

"Why! Keep you safe from . . ." Zoë's voice dropped to a whisper, "you-know-what. Now they know you're not little witches, you see."

'What's 'hosts'?" quavered Lady Sara.

"The heavenly hosts," answered Zoë. "You know— angels. Now the angels are keeping watch over you. Still, if I were you, I shouldn't want to take any chances. Behave like little witches, and even the angels may forget whose side you are on."

"You're making this up," said Lady Emily doubtfully. She was beginning to think that her new Aunt Zoë was an adversary worthy of her steel.

Zoë was spared the necessity of a reply by the entrance of Miss Miekle. "Is . . . is everything all right?" asked that breathless lady, her eyes anxiously scanning her unnaturally subdued charges.

"Everything is fine," said Zoë, and with one last pointed look at her nieces, swept from the room.

As she gently closed the door, she heard Lady Sara's childish voice piping, "Miekle, Miekle! What do you think? Aunt Zoë is an angel!"

Lady Emily snorted derisively.

Later that evening, over dinner, Charlotte ventured a shy, "Miss Miekle tells me that you paid a visit to the nursery this morning?"

"I did," answered Zoë, squirming in her chair.

"What's this?" asked Rolfe, in the act of helping himself from one of the servers a footman was tendering. He had arrived at the Abbey in time for

141

dinner, and was more than a little relieved to find everything very much as he had left it.

"Zoë," answered Charlotte. "Nurse says that she made a great impression on the children."

"That doesn't surprise me. Zoë has a way with children." Rolfe's smile brought a guilty heat rushing to Zoë's cheeks.

The dowager chose that moment to regale her captive audience with the merits of her new physician. Zoë, for once, was not sorry that her mother-in-law was impatient with every conversation where she did not figure prominently.

One week followed upon another. The snow melted. The first snowdrops came and went. Soon, the park around Rivard Abbey was tinted delicately as narcissi and crocuses pushed their way through the black earth.

By and large, Zoë's days were as empty as they ever were. Occasionally, the tedium was broken by a shopping expedition to Canterbury, or when neighbors made an obligatory call to pay their respects, ironically, to the new mistress of the Abbey. But Kent was very thin of company. The London season was in full swing. Only the aged and infirm seemed content to bury themselves in the country. Young people of an age with Zoë were as rare as swallows in winter. Rolfe was scarcely ever there.

But when he did tear himself away from the press of business which occupied him in town, Zoë's days took on a different color. They went riding, or took long walks. And in the evenings, after dinner, they would retire *en famille* to the music room where Rolfe insisted that Zoë entertain them at the piano. Occasionally when his eyes absently rested on her, she would surprise a brooding quality in him. On coming to himself, he would flash her a grin and make some observation which invariably stifled any romantic hopes she might be entertaining.

And yet, she did entertain hopes that her husband was coming to see her as something more than a child. He enjoyed her society. Zoë was sure of it. They were never at a loss for words when they were together, though, to be sure, Rolfe's interest seemed bent on broadening her education. There were books she must read, places of interest in the neighborhood she must visit, and the music of English composers with which she must become familiar. In everything, she strove to please him, and never more so than in his wish that she should take an interest in his heritage.

Rivard Abbey. Rolfe was inordinately proud of the place. To Zoë's way of thinking, a converted Abbey left much to be desired as a habitation for humans. Its beauty, its grandeur were unquestionable. No less so was the forbidding aspect of its huge drafty chambers and its cold, flagstoned floors. She itched to be given a free hand in refurbishing the place. She knew exactly how she would achieve a warmer, more intimate atmosphere. She kept her thoughts to herself. The dowager was the indisputable mistress of the Abbey. The master of the house was there so infrequently that it was pointless to offer suggestions.

Zoë was lonely. But she made friends in an unexpected quarter. Ladies Emily and Sara became Zoë's shadows. It seemed that in that first brief encounter with their Aunt Zoë, she had fired their childish imaginations. It was more spells and incantations they craved, not the pleasure of Zoë's society.

She took to spending a good part of each day with her nieces and their nurse. Her influence on the children's conduct was salutary, if not dramatic, and was viewed by the long-suffering servants as nothing short of divine intervention. Zoë *was* an angel.

The dowager took a different view. Her younger daughter-in-law was cold and unfeeling. She was too strong-willed for comfort. Defiance was not too strong a word to describe the chit's neglect. The dowager's vituperation became more cutting.

Over dinner one evening, she regarded the carefully composed features of her son's young wife and she knew an urge to shake Zoë from her usual poise.

"I wish you would tell me," she began dulcetly, "why my son finds it necessary to spend so much time in town?"

The question was one which had troubled Zoë for some time past. She gave the dowager the answer Rolfe had proffered when she had quizzed him about the weeks he spent away from the home he professed to love. "There is so much business . . ."

"Business!" scoffed the dowager. "My dear, this is the height of the Season. Don't you think it a trifle odd that a newly married man should run off and leave his bride of a few months to rusticate in the country?"

Zoë's eyes sought reassurance from Charlotte. It was pity that she saw in her sister-in-law's stare before the girl looked away.

Zoë's head came up. "What are you suggesting?" she asked quietly.

"I'm not suggesting anything!" snapped the dowager, suddenly conscious that if her words were carried to Rolfe she might very well come under the bite of his censure. "All that I am saying is that my son is scarcely ever here." She sniffed, and dabbed delicately at her eyes with a lace handkerchief. "One son was torn from me. Is it any wonder that I should wish to see something of Rolfe when he is all that remains to me? But you cannot know a mother's feelings."

Zoë's thoughts immediately flew to her own family in France. The dowager had been told something of her circumstances, but she rarely made mention of Zoë's family, and then only to imply that Rolfe had bestowed a great favor in raising her to the exalted state of marchioness.

"But that is neither here nor there. No. What I wished to say to you is this. You will refrain from seeking out the society of my servants. Miss Miekle is not paid to be your companion. She has work to do, and it has been brought to my attention that you are taking advantage of her kind nature."

"Mama!" remonstrated Charlotte quietly.

Stung, Zoë cried out, "That's a lie!"

The dowager straightened in her chair. "You dare to call me a liar?" she demanded.

Zoë jumped to her feet. Defiance and injury shimmered in her dark eyes. A confusion of thoughts jostled each other in her head. When she spoke, anger shook her voice. "I dare! Yes, I dare! You're cruel, and you mean to be! You don't want me to have any friends. Deny it if *you* dare."

The dowager's brows lifted. "Friends?" she asked scornfully. "With the servants?"

"Miss Miekle is a lady!"

"She is an employee!"

"She is more of a lady than . . . than *you* are."

The dowager uttered a strangled gasp and fell back against the cushions in a semiswoon. Zoë stared horrified as Charlotte jumped to her feet and ran to help the dowager. Coming to herself, Zoë quickly moved to the console table against the wall where she found a decanter of brandy and a small glass. A moment later, she was pressing the dowager to drink.

The dowager swept the glass from Zoë's hand, spraying the brandy over the front of her gown. "You-you ungrateful wretch!" she spluttered. "Now see what you've done. I want nothing from you!" And she closed her eyes as if the sight of Zoë disgusted her.

With a little cry, Zoë ran from the room.

As ill luck would have it, Rolfe arrived at the Abbey late of that very evening. Zoë was on the stairs when she heard the commotion of his arrival at the front doors. Her heart leapt to her mouth. She lost no time in repairing to her own chamber where she quickly undressed and doused the lights before crawling into bed.

This time, she felt no joy in her husband's homecoming. Her sense of injury was too acute. The dowager had put the demon of jealousy into Zoë's breast. She remembered the beautiful lady at the Devonshires' party who had seemed to be one of her husband's intimates. He would know many beautiful women, she reflected. Mimi and Fifi must be of their number. She felt as if a knife was twisting in her heart.

As Zoë had feared, the reckoning for her misdemeanors could not be long delayed. After a restrained greeting over breakfast the following morning, Rolfe told her to fetch her pelisse and bonnet since he wished for her company as he walked.

"This is a pretty kettle of fish to come home to," he said mildly. They had reached the top of the rise which overlooked the Abbey and all its outbuildings.

"Your mother doesn't like me," said Zoë defensively.

"Have you given her cause to like you?" Rolfe paused to take in the view.

Zoë followed his gaze. "From the outside, the Abbey must look very much as it was when the monks first built their monastery."

"Yes. There have been very few changes to the outside of the building," agreed Rolfe. "And don't try to change the subject, kitten. Couldn't you unbend a little? I know you're not quick to anger. But I ask you, to call my mother a liar? You really must apologize, you know."

"Must I?" murmured Zoë, affecting an interest in a flight of birds as they winged their way to a stand of beech trees just coming into leaf.

"What is that supposed to mean?"

Zoë's eyes glinted up at Rolfe and suddenly she was past caring for his good opinion. He did not deserve her love, she decided. He had, quite literally, dropped her on unwilling relatives and then deserted her. For months she had been treated as if she were a leper, with only the conversation of children and servants to keep her from going mad. She was worried sick about the fate of her own family.

Not once since he had sought her out had her husband so much as made a passing reference to them. And yet, he must know how things stood in France. Did he mention such things to her? He did not. It was left to Francoise to write and tell her that the news from home was as black as ever it had been. Robespierre had gone raving mad. Executions were at fever pitch. And all that her husband could do when the world was coming to an end was chide her for not apologizing to the most selfish and demanding woman it had ever been her misfortune to meet. And then there was Mimi and Fifi, and all the other beautiful women of his acquaintance. It was too much to bear.

Eyes snapping, bosom heaving, she said scathingly, "You should never have married me only to bring me here. I was happy where I was. At least I had friends."

A dark tide of color rose in Rolfe's neck. "You dare to say that to me? Let me tell you, you shameless ingratiate, if I had not wed you out of hand, your position today would be insupportable."

For a moment, she could make no sense of his words. When enlightenment dawned, she gave a sarcastic laugh. With no clear idea of what she was saying, but with a burning desire to hurt him as much as she had been hurt, she cried out passionately, "The *carte blanche* of an honest rake would have found more favor with me than this intolerable marriage to you."

These were not the words of a child. Nor did Zoë look that part to Rolfe in that moment. She had long since removed her bonnet. The breeze stirred her hair, veiling her face in tendrils of dark silk. She

148

brushed at them ineffectively with one hand.

Rolfe knew an impulse to punish her for her gross ingratitude. But it was the impulse to kiss those sweetly sensual lips which was irresistible. He did not stop to think of the wisdom of what he was doing. His hands cupped her shoulders, and then his mouth came down hard on hers.

His name, choked off deep in her throat, like a kitten's purr, burned into him. He forced her mouth wider, letting her taste the force of his rising passion. For a moment, she tried to fight him. In answer, he pulled her body more fully against his, wrapping his arms tightly around her till she could scarcely breathe. The moment he felt her yield to him, he gentled the embrace.

He caught hold of her hair, wrapping it around his hands, arching her throat to receive his kisses. The soft sounds she uttered made his head swim. "Satin and silk," he whispered. "I knew you would feel like this. Soft. So soft," and he breathed endearments he had never thought to utter to any woman.

Weeks of denying the attraction Zoë held for him were forgotten as she grew pliant in his arms. His conscience clamored to be heard. She was too young. She was an innocent. She could not possibly imagine the fantasies he entertained when he thought of her in his bed. *Later,* Rolfe told his conscience, *tell me later,* and he molded his wife's softness to his hard length.

His hands roamed, discovering each delicate bone, tracing each soft contour. She was small made, but there was nothing childish about her figure. There was nothing childish about her response to him. She was emphatically female to his

149

male. Desire flamed through him. His embraces became rougher, more demanding.

He pulled back and gazed down at her. It took a moment before he had his breathing under control. His voice was hoarse and scarcely recognizable. "You're my wife."

"Y—yes."

"I want to do everything to you. Do you know? I want to touch you in ways I've never touched you before."

Under the blaze of passion in his eyes, Zoë faltered. The unfamiliar sensations which had held her in thrall to him began to dissipate. This was Rolfe, she told herself. She loved him. And yet, her mouth went dry with fear. She had never seen that look in a man's eyes before. She had never been so aware of the sheer power of the male animal, and of her own vulnerability. Beneath her fingertips, she could feel the straining virility in the rigidly controlled muscles. Instinctively, weakly, she murmured, "Please, Rolfe. No . . . I can't . . ."

The change in him was instantaneous. His lashes swept down, veiling his expression. His body went rigid, then slowly relaxed. He opened his eyes and set her away from him. He chuckled. "So! You would rather accept the *carte blanche* of an honest rake, would you, kitten? Let that be a lesson to you, my girl. Look at you! You're shaking. And that was only a kiss."

She saw at once that she had made a blunder. Her natural fear of the first experience of a man's passion had led her to reject his lovemaking. "No," she said, protesting the thoughtless words which had turned him away from her.

150

He flicked her playfully on the nose. "Don't be alarmed, kitten. I have no intention of forcing myself on you."

"You don't understand," she cried out.

The screech of children's voices close at hand put an end to their conversation. Ladies Emily and Sara swooped out of a clump of bushes and bore down on them.

"Aunt Zoë, Aunt Zoë," lisped Lady Sara, "Tell Emily that it's my turn to be the angel!"

"No 'tisn't. It's my turn," said Lady Emily.

"But I don't want to be the witch," wailed Lady Sara. Her huge, pleading eyes were fastened on Zoë. 'Tears welled up and overflowed. She gave a pathetic sniff. "Witches are horrid!" she said.

"No, they're not," contradicted Lady Emily. "Aunt Zoë is a witch."

Lady Sara rounded on her sister. "Aunt Zoë is not a witch! She's not! She's an angel! Tell her, Aunt Zoë!"

"What's this about angels and witches?" asked Rolfe, and scooped Lady Sara into his arms. He pulled a handkerchief from his pocket and proceeded to dry her wet cheeks.

"Sara's a watering pot," observed Lady Emily.

"I'm not a watering pot! I'm not," averred Lady Sara. She wriggled furiously. "Put me down, Uncle Rolfe. I'm a big girl. Only little girls get picked up." Rolfe obediently set Lady Sara on her feet.

"You're only four," pointed out Lady Emily with infuriating logic.

"Four is old, isn't it, Uncle Rolfe?" appealed Lady Sara to that sage gentleman.

"Very old," agreed Rolfe gravely. "But I wish you

would tell me why you are squabbling about angels and witches."

Two querulous voices piped up at once. Rolfe held up one hand to silence them. "Aunt Zoë will explain it to me," he said, and looked a question at Zoë.

She cleared her throat. "It's just a game, you know, like . . . like war games."

"The forces of good against the forces of evil?"

"Something like that."

"And you taught the children this game?"

"Aunt Zoë knows all the rules," confided Lady Emily.

"And all the thpells," interjected Lady Sara, her little face brightening.

"Only good spells," explained Zoë quickly. "We don't know any bad spells, do we children?"

"Not yet," allowed Lady Emily, "but . . ." For that indiscretion, she earned a ferocious glower from her aunt which immediately bullied her into silence.

Rolfe passed a hand over his eyes. "I see," he said. "Only good spells."

"It's quite harmless," said Zoë desperately.

Rolfe smiled. "I believe you, kitten." His look became thoughtful as he continued to gaze at her in silence.

The children became restive. "Are you going to play with us today, Aunt Zoë?"

"Oh no, I don't think—"

"Yes, why don't you?" said Rolfe abruptly. "There are a score of things on my desk which beg my attention. I'll see you at dinner." And before Zoë could protest her dismissal, he turned on his heel and strode off.

Later that night, when the house was quiet and

everyone had gone to bed, Zoë stood hesitating with her hand on the key of the door which led to her husband's chamber. She had made up her mind to brave his anger, his scorn, his amusement—everything that kept him from her. She'd had time and enough to regret the misgivings which she'd betrayed when his rough passion had shocked her. He was Rolfe. She knew that he would never do anything to hurt her. And she was determined that she would not fail him, if only he would give her a second chance to prove that she was a woman in every sense of that word.

She pushed open the door and stood for a moment on the threshold, accustoming her eyes to the dark interior. With heart pounding painfully against her ribs, she moved towards the shadowy form of the great tester bed. It was empty. Nor had the covers been disturbed.

It was to be the following morning before she discovered that Rolfe had left for London immediately after dinner. He had taken leave of his mother. For Zoë, there was not one word of farewell.

Rolfe made town in good time for the final curtain at Covent Garden. He made his way to the Green Room and imbibed a glass of the obligatory champagne, all the while his eyes studying the scantily dressed opera dancers and who paraded themselves in the hopes of attaching a rich protector.

Since he had given Roberta Ashton her *congé*, no woman had been his mistress. There had been women in his bed, but very infrequently, and none since his marriage to Zoë. There had not been the time or inclination for amorous assignations.

A muscle clenched in his cheek as a picture of Zoë flashed into his mind. He did not think he would ever forget the fear which had shimmered in those wonderfully expressive eyes of hers when he had told her what he wanted from her. Never again, he promised himself, would he subject his little Zoë to his unbridled lust. When that day came when he must consummate the marriage, he would not come at her after months of deprivation, like a callow youth starved of a woman. He would, he must, take a mistress to slake his carnal appetite. Zoë would have his affections. She would be the mother of his children.

A girl caught his eye. Rosamund. She had shared his bed once before. She was not much older than Zoë, and had something of the look of his wife in her finely chiseled features and dark coloring. But that was where the resemblance to Zoë ended. Rosamund had a harlot's heart. She was all fire and passion. As he remembered, she had damn near worn *him* out with her insatiable demands and that was after he had paid her for her night's work. At that moment, she smiled an invitation at him. Rolfe sauntered over.

It was only later, when he had been serviced with more expertise than he'd ever met with in his life, that be began to see other glaring differences between Rosamund and Zoë. The woman talked without ceasing, and in nothing but trivialities. There were no comfortable silences, no quiet moments of reflection. She fidgeted and could seem to find no serenity in herself. Rolfe did not stay long after the pleasuring was done.

He'd offered Rosamund *carte blanche* and had been accepted. Unlike Zoë, this woman could never be a companion to him. He did not particularly care. Rosamund's role in his life would be a negligible one, but a necessary one for all that.

Zoë. He couldn't stop thinking about her. She would make a wonderful wife and mother, he decided, and felt his lips quirking when he thought of how she had tamed his young nieces to her hand. Spells! Incorrigible girl! Now why couldn't she work her magic on his mother?

The dowager had taken Zoë in extreme dislike. The feeling was mutual, from all appearances. Zoë was unhappy at Rivard Abbey. She must wonder at his frequent absences. If it were possible, he would send for her. He toyed with the idea for only a moment or two. No. At the present moment, his work was too dangerous.

Before his return to France, Housard had occupied much of his time. The Frenchman was almost obsessive in the hunt for his quarry. No piece of information on the suspected members of *La Compagnie* was too trivial to pursue. Old reports must be recalled and thoroughly sifted. New émigrés must be thoroughly investigated. And each piece of the puzzle must be carefully set down until the whole began to take shape.

Their meticulous investigation was at last showing results. The printer had led them to *La Compagnie*. It turned out that *La Compagnie* was broken down into cells. So far, they had infiltrated only one of them. Housard's agent had passed on the name and identity of his section leader — Betrand.

Betrand was young to be a section leader, in

Rolfe's opinion. He was no more than twenty or so. He was as fanatical as they come. He was also more reckless than he ought to be. Betrand had broken— so their own agent had informed him—one of *La Compagnie*'s cardinal rules. He had taken up with a young English girl, an actress whose identity they had yet to discover. It was something to watch. Soon, Betrand must lead them to the other cells, and perhaps even to *Le Patron* himself.

Whether or not they ran *Le Patron* to earth, they must move against *La Compagnie* soon. Already, three assassination attempts, all against prominent French Royalists, had been foiled. Their luck could not hold for much longer.

La Compagnie was not the only matter to occupy Rolfe's attention. In the last number of weeks, he had inveigled Housard into garnering intelligence on Zoë's family. The brother and sister seemed to have disappeared off the face of the earth, and Zoë's parents had been moved to the Conciergerie. He could not bring himself to tell Zoë of these latest developments. The Conciergerie was impregnable and the last stop for those on their way to the scaffold.

Poor Zoë. Oh God, he would make it all up to her. He would protect her from all harm. When it was all over, he would explain everything to her. In the meantime, it was better all round if she stayed at the Abbey. She might not be comfortable, but at least she was safe. And above all things, Rolfe wanted Zoë to be safe.

Chapter Nine

The events of 9 Thermidor burst upon the world like an exploding sun. Robespierre and his cohorts, against every expectation, had been discredited on the floor of the Convention, and were summarily tried and executed. The jubilation in London in the French community could scarcely be contained. The reports from Paris following quickly upon one another raised hopes which a short time before would have been dismissed as mere wishful thinking. The Terror was at an end. Laws which enforced the tyranny were quickly repealed. A climate of idealism had been revived in France.

Rolfe had to search the newspaper for the report which was of most interest to him. He found what he was looking for on the second page. The Marquis d'Arlene, he read, had scarcely set foot on English soil when he was brutally murdered by persons unknown.

There was no doubt in Rolfe's mind that the French aristocrat was *La Compagnie*'s latest victim. The whole thing had blown sky-high. It was inevitable when d'Arlene was an emissary of the Comte de Provence and had come from Verona for secret talks on a British-backed Royalist invasion of France. The

Prime Minister was furious. He had personally vouchsafed the safety of the *comte*'s agent.

The assassination could not have come at a worse time. Their surveillance of Betrand had paid off. He had led them to the other section heads of *La Compagnie,* who, in turn had led them to two other cells. It was only a matter of time before they knew the identity of *Le Patron.*

The Prime Minister, however, could not be persuaded to hold off. He was insisting that they move against all known agents of *La Compagnie* at once. As Mr. Pitt irately told Rolfe, he must have something with which he might placate the second in line to the French throne. It could very well turn out that the Comte de Provence would be the next monarch of France. At the very least, should the young dauphin survive the rigors of his incarceration, his uncle would be Regent.

Rolfe must give the signal to move against *La Compagnie.* God, what a time for Housard to be in France! The Frenchman would not be pleased at this turn of events. *Le Patron* was his quarry. He would set little store in smashing the society if the leader evaded their net.

Rolfe was not so particular. He could scarcely wait to have his present assignment over and done with so that he might take up the threads of his own life. Zoë. She must be overjoyed at the reports that were coming out of France. Her hopes for her family's welfare must soar. He should write to her, if only to depress those hopes. He very much feared that Zoë's parents had not survived the Terror.

"Why is it called the 9 Thermidor?"

The question came from Charlotte. For a month and more, since Rolfe's precipitous departure for town, she had made it a habit to accompany Zoë on her morning constitutional when the dowager was still safely at her toilette.

"It's the French calendar," answered Zoë. "We changed all the names of the months and seasons."

"Does this mean that the war between our two countries will come to an end?"

"Rolfe says that's too much to hope for."

"But the news pleases you?" prompted Charlotte gently.

Zoë turned a radiant face up to her sister-in-law. Tears of happiness were quickly blinked away. "Oh, Charlotte," she said, "the gates of the Conciergerie and all the other prisons have been thrown open. Do you see what this means? My parents . . . my family . . ." she choked back a sob.

Rather diffidently, Charlotte patted the younger girl on the shoulder. "What does Rolfe say in his letter?"

Zoë made a derisive sound. "Rolfe, as usual, says very little. It is my friend, Francoise, who keeps me abreast of what is happening in the world."

"I wouldn't refine too much upon it, my dear. You know what gentlemen are. More than likely, Rolfe doesn't wish to raise your hopes. I'm sure it's no more than that." A thought occurred to her. "Francoise? Isn't she the girl who wed that writer fellow a fortnight since?"

"Charles Lagrange," nodded Zoë. "He's a journalist. They are more than halfway persuaded to return to France." On observing her sister-in-law's shocked expression, Zoë hastened to add, "Charles has received assurances that his name is no longer on the pro-

159

scribed lists. He's a Girondin, you see, and they—those few who survived the Terror, that is—are back in favor."

These observations on France's political scene were evidently beyond Charlotte's comprehension. Zoë tactfully changed the subject. "We had better make tracks for home. Emily will no doubt be at the piano, impatient for her music lesson."

"I can hardly credit the change that has come over that girl," said Charlotte in some wonderment. "I had no notion that she was interested in music, nor yet had the patience to practise so diligently."

"Emily is very talented," remarked Zoë.

A look of pleasure suffused Charlotte's face. "Do you really think so?"

"Really," said Zoë, thinking that Charlotte, with her large blue eyes and a blush on her skin, looked years younger and far from plain. With the right clothes and coiffure, her sister-in-law could hold her own in any assembly of ladies. Not that the dowager would permit it.

"And French lessons too!" said Charlotte.

"Your daughters are born linguists, Charlotte. They'll be conversing in French with their Uncle Rolfe before you know it."

Smiling, Charlotte quizzed, "Is that what you told them?"

Zoë returned the grin. "Of course. Children need something to aim for."

"It's very good of you to bother with the children, Zoë."

"It's nothing," demurred Zoë politely. "Besides . . ." she was on the point of saying that she did not have anything better to do with her time and changed in mid-sentence to, "they were bored. And bored children get up to all sorts of mischief."

"I'll say!" answered their mother with feeling.

It was not to be expected that this new rapport between her daughters-in-law would find favor with the dowager. Not that she said as much to them. Nor could she, with anything resembling grace, complain about the hours in each day which Charlotte began to devote to her children. But she could make life very difficult for the one who had disturbed the harmony of her days.

Matters were brought to a head when Rolfe sent word that the press of business in town precluded his coming down, as was expected, to celebrate his thirtieth birthday. The dowager passed along that intelligence to his wife over the dinner table. Zoë received the news with a show of indifference which had become almost second nature to her.

More words were exchanged. Zoë said something to which the dowager took exception. She lapsed into silence. The dowager's fury knew no bounds.

"I knew, oh yes, I knew at the outset that this was no love match," she brazenly opinioned. "But I wish you would tell me what you have done to give my son a disgust of his home."

"Mama," reproved Charlotte, "Zoë has done nothing wrong."

With meticulous attention, Zoë stirred the soup in her dish.

Eyes blazing, the dowager rounded on Charlotte. "Don't meddle in things which do not concern you!"

Zoë carefully set down her spoon. "You have no right to address Charlotte in that tone of voice," she said quietly. "Nor do I wish to enter upon a discussion on my private affairs."

"Private affairs!" sputtered the dowager. "There's

nothing private about your husband's affairs! Let me tell you, my good girl, the whole world knows that he had mounted a new mistress within weeks of acquiring a new bride."

"I don't believe you!" Zoë cried out.

"If you need convincing, I'll show you the letter I had from my good friend, Sadie Price! Yes, and another which I received from Lady Athol! What's the girl's name? Rosamund. An opera dancer with Covent Garden. Yes, that's it! Rosamund. Not that I blame Rolfe for his peccadilloes. The pity of it is that he thought to make *you* his wife and not his mistress!"

Hot color surged from Zoë's throat to her hairline. "Do you suppose that I should have accepted his *carte blanche?*" she demanded.

"Why shouldn't you? What are you but a little Frog he picked up from some filthy pond? Everyone knows that you French girls are no better than you ought to be. I see it all now! He felt sorry for you! Either that or somehow you trapped him into a marriage he's come to regret. He should have stuck to his own kind. Didn't I tell him so?"

During this tirade, the dowager had started to her feet. She looked around wildly. It was Charlotte's aghast expression which brought her to her senses. Slowly, she sank back into her chair.

"Now see what you have done, you wicked girl!" she sobbed out. She clutched at her heart. "I'm having an attack. Charlotte, help me, please."

Sighing, moaning, half swooning away, the dowager was helped from the room. Ten minutes were to pass before Charlotte was free to go in search of Zoë. She found her still in the dining room, slumped at the table, her head cradled in both arms. She was so still that Charlotte feared she had fallen into a swoon. All at once, Zoë hiccuped.

"Oh my dear!" exclaimed Charlotte, and in a rustle of skirts crossed the room and swept Zoë against her bosom, as if she were comforting a hurt child. Like a drowning man clutches at straws, Zoë clung to her sister-in-law.

The bout of weeping was to last for several minutes. Finally, Zoë's hand groped on the table. It encountered a napkin. She drew it to her face and proceeded to blow her nose. Sniffing, hiccuping, smiling feebly, she said, "If Emily could see me now, she would call me a watering pot."

"She would lose all respect for her favorite aunt!" agreed Charlotte amiably.

"Her *only* aunt," corrected Zoë.

Charlotte patted Zoë's shoulder awkwardly. When it seemed that the younger girl had herself in hand, Charlotte seated herself on the adjacent chair. She drew in a steadying breath, released it, then drew in another before embarking on what she wished to say.

"My late husband, Edward, had a mistress. All gentlemen do. It means nothing."

"Doesn't it?" Zoë's tears dried.

"No. Really. You may take my word for it."

Through the wet spikes of her lashes, Zoë regarded the older girl. "Why do you English wives permit it?"

"Permit it?" Charlotte's face registered perplexity. "Why shouldn't we? It's a blessed relief not to have to tolerate a husband's . . . well . . . one must give one's husband heirs, of course, but, what I mean to say is . . ."

"Yes?"

Breathing deeply, Charlotte concluded, "A gentleman takes a mistress to spare his wife the unpleasantness of the marriage bed."

163

"Is . . . is that why Rolfe has taken a mistress — to spare me the unpleasantness of the marriage bed?" Zoë's look was hopeful.

Though she knew herself to be on shaky ground, Charlotte answered with absolute conviction, "Of course it is!"

Hours later, as she undressed for bed, Charlotte found herself still reflecting on the conversation she'd had with Zoë. She thought of her husband, Edward, and of the day he had introduced her to his younger brother, Rolfe.

He'd looked like a young golden demigod as he'd come forward to take her hand. Laughing, Rolfe was always laughing. She had not believed that he could be related to Edward and the dowager. How she had wished, then, that it was the younger son she was marrying. But he'd had little in the way of prospects. And her guardian would never have countenanced the match.

"Rolfe," she whispered into the darkness. "Rolfe." She had never loved anyone but Rolfe. And he did not even know that she was alive. Ironically, it was Rolfe's young wife who had shown her more kindness than she'd met in a long while. Rolfe was never at the Abbey, and the dowager had no thought for anyone but herself.

Zoë was not as she was. Zoë would make Rolfe notice her. Zoë would have Rolfe's kisses, share his bed, bear his children. It was inevitable.

She was only four and twenty, thought Charlotte, and already she felt as if her life were over. Zoë was not so poor spirited. Zoë was the sort of girl who made things happen.

She took that thought with her to bed.

As the residents of the Abbey retired for the night, the social whirl in Town, such as it was in that stifling indolent August when London was thin of company, was just getting underway. Amy Granger, a young actress of Covent Garden fame, took one last searching glance in the looking glass before flouncing out the stage door.

The marquess's hired hackney was waiting for her. One of the coachmen handed her in with gratifying deference. Amy settled herself comfortably on the leather banquette and considered her good fortune.

She'd had her eye on Rivard for some time past, ever since he had taken up with Rosamund and had set her up in a little house in Duke Street. If Amy played her cards right, she was thinking Rosamund might soon become ancient history and she, little Amy Granger, might be the one to lord it over the other girls in the Green Room.

At the thought of the high and mighty Rosamund, she stifled a giggle. Rosamund had no notion that her protector was straying. Not that the marquess had taken any liberties. Amy frowned, wondering why he had not.

Betrand. It was sheer ill luck that the marquess knew of Betrand's existence. That must be it. A gentleman of Rivard's consequence would not offer *carte blanche* to a lady who had another protector hovering in the wings. She had decided that, as soon as may be, Betrand must be given his *congé*. It was too bad that in the last little while, the young Frenchman had removed from town to visit with friends in the country.

She tried to imagine that moment when she turned Betrand off, and her heart began to race unpleasantly.

Betrand would not take his dismissal with grace. He had a temper, that one. He was young and he was reckless. He would challenge the marquess to a duel, if she knew anything of Betrand.

Her eyes glowed with pleasure as she considered how far she had risen in the world. Two gentlemen of consequence fighting a duel over *her*—little Amy Granger! And her sister had predicted that she would come to a bad end! She snorted derisively. Elsie's life of respectability was not for her—not if it meant a life of drudgery. God, how she wished Elsie could see her now—in her silks and satins, and riding in a fine carriage! She giggled, thinking that Elsie would no doubt find some text from the Bible to try and take her down a peg or two. Poor Elsie! All that beauty gone to waste on an impoverished young farmer in the wilds of Devon. And all she had to show for it was a passel of brats. Elsie would be old before her time.

The coach drew to a halt at the back entrance of Stephen's Hotel on Bond Street. The marquess received her in a private parlor up one flight of stairs. A late supper had been laid on. But though Rivard was flatteringly attentive, there was no mention of setting her up in her own establishment. Amy swallowed her disappointment. She had been right about one thing. Until she had given Betrand his *congé* the marquess meant to keep his distance. By the time the coach was sent for to take her to her own lodgings, she had quite made up her mind. She would pen a note to Betrand and give it into the hands of the innkeeper at the White Hart. Betrand had advised her that, if it were necessary, he could be reached that way. When next the marquess sent for her, resolved Amy, she would be free of Betrand.

From the upstairs parlor window, Rolfe watched the hackney till it disappeared around a corner. Another hackney pulled out of a side street and, within moments, it too disappeared around the same corner. Miss Amy Granger, reflected Rolfe, had never been better guarded in her life, if only she knew it.

He felt a twinge of guilt. He knew exactly what was going on in Amy's avaricious little mind. When it was over, he must present her with an expensive trinket if only to compensate the girl for her time. If she led them to *Le Patron* he would be happy to throw in a handsome reward.

God, what a debacle! Rolfe threw himself down in the overstuffed armchair flanking the empty grate, reflecting that the week past must surely be one of the worst of his whole life.

Under orders from Mr. Pitt, he had given the signal to arrest all suspected members of *La Compagnie*. With support from a detachment of guards, his agents had moved in. Who could have foreseen the blood bath that followed? They knew, of course, that they were dealing with fanatics. What they had not known was that, when cornered, those fanatics would turn their violence upon themselves. Evidently, a tenet of their dogma was that no one should be taken alive.

Of the forty suspected and known members of the sect, more than twenty had been killed resisting arrest or had died by their own hand. The rest had gone into hiding. Betrand was one of them. And it went without saying, *Le Patron* was still at large.

Unlike Mr. Pitt, Rolfe could take no comfort from the thought that *La Compagnie* had been effectively smashed in England. They had been so close to capturing *Le Patron*. They had shown their hand prematurely. Betrand was their last link to that elusive gentleman. Hence Rolfe's determined cultivation of Betrand's mistress, Amy Granger.

The girl knew nothing. Rolfe was sure of it. She had played no part in *La Compagnie*. Their only hope was that Betrand would grow careless. If luck was on their side, he would come out of hiding to be with the girl. And if and when he did, they would be waiting.

Some days after the contretemps with the dowager, Zoë descended the stairs to the Great Hall. She was dressed in a light traveling cloak and carried a well-worn portmanteau in one hand. She'd been refused admission to her mother-in-law's chambers, but Charlotte was there to see her off.

"Say good-bye to the children for me," said Zoë.

Charlotte opened her mouth and shut it again. Nothing she could find to say would dissuade Zoë. She did not know if she wished to dissuade her. When she thought about it, she wished she could go with her. One day, she might.

When carriage and outriders took the last turn in the drive, Charlotte turned back into the house. At the top of the stairs, she was met by the dowager's maid with the message that she was wanted in the dowager's chamber at once.

The smell of burnt feathers assailed her nostrils. Her mother-in-law was propped up in bed, reclining languidly against a mound of cushions and pillows. The maids were dismissed.

"Has . . . has she gone?" asked the dowager.

"She has."

"Frightful, ungrateful wretch of a girl! I hope Rolfe beats her!"

"Do you?" asked Charlotte noncommittally. She toyed with the tassel on the silk rope which held back one of the curtains.

The dowager slanted her daughter-in-law a puzzled look. After a moment, she let out a breath and said, "Well, I, for one, cannot be sorry that she has gone. I wish Rolfe *would* keep her in town. Yes, and I shall write and tell him so. Then we may go on as before. How pleasant things were before *she* came among us."

Charlotte's interest was caught by something outside the window. It was a moment before she replied. "The children have just discovered that their Aunt Zoë has gone. Can you hear them? I must go to them."

"Charlotte!" commanded the dowager. Shock vibrated through her voice.

"Mmm?" Charlotte halted with her hand on the doorknob. "Oh, no. I don't think things shall go on as before. They never do, you know. Shall I send your maids to you?"

"My maids? But-but what about you?"

"I'm promised to the children," answered Charlotte and left the dowager open-mouthed and staring.

Zoë reached town without mishap. That Rolfe was not at home occasioned her more relief than disappointment. There was just enough time, if he so wished it, to have a fresh team hitched to the carriage to return her to the Abbey before nightfall.

With this in mind, she wasted no time in unpacking, but left the maid who had accompanied her to see to it while she set off to pay a call on Francoise. A hired hackney took her to an address in the district of Soho.

Much to her surprise, she found valises and trunks in the narrow vestibule and the furniture under Holland covers. Zoë had known that her friends were resolved to return to France. But by the looks of things, it seemed that their departure was imminent.

With sinking spirits, Zoë followed Francoise to a small, downstairs parlor which was still habitable. Only then, when Francoise turned to face her, did Zoë observe the older girl's unnaturally pale complexion and red-rimmed eyes.

"My dear, what is it?" she asked. "I thought you were happy to be going home to France."

"I was. I am. It's just that I'm sorry to be leaving England." Francoise gave a watery smile. "I shall miss all my friends, you see, yourself most of all."

It was an evasion, and Zoë knew it, though she could not have said how she came by that knowledge. Something was very far wrong, and Zoë had a good idea of the source of her friend's distress.

Francoise had been married for little under a month, and Zoë was beginning to wonder if her friend had come to regret her hasty marriage to Charles Lagrange. Zoë was aware that it was not a love match. Francoise had indicated as much when she had written to inform her that the marriage had already taken place. Francoise was not a romantic. She had no use for love. She wanted security, so she had written. Charles was twenty years her senior. She respected him. She would make him a good wife. They considered themselves fortunate to have found each other. Zoë did not share Francoise's sentiments. Though she was fond of Charles Lagrange, she thought that Francoise could have done so much better for herself.

The older girl made a visible effort to control herself. She forced a smile. As if divining Zoë's thoughts, she said, "Charles thinks I'm foolish beyond permission to take on so. It's just that . . ." She shook her head helplessly before continuing, "Oh God, Zoë, I'm afraid to return to France. Who knows what awaits us there? I can never forget those last months before I came to England. I'm a coward, Zoë, and I can't seem to help myself."

Impulsively, Zoë threw her arms around the older girl's shoulders. "Oh my dear," she said, "things are very different now. Do you see what this means? You may return without fear of reprisal and discover what has happened to your loved ones. Oh I wish . . ." Tears burned her eyes. The words would not come.

Francoise lifted her head. "What do you wish, Zoë?"

Zoë's arms dropped away and she began to pace like a caged wild thing. She pivoted to face her friend. In an anguished tone, she said, "I wish I had never wed! I wish I had remained as Lady Kilburn's companion! Then I might go to France with you to find my family. And I *shall* go with you! Yes! I shall, if he tries to send me back to his mother!" There was a stunned silence. Then, as if the words were wrung from her, Zoë cried out, "Oh, Francoise, I'm so unhappy and I don't know what to do."

Lord Rivard's young footman finally tracked down his master in one of the gaming dens which proliferated around St. James. As instructed by his master's valet, Dere, he handed in a note. Though the footman could not read, he was an intelligent lad, and guessed, quite correctly, that Dere was advising his lordship of her ladyship's unheralded descent on the house in St. James Square.

There was need of that warning, for, only last week, his lordship had comported himself with an almost total disregard for the proprieties. It was shocking, but sadly true, that on that occasion the marquess had returned to the house in St. James in the wee hours of the morning in company of a ladybird, and had kept her in his chamber the whole night through! That his lordship was three sheets to the wind was held, by the female servants, to be of no moment. The marquess was a gentleman. A gentleman worthy of that exalted title was never inebriated to the point of folly. And for a gentleman to dally with a light o' love in the *family* mansion, no less, was an indiscretion bordering on insanity.

It was the upstairs maid, Jessie, who had put her finger on what ailed the master, in the footman's opinion.

"Mark my words!" she said with a sapient wink. " 'Is Lordship's 'ad a disappointment! That's wot! Some lady, or ladybird"—at this point, elbowing the footman playfully—" 'as turned 'im off." A thought struck her. "May'ap 'tis the new un—the young mistress! Cor blimey! And she's a Froggie! I thought they was always 'ot."

At this point in the young footman's reflections, the door to the gaming club opened and his master took a few stumbling steps down the stairs. The footman put out a hand to steady him.

"Fetch me a chair, there's a good fellow," said Rolfe, carefully erasing the slur from his speech. He swayed alarmingly.

The footman obediently hailed a waiting sedan and the marquess laboriously entered it. He gave an address which the young footman countermanded a mo-

172

ment afterwards, but not so that his master would notice.

Inside the sedan, Rolfe held up the folded note and tried to decipher Dere's scrawl. He soon gave up the attempt, and let the note fall where it might. Intermittently humming to himself and bursting into a snatch of a bawdy song he'd picked up in school days, he settled back and forced himself to contemplate the sensual delights awaiting him once he arrived at the little nest he kept for his mistress. Within minutes, his thoughts had wandered.

He had good reason to drown his sorrows, reflected Rolfe. Betrand was dead, and Rolfe still could not believe it. The boy was no more than twenty or so. He blamed himself. He had set a trap for the boy, using as his bait Amy Granger. When the boy had come for her, they were waiting for him. They had expected to take Betrand alive. It was not to be. When cornered, he had shot and killed one of Rolfe's agents. In the ensuing melée, Betrand, himself, had been shot dead. And now there was no one to lead them to *Le Patron*.

A furious oath burst from Rolfe. He could not find it in himself to care one way or another whether or not they ever caught up with *Le Patron*. But Betrand — oh God, what a waste of a young life! His eyes were burning. He stared out at the dark night, seeing nothing. Before long, his lashes drifted down. By the time the sedan stopped outside his house in St. James Square, Rolfe was snoring softly.

Chapter Ten

He awakened with a feeling of complete and utter disorientation. Though it was dark, he knew that the woman sleeping beside him must be his mistress. But her fragrance, as fresh as field lilies, brought to mind the vision of another lady. Zoë. Oh God! Rolfe groaned and flung one arm over his eyes. Waking. Sleeping. Drunk. Sober. He had developed an obsession for little Zoë.

"Rolfe. Are you awake?"

He flinched. He must be going crazy, he decided, to think that Rosamund's voice sounded anything like his wife's. Or perhaps he was in a drunken stupor? Or perhaps it was just wishful thinking that made him imagine that the women by his side had the feel and smell of Zoë. Good God! Surely he had not said her name aloud?

Quickly, he rose above the woman in his bed. "Don't spoil it," he said, sensing that Rosamund was about to say something. "Just let me imagine . . ." He shook his head, trying to get a grasp on reality. This was a dangerous game he was playing. How much longer could he protect Zoë from himself if he once began to pretend that the woman he took to bed was his wife?

"Rolfe?" His name was a brush of silk against his skin.

This was torture. He was only human after all. Once, just once, surely there could be no harm in a little deception? And no one but he need ever be the wiser . . .

"Kitten," he said, and wished he could say "Zoë." "Don't talk. Just kiss me."

It was going to be all right, thought Zoë. Rolfe wasn't angry. He hadn't ordered her from his bed. He wanted her to kiss him. She must be careful not to shrink from whatever he asked of her. He was her husband. She loved him.

Lips molded gently to lips. Breath mingled. Skin whispered against skin. And for Rolfe, conscious thought gradually receded as he let the obsession take hold. Zoë. Her name drummed inside his head. Zoë. Reality slipped into fantasy till he could scarcely distinguish one from the other.

She was shy. He knew she would be. But she accepted each kiss and caress the way he had dreamed she would. Oh God, his imagination was more powerful than he had ever suspected. And yet, it all seemed so real.

"I've wanted you forever, kitten," he told her frankly, and his hands moved under her nightdress, gently easing it upwards, removing it completely so that there was no barrier for what was to follow. "If only you knew!" he whispered. "Oh God! What I've dreamed of doing! I've wanted to kiss you and touch you all over, from your silky head of hair to the tips of your little toes."

His fingers ploughed into her hair combing through it, wrapping it around his throat like silken bonds. He laughed softly. "God, how it would shock

175

her if she only knew what I've dreamed of doing to her!"

"Rolfe?" He wasn't making sense to Zoë.

"Hush. Be still. Let me touch you. I want to know every inch of you."

It took every ounce of her willpower not to jerk as his hands began a slow exploration. She was shy—unbearably so. But she knew better than to object, or show reluctance to follow his lead. He was too sensitive to her feelings. One protest from her and he would put her down as the child she was determined to demonstrate, once and for all, was only a figment of his imagination. And then, incredibly, as his hands and lips moved over her, the shyness left her, and she yielded to a strange sense of floating, of languor. It was like drowning, she thought, and touched her hands to his powerful shoulders to steady herself.

It was Rolfe who jerked at that first tentative touch. "Ah God, yes, kitten! Like this!" and he moved her hand slowly from his throat to his groin, forcing her to spread her fingers through the coarse mat of hair on his chest, down, down, over the granite-hard muscles of his stomach to his loins.

Zoë braced herself for what was coming. Nothing could have prepared her for the reality of the aroused male. She couldn't help herself. She tried to wrench her hand away, but Rolfe steadied her as if he had anticipated her rejection. "I'm only a man," he said with a trace of humor. "Now touch me," and to ensure her obedience, he thrust himself boldly into her cupped hand, smoothing her fingers over the pulsating length of him. Awkwardly, fearfully, Zoë traced the powerful root of his masculinity.

Her mouth was taken in such a ferocity of hunger that she gasped. Her hands fell away from him and

176

clutched at the sheets, twisting them into knots. She had a sudden urge to confess that it had all been a terrible mistake, that she was, in truth, too young for what he wanted from her. She forced herself to relax, recalling every sage word her mother had told her respecting the marriage bed. She must yield herself completely to her husband. There would be pain at the moment of their joining, but it would soon pass, and all the more quickly if she did not tense herself for what was to come.

So involved was she in her thoughts, that his hand was *there*, between her legs, before she could do more than suck in her breath. She grabbed for his wrist, but his fingers had already begun the gentle invasion, stroking through the sensitive folds of her femininity. Zoë choked out a strangled sound of protest, but he was attacking on all fronts, his mouth fastening on one sensitive nipple before teasing the other. Air expanded in Zoë's lungs and whooshed out like a deflated balloon. She moaned, and this time the sound was unmistakably one of pleasure. Beneath him, she softened like melting wax, molding herself to take his impression. Her fingers caught in his hair. Surrender trembled all through her body.

The male in Rolfe exulted in her feminine submission. He sat back on his heels and eased her legs apart to lie over his flanks, opening her body to his whim. He'd long since given up the effort to regulate his breathing. "I've dreamed of you purring for me, kitten, do you know? Ah, love, what odds? This is nothing but a fantasy. Nothing I do can shock you," and his head dipped to that secret place between her thighs.

Bewildering, hot tremors of sensation swept through Zoë. She tried to speak, but only choked moans, remarkably like a kitten purring, escaped her lips. Her hands clutched at his sleek head, tugging him into an awareness of her dire extremity. She thought she might be on the verge of an attack of palpitations, so erratically was her heart racing. Oh God, she was going to die.

Suddenly, he covered her with the weight of his body. In a rush of passion he kissed her brows, her chin, her nose, before his mouth settled on hers. His kiss was as shockingly voluptuous as the rest of his lovemaking, his tongue surging and receding in an age-old rhythm. Zoë reveled in it.

When he pulled back, they were both panting hard. Rolfe closed his eyes, trying to get a hold on himself. He was on fire for her as he had never been on fire for any woman. He mustn't hurt her. Zoë. Good God! What was he thinking? He could never make love to little Zoë like this. The illusion blurred at the edges. The woman in his arms was not Zoë. "Oh no!" he groaned. "Rosamund!" He would not accept it. It was Zoë he wanted. He would make it so.

It took a moment for Rolfe's words to pierce the sensual fog in Zoë's brain. She spread her hands against the bunched muscles of his shoulders restraining him. Rosamund was the name of his mistress. Hadn't the dowager said so?

Horror-struck, she whispered, "Say my name."

Name. He must think of a name. Not Zoë. "Rosamund," he said aloud.

Rosamund? Oh God! Feebly, she tried to push out of his arms. "I shouldn't be here." Rather hysterically, she wondered if she could creep from the bed and gain the sanctuary of her own chamber before Rolfe realized who she was. "I must go," she said, and raised her head from the pillow.

178

"Kitten, easy," soothed Rolfe, refusing to give up the illusion. He positioned her beneath him, and holding her down, slowly began to enter her.

Zoë was beside herself. Rosamund! He thought that she was Rosamund! Her body went rigid. She tried to lunge away from him. He adjusted his weight, pinning her more securely to the mattress. Her frantic struggles to dislodge him only drove him deeper. Feminine muscles, deep in her body, clenched against him, resisting his masculine intrusion, staving off his deeper, surer penetration. "Ah, kitten," he said, "it's kinder this way," and holding her still, he thrust into her.

Zoë gasped. She beat at him with her fists. She wanted to die with the fiery pain of his possession. She wanted to die of shame. Gradually, the pain receded, but still she fought him.

The woman in his arms was a virgin. Rolfe stilled. Reality and fantasy had become inextricably woven together. "Zoë," he said, but so softly he knew she did not hear him. Zoë was on fire for him, wanting him as much as he wanted her. "Be still!" he warned, gritting his teeth as her frenzied movements drove him deeper, pushing him to the edge. But it was too late. Already, the pleasure was coming at him in waves. "Ah love!" he cried out. "Forgive me!" and he drove into her, claiming her with a violence that left him shaken.

Several minutes were to pass before he could bear to allow reality to intrude. And then it came to him that his mistress was weeping uncontrollably into the bedclothes.

"Rosamund?"

No response, but the weeping subsided into muffled sniffles and gulps. He pulled back the bed drapes and groped on the bedside table. It took some doing, but he finally got a candle lit. He had a premonition of disaster the moment he recognized that he was in his own chamber in his house in St. James. He could not credit that he had committed the folly of taking some woman of the streets to his bed. Hadn't he told Dere never to permit such a thing again?

Swearing under his breath, Rolfe turned to face the woman in his bed. Shock and horror held him speechless. Zoë! He closed his eyes as the remorse washed through him. Oh God, what had he done to her? He'd abased her, used her with more intimacy than he'd used with any woman. It wasn't his fault. He'd been acting out a fantasy. Zoë wasn't supposed to be *there!* He could not bear so much guilt.

"Are you all right?" His voice was hoarse.

"I—I think so." Hers was tremulous.

Reassured on that point, Rolfe leapt from the bed and roared. "What the hell are you doing in my chamber?"

Zoë was biting down on her lip, looking up at him with sad, accusing eyes as if he were an ogre. He felt like an ogre—a debaucher of innocents. But *she* had done this to him! The thought made him angrier.

"I refuse to take the blame for what happened," he said with a rather determined defiance, and groped in his mind for a way to explain his behavior. The truth, that he had dreamed he was making love to his own wife, he instantly discarded. Zoë would be shocked, and rightly so. "I had too much to drink. I was dreaming," he said. "I thought you were another lady."

"Rosamund," said Zoë, "your mistress."

Relief flooded Rolfe. Better by far that she accept that lie than divine the awful truth. Her opinion of his character would be even lower, in those circumstances. He was being let off lightly, and thanked God for it. Moreover, Zoë did not seem particularly overset by what had just transpired. He had expected . . . well . . . hysterics.

Zoë had other things to occupy her mind. Before he had turned on her, she'd had a chance to look under the sheet. There was blood on her legs. She wondered if she dared ask him to send for a physician. Her mother had never mentioned anything about blood. But, all things considered, she was beginning to perceive that her mother had deceived her abominably. It was Charlotte who had the right of it. No women in her right mind would welcome a man's embrace. Never again would she submit herself willingly to such agony, no, not even if she, like Rosamund, were paid for it! She moved her legs and felt something sticky. Oh God, perhaps she was dying? She wondered if she should mention it.

"Who told you about Rosamund?" asked Rolfe. Where the hell was his dressing gown? He felt ridiculous stalking about as naked as the day he was born. He saw his breeches, and reached for them. "And you still haven't answered my original question. Why are you here?"

"I quarreled with your mother," said Zoë. "I can't go back there. I came to tell you."

"You can't possibly stay here!" The thought appalled him. He'd take her again. He knew it. It would be torture to have her under his roof.

"I don't intend to," said Zoë. As he pulled on his breeches with his back to her, she surreptitiously peeked under the sheet. The flow of blood seemed to have stopped. Perhaps she would survive after all?

"What does that mean?" asked Rolfe.

Zoë gave him her full attention. "I thought I might

181

put up with my friend, Francoise. If you have no objection, that is. It's months since we've seen each other." She saw the indecision in his eyes, and, as an added persuasion, threw in, "Your mother and I are in need of a respite from each other's society, Rolfe."

"It's been difficult for you, has it, kitten?"

Zoë had no wish to enter upon an acrimonious discussion involving her mother-in-law. In the space of a few minutes, her world had tilted crazily. All her hopes for her marriage lay in ruins. She had a new purpose and must be single-minded in its pursuit. "It hasn't been easy," she allowed cautiously.

"I didn't abandon you, you know." He sat down on the edge of the bed and captured her hand.

"Didn't you?" She eyed him warily.

"I just wanted to keep you safe."

His fingers were massaging her wrist. The touch was surprisingly . . . sensual. He'd been such a tender lover, Zoë was thinking, until he'd gone and spoiled it all. Or perhaps it wasn't his fault. Perhaps nature had never intended them for each other. They just did not . . . fit.

And they did not suit. She had hoped, when he wakened and found her in his bed . . . oh God, she did not know what she had hoped. And all the time, he had supposed that he was making love o his mistress! A sob caught at the back of her throat. She choked it down and deliberately removed her hand from Rolfe's disturbing clasp.

"You needn't think I shall expect you to be at my beck and call," she said, determinedly pursuing her goal. "Far from it, Rolfe. Francoise and I are quite capable of entertaining ourselves. A husband would only be in the way." And she hoped he didn't learn the truth of that statement until it was too late.

In that moment, Rolfe would have promised Zoë anything within reason to make up for the experience he had just put her through. He knew that there would be talk in *ton* circles if it became known that they had not shared the same roof while they were both in town. The alternative was to send her home to the Abbey, or keep her with him.

The thought of keeping her with him was an almost irresistible temptation. He *must* resist it. Even now, knowing how much he had hurt her, shocked her, his senses were stirring. He wanted her. He had tasted her surrender. Surely *that* had not been part of the illusion? Oh yes, he wanted to make love to Zoë, but having once allowed himself the complete freedom of her body, he did not know if he could trust to his restraint.

There was a more cogent reason, however, for keeping Zoë at a distance. Until all the members of *La Compagnie* were traced and captured, he did not wish her to run any risks. He did not think his cover had been penetrated. But that possibility was always there. He could be a marked man.

Abruptly rising to his feet, he said, "How long do you intend to visit Francoise?"

"Two weeks. Three at the most."

"That doesn't seem so long. Then, of course, you'll return to the Abbey."

"Thank you," said Zoë. "Would you mind turning your back while I get dressed?"

He escorted her to their adjoining door. "You never did tell me why you were in my bed, kitten," he said, and flashed her one of his heart-stopping grins.

Zoë ignored it. "It's a long, boring story," she said. She had gamble and lost. She had yielded her body to him, and see where it had brought her. She wasn't about to do the same thing with her heart.

Rolfe was strangely reluctant to let her go. He knew he had to make amends, but wasn't sure how to go about it. "Zoë, wait." She regarded him half fearfully, her hand already pushing open the door to her chamber. "Zoë, rest assured, when the time comes to make you mine, it won't be anything like it was tonight." And he hoped he could hold himself to that promise.

She said nothing, but stared at him gravely.

He coughed. "What I mean to say is this, kitten. A man doesn't make love to his wife the way he makes love to his mistress." Surely the knowledge that he had a mistress would lay her fears to rest?

"It doesn't signify," answered Zoë, and made to push past him.

"Wait! Zoë, I was half dreaming. You must believe me. You should have wakened me. Why didn't you?"

Her eyes fell before his. What could she say? She'd fought him like a jungle cat. Hadn't he noticed? Evidently not. "I must have been dreaming too," she said. "Yes. That's what it was. It was all a dream, a stupid dream."

She sounded so lost, so achingly alone. A constriction tightened Rolfe's chest. He wanted to gather her in his arms and comfort her. He dared not. Still, he detained her, not knowing what he hoped to gain.

"Kitten?" He didn't know what he wanted to say. Smiling, he invented, "Perhaps I should be the one to look after the key to this door?"

"Oh, no," said Zoë. "Now that I know what to expect, I shall guard it with my very life."

The smile on Rolfe's lips died. She brushed past him and shut the door in his face. The grate of the key in the lock was almost instantaneous.

They breakfasted together in the morning like any civilized couple, and if their conversation was a trifle strained, neither mentioned the reason for it.

For a week and more, as the date for the Lagrange's departure for France loomed nearer, Zoë was in an agony of indecision. Should she stay with a husband who did not want her or should she cast caution to the winds and throw in her lot with the returning émigrés?

She came to her decision the night they made up a party for a performance at Covent Garden. At one of the intervals, Roberta Ashton, Rolfe's discarded mistress, swooped down and carried Zoë off to her own box for a quiet tête à tête. The next twenty minutes were the most mortifying and the most enlightening of Zoë's young life. And though she saw at once that Roberta Ashton spoke with all the venom of a scorned woman, she also recognized, intuitively, the truth of what she had been too blind, too gullible, to admit. Her husband was not the hero she had imagined but a rake of the first order.

When the curtain went up for the second act, Zoë was in shock. By the time she returned to Soho Square, she was a broken girl. No one would have known it. She reserved all her tears, all her scathing self-recriminations for the privacy of her chamber. When she awakened in the morning, her mind was made up. Her destiny lay in France.

It was weeks before Rolfe discovered Zoë's direction, and months before he was in a position to track down his errant wife. Only days after her departure, he was ambushed as he exited from the theatre with a young actress on his arm. The girl died instantly. Their attackers, themselves, came under a hail of bullets. There were two of them, one of whom lay dead.

For weeks, Rolfe hovered near death. Housard, himself, came over from France to take charge of the investigation. When Rolfe had recovered sufficiently from his wounds, he was informed that *La Compagnie* in England was smashed. No one could or would tell him what had happened to Zoë.

Chapter Eleven

The winter of '94 was the coldest in living memory. The Seine froze over, and for the first time in years, wolves were spotted on the outskirts of Paris.

In the city, the general populace deemed themselves little better than the wolves. Bread, as usual, was rationed and fuel was scarce. Coal became a luxury, and swarms of men, women, and children descended like locusts on the Bois de Boulogne to hack at trees for their firewood. Prices for the basic necessities of life were so inflated that a laborer's wages were scarce enough to keep starvation from the door.

Not all, however, suffered to an equal degree, and for those who had money, pleasures which the severely moralistic Robespierre had attempted to suppress during his tyranny were entered into with frenetic abandon. Gambling dens, theatres, and dancing halls threw open their doors. Prostitutes who had formerly hidden themselves behind the colunms in the gardens of the Palais Royal now cast discretion to the winds and touted their wares brazenly. Dandies adopted the most extravagant fashions and sped through the streets in their equally outlandish carriages. Luxury and destitution were glaringly obvious. It was evident that the gap between rich and poor was as wide as ever it was before the Revolution.

The Lagranges were fortunate. Charles Lagrange had found himself a position as secretary to a former friend, a Girondin like himself, who had been recalled to the Convention. The salary was not large, but it was adequate to meet the needs of his small household, his wife, Francoise, and her friend, Zoë. They had taken rooms in a house just off the Rue de Bac.

In the front parlor, a coal fire blazed. Francoise, at her needlework, from time to time cast surreptitious glances at Zoë. She was seated at a small spinnet and though her fingers moved over the keyboard and the strains of Mozart filled the small room, Francoise could tell that her friend's thoughts were miles away.

She waited until the piece had come to an end before she casually observed, "I thought we might go to Madame Dugazon's tomorrow and order some muslin for our new gowns."

"Muslin?" said Zoë absently.

"Charles says that all the ladies have adopted the new fashion."

"What ladies?"

"Oh, you know, Madame Tallien and her friend Josephine, what's her name?"

"Beauharnais," answered Zoë. "Barras's mistress."

"Yes, that's the one. And that beautiful child, Récamier's little bride."

"Juliette Récamier. God, he's old enough to be her father!" Zoë drew in a sharp breath as she suddenly recognized the infelicity of her remark. Stricken, she swiveled to face the other girl. "Francoise . . ."

"Don't give it another thought," interposed Francoise quickly. "Truly, I'm not offended. I know that Charles is considerably older than I, and frankly, I'm glad of it. Younger men, or the ones I've observed, seem too bent on gratifying their own heedless pleasures. Oh dear. Now I'm the one who should be apologizing."

A smile touched Zoë's lips, but her lashes swept down, and her fingers became involved in turning the pages of her music.

Francoise set her needlework to one side. "Zoë," she said, her voice as gentle as she could make it, "have you come to any decision with regard to whether or not you are going to divorce Rivard?"

"There's plenty of time, and—and it seems so final," said Zoë faintly.

"Final, yes," agreed Francoise. "But don't suppose that you have all the time in the world to make up your mind. Charles says that many of the laws which were enacted in the last number of years are being struck down by the Convention. For the moment, divorce is a mere formality, but who is to say that we won't return to the old ways? If you are going to do it, do it soon, before it's too late."

Zoë's answer was a bare nod of the head. She flexed her fingers in readiness for the opening bars of the music she had selected.

Francoise made haste to get in one more word before Zoë's music cut off any attempt at conversation. "You've already reverted to your maiden name, Zoë. I can't think why you are balking at cutting the connection altogether. It's the logical thing to do. You'll see! One day you'll meet another gentleman, someone from your own milieu. A Frenchman. That English lord? He was not for you, and you know it. There's no stigma attached to divorce these days. Look at Madame Tallien. You'll find happiness with the right man, I promise you, Zoë."

Zoë brought her hands down forcefully, and the impassioned opening bars of Scarlatti's Sonata in C

Major fairly made the crystal chandelier overhead jump before it began to hum a tuneful accompaniment.

Happiness. The word seemed to stick in Zoë's brain, drumming a litany to Scarlatti's furious tempo. The pursuit of happiness. Now where had she heard that expression? Oh yes, it was written into the American Constitution. How foolish the Americans must be if they made the pursuit of happiness their goal! It was too elevated, too whimsical, too much like wishful thinking. Could they banish sickness, or pain, or death? And did not one man's pursuit of happiness lead, more often than not, to misery for his companions? Happiness was an impossible goal, yes, even if every man, woman, and child in the whole world was of a benevolent nature. Better by far to set one's sights on what was attainable. Happiness was for the fortunate few.

Her fingers flew over the keyboard as she gave herself up to pure sensation, letting the music express a frustration, a passion, which she could never articulate in words. It seemed that she played for hours, deliberately evading all conversation with her friend. What was there to say about the husband she had deserted? She could never confide to anyone what had driven her to the course she had chosen. Simply to remember that episode in her life made her flinch in the deepest chagrin. She had been humiliated in the most painful way that it was possible for a woman to be humiliated. And she had brought it all upon herself. She had tricked the Englishman into a marriage he had never desired. Francoise was right. The logical thing to do was to divorce him, oh, not for her sake, but for his. She should set him free to find another. It was the only honorable thing to do.

In retrospect, she could see that she had never

truly loved him, not the way her mother had loved her father. As is the way of young girls, she had made an idol of him, endowing him with every imaginable virtue under the sun. That was not love. That was a schoolgirl's folly taken to the point of absurdity. She should be laughing, not blinking back tears.

And in the great scheme of things, how utterly trivial this grief for a lost lover who was never a real lover must seem. With France's tragic history, it was almost a profanity to waste one regret on something that was never meant to be.

By the time Zoë had retired for the night to her small chamber at the front of the house, a deep melancholy had taken possession of her. She stood immobile, in the center of the room, remembering a time when her life was filled with happiness. Only, she had not known what a gift she possessed — ordinary days with nothing of much moment to disturb their tranquillity. The door opened and her maid stood on the threshold.

"Ma petite."

"Salome!" Zoë shook her head, a gesture of helplessness that seemed to sum up an inexplicable inertia which had crept up on her. She did not know whether she should undress and get into the bath which was readied for her, or go to bed, or simply sit and contemplate her hands, or pick up her sewing. She didn't want to do anything.

Sizing up her young mistress at a glance, Salome quickly crossed the room. "Old Salome is here," she said crisply. "You had better be a good girl and do exactly as she tells you."

It was a relief not to have to make any decisions. Like a child, Zoë stood while Salome disrobed her. Obediently, she stepped into the warm bath water. She didn't seem to have the energy to wash herself.

191

Salome did what was needful.

When Zoë was under the covers, and sipping obediently at the cup of tisane which her maid insisted she drink, she said softly, "Tell me again, Salome, about my mother and father."

Salome had drawn up a chair near Zoë's bed as had become her practice every night since joining the Lagrange household. Her reunion with Zoë had been filled with pathos and a bittersweet joy. Salome's place in the Devereux household, as nurse to first the mother and then her three offspring, had always been a privileged one. It was only natural that in the present circumstances she would look upon her baby with a fierce protectiveness. Until Zoë's eyes closed in the blessed numbness of sleep, Salome would remain by her side.

Setting aside a piece of needlework which she had been examining, Salome crossed her plump black arms over her bosom and said, "Salome's eyes are getting too old to help you with your stitches, eh?"

"Please, Salome," pleaded Zoë, "tell me about *Maman* and Papa."

Sighing, shaking her head, the elderly maid embarked on a story she had related to her young mistress time and time again. As Madame Devereux's maid, she had been allowed access to her mistress through the many months of her incarceration. She was in the unique position of being a witness to much of what had taken place in those last days. Though she related the facts in stark terms, her voice grew husky as her recitation progressed.

Leon Devereux and his wife had been moved to the Conciergerie in the latter days of the Reign of Terror. They were under no illusions as to what would be their eventual fate. Nevertheless, even in the midst of that overcrowded, foul-smelling hell, they never lost their courage. They were sustained by the knowledge that their children were safely hidden away in the city of Rouen. Madame Devereux, in particular, though separated from her husband, and able to communicate with him only through smuggled letters, seemed to develop an unshakable serenity. Her very presence in the *cour des femmes,* that courtyard where the female prisoners were daily allowed to take their walks, created order among women of widely disparate backgrounds, from duchess to the lowest streetwalker. She became the source of advice, kindness, and consolation to many. On the day she was to be tried, she came down with a fever. She was taken to the infirmary that very morning, but nothing could be done for her.

When Leon Devereux heard of his wife's death, it was as if a terrible burden had been lifted from his shoulders. She was beyond pain, beyond torment, and he thanked God for it. He went to his trial with a lighter step. The verdict of "guilty" was a foregone conclusion. That same day, before the barber came to cut his hair, he wrote a letter to his children describing his sentiments and state of mind. The barber was bribed and agreed to pass the letter on to Madame Devereux's maid. To his everlasting credit, the barber kept his promise.

At six o'clock that evening, in company with other victims, men and women both, Leon Devereux's arms were tied behind his back and he mounted the tunbril that was to take him on the hour-long ride to the Place de la Revolution where the guillotine had been set up. At the corner of the Pont Neuf, Salome had stationed herself. Leon Devereux was calm and erect, and he acknowledged Salome's presence with a slight inclination of his head.

At this point in the narrative, Zoë interrupted to

ask, "Why did you go to the Pont Neuf, Salome? Why did you want Papa to see you as he passed?"

Salome hesitated, groping for words. "Who can say?" she said. "Somehow it seemed the right thing to do."

"I think I understand. I'm glad you were there. I'm glad Papa knew that he was not alone."

Zoë gazed at her empty cup, her thoughts shifting to the letter her father had written. Leon Devereux's final farewell to his children was long since committed to her memory. He began by commending them to God's care, said a few comforting words about their mother and his sure hope in the hereafter, then went on, in concise terms, to advise his heirs how and when they should claim their inheritance. Though it was beyond her at the moment, one day Zoë expected to read that letter and smile at her father's characteristic practical turn of mind. That in his last hours, he should set his affairs in order was the most comforting gesture of all.

Incredible as it seemed, his house in St. Germain, his wealth, had not been confiscated. His heirs, so long as they were citizens in good standing, were free to claim it. Though the bulk of his estate was to go to his son, he left his daughters wealthy women. Charles Lagrange, in the last number of weeks, had been working on Zoë's behalf to have her fortune turned over to her as well as the house in St. Germain, until such time as Claire and Leon could be located or their fates determined.

Thoughts of her brother and sister were always the worst torment for Zoë. It was a year almost to the day since she had last seen them. Of Leon, only one thing was known with any certainty. He had run away from the boarding school in Rouen before she had ever set out for Coutances. Claire must have known it

194

on that very last day when they had said their fare-wells. Yet, she had said nothing to Zoë, wishing, no doubt, to save her young sister anxiety. Zoë refused to accept what everyone else supposed as a matter of course, that Leon was long since dead. No one, in her hearing, dared mention his name in the past tense.

And there was Claire. She had been Commissioner Duhet's mistress. According to Charles Lagrange, that fact was incontrovertible. And when Zoë had been languishing at Rivard Abbey in Kent, Claire had disappeared from Rouen without a trace. What was known was that, at the same time as Claire van-ished, in the Spring of '94, Commissioner Duhet was recalled to Paris, denounced for corruption, and sum-marily executed. But what had become of his beauti-ful mistress, no one could say.

Claire. Leon. It was the not knowing which was tearing Zoë apart. Her friend, Francoise, had come to accept that no member of her own family had sur-vived the Revolution. And so might she, Zoë, if, like Francoise, she had indisputable proof of their respec-tive fates. As it was, her thoughts wavered constantly between a deep despondency and the brave hope that all would yet be well.

Her thoughts gave her no peace, returning time and time again to every possible eventuality that might have befallen her brother and sister. Boys were sometimes pressed into the army, or lured into bands of marauding brigands. Either of them might be ill or injured and in strange surroundings, not knowing who and where they were. And as for beautiful girls like Claire—but Zoë's thoughts shied away from this unpleasant and wholly unacceptable conjecture.

She must do something. But she did not know where to begin. Charles Lagrange had done as much as was possible to ferret out information, but it was all very sketchy. Someone, somewhere, must know something of Claire and Leon.

She surrendered her empty cup into Salome's outstretched hand. "I don't know what to do," she said, and Salome knew that her nurseling had no notion that she had spoken the words aloud. "I never told them, you see."

Salome blew out the candle on the bedside table. She touched a hand to Zoë's brow. The mild dose of laudanum was beginning to take effect. "Never told them what, *ma petite fleur?*" she asked soothingly.

"I never told them . . ." The eyelashes quivered. "Salome, have I ever told you?"

"Told me what, *cherie?*"

"That I love you?"

The maid chuckled. "No need to tell old Salome. She already knows."

"How do you know?"

"The same way you know that old Salome loves her little flower."

Zoë's eyes grew heavy. Her lashes lowered to lie like fans across her cheeks.

"They know," soothed Salome. "Just as you know that they love you. Go to sleep, little Zoë, go to sleep." Quietly, Salome extinguished the few remaining candles and quit the room.

As the latch clicked into place, Zoë's eyes fluttered open. Wide-eyed she stared into space. The darkness seemed to press in upon her. From somewhere came the sounds of a child sobbing uncontrollably. By degrees, the sobbing subsided and Zoë's breathing became more regular. She turned her face into the pillows, and the fragrant linen absorbed her tears.

* * *

As January drew to a close, Zoë's affairs were settled. The keys to the house in St. Germain were given into her hand, and her fortune, left to her under the terms of her father's will, in its entirety, was put at her disposal. There was never any question in her mind of how she intended to make capital of this happy turn in events. In the certain hope that Claire or Leon, circumstances permitting, would seek out the home of their childhood, she proposed to take up residence there with her friends, the Lagranges, and await developments.

When it became evident that Charles Lagrange would not countenance a move to St. Germain, Francoise did everything in her power to dissuade Zoë from her course.

"A woman alone, Zoë? Charles says it's not fitting."

"Then come with me."

"You know Charles's sentiments. His pride would never allow him to live off a woman's charity."

"What nonsense! Haven't I been living off his charity these many months past?"

"That's not the same thing, dear. And the expenses to run such an establishment, even supposing we share them, are simply beyond our means. Won't you reconsider?"

But nothing could dissuade Zoë. For the first time in months, her melancholy was lifting. She was beginning to take up the reins of her own life. In company of thousands of women throughout France who had formerly led a sheltered existence, she found herself with no father, no husband, no guardian to order her life. She was mistress of her own fate. At one and the same time, the thought terrified her and exhilarated her.

She removed to her former home at the beginning of February. Though Lagrange had warned her what to expect, her first sight of the house since she had fled from it more than a year before was almost enough to plunge her into a fresh wave of despair. She stood in her mother's yellow *salle* and could have wept. Though the house had been boarded up and still displayed the official seals prohibiting unauthorized persons from making free with the property, thieves had broken in and ransacked the place. This Zoë could have borne with equanimity, but not the desecration, the violation, the wanton destruction of everything of beauty which could not be carried off or was of no monetary value.

When she retrieved her mother's blackened tambour frame from the ashes in the grate, the first tide of self-pity gave way to slow-burning anger. It was this anger which fueled her flagging energies and made her more determined than ever to restore the house to its former magnificence.

She became untiring in her purpose. Slashed paintings were removed and substitutes found for them. Cabinetmakers were employed to restore smashed furniture. Her piano, with new sounding board and strings, was completely rebuilt. Walls were given a fresh coat of paint and soon after, carpets, curtains, and chandeliers were purchased and set in place.

"I can't see the point in any of it," Charles Lagrange was to remark to his wife. They were in their carriage, having at that moment taken leave of Zoë, after she had shown them her latest improvements.

"Zoë's done wonders with the place!" exclaimed Francoise. "Don't you approve?"

"I can never approve of luxury on that scale."

Slightly taken aback, Francoise protested, "She's a wealthy woman in her own right. And besides, think of what this project has done for Zoë. She was falling into a decline until she took over the house. It's been the making of her."

"She might have turned the house into an infirmary for the poor. Now *there's* something a woman of means ought to consider."

"Charles! Zoë's not doing this for herself. The house belongs to her brother, Leon. She thinks to restore it and hold it in trust for him."

Lagrange patted his wife's hand placatingly. "I don't mean to find fault with your little friend. I like Zoë, as you well know. I should have known, I suppose, when she deserted her English husband and came to France with us that beneath that demure exterior is concealed a will of iron."

"Zoë? Willful?" The thought seemed to amuse Francoise.

"There's no persuading her once she makes her mind up to do something. I cannot like her living in that house with only her maid as a chaperone."

"Not everyone thinks as you do," pointed out Francoise prosaically. "In point of fact, some would say that you are inclined to be old-fashioned in your notions."

"If I am old-fashioned," rejoined Lagrange, "then so is the majority of my sex. And I tell you now that a lady on her own, whether on the streets or in her own home, is inviting trouble."

Zoë was to learn the truth of this statement when she made her first outing to Picpus, in the Faubourg, St. Antoine, where her parents were interred. The place was desolate, like a wilderness, with nothing to show that beneath its fresh shroud of snow the bodies of more than a thousand victims of the last days of the Terror had found a common grave. "The Field of Martyrs," some called it, and came to mourn. Others crossed themselves, and hurried by.

It was here, strangely, that the violence of Zoë's

grief slackened till it became something more manageable. For here was sorrow on a scale that humbled her. Here was represented every class, every segment of society from common laborer to titled aristocrat. The hopes of some of the most noble houses ever to flourish in France no less than those of the most miserable peasant family had come to ruin in this final resting place. And there was no logic to it.

When Zoë returned to her carriage, she was white faced and silent. Salome, equally silent, unobtrusively adjusted the traveling rug around her young mistress's slight form. The silence was preserved until they reached the corner of the Palais Royal and the Rue de Richelieu. Something hit the side of the carriage and Salome cried out. The horses plunged, then came to a shuddering standstill.

"What is it?" Zoë called to her coachman, but already her eyes had taken in the swarm of young men who streamed out of the gardens of the Palais Royal. She knew at once what was afoot. A roving band of the *jeunesse dorée*, that gilded youth, young fops who were easily identified by their white cockades and long powdered hair, and who invariably carried short sticks weighted with lead, were staging a pitched battle with their bitterest enemies, the *sans-culottes*.

"Get us out of here!" Zoe's cry was desperate. But there was nothing her coachman could do. It was enough to keep his terrified team steady as the hordes of yelling combatants hedged them about.

The carriage door was wrenched open and the hostile face of a laborer, a *sans-cullotes*, thrust itself at Zoë. "La-de-dah lady. I thought Madame Guillotine had rid France of all your lot," the voice jeered.

Bloodied hands made a grab for Zoë. There was a scuffle. With a roar of rage, Salome threw herself at Zoë's attacker and bore him backwards out of the car-

200

riage. His place was immediately taken by another man. With great presence of mind, Zoë grabbed for one of the bricks which had warmed her toes on the way to Picpus. She threw it at the man who threatened her.

He dodged it easily. "Whoa, milady!" he said with a flash of white teeth. "Is that any way to thank your rescuer?" and just as her hand was groping for the second brick, he surprised her by giving her, her name. "No time for explanations," he said, cutting off her spate of questions, and he swept her into his arms.

They would never have made it through the crush of people to the gardens of the Palais Royal if the *jeunesse dorée* had not given them aid.

"*A moi! A moi!* Alphonse! Henri!" shouted the stranger, and young fops disengaged from *sans-culottes* and flanked him, their short sticks viciously cutting a path through the press of their attackers. Not until they reached the safety of the gardens did the stranger lower Zoë to her feet in one of the arcades.

"My maid," said Zoë, and subsided when Salome, seated with queenly grace in the saddle of the joined hands of two members of the *jeunesse dorée*, was borne into the gardens. They set her down, then raced back to the fray.

A sudden roar from the Rue de Richelieu signaled that one side in the confrontation had decided to cut its losses and run.

"You're quite safe here," said the stranger, his eyes studying Zoë's set face. "The *jeunesse dorée* will make short shrift of that lot."

A tremor passed over Zoë. She looked around wildly. Outside one of the gallery cafés, waiters were setting tables and chairs to rights. Elsewhere, people were going about their business or pleasures as if nothing of any importance had taken place.

"What if they return?" she asked, catching her breath.

"Who?"

"Those young fops—the *jeunesse dorée?*" As the words left her lips, two members of that dread society sauntered through one of the arches and came towards them. Zoë inched closer to the stranger.

He laughed softly. "No, no, Mademoiselle Devereux. Don't be afraid. These two outrageous *muscadins,* I'm ashamed to admit, happen to be my friends. It doesn't surprise me that you don't recognize them. I see what it is. You don't wish to, and who could blame you? Such affectation, such exaggeration! It's the new fashion, don't you know, but only for untried whelps." He spoke with such affection that no one could take offense at his words.

Zoë's eyes flicked over the two young dandies who were rapidly approaching. They were, she decided, something approximating her own age. She knew of a certainty that the *jeunesse dorée* were of her own class—the scions of wealthy property-owning or professional families. Since Robespierre's overthrow, the *jeunesse dorée* had become as frightening a force as the *sansculottes* had once been, but with far different aims. Former Jacobins and their sympathizers were *their* quarry, and the authorities supported them. Their short sticks weighted with lead had become as fearsome a symbol as the red caps of the preceding years. Zoë could not suppress a shudder. She abhorred violence in any form, and looked forward to the day when the short sticks, like the red caps before them, were also banned.

Yes, there was something familiar about all three gentlemen, she was thinking, and turned her scrutiny to the stranger by her side who was regarding her with a quizzical expression. She judged him to be in his late twenties. He was of medium height, and, in contrast to the young fops who had joined them, was dressed impeccably in the sober elegance of the new mode. His hair was long, a shade darker than her own locks, and tied in back in a queue. His features made a pleasing though by no means memorable impression. But it was the laughter at the back of those beautifully fringed brown eyes which jogged her memory.

"Jean Tresier!" she said. "How splendid!" and she offered him her gloved hand. Like her own family, the Tresiers had been bankers. At one time, Jean Tresier was considered a good catch. If he was not already wed, Zoë thought that he must still be considered as such, if outward appearances were anything to go by.

"You were at one time, I think, acquainted with these disreputable characters—Alphonse and Henri Destez, of the Destez banking family?"

Zoë could not think now why she had ever judged that the *jeunesse dorée* posed any kind of threat, so bashfully and maladroitly did these two members of that feared sect make their bows to her.

"Alphonse," she murmured, then again, "Henri. You were both away at school last I heard."

They returned something suitable, and lapsed into silence. There followed a slight awkwardness as each groped for a subject which would not cast a shadow on their conversation. It was impossible. Zoë's eyes brushed Tresier's and she knew that he was thinking the same thought.

Her expression grave, she asked, "What of your family?"

"Sadly, I am the remnant," he answered quietly. "And yours?"

Her eyes dropped. "The same. Just me."

It was at this precise point that Salome, rather pointedly, chose to clear her throat. Zoë looked a question at her maid, then followed the path of her eyes. She saw at once what Salome intended her to see. The ladies who were strolling about under the arcades, arm in am, and calling out brazenly to the patrons of the gaming houses and cafés, were not precisely ladies. Never in her life had Zoë ever thought to find herself in the precincts of the Palais Royal. "A den of iniquity," her father was used to call it.

"I must go," she said hurriedly. "Please accept my thanks for your very timely assistance. I shall never be able to repay you for what you did."

The laughter in Tresier's eyes betrayed that he had divined the cause of her sudden unease. "You may consider the debt cancelled, Mademoiselle Devereux," he said, "by granting me the honor of calling on you."

"The honor shall be mine, sir," answered Zoë, dimpling, and with her eyes she carefully included all three gentlemen.

When she entered her carriage, she thought to take her leave of them. But Tresier would not permit her to travel the streets of Paris without an escort.

Referring to his companions, he joked, "These gilded lilies are not good for much, but they'll see you safely to your door. *Á demain*, Mademoiselle," And with catcalls and much joking and back slapping among the gentlemen, Tresier instructed her coachman to make for home.

Chapter Twelve

The advent of Jean Tresier into Zoë's life marked a turning point. He was young, he was wealthy, he was received in the most prestigious salons of that new breed which now held sway in France, and he brought others with him. With the exception of her good friends, the Lagranges, and their small circle, Zoë had few friends. Suddenly, she was sought after. Scarcely a day went by that someone did not pay a call on the house in St. Germain, or take Zoë for a spin in his carriage. And none was more flatteringly attentive than one of the first friends Tresier brought with him.

Zoë recognized him at once. Paul Varlet had occasionally been a guest in the house in St. Germain. Like her father, he was a financier. According to Tresier, he was one of the richest men in France and had made his fortune in the last number of years as a supplier to the Revolutionary government for everything from tent poles to cannons.

By Zoë's reckoning, Varlet was close to forty. His hair was dark with silver wings at the temples and cut in the new mode, just brushing the collar. With his aquiline features and somnolent expression, to

Zoë's eyes, he had the stamp of an aristocrat. She vaguely remembered her father having commented upon it at one time.

Though Varlet's manners were charming, Zoë could never be quite comfortable in his company. She put it down to the difference in their ages. Or perhaps it was because he had a way of speaking to her that made her think he was playing Pygmalion to her Galatea.

"Zoë could be one of them if she had a mind to," he remarked idly, his eyes scanning with approval Zoë's yellow *salle* with its fine furniture waxed to a satiny patina, and its silk drapes and upholstery in shades of gold, the perfect complement to Zoë's beauty. "What do you think, Jean?"

"Indubitably," answered Tresier. His eyes were watchful.

Zoë lowered the lid of the piano and swiveled to face her companions. "What could I be if I had a mind to?" she asked.

With leisurely grace, Varlet crossed to the piano and lounged against it. "One of the lionesses of Parisian society."

"You're hoaxing me!"

"Why should you think so?"

"I don't know the first thing about society or how to go on in it. You forget, I was barely out of the schoolroom when I fled to England."

"How old are you?"

"Eighteen."

"You look older," commented Tresier from across the room in his comfortable chair.

Surprise and pleasure etched Zoë's finely sculpted features. Her eyes danced. "Do you think so?"

Varlet laughed. "You should be glad that you are

so young. Innocence is a priceless commodity. Once lost it can never be regained."

Zoë blushed, not quite knowing why she should do so. She was glad when Tresier joined them at the piano.

"What exactly have you in mind, Paul?" he asked pointedly.

Varlet made a leisurely study of the blushing girl. "I should like to make Mademoiselle Devereux over," he said. "If she will permit it, that is. With the right clothes and coiffure, she would outshine every other lady of my acquaintance."

"Why should you be the one to make her over?" asked the younger man, a note of hostility creeping into his tone. "Why not I?"

"I haven't said that I wish to be made over," protested Zoë. Her eyes dropped to take in the fresh white muslin, and her hands wandered to the neatly braided coronet on the crown of her head. "What's wrong with the way I look?" she demanded.

"You look charming," soothed Varlet, and then spoiled it by adding, "if you like the *ingénue* look."

What Zoë wanted was that sophistication, that polish which was the mark of all her husband's women, and which he had once denied that she possessed. And if she had to choose a mentor from between her two companions, she knew that she would chose Varlet over Tresier.

Varlet was older, more urbane, a connoisseur of everything from fine wines to correct etiquette. She sensed intuitively that he would know to a nicety how to help a lady acquire the polish she so much desired. Oh yes, as a mentor, Varlet would be without peer. But she knew that she would rather have

Tresier for a friend.

"I have no wish to be made over," she said, and rising to her feet, led the way to a circular table in front of the grate. "You'll take a glass of chocolate?"

"Thank you," said both gentlemen in unison.

Zoë graciously poured chocolate from the silver pitcher which Salome had set down only moments before. The door opened, and for some few minutes, conversation flagged as a magnificent black man, a giant of a person, resplendent in white satin breeches and scarlet tunic came sauntering into the room.

"My new footman," said Zoë in an undertone and almost cringed when the giant bent over her. "Thank you, Samson." She saw that he was offering her a tray of sweets and indicated that he should set it on the center of the table.

Having done this he straightened and stationed himself behind Zoë's chair.

"You may go, Samson," encouraged Zoë. She breathed a sigh when, after a slight show of reluctance, the footman withdrew.

With a gesture, Zoë invited the gentlemen to help themselves to the sweets. Varlet demurred, but Tresier selected a marzipan and proceeded to munch his way through it. The conversation, quite naturally, turned to the friends and acquaintances the two gentlemen held in common. From there it moved to the salons of the foremost Parisian hostesses.

By a remarkable coincidence, these ladies were mostly known to Zoë, though distantly. Through marriage or birth, they were related to the great international banking families.

Madame de Staël, the wife of the Swedish ambassador, was the intellectual of the group. Poets, philosophers, and men of letters were the patrons of her salon. Madame Tallien was close to government circles. Her former lover, who had since wed her, was a powerful member of the Convention. And Madame Récamier, that child bride of Récamier the financier, attracted an audience of those who came merely to worship at the shrine of her beauty and charm. Of the three, Zoë had paid a morning call only on Madame Récamier, and with good reason. Salome, turning belligerent, had warned her young mistress off cultivating the acquaintance of ladies of tarnished virtue. Juliette Récamier was acceptable since she was as virtuous as she was beautiful.

"Does Madame Récamier frequent Theresia Tallien's salon?" asked Zoë.

"She does. Why do you ask?"

"No reason.

Laughter glimmered at the back of Varlet's eyes. As if reading her thoughts, he remarked, "We live in a new era, Zoë. The old manners and modes have all but vanished. Very few of us can afford to have the embers of our past histories raked over. You must either accept things as they are, or make up your mind to live in a cloister." More gently he added, "Theresia Tallien is accepted everywhere. There is nothing amiss in your attending the salons of Theresia or Germaine, yes and even Josephine Beauharnais's. However, it would be ill-advised for one of your innocence to make a confidante of these worldly ladies."

Soon after, the two gentlemen took their leave, and Zoë flew to the long pier glass between the two windows. She turned herself first one way, then the other, and wondered, rather sadly, how it was possible to make herself over. Perhaps, if he raised the subject again, she would accept Varlet's offer.

As she studied her reflection in the mirror, Salome wandered in unobserved. For a few moments, she regarded Zoë posturings before interrupting, "What was he doing here?"

"Who?"

"Varlet."

"Just a morning call, nothing more."

"He was here before."

"Yes, Monsieur Varlet has called a time or two this past week."

"No, no! Salome means long before. She had forgotten, but now she remembers. He came the morning after you set out for Rouen, when your *Maman* and Papa were arrested."

"Really?" Zoë gave the matter some thought. "How strange that he never mentioned it. What did he want? Did he say?"

Salome snorted. "He said he had come to help after he heard your parents were arrested. When he found that you were not here, he was very angry."

"How . . . how kind of him," said Zoë. "I wonder if Monsieur Varlet was one of Papa's special friends." Suddenly, she was feeling very much warmer towards Paul Varlet.

"Salome sees the way he looks at you and she doesn't like it," said Zoë's maid.

"By the holy virgin, Salome, he's old enough to be my father! We're friends, that's all."

"A man and a woman can never be friends," disclaimed Salome. "He kissed your fingers."

Zoë's back was to her maid, the delinquent fingers busily adjusting the music on the piano. "What of it? With you and Samson always spying on me, what can go wrong? Lord, it's embarrassing, sometimes, the way you both trot in every few minutes on some pretext or other. Nobody would ever think that I was the mistress of this house."

"That's not it," said Salome. "Neither Varlet nor Tresier is the man for you. It was in the cards. There is one coming who—"

Zoë spun to face her maid. "Good God, Salome!" she cried out. "We'll soon be stepping into the nineteenth century! We're Christians, for heaven's sake. You mustn't practice that . . . that hocus-pocus which you brought with you from the islands. You'll have us all taken for witches and burned at the stake if you're not careful, that's what you'll do."

Salome drew herself up to her full height. "Salome is a good witch and a good Catholic," she said.

"Oh God!" groaned Zoë. "I didn't mean to imply that you were a bad witch or—"

"Your *maman* knew it. She listened to old Salome." Arms akimbo, head nodding, Salome went on inexorably, "You had better listen to old Salome's words. Only bad cards have turned up for this family for years past. Now the cards have turned in our favor."

"I don't want to hear this," said Zoë.

"You'll see. Salome will know him when he comes. And you had better not let this one slip through your fingers."

"*Who* is coming?"

"You'll see." And with that unsatisfyingly cryptic rejoinder, Salome turned on her heel and left her mistress to the dubious consolation of her music.

When next Varlet paid a call on Zoë, Tresier was

not present. He found her far more amenable to his suggestions than formerly. And when she shyly thanked him for coming to the house so soon after her parents' arrest he understood the change in her. By the time he rose to leave, Zoë had agreed to allow him a free hand in preparing her for her entrance into Parisian society.

"We shall begin with the dancing master," he said.

Zoë just looked at him as if he had gone stark, raving mad. She knew the steps of all the dances.

"Reserve all your mornings for the dancing master," were the last words he called out before Zoë shut the front doors upon him.

The dancing master who introduced himself to Zoë the following morning was of the old school, that is, the instruction of dancing was only a very small part of his repertoire. Monsieur Montmercy regarded himself, first and foremost, as an educator, a purveyor of style, of that polish which a gentleman or lady of fashion must acquire. "Rank is nothing. Quality is everything" was his motto.

Laughing with disbelief, Zoë heard him out as the old chevalier instructed her on how to enter a roomful of people. The laughter was wiped from her face when she discerned that the old gentleman was perfectly serious. Over and over, time without number, he made her rehearse her steps, her smiles, her curtsies, her opening remarks after imaginary introductions were made.

"The entry of a young lady or gentleman into society requires serious study," he was to repeat without ceasing in the days that followed. No gesture, no movement, was so elevated or so trivial that it could not be practised with profit.

She had not known that there was an art to putting on and taking off her bonnet. And who would have suspected that a lady's skirts must be shaken out just so, as if she were a dancer in the chorus of the Opera? And it went without saying that the correct mode with a fan was a science which would take a lifetime's study to master with anything resembling style.

Zoë set herself to practicing with religious zeal. Once having made up her mind that she would acquire "polish" or die in the attempt, she let nothing stand in her way. Nor did she make the slightest objection when Varlet engaged a modiste for her. She was paying the shot, she reminded herself. She was under no obligation to him. Still, she was curious.

"Why are you doing all this?" she was finally moved to ask. He had taken her to Tourtoni's for one of its famous ices. She could not help remembering another occasion when a gentleman had taken her out for an ice. But that was in another lifetime. Rolfe's face, as clear as a picture, flashed into her head. She stifled a pang and with great deliberation she forced the image to retreat. Giving her full attention to her companion she repeated, "Why are you doing all this?" Suddenly, she sliced him an affronted look and exclaimed, "Paul, if this has anything to do with a wager . . ."

"You misjudge me!" he protested. He stroked one long finger under his chin. He caught her stare, and smiled. "I've known you since you were in the cradle," he remarked.

Zoë's eyebrows winged upwards. "Have you?" she asked. "I had not known you were so old."

Feigning an air of injury, he quizzed, "I attended

many a reception at your parents' home. Surely you must have noticed me?"

"Naturally! But only from a distance. I wasn't permitted to attend grown-up parties."

"I noticed you."

"Did you truly?" She made no attempt to conceal her surprise.

"Peering over the balustrade in the gallery, your eyes as big as saucers."

"I remember." A small smile turned up her lips. Her eyes wandered and gazed into space. As from a great distance she murmured, "In those days, the ladies were all so beautiful, and the gentlemen looked like demigods."

Covering her clasped hands with one of his own, he spoke softly, as if afraid to shatter the moment. "I think I lost a little bit of my heart to you even then."

Her withdrawal was so gradual it was scarcely noticeable. Varlet was aware of it, and said in a more natural tone, "I always promised myself that one day, when it was time for you to enter society, I would be there, just for the pleasure of watching that little cygnet turn into a swan."

His words startled a laugh out of her. "Cygnet! That's not very complimentary!"

He guided her out of Tourtoni's and handed her into his waiting carriage. She was comfortable with him again and on the return drive to St. Germain, he was careful to steer the conversation into neutral channels.

Later, as his *valet de chambre* assisted him to dress for a night on the town, his thoughts wandered to Zoë as he had remembered her as a little girl. It was the elder sister, Claire, who was always referred to as the beauty of the family. But it was the younger girl with her lost, doe-eyed air which had made the lasting impression on him. She still had that same look of innocence.

It was fortunate that he had not declared himself that afternoon. To do so would have been premature. She would have refused him. He must approach her cautiously, persuade her by degrees that marriage to him was eminently suitable.

Varlet was not the only gentleman who harbored thoughts of wedded bliss with Zoë. Jean Tresier was reflecting that already he felt a great affection for the girl. In the meantime, it could only do him good to be seen in her company. His creditors would know what to make of it. The thought that his motives were entirely mercenary, he rejected out of hand. He was genuinely fond of Zoë. She needed someone, some man, to manage her affairs. It was no fault of his that the Tresiers had lost their vast wealth. While other speculators had made capital of the upheaval in France with the advent of the Revolution, his father had seen fit to squander the Tresier fortune on the losing Royalist cause. The knowledge that the debts which he had since incurred were for nothing more pressing than to maintain a style of living well beyond his means, did not trouble him overmuch. Once he married Zoë, his troubles would be at an end.

He must warn her off Varlet. Without conceit, he knew himself to be a far more preferable suitor for the girl's hand than the debauched older man, even supposing his debts were astronomical.

"Jean?"

Rose was restless. He adjusted his naked body to the fit of hers. "What is it, *chérie?*"

215

"What are you thinking, Jean?"

He would have to tell her soon, of course. But not yet. He would delay for as long as possible. Rose might be only his mistress, but she truly loved him. He cupped a hand round her breast. "That is what I am thinking," he whispered. And very soon after, he proved the truth of his words.

How odd, thought Zoë, a fortnight later, that having just acquired a whole new wardrobe of gowns and having paid no inconsiderable sum for that pleasure, all she could see when she opened the press in her chamber was a cloud of white fluff.

"They're all white," declared Salome gratuitously. She peered into the cavernous depths of the clothes press.

Immediately on the defensive, Zoë protested, "Yes, but no two gowns are alike."

"They all look the same," insisted Salome.

Stifling her own thoughts on the subject, Zoë adopted a superior air. "If you look closely, Salome, you'll observe that the muslin of each gown is vastly different." Those were the very words the modiste had used when Zoë, herself, had voice a similar misgiving. She tried to recall more of what the modiste had said. "Details, Salome," said Zoë airily. "It's the details that make the difference in the new fashion. Sleeves, hems, embroidery, ribbons, feathers, and such like — ladies of discriminating taste know what to look for."

Salome pressed her lips together, and Zoë was saved from further defense by the arrival of the hairdresser. Clad only in a silk wrapper, she stared solemnly at her reflection in the mirror as Monsieur André brushed out her waist-long hair.

"Your hair is very beautiful," remarked that gentleman, cocking his head first one way then the other, "but so *démodé*. When I have finished with Mademoiselle, the transformation will be astounding. Not all ladies have the head and face to carry off the new mode. This long neck?" He held the weight of Zoë's hair over her crown to make his point, "It will show the ringlets to advantage. And those enormous eyes of yours? We shall brush the tiny curls forward to emphasize them even more. Oh yes, when I have finished with you, Mademoiselle, you will resemble Aphrodite herself."

The scissors were poised to sever the offensive mane when Zoë cried out, "Wait!"

"Ah," said Monsieur André, lowering the scissors, "I know how it is. It feels like an amputation, *non?* It is always the same with ladies who have preserved their locks for so many years. May I suggest, Mademoiselle, that you close your eyes?" He angled her an encouraging smile. "The surgery is quite painless."

But it wasn't painless, not really. Her waist-length hair symbolized her last link to Rolfe. He had forbidden her ever to cut it. At each slice of the shears, something inside her seemed to wince in pain. Tears squeezed from beneath her lowered lashes.

It was absurd to be moved to tears by the loss of her hair when she had been dry-eyed on the day she had taken the irrevocable step of divorcing her husband. Charles Lagrange had accompanied her to the law courts. In a matter of minutes, the thing was done. And she had a piece of paper to show for it.

217

Divorce, as she understood, was almost impossible to obtain in England. Short of murdering her, there was no way Rolfe could have extricated himself from his unwanted marriage. She could almost imagine his relief when he was informed that she had no claims on him. Charles had undertaken the office of conveying the report of the divorce to Rolfe. Zoë had no notion how this might be achieved, especially as their two countries were at war. But Charles had assured her that, for those in the know, the lines of communication between France and England were still open.

Rolfe's sense of relief, she was persuaded, could not be greater than her own. She could never think of him without experiencing the humiliation she had suffered at his hands. She had tried to put it from her mind, to no avail. It seemed that she must relive, in minute detail, that last scene between them, when he had called her by another woman's name.

In the days which had followed, during that last week in England, she'd been tormented by thoughts of Rolfe with the girl called Rosamund. Without betraying her interest, she had persuaded the Lagranges to take her to Covent Garden. For her vulgar, almost obsessive curiosity, she had paid an exorbitant price. Roberta Ashton, the lady at the Devonshires' Christmas party, pretending to be her friend, had carried her off to her own box during one of the intervals, and had put her wise to what Rolfe had been up to whilst his wife was buried in the depths of the country, callously abandoned to the mercies of his mother.

And this was the man she had hero-worshipped? This was the man whom she'd considered the brightest and best of everything England had to offer, the epitome of the English gentleman, the flower of English manhood? The man was a faithless libertine, indulging in every debauchery her young mind could conceive. And if he had not made her a laughingstock, it was because scarcely a person knew of her existence. How should they? He had made no attempt to introduce her to any of his friends. He was ashamed of her. He didn't want her, had never wanted her, and she was coming to realize how wise she was to return to her own kind.

But there was one more wrenching mortification to endure before the awful, horrible evening came to an end. As Charles Lagrange handed her into his hired carriage, she looked over his shoulder and she saw him, there, in the shadows, coming out of the theatre, his arms wrapped around a woman, dragging her to him for an openmouthed kiss that had Zoë's stomach clenched in knots. She knew the color rushed from her face. Lagrange twisted his head, following her gaze. Thankfully, he did not know her husband, did not recognize the face of the man who was embracing the woman so passionately, making a public spectacle of himself.

Lagrange had made some biting comment about the vulgarity of the younger generation and had thrust Zoé inside the carriage. She had not said two words on the drive to Soho Square, but her thoughts were killing her.

Wave after wave of shame washed through her. His mother had told her the truth, and she had not believed her. Charlotte had tried to explain the English mode for married couples, and she had supposed that she knew better. Oh God, in her abysmal ignorance and innocence, she had offered herself to a man she must, in her saner moments, despise. She did despise him. It was an illusion she had loved. That man of her dreams was only that—a dream. He had no existence outside of her imagination. And soon, she would cease to think of him altogether.

She was free. She was independently wealthy. And she had an entrée into the most prestigious salons in the world. Paris was her oyster, and she would be a fool if she could not be the happiest of girls.

There, it was done. Her head was shorn and the heavy weight of her hair lay in discarded skeins at her feet. She tossed her head, testing the new freedom.

"Mademoiselle is pleased?"

"Oh yes," she said without having to think about it. She ran her fingers through her short crop of dark hair and admired the way in arranged itself into tiny waves and curls. She smiled cockily at the image in her mirror, and the new Zoë, remarkably matured, smiled back at her.

Later that evening, decked out in one of her new transparent, gauze evening dresses and with her shorn locks clinging like a silk cap to her shapely head, Zoë made her entrance into Madame Tallien's salon on Paul Varlet's arm. Her manners, her address, no less than her beauty, won instant admiration. There was nothing unusual in this. Paris had a surfeit of beautiful women who could hold their own with rapier-sharp wit. But it was soon perceived that Zoë had a talent which few could boast. She had an unerring tact which deflected the poisoned barb before it could find its mark. She was a soft-hearted girl, virtuous without being a prude. Oh yes, Mademoiselle Zoë could flirt with the best of them, and remain politely but firmly chaste. And who could deny that she played the piano like an angel? By the end of the week, Zoë was acclaimed as the darling of society. When she opened the doors to her own salon, all Paris flocked to it.

Chapter Thirteen

"Divorce!" The roar split the stunned silence like the crack of a thunderbolt. "Divorce," repeated Rolfe in a more moderate tone.

His companion's lips were suspiciously folded together. Monsieur Housard lounged against the leather armchair in Rolfe's study in the house in St. James and studiously examined the amber liquid in the crystal glass in his hand. "This is excellent brandy," he remarked conversationally, "but it's not really my tipple. I brought a couple of bottles of burgundy with me, do you know? It would be a shame to let them go to waste."

Ignoring this non sequitur, Rolfe demanded in barely suppressed fury, "On what grounds, may I ask, has my wife divorced me?"

"Adultery," stated the Frenchman unequivocally.

"Adultery?" queried Rolfe. "A trumped-up charge, if ever I heard one. I have never committed adultery."

"She named several ladies."

"May I be permitted to know their names?"

"A certain Mrs. Roberta Ashton—"

"That was before my marriage," cut in Rolfe.

"An opera dancer with Covent Garden who goes

222

by the name of Rosamund, and two others—now what were their names? oh yes, now I remember—Mimi and Fifi."

"Adultery? With the likes of those vestal virgins?" he said sarcastically. "That could never be considered adultery, surely?"

"I assure you, my lord, in France, under the new laws, a faithless husband has no more protection than a faithless wife."

At these inadvertently polemic words, Rolfe's eyes blazed, then glittered dangerously.

Hastening to amend matters, Housard offered, "There's talk of repealing the laws which put men and women on an equal footing. Oh yes, there's a definite swing to the right. Though, of course, I don't suppose that is any consolation."

"To the right? What does that mean?"

"Tradition." There was an ironic twinkle in Housard's eyes when he blandly offered, "Women are simply flocking to the courts to obtain divorces before the laws of the ancient régime are restored, and who can blame them?"

"I never heard of anything so insane—to treat men and women equally under the law. Men have always made free with women of a certain class."

"Quite," said Housard with mock commiseration.

Rolfe sliced his companion a hard stare, but Housard's eyes were carefully averted. There was a protracted pause in the conversation as both gentlemen made inroads into the brandy decanter. They sipped their drinks in considered silence.

Rolfe eased back in his chair. He crossed one booted foot over the other and surveyed his companion through half-hooded lids. Smiling languidly, he said, "And now, Monsieur Housard, perhaps you will be good enough to come to the point. What, may I ask, is the *real* purpose for this unhoped for visit?"

Housard settled himself more comfortably before replying. "I think you know why. It has come to my attention, my lord, that you are making plans for a little foray into France."

Rolfe took a long swallow of his brandy before responding, "Tinténiac told you, I suppose?"

"He did."

"And if I am?"

"Surely, there's no necessity?"

"Oh?" murmured Rolfe.

"Your wife has divorced you. She neither wants nor requires rescuing. And what could you hope to gain? Think of it, man! To abduct an unwilling woman behind enemy lines and flee with her to England? The task is beyond you."

"Perhaps I only hope to *murder* her," drawled Rolfe.

Housard started, then gave a low laugh. "I'm afraid I can't permit it."

Rolfe's expression turned savage. "Nothing on God's earth is going to stop me going after my wife, do you understand, Monsieur Housard? Not the war, not the Revolution, not the King of England, and least of all a stupid girl who does not know her place."

"I think I could stop you, if I had a mind to," was the quiet rejoinder.

The silence pulsed with controlled violence as both gentlemen took each other's measure. Finally, his voice soft with menace, Rolfe said, "Try it, Monsieur Housard, and you'll have the fight of your life on your hands, I promise you."

A long audible sigh fell from the Frenchman's lips. "I just knew you would prove to be awkward

Take 4 FREE Books!

We created our convenient Home Subscription Service so you'll be sure to have the hottest new romances delivered each month right to your doorstep — usually before they are available in book stores. Just to show you how convenient Zebra Home Subscription Service is, we would like to send you 4 Kensington Choice Historical Romances as a FREE gift. You receive a gift worth up to $23.96 — absolutely FREE. You only pay for shipping and handling. There's no obligation to buy anything - ever!

Save Up To 30% On Home Delivery!

Accept your FREE gift and each month we'll deliver 4 brand new titles as soon as they are published. They'll be yours to examine FREE for 10 days. Then if you decide to keep the books, you'll pay the preferred subscriber's price. That's all 4 books for a savings of up to 30% off the cover price! Just add the cost of shipping and handling. Remember, you are under no obligation to buy any of these books at any time! If you are not delighted with them, simply return them and owe nothing. But if you enjoy Kensington Choice Historical Romances as much as we think you will, pay the special preferred subscriber rate and save over $7.00 off the bookstore price!

We have 4 FREE BOOKS for you as your introduction to KENSINGTON CHOICE!

To get your FREE BOOKS,
worth up to $23.96, mail the card below
or call TOLL-FREE 1-800-770-1963
Visit our website at www.kensingtonbooks.com.

4 FREE
Kensington
Choice
Historical
Romances
are waiting
for you to
claim them!

(worth up
to $23.96)

See details
inside....

in this," he said, and tipping up his glass, he drained it in one gulp. He offered a placating grin. "I suppose it's better if we work together, rather than at cross purposes."

"Meaning?"

"Meaning that—how do you English say it?—oh yes, I'll scratch your back if you will scratch mine. And now, before I take you into my confidence, do be a good fellow and offer to crack a bottle of burgundy with me."

Long after the Frenchman had broached his second bottle of burgundy, Rolfe remained hunched in his favorite chair, his mind grappling with the story Housard had just related to him.

Housard was still hot on the trail of *La Compagnie*. He had made some progress. *Le Patron* was known to be active in Paris once more, though Housard was no nearer to unmasking the man than he ever had been. Of more interest to Rolfe, however, was the intelligence that several suspected members of *La Compagnie* moved in the same salon circles as Zoë. It was a perfect cover, since it was almost impossible to trace one man's contacts in these circumstances.

"Why are you so determined to net *Le Patron?*" struck in Rolfe at one point. "Why not simply pounce on his agents? Without a body, the brain is useless."

"Two reasons," replied Housard evenly. "In the first place, something is afoot, and your government does not wish to take any chances."

"Pshaw!" derided Rolfe.

Housard's bushy eyebrows lifted.

"If my government is backing a Royalist landing in France, then my government is an ass," exclaimed Rolfe.

"Quite," concurred Housard, eyes twinkling, "but you did not hear of this projected invasion from me. Kindly remember that, should you be asked."

"And the second reason?" demanded Rolfe.

"Oh, merely that I have a debt that must be repaid."

For some reason, Rolfe immediately thought of Housard's agent, the woman who had been murdered after infiltrating the society. "Marie," he murmured and Housard's eyes flashed. Rolfe did not notice. His thoughts had drifted to the young actress who had paid with her life for the help she had given him.

After Betrand's death, it had taken very little to persuade Amy Granger to tell them as much as she knew of her young protector's acquaintances. She had been terrified out of her mind and Rolfe had unashamedly played on that fear to obtain information, not supposing for a moment that the girl stood in any real danger. He still could not say with any certainty whether her death was by design or whether she had taken a bullet that was meant for him.

In that last week, he had grown careless. *La Compagnie* was smashed. Its agents were being hunted down. He should have foreseen that those same agents would exact retribution against their persecutors.

He was escorting the girl from the theatre when the attack came. They were gunned down. The young actress—could she have been all of seventeen or eighteen?—had died instantly.

Rolfe felt the bile rise in his throat and he choked it down. "I wish you well," he said, breaking the silence. "But I still don't see how any of this makes a lot of difference to my plans. Zoë is my wife. I have every intention of going after her."

"Unfortunately . . ." murmured Housard, and fell silent.

"Yes?"

Housard stifled a sigh. "There's no gentle way of breaking this to you. I'm very much afraid that your former wife is a suspected member of *La Compagnie.*"

Shock held Rolfe speechless. After a moment, his teeth ground together. "That is the most ridiculous thing I've heard in my life," he snarled. "And Zoë is not my *former* wife. English law does not recognize your French courts. Her divorce isn't worth the paper it's written on."

"Still, she has reverted to her maiden name. In point of fact, only her friends, the Lagranges, are aware that she was formerly — I beg your pardon — that she is a married lady."

Rolfe's brain had begun to function again. "What the hell do you mean — Zoë is a member of *La Compagnie?*" he roared.

"Suspected member," corrected Housard quietly. "She is not a big fish, I'll give you that. It's even possible that she does not know that she is involved. But you must see that your advent into the game at this point could only tip the balance in favor of *La Compagnie.* Should you abduct your wife, the others may run for cover. I regret that I cannot permit it."

"You must have some grounds for your suspicions!"

"She has a younger brother, Leon. At your request, I put my agents on to discovering what had become of him."

"Yes," said Rolfe cautiously. "His case seemed hopeless. And her sister's also."

"Leon Devereux is a member of *La Compagnie,*

and one of its most ruthless assassins."

Rolfe's mind was reeling. With a visible effort, he brought himself under control. "That may be. But I'll wager my life that Zoë is no conspirator. Damn it all, I know my wife!"

Ignoring Rolfe's heated avowal, the Frenchman continued, "And two of her most constant escorts are also on the periphery of *La Compagnie*. Paul Varlet and Jean Tresier. Do you know of them?"

"No," said Rolfe.

"They may be couriers—unsuspecting ones, that is, or nothing at all. It's too soon to say."

Rolfe straightened in his chair and gave his companion a long, level look. "You haven't said one thing to stop me going after my wife. Quite the reverse."

Housard permitted himself a small smile. "It was not my intention to dissuade you from going after Zoë. I merely wanted to impress upon you that the game must be played my way or not at all. Do I make myself clear?"

"Perfectly," drawled Rolfe, inwardly seething. "But nothing will persuade me, Monsieur Housard, that you, yourself, believe one word of what you've been spouting. Zoë a member of *La Compagnie*? It's preposterous and you know it!"

Housard laughed. "I don't believe it. Not for one minute, otherwise I should not permit you to enter France. Nevertheless, she is part of whatever is going on, and must remain in place until I give you the word to take her away. I must have your word on it, Rivard, before we go any further."

Rolfe closed his eyes. He was thinking that he had his own friends in France, men who would come to his aid if he gave them the nod. That he could remove Zoë from under Housard's nose wasn't entirely beyond the realms of possibility.

He opened his eyes and studied his companion. The man would make a formidable enemy, he decided. Aloud, he said, "I shall give you my word to play the game your way, Monsieur Housard, if you promise to release my wife into my keeping when the time comes, whether or not she is a member of *La Compagnie.*"

"Agreed!" said Housard at once. "My God, man! You had me worried there for a moment! I was thinking that I shouldn't like you for an enemy."

Rolfe's tone was considerably warmer when he said, "I shall need a cover. Any suggestions?"

"That has already been arranged."

A start of laughter was won from Rolfe. He shook his head. "Amazing," he said. "You are absolutely amazing, do you know? I'm all ears, Monsieur Housard."

"You are to pass yourself off as a diplomat attached to the Swedish Embassy," said Housard. "That is where I have set up my headquarters, by the way. The Swedish ambassador and his wife are in my confidence, to some extent. They won't ask any questions. I understand you know Madame de Staël quite well."

"Germaine and I were introduced when she was an exile here in England," answered Rolfe. He could foresee a number of problems. "Germaine is a known anti-revolutionary," he pointed out. "She is certain to be under surveillance."

"That has been resolved," answered Housard.

"Oh?"

"We have a powerful ally in the Convention. Deputy Tallien, to be precise. *La Compagnie* has made him a target. He's incensed. He'll do almost anything to crush them. He, privately, vouchsafes the progress of our investigation."

"*Our* investigation?" drawled Rolfe, one eyebrow arching.

Housard laughed. "Look at it this way," he said. "We work well together. You know as much as anyone about *La Compagnie*. Naturally, I expect something in return for the promise I've made respecting Zoë."

"Naturally," agreed Rolfe with a small ironic smile. "But there is one problem." To Housard's questioning look, Rolfe answered, "I don't speak Swedish."

Housard dismissed this objection out of hand. "Neither does anyone else in France, not even Madame de Staël." Grinning, he went on, "Just try to look intelligent if anyone addresses you in a language you do not know."

Much later, when the Frenchman had taken his leave, Rolfe found himself a fresh glass and reverted to the decanter of brandy. His brain was chirping like a bloody cricket. He'd lived through the worst six months of his entire existence, he was thinking, and of those, the last few hours must surely be the nadir of all nadirs. Zoë had divorced him. She was a suspected member of *La Compagnie*. How the hell had everything gone so wrong, and just when he had come to believe that everything was going to be all right?

Without knowing what he was doing, he had made love to her. How aghast he had been when he had come to his senses. She had been an innocent and he had taken her roughly, with a passion of which he had not even suspected he was capable. In the days which followed, his remorse had undergone a material change. In his dreams and in his waking hours, he had relived every minute of that blissful encounter. Surely he could not be mistaken? She had wanted him, responded to him, offered herself with shy abandon. The very thought had electrified him.

There was no thought, then, of banishing Zoë to the Abbey. When his assignment with Housard was over, he meant to court her, woo her, gentle her to his hand and initiate her, step by slow step into the glorious mysteries of love. God! Was ever a man so happy with his lot?

An assassin's bullet had changed everything. For weeks he had hovered in and out of consciousness. For months, he had made a slow recovery from the wound which had almost put a period to his existence. And where was Zoé? he had weakly demanded of everyone who had entered his sickroom. They had put him off with evasions until he could stand it no longer. Only when he had dressed himself and had come tottering down the stairs on shaky legs was his wife's perfidy finally revealed to him. Without a word to anyone, with the first wave of emigrés, she had returned to France.

The shock had restored him to health as nothing else could. He was demented with worry, petrified for her safety. It was to Tinténiac he had appealed for help. Who better could find her direction than this master spy? And Tinténiac, no doubt following *his* master's orders, had fobbed him off with more evasions, more delays, till Rolfe thought he would go mad with the uncertainty about Zoë. As a last resort, he had determined to go to France himself. He had said as much to Tinténiac and was impervious to every argument put forward to deflect him from his purpose. Hence, no doubt, Housard's sudden appearance on his doorstep that very evening.

She had run off to France and shortly afterwards

she had divorced him. She was a suspected member of *La Compagnie,* and her brother was one of its known assassins.

For several minutes, he tried to consider these facts with dispassionate interest. Unbidden, there came to him the faces of the young assassins who had gunned him down on the steps of Covent Garden. Surely neither of those boys could possibly be Zoë's brother?

A thought struck him, and he went perfectly still as he considered it. Was it possible that he had been mistaken in Zoë's character from the first? Could it be that she was not the innocent she pretended, but that she really was up to her neck in intrigue from the moment she had surrendered herself into his custody in Rouen? She was a consummate actress. That much was proven. Was it possible that she had been deceiving him all along?

One thought led to another. His imagination ran riot, taking him down paths that, in his saner moments, he would have rejected out of hand. Zoë as a member of *La Compagnie.* Zoë setting up a cell in London, using him as a screen for her nefarious activities. And when his usefulness was at an end, Zoë . . . !

Christ! The idea was so shocking he could scarcely entertain it! What better way to rid herself of an unwanted husband than to arrange for his demise? And when that failed, naturally, divorce was the only alternative.

By the time Rolfe climbed the stairs to his bedchamber, he was imagining the silky feel of Zoë's hair in his hands, but only in the split second before he wrapped it round her white throat and strangled the life out of her.

He slept fitfully and came awake with a start. Something that Housard had mentioned came to the fore. *Mimi? Who the devil is Mimi?* wondered Rolfe, but the moment he rose the thought was lost.

Chapter Fourteen

With their high waists, low-cut bodices and almost transparent gauzes, never had ladies' gowns appeared more scanty or diaphanous. Petticoats were left off, and the flesh-colored silk pantaloons which showed beneath softly draped skirts left little to the imagination.

Jean Tresier's glance skimmed over the throng of ladies in Germaine de Staël's salon in the Swedish Embassy, and he was not quite sure whether or not he approved of the current mode. A moment later, he smiled wryly as it occurred to him that, having forbidden his mistress, Rose, to make an exhibition of herself with the new fashion, he was scarcely likely to encourage Zoë, the lady he intended for his wife, to appear in public with less decorum.

At the thought of marriage to Zoë, he frowned. Only that afternoon, he had paid his addresses, and had been gently, though firmly, refused. He'd acted too hastily, spurred by the demands of his creditors. He had not given up on Zoë, however. It was common knowledge that ladies rarely accepted a first offer. In another week or so, he would try his luck again. In the meantime, he wondered if, having refused his offer of marriage, she might be willing to advance him a loan.

Rose. Zoë. Neither knew of the other's existence. When he married Zoë, he was aware that Rose must be told. The thought was more than a little unpleasant. He had no wish to hurt Rose. He loved her. But he must marry money. Rose could not accept it.

She was a gently bred girl, the daughter of one of his former university professors. In other circumstances, he would not have been allowed near her unless his intentions were honorable. But in the upside-down world in which they lived, she had been left a pauper with no male relatives to look out for her interests. He had offered his protection and had been accepted. Marriage was out of the question. She had no dowry. His debts were astronomical. He lived by his wits. If he had not taken her, some other man would. Rose was too beautiful, too easily persuaded for her own good.

Zoë's voice put an end to further reflection. "I beg your pardon," said Tresier.

"I don't see Theresia Tallien," she repeated.

"Haven't you heard? Tallien was attacked this evening outside his house. Lucky for him, the *jeunesse dorée* was at hand. They drove off his attacker before he could finish him off."

"The deputy is all right?"

"He suffered a mild concussion, but his assailant didn't get off scot-free either. In the scuffle, somebody got hold of a pistol and winged him. Still, he managed to escape. They are saying it was that *Cache-Cache* fellow."

"*Le Cache-Cache?*" said Zoë, and shivered. *Le Cache-Cache*—hide and seek—was the nickname applied to a young terrorist who in the previous year had cast a sinister shadow over Paris. To some he was something of a folk hero. To Zoë, he was a common criminal. There seemed to be neither rhyme nor reason to his choice of victims. Reputed Royalists, Jacobins, *sans-culottes* — he attacked indiscriminately.

"These are terrible times we live in," she commented. "First Barras, then Fournier, and now Tallien."

"They all survived, though."

"So?"

"What? Oh, I was just wondering if *Le Cache-Cache* was beginning to have a change of heart."

"I don't follow you."

"It probably means nothing."

A footman bore down on them bearing a silver salver with glasses of champagne. Tresier selected two and handed one to Zoë. Between sips, he said, "It wouldn't surprise me if poor *Cache-Cache* takes the blame for far more than he deserves."

"I suppose. Where is it all going to end, Jean? Old scores are being paid off, parties are jockeying for power, the *sans-culottes* are on the rampage. It seems as if France is hurtling towards anarchy."

"Why are we talking politics?" asked Tresier, abruptly lightening his tone. "This is a party, for heaven's sakes. I should be paying you compliments and you should be flirting madly with me. Didn't the dancing master teach you anything?"

In answer, Zoë shook out her fan, and Tresier's eyes warmed with admiration as they followed each dip and delicate flutter of swansdown feathers which graced Zoë's hand.

"Is this what you mean?" she murmured, her eyes dancing with enjoyment.

Charles Lagrange chose that moment to join

them. Zoë greeted him with a smile. Tresier, suppressing a small frown of distaste, soon made his excuses and sauntered off.

To cover what she perceived was a snub to her friend's husband, Zoë plunged into speech. "What do you think, Charles? Tallien was attacked outside his house."

"So I've heard. It doesn't surprise me."

"No?" Zoë resigned herself to the predictable lecture. She had heard it all before, and, though she concurred wholeheartedly with Lagrange's sentiments, it did not, for one moment, mitigate her boredom. The Revolution, according to Lagrange, had failed in its objectives. The poor were in a worse case than they had been under the ancien régime. If those in authority did not soon redress these wrongs, France would be plunged into a civil war.

"You're preaching to the converted!" The comment came from Francoise who had unobtrusively interposed herself between her friend and her husband. "Charles," she reproved, "this is a party. Can't you forget politics for one evening?"

Lagrange's stern expression softened as his glance rested on his wife's upturned face. His tone was close to jocular when he answered, "You think I'm boring Zoë? Just wait till Madame de Staël takes the floor!"

Francoise made a moue of distaste. "It's the price one pays for the privilege of being invited to her salon, though why any sane person would wish to endure an hour of her rhetoric simply for the privilege of boasting that one was here in the first place is beyond my intelligence."

"You said that, not I," murmured her husband.

"Ah. Will you excuse me, ladies? Monsieur Pétien has just come in. I want to have a word with him on a subject which would simply bore you to tears."

"Politics!" said Francoise disparagingly as her eyes followed her husband's retreating back.

Relieved of Lagrange's presence, the two ladies began to take stock of their surroundings.

"Who's that little man over there?" asked Francoise. "The one who's in conversation with Joséphine de Beauharnais."

Zoë looked in the direction her friend had surreptitiously indicated. "He's Napoleon Bonasomething-or-other. He's the soldier who relieved the blockade at Toulon, don't you remember?"

"Italian?"

"Corsican. He's very particular on that point."

"Mmm. He's falling all over Joséphine. Barras won't take kindly to his mistress flirting with another gentleman. What do you know of him?"

"Not very much. He's Barras's protégé, as I understand."

Francoise giggled.

"What?" asked Zoë.

"How did we ever get mixed up in such a den of iniquity? And you can take that supercilious look off your face. This is Francoise you're with, remember? We don't really fit in with this crowd, Zoë, and you know it."

"They're really charming people once you get to know them," said Zoë, trying to inject a little enthusiasm into her voice.

"What? Germaine de Staël? Charming? The woman is all affectation." The eyes of the two ladies, without volition, found the imposing figure of their hostess. Madame de Staël was easy to find in any crush of people. On her head, she invariably wore a turban, the only lady to do so.

Francoise jabbed Zoë with her elbow. "Will you look at that!" she exclaimed. "She's flanked on one side by her husband and on the other by her lover. I just don't understand it."

"What don't you understand?" asked Zoë.

"Germaine! She never wants for lovers. And she's not exactly beautiful, not a patch on Juliette Récamier, for example. If it weren't for those fine eyes and that enormous bosom, Madame de Staël would be as plain as porridge. I suppose Charles has the right of it."

"What does Charles have to say on the subject?"

"Charles says that Germaine is lusty and that gentleman can sniff out a lusty wench a mile off."

"Francoise!" Zoë was truly shocked at the tone of her friend's conversation. "Germaine possesses a prodigious intelligence. She's a clever woman. What could be more natural than for like to be attracted to like? Benjamin Constant isn't her lover, if you want my opinion. They're simply friends."

There was a moment of silence before Francoise replied, "If that's all you know, you're more innocent than I thought you were. Have you heard the latest?"

"I don't think I want to."

Francoise pressed her lips together. Zoë affected an interest in the appointments of the room. The silence lengthened. It was Zoë who gave in.

"All right, what's the latest?"

"Oh, so you are human!"

"Francoise," warned Zoë.

Francoise's voice dropped to a little more than a whisper. "Benjamin Constant isn't the only arrow in

239

Germaine's quiver," she said. She paused to see the effect of her words. Not a flicker of understanding registered in Zoë's face. Sighing, Francoise went on, "She has another lover who resides right here at the embassy. The word is that she brought him back from Switzerland with her. He's passing himself off as a diplomat. He's around somewhere. And the oddest thing, Zoë—"

Francoise stopped in mid-sentence as Madame de Staël's strident accents cut across all conversation, indicating that she was ready to begin. With varying degrees of eagerness, her guests idled their way to their places.

The small, restless sounds of the audience stilled as Madame de Staël made her opening remarks. It seemed that they were to be treated that evening to passages from two of her works, *Apologie de Rousseau,* and her dramatic essay in defense of suicide, *The Influence of the Passions on Happiness.* There was a small burst of applause before her guests stoically set their features in various poses of intelligence.

As Madame de Staël's impassioned, singsong rendition progressed, Zoë's thoughts wandered. Her eyes brushed those of Madame Récamier. The two ladies gave each other a silent salute. At Madame Récamier's salon, there were concerts, and occasionally, as the *pièce de résistance,* madame would perform her famous shawl dance. Everyone went into ecstasies over it. So did Zoë. She really was a fortunate girl, she told herself, to move in such talented, exalted circles. Her friends and acquaintances included poets, actors, writers, not to mention the most influential men in French politics, and the most sought after women in Parisian society. Even she, Zoë Devereux, was credited as one of the brightest stars in her galaxy. And she would not have been human if she had not wished, fleetingly, that Rolfe could see her now and recognize how much he had carelessly forfeited.

Her gaze absently traversed the rows of spectators, stopped, then suddenly retraced its path with the shock of recognition.

At her ear, Francoise intoned from behind her fan, "That's the gentleman I was telling you about, you know, Germaine's latest lover. Doesn't he remind you of you-know-who?"

The resemblance was uncanny. Zoë gave herself a mental shake. No. This gentleman could not possibly be her husband. This gentleman had brown hair tied in back in a queue. This gentleman looked older, much older. He was slumped in his chair. Rolfe was known to lounge. She had never seen him slump. On closer inspection, she noted the walking cane at the gentleman's knee. At that precise moment, he turned his head and caught her stare. Indifferent eyes brushed over her, and looked away. No. This gentleman could not possibly be her husband. Her breathing steadied. The small leap of her pulse regulated itself.

"What do you think?" asked Francoise in a stage whisper. "I only ever saw your husband a time or two, but the resemblance is remarkable."

"Remarkable," agreed Zoë. "But . . ."

Madame de Staël, perceiving that her audience was not quite with her, abruptly came to a halt. Her eagle eye pinned Zoë unerringly. All heads turned to stare. Zoë feigned absorption in Madame's regal figure, and, to her great relief, the recitation continued.

The most difficult part of the evening was yet to

come. At Germaine de Staël's salon, one made one's mark by the tone and cleverness of one's conversation in that interval after the formal program was concluded and before supper was announced. Intelligence, erudition, and argument for the sake of argument were de rigueur. A stupid or ignorant person, however elegant, was never invited to return.

Madame de Staël brought her recitation to a dramatic close. The applause was thunderous. Zoë girded herself for the coming ordeal.

She began by addressing the gentleman on her right, and recognized him as Monsieur Bonawhatever-it-was.

"Germaine is the cleverest woman of my acquaintance," observed Zoë with all the erudition of which she was capable.

In answer, the young man covered a huge yawn behind his hand. He gave every evidence of awakening from a deep sleep.

Zoë tried again, but this time she went on the offensive. "I should like to know Monsieur Bona . . . ?"

"Bonaparte," supplied the young man helpfully.

"I should like to know, Monsieur Bonaparte, whom you consider to be the cleverest woman of your acquaintance?"

He gave Zoë a very direct look and said baldly, "The one who has borne the most children."

Mentally, Zoë gasped. Her eyebrows lifted. The clod was serious. She searched her mind for a crushing set-down.

Before she could think of one, he stated argumentatively, "There isn't a man here who wouldn't be happier if all you women would stick to your knitting."

This time Zoë did gasp. "What an antiquated notion!" she burst out. "Let me tell you Monsieur Bonapadre—"

"Bonaparte!" corrected the young man testily. "No, Mademoiselle Devereux, let me tell you . . ." and he launched into a scathing diatribe on every liberty that French women had won for themselves with the advent of the Revolution.

The bile rose in Zoë's throat. Her eye fell upon Joséphine de Beauharnais, who was not known for the quality of her knitting, and her lip curled. She hoped, then, quite uncharitably, that the worldly widow would lead young Bonawhatever-it-was on the dance of his life.

Monsieur Bonaparte's eye had also fallen on the alluring Joséphine. With a great deal of alacrity, and a demonstrable want of courtesy, he decamped for greener pastures.

" 'Pon my word!" exclaimed Zoë, turning to Françoise. "We women can thank our lucky stars that Monsieur Bona . . ."—she had to think before she got it right—"Monsieur Bonaparler has no influence in France's affairs. Boor!"

"What, dear?"

But Zoë's attention had wandered as her eyes chanced upon the gentleman who so forcibly reminded her of her husband. He was standing in the center of a group of very pretty ladies, holding forth on some topic which had them all convulsed in laughter.

"Old goat," said Zoë under her breath, and could not understand why the sight of him annoyed her.

For the next hour, she had her hands full as hordes of young men descended upon her and vied

with each other for her favors. She was more than a
little partial to the *muscadins,* the young fops, members of the *jeunesse dorée,* who swaggered about as if
they were at the court of Versailles. For the most
part, they were little more than adolescents. They
put her in mind of her own brother. And if the
thought saddened her, few would have known it, for
she smiled a little brighter, laughed a little harder.
Even so, her unwary glance was continually drawn
to her husband's look-alike. He was limping rather
badly, Zoë noted, and from time to time, pain
tightened his features. Madame de Staël was all so-
licitation, one arm supporting him like a crutch.
The gentleman, nothing loathe, frequently leaned
into the warm curve of her ample bosom as if to
pillow his weight. The spectacle, thought Zoë,
frowning, was quite amusing.

For some reason she did not examine too closely,
she chose to avoid Madame de Staël and the gentleman who, to all appearances, was the guest of
honor. As they approached the group to which Zoë
had attached herself, she promptly detached herself
and moved on.

Over the rim of his wine glass, Paul Varlet's eyes
followed Zoë's path through the crush of people.
"Someone has warned her off me," he observed conversationally.

At his side, Tresier straightened. He set his glass
on a table. Forcing a smile, he quizzed, "I thought
perhaps you had quarreled."

"No," murmured Varlet, "there was no quarrel.
Which leads me to wonder why Zoë is keeping her
distance. There is a reserve in her manner, a some-

244

thing I cannot quite name. Oh, she is civil to me. Don't mistake me. But she is wary."

"Perhaps some of the ladies have put her wise to your reputation."

"Perhaps." Varlet brushed the rim of his glass against his full lower lip, then tipped it up and imbibed slowly. There was a certain sensuality in the gesture. When he turned his gaze on his companion, he smiled easily. "But in my experience," he drawled, "an offer of marriage covers a multitude of transgressions."

"Marriage!" Tresier's jaw went slack. "You are thinking of offering for the girl?"

"Certainly. Don't you think it's time and enough that I was wed?"

"But the difference in your ages!" Tresier visibly made an effort to cover his shock. "I beg your pardon," he said. He was thinking that he, more than anyone, should know of Varlet's predeliction for the young and innocent.

"Something tells me," said Varlet in the same conversational tone, "that you and I are rivals for the lady's hand. Is that not so, Jean?"

"I . ." Tresler coughed and found his voice. "Yes," he managed. "It would seem so."

Varlet laughed. His eyes found Zoë again. "I hear the girl is well dowered. If she accepts you, you'll be the most fortunate of fellows." The innuendo that Varlet was one of Tresier's biggest creditors hung on the air.

"You have been most generous in extending my credit," said Tresier stiffly.

"Mmm . . . the thing is, Jean, I may have to call in your note. I'm investing in something which is eating up all my capital, I regret to say."

Tresier said nothing.

"Do you know, I would give almost anything to have such a woman in my possession?" The bribe could not have been more blatant.

"I . . ." Tresier hesitated.

"Time and enough to discuss this in my office tomorrow," drawled Varlet. "Think about it, Jean." And he sauntered off.

There was no need to think about it. Tresier knew that he faced ruin if Varlet called in his note. And no one would advance him a sou. His circumstances were too well known. His eyes found Zoë.

Zoë was momentarily distracted from keeping a watchful eye on Madame de Staël and her companion when Jean Tresier bore her off to a private alcove. Though she stood quietly and pretended an interest in what he was saying, she was acutely conscious of Germaine de Staël's penetrating voice somewhere at her back.

Tresier wanted a loan, that much Zoë did understand. She was a little surprised, but not unduly. Many of the young men of her acquaintance frequently found themselves temporarily strapped for money. They spent too freely on their tailors or at the gaming tables. She was glad to help Tresier out of his difficulty, and told him so. His gratitude, she thought, was excessive.

When another lady claimed his interest and carried him off to supper, Zoë turned back into the room and found herself face-to-face with Germaine de Staël.

"Germaine," said Zoë, extending her hand. She dragged her gaze to the gentleman who was an older version of Rolfe, except that this gentleman's eyes were blue, not gray. She observed the fine pair of shoulders, the manly form, the muscular thighs. The cane, the dark hair, and the gray complexion seemed, somehow, incongruous. Still, she could not believe that this gentleman and her husband were one and the same person. And then she noted the teasing glint in his eyes.

"Emile Ronsard at your service," he said.

"Devereux," murmured Zoë. "Mademoiselle Devereux." There was only one sure test that could prove her husband's identity. She wondered if she were bold enough to chance it.

Monsieur Ronsard chuckled and observed, "You were studying me so closely, Mademoiselle, that I began to think you had taken my tailoring in aversion?"

"Oh no," disclaimed Zoë, coloring faintly. "To be perfectly frank, Monsieur Ronsard, you remind me of someone I used to know."

"A lover?" His tone was provocative.

The old lecher! Zoë was thinking. His resemblance to her husband was becoming more marked by the minute. There was a glint in her eye when she blandly baited, "Not a lover, Monsieur Ronsard. More in the nature of a . . . satyr."

No sooner had the words left her lips than she knew, with startling, awful clarity, that Germaine de Staël's new lover and her former husband were one and the same person. Mesmerized, stricken into immobility, she watched those blue eyes take on an arctic transparency. There was only one person she had met in her whole life who had those trick eyes.

She gave an instinctive gasp and looked around wildly. Her thoughts fell over themselves. Though logic had long since persuaded her that, having tricked Rolfe into marriage, she had nothing with which to reproach him, her heart had given her a different message. She'd indulged the odd fantasy of punishing her errant husband. She'd relished the thought of having him in her power to dispose of as the whim took her. He was in her power at that moment and all she could think was that he was mad to take such risks. Was he too stupid to know the peril of his position? He was English. This was France. Their two countries were at war. At any moment, someone might recognize him and denounce him. He could be shot as a traitor, or a spy or . . . The room tilted, and Zoë sagged against a marble pillar.

"Quick, Germaine! Fetch a glass of wine."

A strong arm supported Zoë. She lifted her lashes and gazed up at the face she'd never thought to see again. "You!" she said, and could say no more.

"Easy," he said, so softly she had to strain to hear him. "Don't distress yourself. Everything will be fine." As Madame de Staël came up, he went on in a more normal tone, "Here. Drink this, Mademoiselle. You'll soon be feeling more the thing," and he pressed a glass to her lips.

"She looks as if she'd seen a ghost," observed Madame de Staël, and helpfully waved her fan in Zoë's face.

Paul Varlet appeared at Zoë's elbow. *"Chérie!* What happened?"

"Nothing." She had to search to find her voice. "Nothing," she repeated, more strongly this time. "A stupid faint, 'tis all."

And there began a discreet tussle as the two gentlemen tried to elbow the other aside for possession of the fair damsel in distress.

"Sir!" Varlet's affronted glare was almost comical. Through sheer nerves, Zoë giggled. "I am Miss Devereux's friend. If you would kindly step aside?"

"Beg pardon," mumbled the elder of the two gentlemen. "This damn stick of mine is forever getting in the way, don't you know?" With his full weight behind it, he moved his cane out of the way, and straight onto the toe of Varlet's black patent pump.

Varlet let out a roar of pain. He hopped on one foot. "Clod! You did that on purpose!"

"Nothing of the sort!" snapped the gentleman who was passing himself off as Monsieur Ronsard. "Your foot got in the way." His free arm, if anything, tightened about Zoë.

Zoë was sure she was on the point of hysterics. A group of interested spectators had gathered round. The last thing she wanted was for Rolfe to call attention to himself. Didn't he realize the danger he was in? Summoning her scattered wits, she made an effort to put an end to the contretemps.

"Paul, please, find Francoise and get me out of here?" She handed the glass of wine, untouched, to Madame de Staël.

For a moment it looked as if Varlet might argue the point.

"Please?" repeated Zoë with such a look of appeal that Varlet, muttering an imprecation, allowed himself to be persuaded. Only then did Zoë push out of Rolfe's arms.

"I beg your pardon," she said, "I don't know what came over me."

"The color is coming back into her cheeks," noted Madame de Staël with a degree of satisfaction. "Ah, here is Madame Lagrange. You'll be in good hands now, my dear. You're sure you won't stay for supper?

It was evident that Madame de Staël was impatient to be rid of her troublesome guest. She clung to Rolfe's arm and urged him away. Monsieur Ronsard displayed more courtesy than his hostess. He stood his ground, and bent over Zoë's limp hand.

"A bientôt, ma petite fleur," he murmured. His voice and look were weighted with meaning.

Zoë trembled.

Chapter Fifteen

Zoë arrived home from Germaine de Staël's salon earlier than expected, which, she decided, more than likely accounted for Salome's absence from the front hall. Either Salome or Samson made it a point to be on hand when she came home of an evening.

The candles were lit, but the house was unnaturally quiet. Zoë wandered through the great empty foyer and into the yellow *salle,* removing her cloak and stripping her gloves as she went.

A bientôt, ma petite fleur were the last words Rolfe had said to her. Nothing was more certain than he would seek an interview with her as soon as possible. How soon was a matter of conjecture.

She seated herself at the piano and stared into space. She felt like weeping and could not think why. She touched her fingers to the keyboard, but the movement was mechanical. She wasn't in the mood to play the piano.

Rolfe was a spy. Of that much she was certain. And she was one of the few people, if not the only one, who could betray his identity. She cast her mind back, remembring.

The recent past was of no consequence. She owed

251

Rolfe a debt of gratitude which could never be repaid. As a husband, he left left much to be desired, and that was letting him off lightly. She could never be sorry that she had divorced him. A man of that kidney could never make her happy. But she could not forget that if it had not been for Rolfe, she might have perished during the Terror like the rest of her family. He would want to know if he could count on her silence. The answer was an unequivocal "yes." She supposed, by association, that made her a spy, too.

Sighing, moping for reasons she could not quite fathom, Zoë rose to her feet and idled her way toward the back of the house where the kitchens were located. Before she retired for the night, she meant to advise Salome that she had returned home. Salome could never be persuaded to relax her vigilance until Zoë was safely tucked up in bed.

At the end of the long, dark corridor, a light peeped under the kitchen door. Zoë heard voices, but indistinctly. She recognized the musical intonation of her maid's voice, and smiled when it came to her that Salome was scolding. It brought to mind memories of the nursery when one of the Devereux children, usually Leon, had been discovered in some mischief. The next thought startled her. She could have sworn she heard Leon's voice, as she'd heard it time without memory, jogging their nurse from her wrath through sheer charm. She and Claire had always envied their brother his talent for getting out of trouble.

She stopped and leaned against the wall, trying to compose herself. Inhaling several deep breaths, she pressed her hand to the kitchen door. She heard

Samson's low tones say something about "hide and seek" a moment before the door gave way, soundlessly, beneath the pressure of her hand.

A young man of muscular physique was sitting on the kitchen table. One shoulder was encased in white bandages. Salome was helping him into a clean shirt. Samson was kneeling by the grate, stuffing some article of clothing into a fire which had been newly kindled. The curtains at the windows were drawn tightly against prying eyes. The only light came from a lantern set on the mantel of the huge stone fireplace. The tableau would remain frozen in Zoë's memory for years to come.

"Leon?" she whispered.

As he swung to face her, for the first time, she noticed the pistol in his hand. And suddenly, everything became clear to her. Even as she quickly crossed the distance between them and flung herself into his arms, even as he groaned some rough expletive before hugging her with his good arm, even as the tears of joy welled over, she knew who and what Leon was.

Salome and Samson hung back, hesitating to intrude on the tender drama which was unfolding. As of one volition they moved about the room, finding things to do, carefully averting their eyes from this very private and emotional reunion. Broken sentences, inarticulate murmurs, the occasional sob, filled the silence. From time to time Salome looked at the clock on the mantel.

Five minutes were to pass before she emitted a warning cough. Leon looked up. "Better get dressed," she said gruffly. "Just in case."

Slowly Leon set Zoë away from him. He flashed

253

her an amused grin. "Salome is right," he said. "I was mad to come here. They cornered me, you see. I didn't know where else to go. They might come looking for me. If they find me here, you'll be implicated."

"You're not leaving?" Zoë could not believe that fate could play such a cruel trick on her, that she had found her brother only to lose him again. Her mind frantically groped for reasons to keep him with her. "I have friends, Leon. Powerful friends. They can help you, protect you. Barras, Tallien. They will—"

"No!" The word had all the force of an oath. He winced, as Samson solicitously helped him into a dark coat. "I wish I could make you understand. I don't have the time."

He was going to leave her. Just like that. Already, he was stuffing the pistol into the waistband of his breeches.

"Make me understand," she implored. "Make me understand." Her voice cracked. She bit down on her balled fist to choke back the sobs. "I don't care what you've done. You're my brother. My brother, do you see? I know who you are and it doesn't mean that"—she snapped her fingers—"to me. You need me, Leon. I can help you. Please . . . oh God . . . please?"

In the act of reaching for his cloak, his hand stilled. "What do you mean, you know who I am?"

"You're *Le Cache-Cache*," she answered at once.

He gave a derisory laugh. "What a romantic turn of mind you have, little sister. Nothing so fanciful, I assure you. I won't try to deny that I'm a wanted man—"

This time, it was Zoë who gave a derisory laugh.

Leon frowned and went on determinedly, "But you're letting your imagination run away with you. *Le Cache-Cache* is an assassin. Can you really see me in that role?"

She made a gesture of impatience. "I'm not a fool. I know how you came by that injury." As he started to answer her, she cut him off angrily. "You're wasting your breath, Leon. If you denied it on a stack of Bibles, I still wouldn't believe you. But, darling, it doesn't matter. Don't you see? I don't care."

He gazed at her in brooding silence. Zoë was painfully aware of the furious pounding of her own heart.

Salome moved between them. "Tell her," she said, giving Leon a very direct look. "All of it. Else she'll never rest till she finds you." She signaled to Samson. He nodded and followed her from the room.

"Sit down."

Zoë obediently sank onto a wooden chair and accepted the handkerchief Leon offered. She blew her nose, dried her eyes, and tried to compose herself. Leon leaned against the table in a posture of indolence which Zoe instantly recognized. It won a watery smile from her.

"What I can't understand," she said between sniffs, "is that Salome said nothing to me when she must have known that I was frantic to find you."

"Don't blame Salome. She did not know till tonight. It was better that you didn't know what had become of me." Before she could protest, his tone hardened and he asked, "What makes you say that I'm *Le Cache-Cache?*"

"I . . . at the Swedish Embassy tonight there was talk of the attack on Tallien. I suppose I've been thinking of *Le Cache-Cache* on and off all evening. Then just before I walked in here, I heard Samson say something about 'hide and seek.' Everything fits."

A look of patent relief crossed his face. "Then no one else suspects my identity? No one suggested to you that *Le Cache-Cache* and your brother were one and the same person?"

"No." And then, as if the words were wrung from her, she cried out, "But what I don't understand is . . . oh God, Leon . . . why?"

For a moment, he studied her face. He gave an imperceptible shake of his head. "I'm a member of *La Compagnie*," he said. "Have you heard of it?"

She'd heard the name before, but could not remember exactly what she had heard. "It's a secret society or some such thing, I think I heard?"

"You heard right. And once a member of *La Compagnie*, always a member. Do you understand what I'm saying?"

"I . . . I think so. They won't let you go?"

He gave a mirthless laugh. "They'll kill anyone who tries to break ranks. And those who are fool enough to try jeopardize not only their own necks but those of their friends and relations. My God, do you see what a hold they have over me?"

"No. I don't see. You're not on any proscribed list. You could take your place openly. Surely the authorities would protect you? You're a wealthy young man, Leon, and—" His harsh expletive cut off the flood of words.

"Zoë, listen to me." He leaned forward and gently touched a finger to her cheeks. "I've done things that could send me to the guillotine several times over. I'm . . . an assassin, for God's sake. Your powerful friends — Barras? Tallien? Haven't you heard that *Le Cache-Cache* tried to kill them?"

"Yes, but . ." She'd heard something else that very evening. It came back to her now. "You didn't kill them. What happened? Did you have a change of heart?"

He straightened at her words. "Devil! How did you . . . ?" He shook his head. "That's all I need! If they once begin to suspect that I've grown fainthearted, it will be all up with me. Oh God, it's hopeless."

Anger, hot and heedless, brought Zoë to her feet. "Don't ever say such words to me! I'm ashamed of you. Hopeless? How can it be hopeless as long as you have breath in your body? And when I think what Claire did so that you and I could have our chance, yes, and how our parents were comforted at the end, knowing that their children would survive them to live a better life. I left a husband in England — do you know? — and came back here to this this *wasteland* to find you and Claire. Are you telling me it's all been for nothing?"

The fight suddenly went out of her. Wearily, she turned away from him, and took several paces about the room.

Very softly, he said, "Little Zoë, married?"

Abruptly, she answered, "I divorced him. He was English. No one here knows, not even Salome. And I want to keep it that way."

"Fine. Whatever you say, little sister."

He was using his charm on her to get out of a scold. She tried to repress a smile and almost failed.

"I want to hear what happened to you after you ran away from the school in Rouen," she said. "I want to know exactly how you got involved with this secret society."

She settled herself on a chair, and looked up at him expectantly. "Well? Go on."

Smiling, he shook his head at the picture she presented. "You have a way of pursing your lips. You look just like *Maman,* do you know?"

"Thank you," said Zoë, "but let's not change the subject. You ran away from the school in Rouen. Where were you going? What did you hope to gain?"

A shadow crossed his face then was quickly gone. He shrugged carelessly. By degrees, his posture became more relaxed. "I thought, somehow, to rescue our parents. Don't ask me how. I had a plan, which I won't go into. It's not important." He stopped abruptly, and Zoë heard the quick rasp of his breath as he inhaled. In a quieter tone, he continued, "I made it as far as Giverny where I fell in with a band of Vendeans—a remnant of the Grand Army. We had a disagreement. I wanted to go to Paris. They wanted me to become one of them. They won, I lost. Good-bye Paris. Good-bye parents. Good-bye everything."

For just a moment he lost the cool aloofness he had adopted and Zoë caught a glimpse of something, pain or passion, in the depths of his eyes. It was as if she had been granted a glimpse into his soul. She knew, then, that she would never be able to question him about his life with the Vendeans. They had suffered unspeakable atrocities at the hands of Revolutionary forces, and, in their turn, had committed the most demonic acts of revenge.

"Oh, my dear," she said, her breath catching at the back of her throat. "Oh my dear." She looked at him then, really looked at him, and saw how mistaken she had been to think that she had found her brother Leon. This boy was not the negligent, carefree companion of her childhood. This boy was already a man, a young warrior molded by experiences she could not imagine, did not wish to imagine. This darkly good-looking youth with the lean, hard face was not her brother, and yet, strangely, he was the same Leon she had always known.

Leon had looked away from Zoë when he had stopped speaking. When he glanced at her next, his expression was remote, almost indifferent. "We were ambushed one day and left for dead. As you see, I survived. I made my way to Rouen to look for you and Claire. You were both gone. I supposed that you had somehow managed to make your way to England."

"You were right, about me," Zoë interposed. "But no one seems to know what happened to Claire."

"Not an uncommon story in modern France," responded Leon bitterly.

"You've heard nothing?"

"I heard that she was Duhet's mistress. There have been rumors, but nothing of any significance."

"What rumors?" asked Zoë.

"That she went to the guillotine with her lover." At the look that came over Zoë's face, his tone instantly gentled. "Zoë, it's more than likely that, that's what happened. You must learn to accept it. I have."

Her eyes searched his face. "But you've heard other rumors about Claire, if I'm not mistaken."

Almost reluctantly, he answered, "I have a friend who swears that he saw her in Bordeaux."

"When was this?"

"The spring of '94. Zoë, don't get your hopes up. Don't you think I tried to verify it? I went there in person. If Claire was there, no one knew of it. There's not a trace of her anywhere."

She bit down on her bottom lip, striving to contain the excitement his words had raised in her breast. It probably meant nothing, and yet, she could not help clutching at any hope, however faint. At length, she said, "What did you do when you found that Claire and I were not in Rouen?"

"I went on to Paris. By this time, it was too late to save our parents. I fell in with friends, people I had known before. They helped me."

"And . . . and *La Compagnie?* How did you come to be involved with them?"

"You misunderstand. My friends in Paris? They were all members of *La Compagnie*. So was I before we ever hid out in Rouen. Call it a boyish escapade if you like. Thank God, I wasn't quite crazy. I joined the society under an assumed name. No one knows me as Leon Devereux as far as I am aware, not yet, at any rate."

At the look of revulsion which crossed Zoe's face, Leon burst out, "I did not know then what I know now. It was all talk. How could I know that I was being trained to become an assassin?" Almost defiantly, he flung at her, "Yes. I've killed. And I did it without regret. I've never killed anyone who didn't deserve to die."

She tried not to let the horror show in her face. "I don't understand. What does *La Compagnie* hope to gain?"

"Power, of course. When the time is right, they'll crawl out from the rocks under which they are presently hiding. In the meantime, the only sure way of thinning the opposition is by eliminating them one by one."

Zoë was silent, staring at him with huge unblinking eyes. The silence lengthened till Zoë thought she would break under the strain.

"Now you know," he said, and before she could stop him, he was up and moving swiftly to the back door.

"Leon!" She was on her feet and running to catch up with him. "Where do you think you are going?"

His eyes gleamed brightly, but whether from tears or anger was not clear to Zoë. "My God, you never give up do you? I should have remembered that you were always a determined little thing." He smiled briefly. "Zoë, I'm going back where I belong. Haven't I just told you? No one leaves *La Compagnie* and lives to tell the tale."

"Do you really want to leave *La Compagnie*?"

"My God! If only it were that easy! Of course I want to leave. I'm sick of it all—the hatred, the killing!" He passed a hand wearily over his eyes.

"Who are these people? What are their names?"

"They are everywhere, at every level of society. I'm very small fry. I only know the members of my own cell."

She spoke quickly, brokenly, "We'll go to America, England. There must be a way to get you out of their clutches. I'll think of something. I'll ask

Varlet—"

"Zoe! Don't do anything foolish. It could cost me my life. Do you understand? Look, I must go. I should never have come here. Forget about me. It's better this way."

It was the wrong thing to say. For the fraction of a second she looked as if someone had just doused her with a pitcher of cold water, and in the next instant she went for him.

"Zoe!" Even with one arm, it was easy to subdue her. Leon winced as one wild blow caught him on the shoulder. It was all over in a matter of seconds. She collapsed against him, cursing him, pleading with him, lapsing into an incoherency which would have made him smile in other circumstances.

At the last, she took a deep, shuddering breath and said brokenly, "You can leave if that's what you wish, Leon. I can't stop you. But I promise you, I'll never stop trying to find you as long as I have breath in my body. And you know in your heart that if things were different, if our places were reversed, you would do the same for me. I'm thinking of *Maman* and Papa, I'm thinking of Claire and what they would want, don't you see?"

Their eyes held, and just for a moment she thought she caught a glimpse of that younger, softer boy who had once been her brother.

"You win," he said. "But don't come looking for me. I'll find you. Now douse the light."

She felt like laughing, she felt like crying. Her spirits soared. Together they would find a way of escape. There was a haven for them somewhere if only they could find it. She crossed quickly to the big stone fireplace. It took only a moment to remove the shade and douse the lantern.

"Leon?" she whispered, and even as she listened to the sound of her own voice, she knew that she was alone.

She awakened in the middle of the night, cold and clammy, with her heart pounding as if she had just run a mile. Of course! In her dream, she had been running for miles. They were children again. The dogs were on their scent. She was clasping Leon's hand, dragging him with her. Safety lay just ahead. But Leon kept insisting they go back. He was stronger than she, and she refused to let go of his hand. Back, they were going back to be torn to pieces by the hounds. The dogs had faces. Varlet, Lagrange, Madame de Staël, Francoise. Oh God— all the people she had been with that evening! They all wanted to tear Leon to pieces. And the dream was so real, she could almost feel the warm breath of the dogs at her throat.

Shivering, she threw back the covers and reached for her robe. Suddenly, she froze. She hadn't been dreaming. She really could hear someone breathing close by. She acted instinctively. At one and the same time, she lunged away and let out several piercing screams.

"Hell and damnation!"

Rolfe dropped the tinder box with which he'd hoped to strike a light and went for Zoë with some idea of cutting off her caterwauling. He'd forgotten about his walking stick. It caught him smartly on the ankle. He let out a bellow of pain and went sprawling across the bed, on top of Zoe. At the top of her lungs, Zoë screamed for help. There was only one sure way of silencing her, and Rolfe took it. He'd been wanting to do it since he'd first clapped eyes on her at the Swedish Embassy. His hands closed around her throat, holding her steady, and his lips came down hard on hers.

In the space of a single heartbeat, Zoë recognized the smell, taste, feel of the man who was attacking her. The hands which had been pushing him away suddenly dragged him closer. Vestiges of her dream clung to her mind. This was Rolfe. Safety. A haven. Later, she would excuse her odd behavior by blaming it on the nightmare. For the present, she was too relieved to care. She burrowed under him, pulling him more securely on top of her, hugging him to her, reveling in the comfort she experienced in the shelter of his powerful muscular body. Lust was the furthest thing from her mind.

Lust was the furthest thing from Rolfe's mind, too. But when he adjusted the lower half of his body against the cradle of her spread thighs, the inevitable happened. He was, as he later philosophically consoled himself, only a male. And no woman had ever given him the warmth of Zoë's welcome.

Zoë felt the press of the masculine arousal and went perfectly still.

Rolfe pulled back his head and tried to gauge her reaction. It was too dark to make out her features. But the pulse at her throat seemed to leap up at him. The quick rasp of her breath feathered his lips. He could feel her body trembling all the way to her toes. Smiling, Rolfe lowered his head.

"No," quavered Zoë.

"Kitten, you know you want this," crooned Rolfe,

with so much masculine satisfaction that Zoë almost took offense.

It was the surprising tenderness which disarmed her. Lips, whisper soft, brushed over hers, tasting, nibbling, before settling to claim her completely. The pressure of Rolfe's mouth became bruising, demanding entrance for the thrust of his tongue. Surrender flamed through Zoë. She was boneless, helpless, pliant. His head dipped and the lash of his tongue at first one tight nipple then the other had her writhing with pleasure. She whimpered.

"I'm going too fast," muttered Rolfe, and he stilled, fighting back the rush of passion. Zoë moved sinuously beneath him. "Don't move," he groaned the moment before he lost control.

His hands were everywhere at once, sweeping over her soft woman's contours, roughly urgent as he yanked up her nightdress, gentling to probe between her thighs for the entrance to her body.

"Ah, kitten." He sighed the words into her mouth.

At the first touch of his fingers, Zoë jerked. Rolfe's hand spread out across the soft flesh of her bottom, kneading reassuringly. "Be still, love," he murmured. "I don't want to hurt you."

Not hurt her? Like a bursting bubble, Zoë's desire evaporated. *Not hurt her?* Belatedly, she remembered the pain of his possession. Instinctively she arched away, but one strong arm slid around her hips, locking her body more securely to his.

Sensing her alarm, Rolfe soothed, "I won't hurt you. I promise." Zoë trembled, undecided. That beguiling, incredibly seductive masculine voice went on, "Ah, kitten. There's never been anyone for me but you. Only you."

265

Only her? She thought of Roberta Ashton and Rosamund and Mimi and Fifi, not to mention Germaine de Staël. *Only her?* That did it! "What do you think you're doing?" she burst out, and raked her fingernails across the width of his shoulders, compelling him to release her.

Rolfe laughed softly, a sound of sheer masculine triumph, and he fumbled for the closure on his breeches. Zoë went wild. She went for his hair. One yank was all it took. She screamed when it came away in her hands. My God, what had she done to him?

Several things happened in quick succession. The door burst open. Light flooded the room. A gun went off, shattering a pitcher of water on a commode near the window. Zoë screamed and bolted upright as Rolfe rolled from the bed.

Grim faced, Salome advanced into the room. In one hand she had a candelabrum, in the other, an upraised broom. Behind her, Samson was cursing and valiantly trying to reload an antiquated pistol. Several faces, which Zoë recognized as belonging to the various members of her staff, peeked around the doorframe.

"A w-wig!" sobbed Zoë. "He was wearing a w-wig," and she threw the horrid thing from her.

Chapter Sixteen

The clock on the mantel chimed the hour. Three o'clock of the morning, thought Zoë, and could scarcely credit that she was entertaining a gentleman caller in her mother's yellow *salle* at such an ungodly hour. It wasn't proper, but then, the gentleman caller wasn't precisely proper either. In point of fact, everything about the situation was ludicrously *improper*, and if she were in her right mind, she would show him the door. Oh God, what a night it had been.

"You haven't heard a word I've said," said Rolfe, halting in his pacing to pin her with a look.

To prove him wrong, Zoë recited his words back to him. "You are representing your government on a very delicate mission."

"Peace talks," he reminded her.

She believed him. The war was going remarkably well for France. England's allies were falling to French armies one by one. It was only natural that England would wish to sue for favorable terms before she, too, succumbed. Somehow, Zoë could not find it in herself to care one way or another which side eventually won the war.

He was waiting for her to make some response.

267

"Yes, peace talks," she agreed. "And since there are some in the Convention who are diametrically opposed to peace with England, you are passing yourself off as a Swedish national, a diplomat, until you sound out the opposition."

"It's imperative that my real identity remains a secret for the present. This is all highly irregular, you understand."

"Quite. Though I don't think much of your disguise. Anyone might recognize you. Francoise almost did."

"It's a chance I'm willing to take," he answered with a carelessness Zoë could not approve.

He could scarcely credit that she was so—the word *gullible* came to mind. He rejected it guiltily in favor of the far more acceptable *trusting*. No sooner had he done so than he lost patience with himself.

Rather sternly, he reminded himself that the subdued young woman who gazed up at him with such mournful, innocent eyes was, contrary to appearances, as guilty as all hell. At the very least, she was a runaway wife whom any self-respecting husband would beat soundly for her misdemeanors. She might well be worse—a member of *La Compagnie* who had connived at his death. To forget that fact was worse than folly. It was dangerous. It might very easily cost him his life.

His eyes roamed over Zoë's slight form, and his logic developed a crack. Every instinct repudiated the suspicion he had nursed since the night Housard had taken him into his confidence. Whatever else she might be, his little wife was no murderess. It wasn't in Zoë to harm a fly. He knew her too well. And it had only taken the sight of her to give his thoughts a proper direction.

Still, there were things that flicked at him like the sting of the lash. He didn't like the company Zoë kept. The gentlemen were too French by half, libertines to a man, if he knew anything of gentlemen. And the ladies were little better than barques of frailty. Rolfe had no real quarrel with the prevailing morals in Paris. He felt quite at home in such society. What set his teeth on edge was that his little wife should be one of its brightest stars.

From the moment she had stepped inside the Swedish Embassy, his eyes had been drawn to her. He had been admiring the lady covertly for some time before it came to him that the lady was none other than his very own wife! From that moment on, he had become as sulky as a schoolboy. With her shorn locks and fashionable, transparent muslins, his little Zoë had changed beyond all recognition. But it was more than that. Her gestures, her poise, her confidence were a wonder to behold. As was her flirting.

He was smiling when he addressed her and could not know that his eyes betrayed his volatile thoughts. "You won't give me away?"

Her eyes narrowed slightly, hinting of wariness. "No."

He rewarded her with one of his irresistible grins.

Flustered, she asked, "What news of home?"

"Home?" One eyebrow rose.

"I mean England, of course."

"Of course." The expression in the cold gray eyes warmed slightly. "What do you wish to know?"

The next few minutes were taken up in satisfying Zoë's curiosity about Rolfe's family. It seemed that everyone was jogging along in much the same way as before. There were no messages for her, no references to anyone expressing one iota of regret for her absence and her subsequent divorce from Rolfe. It was as if the months she had spent at the Abbey had never taken place, so little impression had she made. She thought of Ladies Emily and Sara and swallowed the lump in her throat, trying not to betray that she was cut to the quick by their indifference.

"I heard about your parents, Zoë. I'm truly sorry, my dear."

Zoe swallowed. "Thank you," she murmured, and felt comforted by the clasp of Rolfe's hand on her shoulder.

"Have you traced your brother and sister yet?"

She shook her head, not daring to look at him.

"Perhaps I—"

"No!" she cut in. "I . . . I have come to accept that they both perished during the Terror. Really, there's no necessity to pursue this any further."

"I see."

She noted a hardening in him and said casually, hoping to divert him, "I presume Madame de Staël knows your real identity?"

"You presume correctly. Germaine and I are old friends. I was a frequent visitor to Juniper Hall when she lived in England." Something in Zoë's expression moved Rolfe to explain, "It was all perfectly innocent. I was there for talks with Monsieur Talleyrand. And now I wish you would tell me why your maid did a sudden turnabout when I grabbed my walking stick and swung it in the air."

The undignified scene in Zoë's bedchamber would

be forever imprinted on his mind. Rolfe hadn't experienced such extreme mortification since the day his mother had barged unannounced into his rooms in Baker Street and surprised him in bed with the attractive young wife of the portly and elderly earl of Summerfield. His mother had gone into one of her spasms. Zoë's maid, on the other hand, had gone into transports.

What happened next was even more incomprehensible. With all due respect, as if he had been an honored guest, he was ushered down the stairs and into Zoë's drawing room where he was plied with brandy and every sort of mouthwatering delicacy until Zoë should make herself presentable and join him.

Rolfe recognized that there had been some relaxation in the proprieties governing conduct between the sexes in France. Nevertheless, he had been discovered in a most compromising position, to all intents and purposes on the point of ravishing the lady of the house. That Zoë's servants had treated the episode with so little regard for her good name, did not sit well with him.

There was a hard glitter to his eyes when he demanded peremptorily, "I should like to know why I have been treated like an honored guest when I ought to have been set upon and thrown to the dogs. Do you realize that it's after three o'clock of the morning?" He swung his walking cane and pointed it in the direction of the mantel clock. "And you are entertaining a gentleman caller in your drawing room?"

Zoë winced at the volume of Rolfe's voice. She was glad that he had stopped his angry pacing. It

made her nervous. This irate gentleman in the powdered wig bore no resemblance to the Rolfe she remembered.

This man frightened her. He was volatile. She
didn't know what to make of him. One moment, his
glances were almost soft with tenderness and the
next moment sparks were shooting from his eyes.
His control was on a tight leash, that much was obvious. Instinct warned her to proceed with extreme
caution.

"I'm waiting for the dignity of a reply." His tone
promised very unpleasant consequences if she offered him an unacceptable answer.

Swallowing, Zoë said, "It was the walking cane,
you see."

"No, I don't see," said Rolfe, and raised his cane
a few inches from the floor and brought it down
smartly.

Zoë jumped. After a moment, she licked her lips
and said, "Salome, my maid, took it for a . . . a
wand."

"A wand?"

"You're not familiar with Tarot cards?" queried
Zoë. At Rolfe's blank look she went on, "No, well,
I'm not very familiar with them either. But Salome
is, you see. She thinks that she is something of a
fortune teller. And she had taken into her head that
you are in my cards."

"Because of my walking cane?"

Zoë nodded, relieved at Rolfe's quick understanding. "Yes. And because you are fair skinned and
have blond hair."

"Kitten?" Rolfe's smile was deceptively lazy. "What
the devil are we talking about?"

272

"My card," said Zoë. "Salome read my future from the Tarot cards."

"And what exactly is your card?"

"A knight with a wand. Salome gave it into my hand some weeks since. Of course, it's just a piece of nonsense. Intelligent people don't put any stock in it."

There was an arrested expression on Rolfe's face. "No?"

"No," averred Zoë, frowning.

"What did you do with the card, kitten?"

Without thinking, Zoë answered, "It's upstairs in my dresser." Catching the gleam of satisfaction in Rolfe's eyes, she said deflatingly, "It would have been unkind to throw it away."

"Quite."

Rolfe chose that moment to seat himself on the sofa beside Zoë. She was aware of a relaxation in his manner towards her. By degrees, her own guard relaxed. She was beginning to see the humor in the situation. A little giggle escaped her. Rolfe's brows rose.

Shaking her head at the recollection, she said in answer to his questioning look, "If you could only have seen yourself—waving that cane in the air, bellowing, and my maid on her knees, prostrating herself before you as if you were," more giggles escaped before she finally got out, "as if you were the angel Gabriel."

Perfectly serious, Rolfe replied, "And if you could only have *heard* yourself. 'A w-wig,'" he mimicked. 'He was wearing a w-wig!' He thought about it for a moment, and his shoulders began to heave. His eyes brushed Zoë's, and he sobered.

For several seconds, each tried to stare the other down, an impossible feat when their lips were twitching. It was Rolfe who gave in first. He threw back his head and hooted with laughter. Zoë soon followed.

Wiping the tears from her eyes, she said, "And that *wretched* maid of mine now thinks it perfectly proper to leave me unchaperoned with you simply because she sees you as my fate. Can you believe that?"

It was a moment before she realized that Rolfe had gone perfectly still. In some uneasiness, she forced herself to look at him.

Very softly, his eyes holding hers, he said, "In a sense, I thought I was your fate. What happened, Zoë? Why did you leave me? Why did you divorce me?"

She regarded him steadily for a long moment. It would be so very easy, she thought, to give in to the dictates of her foolish heart and fall in love with him all over again. What woman could resist those beautiful eyes and that bone-melting smile? It was a salutary thought, reminding her that while he would be everything to her, she could only hope to be one among many. Her eyes dropped to her hands and she said quietly, "Our marriage was doomed from the beginning. We are too dissimilar. Like should marry like. Evidently, we want different things from life."

Smiling whimsically, he asked, "How can I possibly know what you want, kitten? Did you ever tell me?"

A pervasive sadness had taken hold of Zoë. She ached with weariness. Thoughts of her brother pressed on her mind. She'd had the fright of her life when she'd first found Rolfe in her chamber. And now she was forced to think back on one of the most humiliating episodes of her young life.

It would have helped if she could hate him. When she put her mind to it, she could manage it for two or three minutes together. At this moment, she did not hate him. Her eyes drank him in, the graceful manliness of everything that was Rolfe, and she felt only a deep regret.

With no idea of annoying him, she said, "Once . . . a long time ago, I wanted what my mother and father had. Our home was a happy one. My parents loved each other. They respected each other. Those days were . . . precious. I wish I had known it then." Her voice cracked and she cleared her throat. "Since I don't have what my parents had, I've learned to compromise. I'm content. 'Tis enough."

Somehow, he had managed to capture her hands. He squeezed them gently, and the gesture was almost more that Zoë could bear.

In a voice that strained to remain steady he murmured, "Don't you think that I could want the same things, too, kitten?"

She looked at him carefully. "How can you want the same things I want?" she asked. She thought of his mother and quickly suppressed a shudder of revulsion. "Your family is nothing like mine," she told him. "You can't possibly know what I mean."

When he answered, his voice was very low and very earnest. "You are right in this: our families, our backgrounds, are very dissimilar. But the last thing I want is to make my own marriage a replica of what my parents had." He turned over one of her hands, and traced the palm with the pads of his fingers. "You see, Zoë, I want my children to be happier than I was."

Hearing his own words, Rolfe stilled as the truth of them registered. His home had never been a happy one. Like most of their class, his parents had married for expediency, not for love. It was the way of their world. And while gentlemen pursued their pleasures, their wives learned to turn a blind eye to what must be endured. They had no other recourse. A husband's authority was inviolable.

Nevertheless, wronged wives had their own way of exacting justice, of a sort. They had their children. And children could sometimes be taught to hate the object of their mother's scorn.

As a young child, he had both feared and hated his father, repulsing every overture of friendship. His mother had taught her sons well. And if there was a lessening of antipathy as the years passed, it was because he was outside the sphere of his mother's influence. Boys of his class were sent off to school at a very tender age. It was then, as he remembered, that his mother had become something of an invalid.

He had a vivid impression of his first school holidays, when he and his brother, Edward, had returned to the Abbey. They had found their mother in her bedchamber, propped up in bed. It was the first of many such scenes: their mother tearful and sickly, their father intolerant and taking no pains to hide it. Rolfe and his brother had taken their mother's part.

It was his turn to suppress a shudder of revulsion. No. The last thing he wanted was his own marriage to be a replica of his parents' one.

Choosing his words with care, he said, "I'm willing to make a fresh start if you are."

Zoë was assailed with the sudden unwanted memory of Roberta Ashton's silky voice as she had described in minute detail the sordid amorous adventures and peccadilloes of the man who had once been her hero. Well, he was her hero no longer. "I divorced you," she reminded him, "and with good reason.

In an amused tone, eyes mocking, he carefully enumerated, "Roberta Ashton, Rosamund, Mimi and Fifi? Kitten, is that why you ran away? Were you jealous of those other women?" This, decided Rolfe, was going to be easier than he thought. Little Zoë must surely love him.

"Shouldn't a wife be jealous of the women in her husband's life?"

"Ah, but you weren't my wife then, were you? Not really. You were a wife in name only."

Resentment flared in her. He was lying in his teeth. She herself had witnessed the public spectacle of her husband locked in an embrace with another woman, and that was after she, Zoë, had so stupidly taken matters into her own hands to ensure that she was no longer a wife in name only. She wanted to fling the accusation in his face, but pride kept her silent. He would have proof, then, that she was, in very truth, a jealous woman. In point of fact, she hadn't been jealous. She had been . . . crushed.

Forcing herself to be calm, she said, "And now I am not even a wife in name only. And there is no point to this conversation."

She rose gracefully to her feet indicating that the interview was at an end. Rolfe stretched his arms along the back of the sofa and struck a negligent pose.

"What would you say," he asked softly, "if I told you that our divorce could be overturned?"

Shock held her speechless.

His voice took on a caressing quality. "Kitten, I'm serious. We could start over."

"Are you mad?"

"What?"

"Marriage to you?" Calm deserted her as indignation rushed in. Her voice became agitated. "Don't you understand anything? I hated everything about being married to you. I hated the life I was forced to follow in England."

"Ah, but you didn't hate *me,* did you, kitten?" With slow, leisurely movements, he rose to his feet. A smile of amused tolerance played about his lips.

Zoë threw back her head and stared doggedly into his face. "What does that mean, pray tell?"

His hands cupped her shoulders. Laughing softly, he said, "I could keep a whole stableful of women, and it wouldn't make a jot of difference. I have only to touch you, and you melt for me."

Eyes snapping, she hissed, "I think your conquests must have mounted to your head." Zoë's eyes narrowed on the disbelieving smile and her anger boiled over. Not a quick-tempered girl, nevertheless, when roused, the little kitten could turn into a jungle cat. She unsheathed her claws and drew blood. "Frankly," she purred, "I have no desire for your touch." And to make sure that he got the message, she threw in gratuitously, "When you make love to me, I don't like it."

The smile left Rolfe's face. He administered a rough shake. "You liked my touch well enough a little while ago. If your servants hadn't burst in when they did, I would have finished what you started, and very thoroughly too, let me tell you."

"What I started?" Zoë's mouth opened and closed. "What *I* started? I didn't start anything!"

"God, you were crawling all over me. And those pleasure sounds you made? They nearly drove me over the edge."

"I was frightened. I didn't know what I was doing," she cried out. "I had a bad dream."

"You knew what you were doing, all right. You were wild for me. And I've got the scratches on my back to prove it."

Breasts heaving, color heating her cheekbones, Zoë regarded him in tight-lipped silence. It took a moment or two before she could find her voice. "I'm not denying that I responded to you at first but . . ."

Rolfe made a derisive sound.

"All right, so I responded to you. You're that kind of man. A marble statue would respond to you. It's a knack all rakes possess otherwise they wouldn't be rakes, would they?"

When Rolfe could unlock his jaw, he said tersely, "I never pretended that I was a monk. And if you were a real woman, you would not wish me to be one. God, you still haven't grown up, in spite of appearances."

He could not know that he had insulted Zoë in the worst way possible. "Get out," she hissed. "Get

279

out before I have my man throw you out."

Rolfe practically threw her from him. He snatched up his cane and strode for the door. At the threshold, he turned back to face her. He seemed to be on the point of saying something, hesitated, then closed his mouth firmly. A moment later, the front door slammed as he exited.

Chapter Seventeen

When Paul Varlet called on Zoë the following morning, he was informed that she was not at home. In point of fact, Zoë was still sleeping off the effects of her tumultuous night. Nothing daunted, Varlet returned late of the same afternoon. This time, Zoë received him in her yellow *salle*. She was seated at the piano.

She gave him her hand. He kissed it lingeringly, looked deep into her eyes, and told her that he loved her.

Zoë covered her shock with remarkable aplomb. It was only in the last little while that it had been impressed upon her that Varlet's interest might be less than innocent. Varlet had a most unsavory reputation, Tresier had told her. She had paid scant attention until Charles Lagrange had taken her aside and reiterated Tresier's warning. In spite of finding Charles a bit of a bore, Zoë respected his opinions. That Varlet should offer her his hand in marriage had never once occurred to her.

She tried to stay the words she knew must follow, hoping to save him the pain and embarrassment of a refusal. Varlet, however, was determined to have his say.

"I'm so sorry, Paul," she said, after hearing him out. "I can't marry you."

"You don't mean that, Zoë. You could not be so cruel as to let me pay court to you these many months past, knowing how I care for you."

"I didn't know . . . I never dreamed . . . the difference in our ages," said Zoë feebly.

"That has nothing to say to anything, my dear. Observe Madame Récamier, and your own friend, Madame Lagrange. They married older gentlemen, and see how happy they are."

"But I don't love you," insisted Zoë.

"You like me a little," he said, smiling persuasively. "In time, love will come. And as for my reputation," he shrugged negligently, "naturally, it must offend one of your innocence. When you are my wife, you need never be troubled by that side of my life."

The interview became painful. Varlet would not take no for an answer. And behind his suave compliments and promises, Zoë sensed an unspecified threat to herself should she, indeed, decline his offer. She became frightened. There was a way of putting an end, once and for all, to his addresses if she were bold enough to grasp it.

Quickly coming to a decision, she said, "I can't accept your offer for the simple reason that I already am a married lady."

She knew at once that she had said the wrong thing. He went rigid. The smile was wiped from his lips.

"I . . . I never meant to deceive you," she began, groping for words to deflect his fury. "It was a mistake. My husband and I did not suit."

"And where is this husband now?" His words were soft. His eyes were as hard as diamonds.

Dry mouthed, Zoë answered, "I—I left him in England." She was careful not to betray whether she had married an Englishman or a French émigré. "Perhaps I may divorce him. But for the moment, you see, I am not free to accept anyone."

He stepped back. The light played tricks with the angles of his face, giving him a demonic aspect. His eyes swept over her, damning, insulting. Zoë began to quake visibly.

"You jade!" he sneered. "You slut! You were my obsession! Little, untouched Zoë! You've made a fool of me—me, Paul Varlet! My God, I'll teach you—"

He never completed the sentence. At that moment, the door was pushed open, and Samson entered bearing a folded note on a silver salver. With trembling fingers, Zoë accepted it. Samson set down the tray and stationed himself, arms akimbo, at the open door.

Varlet's face turned purple with rage. His eyes assessed Samson's huge bulk. After a muttered imprecation, he strode from the room. Zoë went limp with relief. Only then did she unfold the note in her hand. It was nothing but a piece of blank paper. She looked a question at her retainer.

Grinning sheepishly, Samson said, "If Salome or I could write, it would say, 'Help has arrived.'"

Samson did not know where to look when his

tearful mistress pressed a grateful kiss on his cheek.

It was guilt that decided Zoë to accompany Tresier to the masquerade. In normal circumstances, she would never have considered attending this kind of function — a clandestine party, made all the more intriguing, according to Tresier, because all the principals would be incognito, and it had yet to be decided where the party was to be held. To her weak objections, Tresier had protested that no harm could come to her with him as her escort. Still, Zoë hesitated. Many ladies of her class, she knew, were not above frequenting the most questionable establishments just for the fun of it, so long as their identities remained a secret. She wondered if this was to be just such an event.

Finally, she consented. Hours before, she had refused Tresier on another matter. She could not bring herself to refuse him a second time.

Her first refusal came when he reminded her of the conversation which had taken place in Germaine de Staël's salon, when she had promised to advance him a loan. Zoë could scarcely remember more than a few words of that particular exchange. At the time, she had been flustered, her mind wandering to the gentleman who reminded her so forcibly of Rolfe.

"Of course," she said to Tresier. "How much do you require?"

He named a sum. Zoë was aghast. It was astronomical and she told him so.

"But you agreed to that sum."

"I'm sorry, Jean. I must have misunderstood," and she offered an amount that was not a tenth of what Tresier has named. She gasped when her wrist was shaken with bone-crushing strength.

"Don't play games with me. Damn, I'm sorry, Zoë. I didn't mean to hurt you. I was counting on you. It's an investment."

But no argument he put forward had the power to persuade her. A plan was forming in her mind. She meant to transfer to America as much of her funds as she dared without rousing suspicion so that she and Leon could have a fresh start. Already, she had made an appointment to see her bankers. What Tresier proposed was out of the question.

"I'm sorry. Most of my funds are invested," she said, and he could see that her decision was final.

She and Tresier had parted with every mark of civility, and when she saw him later that evening, at Juliette Récamier's salon, though all her instincts warned her against it, she agreed to accept his escort to the masquerade, feeling that she owed him some recompense for refusing him the loan.

She should have trusted to her instincts. As soon as Tresier's coach stopped in the Rue de Richelieu, Zoë knew that she should never have agreed to come with him. They were at the Palais Royal where no decent woman dared show her face after sunset.

Rigid with hostility, she permitted Tresier to escort her through groups of *merveilleuses,* common streetwalkers in their transparent gauzes, and *incroyables,* those outlandish fops who were brazenly making their selections for the night's pleasure. Averting her head, Zoë swept past them. They came to the theatre, now dark and empty of patrons. Tresier stepped through an arched doorway and waited for Zoë to precede him. They were in the foyer of a magnificent set of apartments.

"Whose apartments are these?" asked Zoë, the first words she had spoken to Tresier since he had helped her from the carriage.

"Madame Montansier's," he answered without elaboration.

Footmen came forward to take their black dominoes. Zoë adjusted the mask which covered half her face. The gentlemen wore demimasks, but took no other precaution to conceal their identities. Why should they? reflected Zoë, mildly irritated. Gentlemen were permitted a greater freedom than ladies. No one judged them by the company they kept.

She waited silently as Tresier spoke in low tones to the waiting footman. She could not look at him for anger. Madame Montansier was notorious. Some said she was under Barras's protection. What was indisputable was the madame's theatre provided her masculine patrons not only with the expected dramatic fare, but also with a choice of young girls to amuse them after the final curtain came down.

Zoë was suddenly very afraid and, at the same time, reckless with the force of her emotions.

Tresier put a hand on her arm. Almost shamefaced, he said, "Zoë . . ."

"Shall we go in?"

He bowed stiffly and held out his arm. Zoë shook out her skirts before gingerly placing her fingers on his sleeve. A woman's laughter close by turned her head. Joséphine de Beauharnais was present. Zoë was more than a little relieved.

An hour later, Tresier stood at one of the windows, staring into his empty glass. He looked up and gave a slow, ironic smile when he saw Paul Varlet approaching.

"My dear Jean. I was hoping to find you."

Tresier said nothing, neither encouraging nor discouraging.

Varlet studied the younger man quizzically. Very softly, he asked, "Did she come with you?"

"She did."

For a moment or two, they stood in silence, surveying the sets of dancing couples. "Which is she?" asked Varlet. With the new mode and all the ladies wearing masks, it was almost impossible to distinguish one lady from another.

"She is partnering Musset."

Varlet laughed. "She's decked out in a blond wig, I take it?" There was no answer from his companion. "Even so, I should have recognized her," said Varlet. "There is an untouched quality about her which is umistakable, completely sham, of course. Were we ever so innocent, do you think, Jean? But I am forgetting, you are a young man."

Tresier began to breathe deeply.

The older man flicked him a curious look. So that no one could overhear, he said, "She has reneged on a promise to both of us. Remember that."

The words were slow in coming. "I don't forget."

"Ah." That one small sound said everything that needed to be said.

"You'll explain to her that I was suddenly called away?" asked Tresier.

"Don't give it another thought, Jean. Mademoiselle Devereux will never suspect . . ." Varlet's voice trailed to a suggestive halt. Color crept under Tresier's collar. Seeing it, the older man slapped him on the shoulder. "You are too sensitive," he said. "There is a package for you upstairs. You've done well. You deserve your reward."

The wages of sin, thought Tresier inconsequentially, and shrugged off the unpleasant thought. She had reneged on a promise, not realizing the difficulty she had placed him in. Zoë. Poor Zoë. Poor innocent Zoë. But she wasn't innocent, not by Varlet's measure. And she must pay the penalty for deceiving him. His eyes grew misty. He wasn't thinking of Zoë. Absurdly, his thoughts had shifted to his father.

"Thank you," he said. "You are most generous."

"It's all so reminiscent of what happened in London."

"Hm?" Housard turned aside from the picture he was studying and came to stand beside Rolfe's desk. They were in an upstairs room, an office of sorts, in the Swedish Embassy. Both gentlemen were in their shirt sleeves, having long since removed their coats.

"Fetch me another candle," said Rolfe irritably. I can't make out a thing I'm reading." As an after-

288

thought, he added a belated, "Please."

Housard obediently fetched a candle and set it on the desk. "What is so reminiscent of what happened in London?" he asked.

Rolfe folded his arms behind his head and leaned back in his chair, stretching his cramped muscles. It seemed they had been at it for hours. "Lord, I don't know," he said. "It may mean nothing at all."

"What may mean nothing at all?"

"We're ready to move against *La Compagnie*, wouldn't you say?"

"Just about," agreed Housard. "We now know the identities of the section heads of each cell."

"But we're still no nearer to unmasking *Le Patron?*"

"One of those section heads will lead us to him in time. We must be patient, that's all."

"As I said, it's all so reminiscent of what happened in London."

Housard pulled up a chair and seated himself. "What are you suggesting?" he demanded.

"It's just a hunch," Rolfe mused.

Housard's patience was wearing thin. "Well, don't stop there, man, for God's sake! What is just a hunch?"

Rolfe permitted himself a small smile at his companion's uncharacteristic show of impatience. "I have a dreadful premonition that history is about to repeat itself. Let me ask you a question, Housard. At this point in our investigation in London, what happened?"

"What happened?"

"Yes, what happened?"

"You know what happened. We were forced to show our hand prematurely. We lost *Le Patron,* but on the whole, we didn't do too badly. We netted all his lieutenants."

"No, Monsieur Housard. We netted precisely nothing."

"What? Oh, I see what you are getting at. They died resisting arrest or by their own hand."

"Betrand resisted arrest," corrected Rolfe "The other two section heads committed suicide—or somebody got to them first."

"I don't think I—" Housard stopped in mid-sentence. After a moment, he said consideringly, "It's possible, I suppose, that *Le Patron* took matters into his own hands and personally silenced them before we could question them. Is that what you are suggesting?"

"It had occurred to me. We know we are dealing with someone who is completely amoral. Such a man would not scruple to rid himself of any witnesses." Rolfe shrugged. "We have no way of knowing what really happened."

"But *Le Patron* did not silence Betrand," pointed out Housard. "We almost had him."

"True," said Rolfe. He smiled. "And that fact would seem to blow holes in my thesis." He rolled his head on the back of his chair, easing his neck muscles.

Both men fell into a reflective silence. Some time later, Rolfe said, "At least we have some clue to *Le Patron's* identity. We know that he was in England for some time before and after Robespierre fell from power."

"My dear Rivard, so were thousands of other Frenchmen," answered Housard gloomily. "Even your dear lady wife can claim that distinction."

Rolfe uttered a soft expletive. Zoë had become a sensitive subject ever since Housard had informed him that, after the failed assassination attempt against Tallien, Leon Devereux had been trailed to the house in St. Germain. There was no question that Zoë knew of her brother's involvement in *La Compagnie*. "God, I'm confused!" he said. "I no longer know what to believe."

Housard was perusing the paper on which Rolfe had made several notations. "What's this?" he asked.

"Hmm? Oh, I'm probably grasping at straws. It's a list of those members of the salon society who were known to be in England at the crucial time."

"You've omitted Germaine de Staël's name."

Rolfe groaned. "You're right, Housard. That tack won't lead us to *Le Patron*. The list is endless."

A rap on the door brought Housard to his feet. He unlocked it and moved aside as a gentleman, a young clerk, pushed his way in. Rolfe carefully averted his head as the newcomer conversed in an undertone with Housard. The conversation lasted no more than a minute or two. The clerk exited, and the door was carefully relocked.

Without preamble, Housard said, "Not more than thirty minutes ago, your wife arrived at Madame Montansier's Theatre where a masked ball is in progress."

Rolfe was swearing and on his feet in an instant.

There was no need for Housard to enlighten him about Madame Montansier's establishment. It was notorious, but more to the point, it was a known haunt of several suspected members of *La Compagnie*.

Chapter Eighteen

The company was thinning. It was long past time to go home. Zoë's eyes traveled the sets of dancers. She grew anxious. She could not find Tresier anywhere. Paul Varlet joined her and her alarm increased.

"You look particularly enchanting this evening, Zoë."

He bowed over her hand. Zoë tried not to flinch. And then everything seemed more natural. Varlet was smiling and calling himself all kinds of a fool for losing his temper when he had learned that she was not free to marry him.

"Will you ever forgive me for those dreadful things I said to you?"

"Of course," said Zoë, more relieved than she could say that this formidable man was not to be her enemy. Nevertheless, she would never forget the change that had taken place in him when she had told him "no." Trying not to betray her thoughts, she looked over the throng and said, "Have you seen Jean?"

"I believe he is in the cardroom—oh, not the one which is open to all and sundry. Upstairs, a private game is in progress. Perhaps you would care to join him?"

"No . . . no, I don't think so."

"Child, I shall accompany you. There will be other ladies present. What harm can come to you if I am with you?"

And because she was deathly afraid of him and was desperate to be restored to Tresier, she found herself saying, "You are too kind," and she placed her fingers on his arm.

Couples were ascending and descending the stairs. Some of the women had removed their masks. Zoë's heart hammered painfully against her ribs.

On the landing, they were joined by an acquaintance of Varlet's, a young *muscadin,* a member of the *jeunesse dorée.* Zoë recognized him easily. He was an extraordinarily handsome creature. She had seen him with Varlet on several occasions. He had been drinking heavily.

"May I join you?" he asked, his speech so slurred that it took a moment before Zoë could make sense of his words. His eyes looked at Zoë with veiled hostility, but when he addressed Varlet there was a pleading note in his voice. "Paul . . . ?"

Varlet hesitated, his eyes lazily moving from Zoë to the newcomer. He put an arm around the young man's shoulders and said, "Yes, you may join us, André. But only if you promise not to act like a jealous young fool."

The promise was given. Zoë puzzled over it as Varlet urged her up the next flight of stairs. She balked. The next floor up was almost in total darkness. On this section of the staircase, they were the only people.

"I told you this was a private game," came Varlet's amused tones. His breath tickled her ear. "Suit yourself. But I am going up. Are you coming, André?"

Both gentlemen brushed past Zoë. "Will . . . will you send Jean down to me?"

"My dear child," answered Varlet, "evidently, you don't know much about gentlemen. If Tresier is in the middle of a game, he can't simply throw down his cards and walk out."

It was all perfectly reasonable, perfectly innocent, and she did not know why goose bumps were forming on the backs of her arms and on her shoulders.

Varlet put out his hand. She hesitated for only a second, then put her own hand in his. She mounted the next step, trying to conceal her reluctance.

"Zoë!"

Varlet released Zoë, and she half-turned on the staircase to view the owner of the voice. Relief flooded her. Rolfe stood there, one hand on his cane, the other disentangling itself from a very pretty girl who, a short while before, had been blatant in her attentions to another gentleman.

Rolfe took a step forward, and Zoë noted the gray eyes snapping with rage, the stiffly held posture, the mouth tight-lipped with censure. At Madame Récamier's the night before, he had treated her with an almost insulting indifference. She had told herself, then, that if she never again set eyes on the perverse man, it would be too soon for her liking. She lied. She was never more glad to see anyone in her life.

"What are you doing up here?" he demanded.

It was Varlet who answered. "My dear Ronsard, what should Mademoiselle Devereux be doing here? Like everyone else, she has come to be ... amused."

Rolfe put out his hand, just as Varlet had done a few moments earlier. Zoë was sick with fright. The tension in that dimly lit half-landing was almost palpable. Rolfe's hand lifted a fraction, and Zoë instinctively moved to obey the implicit command. When she reached his side, his arm came round her so hard she cried out.

"I'll see Mademoiselle Devereux to her door," said Rolfe.

Varlet and Rolfe stared at each other for a long, comprehending moment. Finally, Varlet's gaze shifted to the young woman whom Zoë had displaced.

"Yvonne, do you come with us?" he said.

The woman gave Rolfe an uncertain look. His gaze was fixed on the two gentlemen on the staircase, completely ignoring her.

"I ... there's someone waiting for me," she said, and picking up her skirts, she moved rapidly along the corridor.

It was the older man who brought the confrontation to an end. With a slight acknowledgment of the head, gracefully, without haste, he made to ascend the stairs on the heels of the young *muscadin*. Rolfe watched them until they were out of sight, then turned on his heel, jerking Zoë after him.

In the carriage, he demanded an accounting of how Zoë had come to be at Madame Montansier's establishment.

"Didn't you know what kind of house madame keeps?" he asked savagely. "Any women there can be bought if the price is right."

Eyes downcast, she wrung her hands. "I knew," she confessed.

Rolfe could not believe his ears. "You knew?"

"There was no harm in it."

"No harm in it?"

"Respectable ladies often go to such places. If they are properly escorted, they have nothing to fear. And everything seemed so normal."

The irony did not escape him. How many times in the past had he escorted avidly curious ladies of the *ton* to just such establishments? It was all very amusing—only he did not feel like laughing.

His anger boiled over. "Oh yes, you had nothing to fear! Then I wish you would tell me why, when I came upon you, you had the look of a cornered hare. You were terrified! And so you should be! God knows what will be the wages of this night's work. I don't trust Varlet. It was too easy. He's not the sort of man to forgive a slight. I half-expected him to call me out."

Though she was trembling in her shoes and reluctant to add another fagot to the flame of Rolfe's temper, Zoë felt compelled to say more. In a voice barely above a whisper, she told Rolfe of Varlet's offer of marriage and how he had turned ugly when she had put an end to his importuning by pretending that she was a married lady who was separated from her husband.

"You told him that?" asked Rolfe.

"I did not betray your identity," she quickly

elaborated. "But that's beside the point. What I wish to say is this: I think you are right about Varlet. He has a ferocious temper when thwarted. Please be careful, Rolfe."

Rolfe was incredulous. "And still you permitted a man of that kidney to escort you to that den of vice?"

"No," said Zoë in a subdued tone. "I went with Jean Tresier." And with the faint hope of exculpating herself, she told Rolfe of how, having refused Tresier's offer of marriage as well as a loan she had promised him, she had accompanied him out of a sense of guilt.

Far from mollifying him, her words stoked his anger to a higher temperature. "What you need is a keeper," he said roughly, "a man to protect you."

What he was thinking was that Zoë had received two offers of marriage in as many days. Who next would offer for her? And what if she accepted?

Baring his teeth, he snarled, "I would not shake the hand of either Tresier or Varlet without washing my own hand afterward. But you, evidently, are pleased to be taken for one of their kind."

Zoë shrank into herself in miserable silence.

Wearily, Rolfe passed a hand over his eyes, his anger suddenly spent. He did not know whether or not he believed his own words. He did not know what to make of the girl who was his wife. Beneath the fine feathers and newly acquired air of worldliness, he sensed the same innocent girl who had captured his heart. But how could he be sure? And he had still to come to terms with the fact that she was seeing her brother—and he a known member of

298

La Compagnie. God, where was it all going to end?

"What were you doing at Madame Montansier's?" asked Zoë from her dark corner of the coach.

"Gaming," he said, and sighed quietly to himself when his answer passed without comment.

When the carriage pulled into the courtyard of the house in St. Germain, Rolfe jumped down and helped Zoë alight. In the foyer, Salome and Samson were waiting.

Zoë wasted no time in offering her profuse thanks for his escort home. Having said her adieux, she went racing up the stairs.

Rolfe removed his cloak and gave it to Samson. Then, coldly deliberate, he dismissed the servants for the night. Salome's head came up and wrath kindled in the depths of her eyes. Wordlessly, Rolfe put his walking cane into her hands. They stared at each other significantly for several moments before Salome's eyes dropped. Rolfe turned on his heel and went after Zoë.

"What . . . what do you want?" She had removed her mask and wig, and was running her fingers through her hair.

Rolfe shut the door softly. Brutally, frankly, he explained what would have happened to her if he had allowed Varlet to take her upstairs. The color came and went under her skin as he graphically described how two men would use a woman, then use each other.

"They let you go because they thought I was your protector," said Rolfe. He shrugged off his dark coat and threw it over the back of a chair.

Shocked, not quite taking in what she was seeing,

Zoë sank down on the bed. At any moment she expected that Salome and Samson would come bursting through the door.

"You see," said Rolfe easily, "Varlet knew that if he had not released you at once, I would have challenged him to a duel."

"Dueling isn't permitted," said Zoë.

Rolfe merely smiled and began to unbutton his shirt. In another moment, he had thrown off his wig and was pulling the shirt over his head. "The way I see it is this. When the whole world knows that I am your protector, you'll be as safe as the bank of England."

Zoë wasn't looking at him. At the first glimpse of bare skin, her eyes, her whole attention, had become riveted on the door.

"It's a fair exchange, wouldn't you say, kitten?"

"Wh-what is?" She was gingerly testing the word *protector* and had decided that it was preposterous to think that Rolfe meant what she thought he meant. The house was unnaturally quiet. Where, oh where, were her servants?

"And there is something more to be considered. You owe me . . . how long were we married before you ran away from me, kitten?"

"Eight months, three weeks, and four days," answered Zoë automatically.

Rolfe grinned from ear to ear. "By my reckoning, you owe me about three months uninterrupted time in bed."

At last, he had her attention. Her delicate brows knit together. "What are you suggesting?" she asked, her eyes darting around the room as if seeking a way of escape.

"What I am suggesting is this. You refused me my conjugal rights when you were my wife. I have decided to collect on that debt beginning as of this moment."

He wasn't making sense. Nothing was making sense. And she was on the verge of hysteria. A sudden suspicion assailed her. She rounded on him. "What have you done with my servants?" Her voice rose querulously.

Calmly, coolly, he began to remove his shoes and stockings. "I sent them to bed. They are not going to rescue you, if that's what you were hoping."

The room was suddenly as hot as a bakehouse. Zoë closed her eyes tightly.

For a moment, a very fleeting moment, he almost felt sorry for her. He ruthlessly crushed what he regarded as a fatal weakness. It was a proven fact that this woman could draw rings around him without half trying. If he didn't watch his step, she would seduce him from his purpose. One look, one word, and he was putty in her hands. He always had been, from the moment she had pushed into his life.

She was his wife. The thought was grimly satisfying. Her divorce might mean something in Paris. In London, it was worthless. And once he had her safely on English soil, he would . . . oh God, he did not know what he would do. He wanted to keep her safe. He wanted to share his future with her.

For the first time in his life, he wanted a real home. He wanted children. And he knew that Zoë was the heart of this new ambition that had taken hold of him. He wanted Zoë as he had never wanted anything. How ironic, he thought, that having adroitly evaded the lures and snares of the most beautiful and sophisticated ladies of the *ton* for any number of years, he should fall victim to a young girl who was barely out of the schoolroom.

She confused him. She did not want him for her husband. But he would wager his life that she was not indifferent to him. He did not know what he should believe about her. That she might be involved in intrigue mattered not one jot. He was less sanguine when he considered that his little Zoë might possibly have taken other lovers since arriving in Paris. He tried to put the unpalatable thought from him. There would be time and enough to sort through all her iniquities when he had extricated her from her present coil and had her under his own roof.

In the meantime, it was imperative that he have some ordering of her life. She had made it abundantly clear, however, that she would accept no authority but her own. He would not accept that. She was his. In their present circumstances, he knew of only one way to press his claims upon her. He was doing it for her own good.

Rising, he said, very gently and quietly, "I'll act as your lady's maid if you wish."

Her eyes flew open. "My servants will kill you," she breathed hoarsely.

"I think not. I'm in your cards remember? The knight with the wand?" He smiled indulgently. "Salome thinks I'm your fate. She won't meddle."

"Oh God!" Zoë made a bolt for the door.

Rolfe was on her in an instant, bearing her back across the bed, pinning her down with his weight. "Easy, easy," he soothed as she began to buck under him.

She whimpered as he lowered his head to touch his mouth to hers. "I don't want this," she said weakly, and tried to pull away.

He assessed her expression carefully. Smiling, he said, "No. I can see that you don't. But I know how to change that 'no' to a 'yes'."

She believed him. Where Rolfe was concerned, she had no willpower. Once, she had adored him with a child's blind devotion. And though she was wiser now, disillusioned, older than her years, he still had the power to move her. And she wished with all her heart that she was immune to him.

He saw everything that he wanted to see in her eyes. She was giving into him, softening beneath him. Something fierce, that same primitive emotion he had experienced when he had found her on the staircase with Varlet, surged through him. The woman was his, the pride of all his possessions. And he would take whatever steps were necessary to hold what was his.

There was a hard glitter in his eyes as he gazed down at her. The look chilled Zoë to the bone. And then the look was gone.

"No," he said, lowering his head to press little kisses across her cheeks and along the line of her jaw. "Don't look at me like that. Give into me. Oh God, kitten, give into me. I've waited forever for this. Don't turn me away now."

It was sheer insanity to give into him. She should

303

have more pride, more sense. But when his kisses were so sweetly imploring, the remnants of her resistance melted like snow on a summer day.

A soft moan caught in her throat as he turned her face up to his. His mouth hovered over hers. Zoë trembled in anticipation. She closed her eyes, waiting for his kiss. When it did not come, her eyelashes lifted slowly and she stared into eyes as blue as a Mediterranean sky.

He seemed to be hesitating, as if he were not quite sure of her. Smiling, Zoë brought her head up from the pillow and touched her open lips to his in an age-old gesture of feminine capitulation.

A spark leapt between them. Those sweetly imploring kisses turned into something quite different. He could not undress her fast enough.

"This time it's going to be different," he told her, and he cast around in his mind for a way to explain what he was feeling.

"Different?" said Zoë. She was enthralled with the sight, smell, and taste of him. Her fingers splayed out, savoring those powerful masculine shoulders, muscles tensed, straining, rigidly held in check to protect her fragility. She shivered, remembering that there was always a cost when a woman gave herself to a man. Hadn't Salome told her so? The wages of being female were pain and tribulation. She touched her fingers to the pulse beating wildly at his throat. His virility was almost overpowering. She cherished it, secure in the knowledge that his strength was her shield. If there was a price for this one night of love, she decided that she was willing to pay it.

She was naked. And Rolfe could not believe how

beautiful she was. "Zoë," he said harshly, and his hands covered her breasts. "How could I have been deceived into thinking you were a schoolgirl? You're so incredibly . . . female. Your skin is like silk. Lovely . . . lovely . . . Zoë."

His hands made a leisurely sweep, following the path of his eyes. Calmly possessive, he claimed every inch of her in a way he had never before claimed any woman. It came to him, then, that this act of love was no empty ritual, not merely the taking and giving of sensual pleasure. This joining was . . . significant.

His eyes glittering, he told her, "I'm going to love you so thoroughly that you'll forget every lover you've ever had but me."

Other lovers? Zoë tried to suppress a smile and failed.

"Damn you!" he said savagely. "Damn you, Zoë!"

His mouth covered hers in a ferocity of passion. Zoë surrendered everything to him, trusting him implicitly. And then began the assault on her senses.

It wasn't only passion that moved him. He'd felt passion for other women—dozens of them. But here was an unfamiliar urgency, an insatiable need to impress upon her that he, and only he, was her masculine complement, her true mate. He would tolerate no others encroaching on his private preserves. Disjointed sentences spilled from his lips. She was his. He would protect her with his dying breath from everything and everyone but himself. And from him she needed no protection. She was his own true lady, the prize he cherished above all

305

Zoë scarcely heard the torrent of words. She was drowning in sensations she had never before experienced. Her body felt heavy, engorged, too sensitive for comfort. She was shivering with pleasure, on the brink of something she could not understand. She was beyond denying him anything. His mouth and hands moved over her, teasing, tasting, learning the intimate secrets of her femininity. She responded with an abandon she would not have believed possible.

When he pulled back to strip away his clothes, Zoë was shaking with the strength of her desire for him. But when he turned to face her, and her eyes moved over his powerful masculine physique, finally coming to rest on the vigorous shaft of his sex, desire gradually faded. He crouched over her, his face taut with passion.

Zoë inched away. "Please, Rolfe . . . no."

He went perfectly still. His voice was harsh when he said, "I won't let you change your mind." He read the fear in her eyes, and he groaned. "Don't be afraid of me, kitten." He buried his mouth against her throat. "Don't stop me, love. Please don't try to stop me. It's gone too far. I can't stop. Don't you see? Oh God, you are so beautiful, so perfectly made. And you belong to me."

He was seducing her with words. And it seemed that nothing had changed. She could never refuse Rolfe anything. He positioned her beneath him and Zoë tensed for the coming agony.

And suddenly, without having to be told, Rolfe knew why she had turned skittish. He braced himself on his arms and regarded her with a lazy grin. "I won't hurt you this time," he told her softly.

"No?" Her look was disbelieving.

He felt like laughing. In spite of the questionable morals of Zoë's intimates, and in spite of finding her in Madame Montansier's notorious establishment, his little wife was as pure as the driven snow. The amusement left him, and he felt suddenly humbled and more fortunate than he deserved to be.

His expression grave, he said, "I hurt you the first time. I'm sorry. I should have taken more care with you."

"It wasn't your fault. You thought I was—" Horrified, Zoë stared up at him. The last thing she wanted was to bring another woman's name into the conversation.

Rolfe tenderly combed his fingers through her dark ringlets. He loved the way the strands of her hair curled lovingly round his fingers. He chose his words with care. "I'm not sure that I can explain what happened that night. I awakened from a deep sleep. I found you in my bed. In my own mind, it was you I was making love to, Zoë, no one else. But afterwards, it occurred to me that it could not possibly be you. For one thing, you'd never come to my bed before. And for another, I thought you were still at the Abbey. I was confused. But I wanted it to be you. I wish you would believe me."

It shouldn't matter to her. But it did. He'd had women, lots of women, before and since. He was a rake of the first magnitude. But at least when he had made love to her he hadn't been wishing that she was one of those other women. Her heart swelled with happiness.

She wound her arms around his neck. "Love me, Rolfe," she said, "please love me."

A soft, unintelligible murmur broke from him. He held her face between his hands. Trembling with passion he kissed her slowly and deeply. He became less controlled, and his lips moved over her urgently, scorching her like flame wherever they touched. Her whole body seemed to swell with desire for him. She knew that she was moaning, panting, inviting every intimacy by offering herself like a wanton. She had to bite back the words of love.

He settled himself between her damp thighs. "Oh yes," he breathed into her mouth. "This is how I've dreamed it would be between us. Welcome me into your body, Zoë. Show me how much you want me."

He smoothed her fingers around the powerful shaft of his virility. He sensed her hesitation and kissed her with rising hunger, melting the instinctive remnants of feminine resistance. Obediently, she guided him to the entrance to her body.

"Zoë," he groaned, "ah, Zoë," and he drove into her.

He gazed down at her face, at the languorous half-closed lids, the lips swollen with the force of his kisses. "Zoë!" he said again, and there was awe in that one word. He knew that he would never get enough of this woman.

Drawing on reserves of control he had not known he possessed, he moved above her, drawing the response he wanted, holding himself in check till he could feel the pleasure rise in her. "Yes," he said, encouraging her, "yes." Never in his life had he ever wanted anything as mush as this—that Zoë should find her woman's pleasure in his arms.

When he knew that she was soaring on the crest, he relinquished his control. His movements became rougher, almost violent. In husky, sensual whispers, he spurred her to greater passion. The stifled cries of pleasure she made deep in her throat made him wild for her. Belatedly, he tried to restrain his ardor, fearing he might frighten her. It was too late. They came together in a storm of emotion, her surprised cry of ecstasy driving him over the edge. Frenzied, in the throes of rampaging passion of the sort he had never before experienced, Rolfe slipped his hands under Zoë's hips, lifting her to him, thrusting violently into her again and again, groaning her name as his seed spilled into her, shuddering uncontrollably with the force of his release.

Long moments later, he raised himself slightly to allow her to draw breath. His own breathing was still far from normal. He could scarcely bring himself to look into her eyes. He knew that he must have frightened her half to death. The words of apology came out haltingly.

Zoë stirred beneath him. She smiled dreamily. "That was . . . nice," she said, and giggled at the inadequacy of her words. Her hand languidly trailed from his cheek to his throat, then fell away.

"Nice?" said Rolfe, and savored the sudden release of guilt. She wasn't shocked by the ferocity of his ardor. He kissed the tip of her nose. "Only nice?" he asked playfully.

She sighed, a sound of repletion that Rolfe found

eminently satisfying. "It was . . . very nice," she elaborated.

She was love-sated and drowsy. Rolfe wasn't. He kissed her again, darting his tongue between her lips in an age-old masculine question. Her drooping eyes widened. At least he had her attention. He felt himself growing hard inside her, and he rotated his hips, inviting her to reciprocate. Her eyes grew huge in her face.

A wicked grin spread slowly over his handsome face as he felt the shudder that began deep in her womb. He moved again, feeding the small flame of her desire. "Oh yes, love, yes. And don't you dare turn shy on me." He tipped back her drooping chin. "You're a deeply passionate woman. And I'm never going to let you forget it."

Was she deeply passionate? Zoë asked herself. And her heart answered. She was deep in love, as deep in love with him as ever she had been. Nothing had changed and yet, everything had changed. She was no longer the love-struck girl. She had learned how to conceal what she was feeling. Rolfe had said not one word of love to her. And she would never again embarrass herself by betraying the state of her emotions.

"Zoë, what is it?"

She smiled to conceal the sudden constriction in her chest. "Prove to me that I'm a deeply passionate woman," she teased.

He did. But the word *love* was never mentioned between them.

310

Chapter Nineteen

By degrees, she came to herself. She stretched languidly, absorbing the faint sounds and scents in the house. She was aware that it was late. The sun spilled to every corner of her chamber. And then she remembered everything.

Abruptly, Zoë sat up in bed. Only then did she realize that she was naked. She hauled the bedclothes up to her chin.

He was at the window, gazing out towards the river. She recognized the robe he was wearing.

"How did you get hold of my father's dressing gown?"

Over his shoulder Rolfe grinned wolfishly. "Scarcely the first words I expected to hear from your lips after what we shared last night."

As he approached the bed, Zoë made an effort to compose herself. This kind of scene must be a commonplace for her former husband. His sophisticated women would know how to conduct an *affaire*. She had only instinct to guide her.

She had to fight back the impulse to throw herself into his arms. To confess that she loved him would gratify his vanity, or perhaps amuse him, or embarrass him. He would patronize her as he had always done in the past. She could not bear it. Last night had been something she would treasure for the rest of her life. She had no doubt that to a gentleman of Rolfe's experiences last night would be soon forgotten. Pride dictated only one course.

Smiling easily, she said, "You are wearing my father's dressing gown."

"Salome was good enough to fetch it for me." He captured one of her hands. "You're trembling," he observed.

"I'm cold. Would you mind?" and she gestured to her own robe which lay on the back of a chair.

For the moment, he ignored her request as his eyes studied her face. "Do you mind that I'm wearing your father's dressing gown?" he asked seriously, and then, with a wicked grin, "You have only to say so, and I shall remove it." He loved the way color stole across her cheekbones.

"I'm surprised Salome was so obliging, 'tis all."

"She told me that you had kept all your parents garments."

"I . . . there has not been the time to go through them and decide to whom they should go."

"I think I understand. When my brother died, it was the same for me."

"Was it?" Her tone was dubious.

"Somehow I felt that by keeping his things about me, I could sense Edward's presence."

"But—but that's it exactly!" said Zoë. "Do you know, my mother's fragrance still clings to her clothes? I just can't bear to part with them." Suddenly chary of the intimacy which these confidences were creating, in an altered tone, she repeated her request for her robe. This was duly handed to her. It came to her belatedly, that to don the robe necessitated her appearing before Rolfe in all her nakedness.

312

His eyes were sparkling when she chanced a quick glance up at him. Ignoring that sapient look Zoë said, "There was no need for you to approach Salome. You should have wakened me."

In point of fact, it was Salome who had approached Rolfe. Dawn was just beginning to creep into the room when he had heard the scratching at the door. Reluctantly untangling himself from Zoë, he had snatched up the coverlet to conceal his nakedness.

When he unlocked the door, he found Salome, candle in hand, in the corridor, proffering the dressing gown. A moment later, with the robe knotted securely around him, he had followed her into a room farther down the hall.

It was evident that, in spite of believing him to be her young mistress's fate, Salome was coming to have second thoughts about Rolfe. He had done everything in his power to reassure her, swearing that he meant to marry the girl just as soon as circumstances permitted.

"Why not marry her now?" Salome had wanted to know.

"Because she won't have me."

Salome thought for a moment. "You know her from before, don't you?"

"Yes," said Rolfe, and would commit himself to saying no more on that subject.

He could see that Salome was far from satisfied with his reticence. She subjected him to a very hard scrutiny before producing a crucifix on which she made him swear that he would marry Zoë. But when he had told Zoë's old nurse the steps he meant to follow to ensure Zoë capitulation, he'd had a fight on

313

his hands. Without giving everything away, he had tried to impress upon the virago that without his protection her young charge stood to lose more than her virtue. If it had come to the point, Rolfe would have had Housard remove Salome without batting an eye. He decided that he would follow that course only as a last resort. Zoë was fond of her maid, and Salome was devoted to Zoë.

Eyeing him distrustfully, Salome had stalked to a dresser. In the top drawer, she found what she was looking for. Tarot cards. Rolfe had watched interestedly as Salome set out the cards, face down, on a small table. Some few minutes later, the ritual was complete. She gazed with rapt attention at the card in her hand.

"What is it?" asked Rolfe.

She held out the card to him. It was the knight with the wand. He had won. And now it was time to tell Zoë of the change in her circumstances.

"Put on your robe," he said.

Zoë licked her lips. "I should like some privacy," she countered.

He stifled that first pang of conscience. "There's no necessity to be shy with me. We were husband and wife; once. Now I am your protector and you are my mistress."

Unconsciously, Zoë began to shred the soft folds of the robe between her fingers. His words seared her and she was furious with herself for allowing this man the power to hurt her still. Grinding her teeth together, she threw back the covers and flounced to her feet.

"I am no man's mistress," she denied passionately and made to slip on her robe.

Rolfe prevented her completing the movement. Wide-eyed, she stared at him. A pulse began to beat at her throat. His hands trailed possessively, from the line of her jaw to the thrust of her breasts and lower, but his eyes, gray as the English Channel, held her inexorably. "You accepted my protection last night," he told her. "You gave me rights that I refuse to relinquish."

Wordlessly she shook her head.

"No harm will come to you as long as it is known that you have accepted my *carte-blanche*."

In quick succession, her face betrayed the emotions of shame and outrage. Rolfe hardened his heart, reminding himself that he was doing it for her own good. "From this moment on, any insult to you is an insult to me. I take care of what belongs to me. A woman needs a man to protect her and—"

Before he could stop her, she jerked out of his grasp. Her eyes were flashing fire as she quickly belted her robe. In a voice vibrating with scorn she said, "Our account was settled in full last night. I have no wish to be thought ungrateful, however. If you still think that I am in your debt, I shall be delighted to give you my banker's name and direction. He will pay you off."

Rolfe smiled unpleasantly. "That's not the kind of payment I had in mind, kitten."

"Possibly not, but that's all you are going to get. And you may believe that no price is too great not to have to endure your attentions ever again."

While she was speaking, she had moved to the door, only to discover that it was locked and that there was no sign of the key. She wasn't frightened, she told herself as she slowly turned to face Rolfe.

This man was not an abuser of women. This man had never so much as lifted a hand against his nieces when the provocation was intolerable. She swallowed convulsively.

This man had the face and form of the Rolfe she once knew, but that was where the resemblance ended. This watchful stranger in her father's robe had an aura of power, a look of leashed violence which aroused feelings of acute helplessness. So must the doe feel, she thought, before the hounds closed in for the kill.

"Come here, kitten," he said softly.

Her posture was proud, defiant, as she stared at him without blinking.

Laughing softly, as if amused by her show of resistance, he crossed to the door. Zoë held her ground, nor did she flinch when his hands cupped her shoulders. The laughter gradually faded from Rolfe's eyes.

"Zoë," he murmured, "you are no longer a child." He kissed her softly, and then with rising hunger, stifling her protests. "You are a beautiful desirable woman. Don't you see? It was only a matter of time before some man claimed you. Ah God, Zoë, tell me you are not sorry that it was I." And abruptly swinging her into his arms, he carried her to the bed.

Zoë was a prisoner in her own house and she still could not believe it. It was very late of the same afternoon. Rolfe had departed for the Swedish Embassy, advising her that he would return in a short while. Before leaving he had conferred with her servants. Zoë did not know what hold he had over them, but it was evident that her wishes did not have

316

the weight of his.

She was bathed, fed, and cosseted by Salome. There was nothing new in this. But when Salome let slip that she was following Rolfe's orders, Zoë was livid.

"I am mistress here," she fumed. "I say when I shall be bathed, and when and what I shall eat."

"Did Salome do wrong by drawing your bath and preparing a nice *déjeuner* to tempt your appetite?" asked Salome innocently.

"No, of course not!" allowed Zoë with sorely strained patience. She glanced at her empty plate. Not a crumb remained of the chicken vol-au-vent with bechamel sauce and the tiny fried potatoes. Knowing that Rolfe was responsible for ordering one of her favorite dishes almost persuaded her to forgo the next course. She reached for the dish of cream custard and changed tactics.

"Was it kind of you, Salome, to leave me alone with him last night? You must have known—"

"He is in your cards," said Salome doggedly, as if that were sufficient reason for her betrayal. "He loves you. You wait and see. He will yet marry my little flower."

At Salome's words, something leapt to life inside Zoë. After a moment's reflection, she shook her head. "It's not possible," she said. "I can never marry him." She wasn't thinking of Rolfe's past transgressions. She was thinking of her brother and her resolve that they would start a new life in America as soon as it could be arranged.

Salome cast a glowering frown upon her mistress. "You will marry him," she said. "It is the only way to make everything right."

317

For a moment, Zoë was tempted to confess that she had formerly been married to the man and had never been more miserable in her life. She still could not think of his mother without experiencing a mixture of humiliation and anger—humiliation for what she had suffered at the woman's hands and anger that Rolfe had been so callous as to permit it. And then there was his infidelities.

Though her look spoke volumes, Zoë said nothing, knowing that Salome would never sanction divorce. When a man and woman married, the bond was indissoluble. It was one of the tenets by which Zoë had been raised. She tried to console herself with the thought that neither Salome nor her mother could have foreseen the circumstances in which she found herself. One thought led to another, and before long Zoë began to wonder if she still knew right from wrong.

She had taken a lover. It was the most memorable, the most pleasurable experience of her life. And it was so wrong. One lapse from grace she was willing to forgive herself. She was only human after all. And she loved Rolfe above anything. But how could she explain that, having resolved that there could be no repetition of the night before, she had gone against her own scruples?

That very morning, when Rolfe had gathered her into his arms, she had meant to fight him like a wildcat. Oh, she had put up a token resistance. But there had been no way to stop him. And somehow her words of rejection had changed to soft, throbbing gasps of appeal.

There swept over her a tide of burning shame when she remembered how she had permitted him to do whatever he wished with her, and when it was over, his words to her.

"I knew I could make you purr for me," he had said with a smile so smug that Zoë wanted to hit him. Instead, she had burst into tears.

And then the smile was gone, and he was lavishing her with tenderness, stroking her as if she were some cherished pet that had come to hand.

"It's all right," he soothed. "Don't take on so! Zoë! Zoë! Don't look at me like that! Everything will be fine. It's all right. It's all right."

But it wasn't all right. He intended the whole world to know that she had accepted his *carte blanche*. People would point at her, and behind their hands, they would refer to her as a "fallen woman," "a Phyrene," "a harlot," or worse. How was it to be borne?

She could not bear it. Nor could she fight him. He would always come out the victor in any contest between them. Hadn't he already proved it? No. There was only one course open to her. She must arrange for false passports for herself and her brother so that they could make for America with all speed. She must transfer funds from her bank. And finally, when all was in place, she must send word to Leon.

Claire. She was not forgetting Claire. But for Leon's sake as much as her own, she must not delay overlong. When they were settled in America, she would write to a few, chosen friends so that, should Claire ever come looking for her, they could give Claire her direction. Under the circumstances, it was the best she could do.

She decided that her first call that afternoon should be on Charles Lagrange. Though Zoë found him a bit of a bore, he had proved a true friend in the past.

She genuinely liked him. And Charles was so placed as to be in a position to secure false passports if he wished. To travel under their own names was not to be thought of—not if the secret society of which Leon was a member was as far-reaching as he had indicated.

Zoë got as far as her front door. She was turned back by Samson.

"What's this?" she demanded.

Sorrowfully, unable to meet her eyes, he referred her to Salome.

"You are to stay until he returns. Those were his very words," was all the satisfaction Zoë got from that quarter, and no appeal of Zoë's could shake her maid.

Nothing daunted, Zoë stomped to the back door. It was locked. Short of climbing through a window and making an undignified exit, she was a virtual prisoner in her own house. Zoë was fit to be tied.

She repaired to the yellow *salle* and proceeded to take out her frustrations on the piano. When she heard the front door open, she fairly slammed out of the room intent on tearing a strip off the man who had so mistreated her.

In the foyer, she came face-to-face with Paul Varlet and Jean Tresier. It looked to Zoë as if Samson, no doubt following Rolfe's orders had turned them away, and they were on the point of departing. Nothing could be more calculated to make Zoë go against her own natural inclinations.

She greeted them effusively and, turning a steely eye upon her footman, ordered him to bring chocolate and sweets to the yellow *salle*.

When the amenities had been dealt with, Tresier

broached the subject which was on all their minds.

"Zoë, how came you to leave the masquerade last night without my escort? I was never more surprised when Paul told me you had left with that . . . what's his name? — ah, yes, Ronsard, the Swedish diplomat."

Paul Varlet's voice smoothly cut in, "As I told you, Jean, Zoë could not be persuaded to show herself where gentlemen were gaming. And who can blame her?"

Shamefaced, Tresier asked, "Zoë, can you ever forgive me?"

Zoë looked from one to the other and the seed of doubt was planted in her mind. Rolfe had warned her what manner of men they were. Her own instincts, at least with respect to Varlet, confirmed Rolfe's opinion. And yet, their manners were so gracious; their appearance was so gentlemanly; and they had been frequent guests in her home when her parents were alive. In her comfortable yellow *salle* the forebodings of the night before at Madame Montansier's seemed distant and far-fetched.

"Of course I forgive you, Jean," she said. "You meant no harm."

At her words, Tresier's eyes dropped away. Zoë wondered at it, but Samson entered at that precise moment with a tray of chocolate and sweets, and her attention was distracted.

When Samson stationed himself at the door, it was no less than Zoë expected. Truth to tell, she felt more secure with the presence of the huge black man. No. She could not believe that Tresier and Varlet were as depraved as Rolfe had painted them, and, at the same time, she knew that she never wanted to be alone with either of them again.

321

The glasses of chocolate were hardly handed round, when a footman announced the Lagranges. Zoë could not believe her luck. She determined to ask Charles Lagrange to stay behind so that she could put the matter of the false passports to him.

As it happened, she scarcely exchanged two words with Lagrange. He and Varlet had found something outside the long window which held their interest. And even when they turned back into the room, they were in no hurry to conclude their private tête-à-tête.

Some minutes later, Rolfe entered the house. A coachman hauled in his valise and deposited it in the foyer. Hearing the sounds of conversation coming from the yellow *salle*, Rolfe entered unannounced, as if he were master of the house.

All conversation immediately died. Rolfe's eyes quickly scanned the occupants of the room. On one level of his mind, he noted their identities, on another level, his thoughts had taken flight.

He could not help comparing his own ancestral home with Zoë's house—what he had seen of it. He knew that the place had gone to ruin before Zoë had taken possession. He could scarcely believe that his young wife had it in her to effect an elegant background without sacrificing one iota to comfort. He remembered, then, the contretemps with his mother, when Zoë had tried to do as much at the Abbey. And in his colossal ignorance, he had taken his mother's part.

She was on her feet, moving towards him, hand extended like the gracious hostess she was. Rolfe smiled at the innocent picture she presented. He wasn't about to allow Zoë to treat him like a stranger.

"Monsieur Ronsard, how kind in you to call," she

said.

Rolfe accepted the outstretched hand, but only to get a grip on her. He pulled her close and dropped a kiss on her shocked lips. He heard her friend, Francoise, suck in her breath. Lagrange looked thoughtful. Varlet's eyes were flashing daggers, and Tresier's mouth hung open.

Leaning heavily on his cane, Rolfe laboriously limped to a chair where he slowly sank down. *"Chérie,"* he said, "would you be so kind as to order Samson to stow my gear?"

"But he is so old!" Jean Tresier could not have been more affronted if Zoë had taken up with a leper. He was staggered to think that such a proper lady would turn down his honorable proposal to become the convenient of a gentleman who was old enough to be her father.

"Not so old," corrected Varlet. "In point of fact, not so old as he would like us all to believe." He was in the process of taking snuff when his coach hit a pothole. Not a grain of snuff escaped his sure hand.

"Why should he pretend to be older?"

Varlet shut his snuffbox with a snap. "My dear Jean," he said, "obviously Monsieur Ronsard has something to hide."

Tresier slanted his companion a disbelieving look. "Like what, for instance?"

Varlet stared out the coach window. "That has yet to be divined. What do you know of him?"

"Very little," allowed Tresier. "His father was French, his mother was Swedish. He is a diplomat attached to the Swedish embassy. That's all I know.

Oh yes, there's talk that he is one of Germaine de Staël's lovers."

There was a silence as Valet considered the younger man's words. At length, he said, "He has some sort of hold over Zoë. That much is evident."

"Look, Paul . . ." Tresier hesitated and then pushed on with more confidence. "Why don't you forget about Zoë? There are plenty more fish in the sea. For whatever reason, she has made her choice. She wants this Ronsard fellow. There's scarcely a woman you can't have if you—"

"I want *her*," broke in Varlet, his face a mask of fury, *her*, Zoë Devereux! Do I make myself clear?" He was breathing hard, as if he had just quit a fencing match.

Tresier averted his head, sickened by the spectacle of the older man. "Perfectly," he answered without expression. "What is it you wish me to do?"

In the Lagrange carriage, the conversation also revolved around the scene which had just taken place in Zoë's yellow *salle*.

"I still can't believe it," said Francoise.

"Neither can I," agreed Lagrange. "But there it is. It's the way of our world. I always said that a woman on her own—"

"Yes, yes!" said Francoise testily. "I know what you said, Charles, and you may believe it doesn't help one whit to hear you say 'I told you so.'"

"Quite," said Lagrange, and wisely lapsed into silence.

"There's no accounting for it," said Francoise, thinking aloud, "unless . . ." She too drifted into silence.

"Yes?"

"Oh, I was just going to say that Zoë's English husband might easily be Ronsard's younger brother. I mentioned it to Zoë, once."

"Mentioned what?"

"The resemblance. It's uncanny. Do you suppose that that's why Zoë is taken with the man—because he reminds her of the man she once loved?"

"Is there a resemblance? I hadn't noticed. I think you must be imagining things, Francoise."

On the point of arguing, Francoise thought better of it and asked instead, "What did you and Paul Varlet find to talk about?"

"What? Oh, this and that."

"I cannot like that man," said Francoise with feeling.

"I'm sorry to hear you say so, my dear. I've invited him to call on us one evening next week. Still, this is business. There's no need for you to speak with him if you prefer not to."

"Business? With Paul Varlet? What sort of business?"

"Investments. I was asking his advice on that little legacy I inherited from my late cousin Albert. There's no one better to advise on investments than Paul Varlet."

Francoise sniffed. In her own mind, she had earmarked Cousin Albert's legacy for a new house and the accouterments to go with it. For the rest of the drive, she gave herself up to contemplating the house on which she had her eye.

Chapter Twenty

The report that Zoë Devereux had taken a lover spread like wildfire. Some few refused to accept it until they had incontrovertible proof. Zoë Devereux, they protested, was cast in the same mold as Juliette Récamier. There had never been as much as a whisper of scandal attached to either lady. Others were more cynical. The Devereux girl, they surmised, was only doing what everyone else was doing. She was bound to accept some man as either husband or protector sooner or later. Evidently, Ronsard, the Swedish diplomat, had pressed his claims more forcefully than any other of Zoë's circle of admirers. Speculation was rife, and all of Paris eagerly awaited the last Thursday in the month, when Zoë regularly held her salon.

Zoë was so ashamed that she could scarcely hold up her head. If it had been left to her, she would have cancelled all her engagements. As it was, Rolfe had forbidden her to show her face outside the house unless he accompanied her. At the opera, at the theatre, at Very's famous restaurant or strolling in the Tuileries gardens — they were seen everywhere together.

"Is it necessary to flaunt me as if I were a piece

of prime horseflesh?" asked Zoë in a tormented voice. Only moments before, they had returned from a shopping expedition to the Rue St. Honoré where Rolfe had made a great show of selecting gowns, bonnets, pelisses, and the sheerest, laciest underthings for his *chère amie*. Zoë had carried the whole thing off with what she regarded as remarkable aplomb until they had entered a jeweler's shop. Two people were being waited on, a young couple who were choosing a ring. Zoë recognized the gentleman as one of her sister's admirers from the old days. And though the young man greeted her with every mark of civility and they spoke for a few moments on how they had fared in the interim, he made no move to introduce her to his companion. The cut touched Zoë to the quick.

His features impassive, Rolfe watched as Zoë moved restlessly about the room. In a short space of time, he had made it abundantly clear that Zoë Devereux was not without recourse if anyone should think to take advantage of her. Soon, very soon, the trap would be sprung on all known members of *La Compagnie* and he would be free of the constraints placed on him. Already, their escape route had been mapped out. But until such time as he had Zoë safely on English soil, he had no choice but to play the cards as they fell.

"You should thank me," he told her. "I've given you my protection with very little recompense." He was referring to the fact that since moving into the house he had not laid a finger on her. He'd wanted to, desperately. But Zoë's bouts of weeping in the aftermath of their lovemaking was a bitter rebuke to him. She was conscience-stricken. He felt like the

327

veriest cad. Though sorely tempted, he could not impose his will on her. He could seduce her without half trying. But nothing he said afterwards had the power to console her. And to be near her—the sexual frustration was driving him mad.

"I don't understand what you hope to gain by all this," she said helplessly. "When your assignment here is over, you must return to England. Who is to protect me then?"

He answered her curtly. "I may be here for longer than you think."

"Then what? Am I to be passed along to some other gentleman? Are you to be the first in a long succession of protectors?" That, of course, would never happen. Before long, she would be making a life for herself in the New World. But Rolfe puzzled her. He had not come to her chamber since that first week. There was something not quite right in their situation if she could only figure it out.

"Don't talk rot," he said explosively. And because he had no ready answers to allay her fears, he interjected, "Who was the young man in the jeweler's shop?"

Her eyes dropped away. "One of my sister's former beaux."

"Beaux?"

A thought struck her, and she dimpled. "Claire was a heartbreaker. She was the most beautiful girl you could hope to meet. All the young men lost their hearts to Claire."

They had broached the subject of Zoë's family a time or two since Rolfe had taken up residence in St. Germain. In spite of Zoë's protests, Rolfe knew that she had never given up hope of finding her sister Claire. Housard had tracked Claire to Bordeaux at a time when a number of American ships had been in the harbor. It seemed possible that Claire had taken passage on one of those ships. If so, there had been more than enough time for the girl to make her whereabouts known. She had not done so. The task of finding her if she did not wish to be found was almost hopeless. Rolfe did not wish to raise false hopes in Zoë, but he had resolved to pursue the matter further once they returned to England.

Zoë had stopped pacing as she became caught up in her reflections. Rolfe eased back into his chair, crossing one booted foot over the other. "Were you jealous of her, kitten?"

"Jealous? Of Claire?" Surprise etched her voice. "She was my sister."

He smiled. "You admired her, then?"

"I adored her. She was everything I wished I could be."

"Like what for instance?"

"Oh . . . you know . . . confident, sociable, vivacious, fun-loving. There was always a sparkle to a party when Claire was there. I was the quiet one, you see."

"What about your brother?" he asked, his tone as casual as he could make it. "Does he take after you or Claire?"

"Neither," she answered at once. "Leon is . . . well . . . I suppose, when I think of it, he takes after us both. He has Claire's charm, but he is moody—you know, he broods about things."

"How odd!" he said, smiling.

"What is?"

329

"When you talk of your sister, you use the past tense. When you talk of your brother, you use the present."

"Do I? I hadn't noticed."

He waited a moment, giving her the perfect opportunity to confide in him. It seemed as if she might, then she tore her gaze from his and said in a choked voice, "*Maman* said it was a terrible failing—this brooding about things. She said I was too sensitive."

He was disappointed in her, though nothing in his expression gave him away. Reluctantly, he followed her lead, "Yes, you are sensitive, but that is one of the things I like in you, but not the only thing by any means. You are sensitive, thoughtful for others, loyal to a degree, and as brave as Achilles."

"I'm not brave," said.

"If you are not, then I don't know who is," and before she could interrupt he went on, "You tamed my hellion nieces to practically eat out of your hand, you reduced my mother to a quivering jelly, and you incited my poor-spirited sister-in-law to emulate your example."

Her expression arrested, she said, "Charlotte? What has Charlotte done?"

"She's demanding that I find her a husband so that she can set up her own establishment."

Zoë giggled. "Charlotte has more backbone than I gave her credit for. What . . . what did she say when she heard of our divorce?"

"Nothing, for the simple reason that no one knows that we are divorced. I told *my* family that you had conceived the insane notion of returning to

France to find *your* family."

"Oh. When do you intend to tell them?"

Never was what he was thinking. "In my own good time," he answered.

"I—I suppose everyone at the Abbey was happy to see the back of me?"

There was something in her voice, something in her look which gave Rolfe pause. And then it came to him. Zoë was not unmoved by the sentiments of the various members of his family.

Zoë was generous to a fault. They did not deserve her consideration, he was thinking, remembering the callous way they had received the news that she had run off to France. His nieces had merely bemoaned the fact that there was no one to teach them spells; his sister-in-law had expressed a faint regret before demanding a season in town so that she might find herself a husband; and his mother had positively smirked.

Their indifference to Zoë's fate had appalled him. The servants had shown more concern. And so he had told them, ranting and raving like a lunatic. It was no wonder, he had raged, that Zoë had run away from the Abbey when she found herself confined with so many unfeeling monsters. Didn't anyone care what happened to her?

She was waiting for his answer. The last thing he was going to do was hurt Zoë. "Why should you think they were glad to see the back of you?" he countered.

"Well, frankly, they didn't strike me as an affectionate lot. Please don't take that the wrong way," she hastened to add. "They're English. I presume that is why they are so . . . undemonstrative."

Ignoring the inadvertent slur, Rolfe said emphatically, "Until you were not there, they did not know how much the had come to depend on you."

"Truly?"

She was smiling, and Rolfe would have damned his own soul to keep that sweet smile in place. "Truly," he averred.

"What a whisker!" she retorted, and flounced to the piano. She was still smiling, touched that Rolfe could be so careful of her feelings. Her next thought sobered her. If he had truly cared about her feelings, he would not have taken up with all those women.

He noted the change in her expression. Without taking his eyes off her, he went through the motions of taking snuff. "What are you thinking?" he asked quietly.

She told him.

"So I sowed a few wild oats in my time," he said. "What of it? Once I took a wife to myself, I fully intended to give up my bachelor ways."

They had had this conversation before. Zoë understood what Rolfe was saying. Until their marriage was consummated, he had felt free to pursue other women. But their marriage had been consummated, and still . . .

"I saw you the week before I left England," she said. "I was staying with the Lagranges. Do you remember? I persuaded them to take me to Covent Garden. I was avidly curious to see your mistress. Rosamund. Wasn't it vulgar of me?" She swallowed before continuing. "She's very pretty, Rolfe, as is Roberta Ashton. Mrs. Ashton was good enough to invite me to her box during the interval."

332

Through set teeth, he said, "And I can well imagine what that viper said to you. But don't you see Zoë, those women belong in my past? God, why am I defending myself? Haven't I already told you that my affair with Roberta Ashton was over before I married you? And as for Rosamund, I went straight to her house and ended our liaison only hours after you truly became my wife."

"Then who was the woman you were kissing on the steps of Covent Garden?"

"What?"

"I saw you. So did Charles. On the steps of Covent Garden. The spectacle was quite amusing."

It came to him that Zoë must have seen him with the actress whose lover, Betrand, had died resisting arrest. He had been playing a part, pretending that he admired her, wanted her. Amy Granger was on the lookout for a rich protector. In point of fact, all Rolfe had wanted was information on Betrand's associates. The girl knew nothing. And still, a week later, *La Compagnie*'s assassins had gunned her down.

That thought made him harsher than he meant to be when he said, "Was this to be the pattern of our life together? Did you intend to kick up a dust every time I looked at another woman?"

"You haven't answered my question."

"Nor do I intend to! Believe what you will. You always do anyway."

"What I believe," said Zoë, distinctly, coldly, "is that we would have made each other miserable—you with your infidelities and I . . ."

". . . with your petty jealousies," he cut in brutally.

". . . abandoned to your mother's mercies," fin-

333

ished Zoë, equally brutal.

"What the hell has my mother got to say to anything?" be roared.

"Everything," she shot back. "Who do you think put me wise to you in the first place? Who do you think—" She cut herself off abruptly. It was not her intention to set Rolfe against his mother. It was not she who had to live with the woman.

"My mother told you about those women?" asked Rolfe incredulously.

"It makes no difference who told me," said Zoë. "We are no longer married, and there is no point to this conversation."

Rolfe's eyelashes dropped. "No," he agreed. After a pause, he went on carefully, "But should we change our minds anytime soon, as I've told you before, it would be a mere formality to have the divorce overturned."

"I don't think so," said Zoë, and giving him her back, she launched into Scarlatti.

Rolfe cupped his neck with his laced fingers and struck a negligent pose. His wife, he was reflecting, had a stubborn streak in her nature which was not apparent on first acquaintance. No. Nor on second, nor third acquaintance either. How had he ever come to believe that Zoë was as soft and malleable as a lump of butter?

It was because of her looks, he decided. She was small made, with delicate bones, and with a helpless way of looking at one from beneath those heavily fringed doe eyes which aroused a man's protective instincts. But Zoë wasn't soft, or malleable, or helpless. She was a resolute little thing, to which her slightly squared jaw gave evidence.

He'd forgotten about her temper, he thought, as the Scarlatti became more impassioned. And then he wasn't thinking about her temper. He was thinking about the fire he could arouse in her, and the soft, throbbing cries she made, before he brought her to climax. Purgatory, he reflected, must be something like this—to have the one thing one desired above all others within reach and, at the same time, beyond reach.

"Why were you laughing just now?" Zoë closed the piano lid and swung to face him.

If they were to have any kind of life together, there were fences that must be mended. He determined to make a start on them at once. "The irony of my situation amuses me. Don't you find it amusing?"

"I might if you explain yourself."

His manner and expression were devoid of all amusement when he leaned forward in his chair and said gravely, "For most of the time that we were wed, I was waiting for you to grow up, Zoë. Don't you see, you had me convinced in my own mind that you were younger than your years? For your sake, I had to keep you at a distance. Do you see what I am saying?"

"No," she said.

He sighed. "In its plainest terms, I am trying to tell you that those other women were merely a way of keeping *you* safe from *me*."

Her brows arched. "How thoughtful English husbands must be!" she said with so much sarcasm that Rolfe winced.

Gritting his teeth, Rolfe pushed on. "I was growing too fond of you. I tried to stay away. But everything changed the night you came to my bed. Since that night, I have held to our marriage vows—and don't throw that woman in my teeth, I beg you. It was only a kiss, nothing more."

He waited for her to respond. When she said nothing but stared at him with those great dark eyes of hers, he said softly, "Zoë, say you believe me."

"I believe you," she said.

"Good, obedient girl!"

That startled a laugh out of her.

"I like it when you laugh. You don't smile or laugh nearly enough. Do you know that?"

The smile left her face. "I smile when the occasion merits it," she said. "There's been little enough to smile about in the last little while."

She rose to her feet and made some excuse to leave the room. He let her go. He was making progress he told himself. She was coming to trust him. He wasn't the complete reprobate she made out that he was. Surely she must be coming to see that? Soon, she would confide everything to him. She would tell him about her brother and her involvement, such as it was, in *La Compagnie*. He would save them both, of course. And there was the faint possibility that he might also restore her sister to her. In a very short while, he hoped to rise in Zoë's estimation to the perch he had occupied once before.

They would all make their home with him in England where they would live happily ever . . . He stopped before his thoughts could complete the trite phrase. He almost combed his fingers through his hair before he remembered that he was wearing a wig. He swore vehemently. He was allowing himself to be swayed by his own wishes, not by logic. Zoë. She had yet to prove where her loyalties lay.

And yet, hadn't she proved her loyalty to him? She might easily have betrayed him to the French authorities or to her associates in *La Compagnie*. But there had been no move of any kind against him. Surely that said something about Zoë's character? Surely she must love him a little? He thought about the way she responded to his touch. His little Zoë loved him more than she was willing to admit. He would stake his life on it. A moment later, whistling, he quit the room.

On those occasions when Rolfe's presence was required at the Swedish embassy, Zoë was confined to the house. For the most part, she was pleased to obey him, having no wish to brave the salacious conversation of acquaintances who knew of her new lodger. She was, however, as firm as ever in her resolve to save Leon. And for this reason, she had to transfer funds to America and obtain false passports as soon as may be.

Rolfe was easily persuaded that there could be no harm in her calling on her friend, Francoise, or in consulting with her bankers to review her investments. And one fine afternoon in late May, Zoë set out, accompanied by Samson at Rolfe's insistence, to set things in motion for her flight to America.

The great banking house of Devereux stood on a corner opposite the Opera House. Its doors had been closed during the worst of the Terror and some months afterwards. Zoë could never forget that it was through the good offices of Charles Lagrange that her title to the largest share in Leon

Devereux's vast financial empire had been finally recognized.

That financial empire was substantially reduced since Britain and her allies had declared war on France. The Paris office was all that remained. Nevertheless, that one remaining branch was vigorous. Before Rolfe had forced his way into her life, Zoë had suggested to her directors that it was time for the branch to send out shoots. The New World was a fertile field.

She met with the chief director in his spacious office on the ground floor. It had once been her father's office. She tried not to let that thought color her thinking. Monsieur Colbet was not an interloper, she told herself firmly. He was merely a male with all the prejudices of a member of that sex for his opposite gender.

Once seated, Zoë wasted no time on the civilities. "When may we expect Devereux's to open a branch in America?" she asked pointedly.

She felt her heartbeat quicken as she waited for Colbet's reply. She knew by the suave smile on his plump cheeks that she was about to be treated to condescension and evasions. She did not know very much about banking. But she had learned a thing or two about bluffing in the last little while. She forced herself to a calm she was far from feeling.

"My dear lady," said Colbert with something close to amusement, "you have no notion of the negotiations which are necessary before we embark on such an enterprise. You don't suppose that the Americans are about to let us open up shop just like that, do you?" and he snapped his fingers under her nose.

Zoë flinched, but covered it well. "My dear Monsieur Colbet," she droned, mimicking his patronizing tone exactly, "if Paul Varlet endorses it, I don't see why Devereux's cannot do it."

At the mention of the financier's name, Colbet straightened. "Varlet?" he said.

Zoë inclined her head gravely. In a conversational tone she went on, "Paul has sometimes remarked that Devereux's is too conservative by half. We have been resting on our laurels, Monsieur Colbet, content with the status quo. If we are not careful, our competitors will forge ahead of us."

Since this little speech of Zoë's was remarkably similar in content to one that Monsieur Colbet had delivered to Devereux's directors a week since, her words were met with smiles.

Zoë, misunderstanding, played her trump card. "I don't mind telling you, Monsieur Colbet, that I have been toying with the idea of selling out to Paul Varlet." She gave a telling sigh. "He promises to treble my capital with very little difficulty. If there is one good reason why I should not sell to him, I wish you would tell me."

Monsieur Colbet could think of one very good reason which he did not divulge to Zoë. Varlet was a man who brooked no opposition. Maurice Colbet and all Devereux's directors could expect short shrift from the financier once he took hold of the reins.

There was a material shift in Monsieur Colbet's manner. He became flatteringly accommodating. Even so, Zoë was disappointed. Notwithstanding bribes and other incentives to highly placed officials, it was far from certain that the Americans would look with favor on any overt move by Devereux's.

The political climate was against it, so Monsieur Colbet explained. Investment in some business enterprise was a different matter, if it were done discreetly. Devereux's, he assured Zoë, was more than eager to establish itself in the New World.

They talked at some length on how best this might be accomplished. Zoë raised the problem of transferring some part of her personal funds to a relative in Boston who had fallen on hard times. Monsieur Colbet was happy to inform her that this was easily arranged.

As Colbet went off to take care of the matter for Zoë, she began to rethink her position. Devereux's was her brother's birthright. She had hoped to secure some part of it for him by opening a branch in America. It had not occurred to her that there might be a long delay before anything could be done.

Leon could not delay. He must set off for America at once. She was not forgetting what Leon had told her — that *La Compagnie* would wreak its vengeance on Leon's relatives should he break faith with them. If this were so, then she must go with him. They would have some capital, but no share in her father's bank unless it could be arranged once they were settled.

Her next thoughts were of Rolfe. He was a complete puzzle to her. On the one hand, he held her up to public ridicule by broadcasting that she was his mistress. On the other hand, he respected her scruples. She was not his mistress. They had separate chambers. What was he up to? she wondered. And why now, when it was too late, did he offer explanations for his past conduct? More than once he had mentioned that it was possible to overturn their divorce. She refused to entertain the hope that he was coming to love her. He would feel responsible for her. It was Rolfe's way. And she knew how Rolfe took care of his responsibilities. She would be sent to the Abbey.

In her mind's eye, she saw herself as Rolfe's wife, returning with him to England. She had a clear picture of the Abbey. For almost a full minute, she enjoyed the reverie. And then, she thought of her mother-in-law.

She was not the girl she had been when Rolfe had first set her down at the Abbey. She was more mature, more experienced, stronger. She would not retreat into herself if the dowager chose to challenge her now.

Shaking her head, she pulled herself up sharply. She was letting her imagination run away with her. Rolfe had not asked her to be his wife, and even if he should, she must think of Leon.

She had not told him of Leon. She did not have that right, just as she did not have the right to betray Rolfe's identity to Leon. In her own mind, she was free of the taint of deceit. She was doing her best to be loyal to them both.

For a moment or two, she gave into self-pity. She was so confused. It was all such a tangle—Rolfe, Leon, Claire, *La Compagnie,* Devereux's—and she did not know how it was to be unraveled. Hearing a step outside the door, she straightened her spine and swallowed her tears.

Monsieur Colbet returned with the intelligence that in due course, monies would be transferred by way of New Orleans to a bank of her choosing in

Boston in the name of one Raoul Devereux.

"It's rather a substantial sum," he remarked, making no attempt to disguise his curiosity.

"Raoul is my cousin," said Zoë evasively. "As I told you, his family has fallen on hard times."

There was only one more thing to be done before she took her leave of Monsieur Colbet. She allowed him to escort her to the door of his office, but stayed his hand when he made to open it.

"I wish to withdraw everything from my personal account and borrow against my next quarter's interest," she said.

She waited until he had recovered from the shock of her words before continuing, "And I'll take payment in gold, if you please, Monsieur Colbet."

"Gold?" Colbet was sure he had misheard her.

She gave him a sly smile and dropped her voice as though they were in a roomful of eavesdroppers. "Gold, Monsieur Colbet. I'm investing it with . . ." She bit her lip, and said helplessly, "It's a secret I'm not permitted to divulge. But payment must be made in gold."

Colbet escorted her to the front doors where her huge footman was stationed. He was remembering little Zoë from the old days when he had been no more than a clerk in her father's bank. Surprising himself, he voiced the thought that Zoë Devereux gave every evidence that one day she might fill her father's shoes.

Zoë gave him a startled look. She knew that he was mistaken, but saw no point in contradicting him. Her father had been as much a gambler as he'd been a financier. He'd enjoyed taking risks. She liked to play safe. One thing she did admit, however. For a girl who preferred a quiet life, she had traveled some very strange paths in the last little while.

A short time later, Charles Lagrange's thoughts ran along similar channels. There was a lot more to Zoë Devereux, he was thinking, than anyone would suppose from her demure, faintly diffident manner. In the short while that it took to drink one cup of coffee, she had secured a promise from him not only to supply her with false passports but also to inquire about passage on the first ship that was bound for America.

"I shall pay in gold," she had told him, and had named an exorbitant figure.

Clever, Lagrange had been thinking. In the first place, the sum was more than enough to cover expenses. His own share of the necessary bribes was generous. And in the second place, gold was a more acceptable currency in these days when paper money was daily losing its value.

He'd tried to quiz her to no effect. She refused to confide in him. Not that it mattered. He had a very good idea of what Zoë was up to.

Chapter Twenty-one

It was the last Thursday of the month, and the day on which Zoë regularly held her salon. As she mixed with her guests, her head was held proudly. Her gaze was clear. Only the death grip on her fan betrayed the turbulence of her emotions.

"Relax." The quiet command came from Rolfe. He was well aware of the reason for Zoë's tension, and just as aware that she wished nothing better than for a hole to open in the floor and swallow him up. "Few of this crowd will raise an eyebrow when they see us together. How should they? It would be a case of 'the pot calling the kettle black.'" He spoke the last few words in English.

Eyes snapping, Zoë turned on him. "For the love of God, keep your voice down!" Her eyes swept over the crush of people. "If anyone should hear you . . ."

Grinning, he baited, "Zoë, does this mean that you care?"

"Of course I care," she retorted without thinking, then quickly improvised. "If you are taken for a you-know-what, then I may be also."

He laughed, and, as if to test her patience to its limits, moved to join Jean Tallien, one of the Convention's foremost deputies. Tallien, Zoë observed, seemed to have fully recovered from the injuries he had received in an attempt on his life. She thought of her brother and hoped fervently that he had spared the deputy's life by design. She still could not reconcile her brother's character with what she had heard of the ruthless assassin, *Le Cache-Cache*.

The sound of Tallien's laughter diverted her thoughts. He and Rolfe, she noted, seemed to be on the friendliest terms. Zoë was not partial to Deputy Tallien. The blond Adonis was not yet thirty. At the height of the Terror, he had been Robespierre's man and one of the most bloodthirsty *enragés* of that tribe. In his turn he had fallen foul of Robespierre. Who could have foreseen that in that final confrontation, it was the master who would be toppled by his disciple? And now Tallien was so far to the right that he was suspected of Royalist sympathies. Monsieur Tallien, Zoë decided, was a man of many masks.

The deputy's wife caught her eye, and Zoë obediently answered the implicit invitation to join her. Theresia Tallien, like Zoë, was the daughter of a great banking family. At sixteen, she had been married to an aristocrat. She had fled Paris only to fall into Tallien's hands. Faced with the choice of the scaffold or life as Tallien's mistress, the beautiful young girl of eighteen had elected the lesser of the two evils. After Robespierre's fall from power, public opinion had forced Tallien to wed the girl.

In that moment, Zoë experienced a surge of intense resentment against men in general. Her face wore a polite smile, but inwardly she fumed against a creation where the male animal was so much more powerful than the female of the species. Women did not stand a chance against that most ruthless and rapacious predator of all God's creatures. How could God permit such a thing? There was no logic to it. It was unjust. It forced women to use their beauty, yes, and their sex, to sue for terms. She thought of her sister, Claire, and Theresia Tallien, and Joséphine de Beauharnais and a dozen other women who were present that evening, including herself, and she wanted to vent her fury. They were branded as fallen women. And yet, it was scarcely through choice that they had accepted some man's protection. And what was the point of this protection? Irony of ironies, it was to save them from the power of other men.

A fragment of conversation came back to her. Marie Roussillon, in the dormitory of the girls' school in Rouen, had wanted to know the meaning of *carte blanche*.

And Zoë had answered, "Some women sell their beauty and bodies for money. Not respectable women, you understand. Not the kind of women gentlemen marry, but the other sort."

And she was now lumped with "the other sort." She made up her mind that from that moment on she would never again judge the morals of any woman, whatever the circumstances. It was men who were responsible for making these distinctions between women, and women who were stupid enough to accept them. When her eyes chanced to brush Rolfe's, she made no attempt to shade the depths of her reproach.

"What the deuce . . . ?" Rolfe scowled, and his eyes raked the people on either side of Zoë. He was almost sure that someone had slighted his wife. He was furious and half-rose in his chair, intending to go to her to give her his support. In his hearing, no one dared to make slighting observations to Zoë, else there would be hell to pay. Another long look from Zoë stayed the impulse to fly to her defense.

It was he who was the object of her spleen. Rolfe smothered the small pang of conscience which Zoë's damning look had kindled. She was ashamed to be known as any man's mistress. He mentally absolved himself of all reproach. The blame lay entirely at Zoë's door. From the very first he had wished only to take care of little Zoë. Hadn't he married her to give her the protection of his name? She had chosen to throw off the mantle of his protection. A man who permitted his wife to direct her own course was no man by his lights. One day Zoë would thank him for the means he was forced to employ to keep her safe from her own folly.

Conscious that Zoë was casting another killing look in his direction, Rolfe averted his head and gave his attention to the conversation of his companions.

Deputy Tallien and Charles Lagrange were discussing the recent unrest which had swept Paris. Mobs had descended on the Convention, demanding bread and the implementation of the '93 constitution. The Convention had declared that Paris was a city under siege. The army had been called out to restore order. Thousands of *sans-culottes*, the instigators of the riots, had been thrown in prison. The prison populations, mostly *sans-culottes* and former supporters of Robespierre, were terrified, and with good reason.

In the provinces, particularly in the south, a new wave of Terror had broken out. The White Terror it had come to be called. Fanatical extremists of the Right, avowed Royalists, were exacting a terrible retribution on those who had carried out Robespierre's policies. Groups of assassins belonging to diverse secret societies were hunting down their former persecutors and summarily executing them. In several towns, hundreds of prisoners were massacred in their cells or in the courtyards of the prisons. Anarchy was the order of the day, and it was creeping closer to Paris.

"God knows where it will all end," bemoaned Lagrange.

"A little blood-letting was to be expected," said Tallien. "Some good may come of it yet." At Lagrange's pained expression, Tallien laughed. "Look at it this way, Monsieur Lagrange: those White Terrorists are doing the rest of us a favor. They are meting out justice to the rats who have disappeared into their holes. That *Cache-Cache* fellow — the one who tried to murder me? It wouldn't surprise me one whit if his days are numbered. One informer, that's all it takes, and the White Terror will descend like an avalanche on that pack of dogs."

"I presume you are referring to the members of that sect . . . I forget the name," drawled Rolfe.

"*La Compagnie*," supplied Tallien.

"But what if an innocent man is informed against?" interposed Lagrange. "I say that law and order must prevail. Justice must be seen to be done."

Tallien shrugged philosophically. "So a few innocent victims pay with their blood. What of it? It's cheap at the price if France is purged of that *canaille*, that scum of our society."

Lagrange could not disguise his distaste for these sentiments. "Monsieur Ronsard," he said, "you are a foreign diplomat. Your views must be without prejudice. What think you of recent events in France?"

348

"What I think," said Rolfe, "is that Royalists abroad must surely think that the tide is turning in their favor."

"You think that a Royalist army will land in France?" asked Tallien sharply.

Rolfe's attention was momentarily diverted as a young *muscadin*, a member of the *jeunesse dorée*, engaged Zoë in a private *tête-à-tête*. They had moved a little apart from the crush, to one of the window alcoves.

His eyes trained on Zoë, Rolfe murmured, "It's possible, but not likely to happen as long as the Dauphin lives." Since the rumor was rife that the young Louise XVII, as he was known abroad, was failing in health, neither of Rolfe's companions took comfort from his answer.

As they embarked on an argument on the merits of releasing the boy king from his incarceration in one of the gloomiest prisons in Paris to permanent exile abroad, Rolfe gave himself up to contemplating his wife and her companion.

Over her shoulder, Zoë flashed Rolfe a furtive glance. She was shaking like a leaf, and expected any moment to hear someone denounce her companion as that most wanted of all criminals, *Le Cache-Cache*.

Her tone low and vibrating, she exclaimed, "You were mad to come here like this! I never thought, I never dreamed that you would take such risks. You must leave at once! Do you hear?"

"I am going nowhere," said Leon Devereux truculently, "until you give me the satisfaction of an answer. You are my sister, Zoë, and under my protection. I could not credit it when I heard that you had accepted the *carte blanche* of some doddering old foreigner. Tell me it is not so."

Zoë wrung her hands. Ignoring her brother's moot question, she implored, "Please, Leon, be reasonable. You are only a boy and . . ." She shrank under the fire from those flashing dark eyes. In a more conciliating tone, she offered, "Monsieur Ronsard is a guest in this house, nothing more."

Leon's gaze swept the telling color which crept across Zoë's cheekbones. His lips tightened. A moment before, Zoë's fears had been all for her brother, an automatic response, a relic from childhood days. She was struck afresh by the realization that this fierce young warrior commanding respect bore little resemblance to the brother she remembered. Her fears, she realized, should be all for Rolfe. From the corner of her eye, she saw Rolfe rise to his feet. He began to limp in her direction. Her nerves were stretched taut.

In desperation more than in fury, she rounded on Leon. "How dare you sit in judgment on me!" she hissed, and for good measure, she added venomously, *"Le Cache-Cache!* By your presence here, you jeopardize not only your own life, but mine also. For the love of God, go before it's too late."

"I'm not afraid," he said with so much arrogance that Zoë had to quell the rising hysteria.

With forced calm, she implored, "Look, this is not the time nor place for explanations. You must go."

"Then meet me in the boathouse tonight when everyone has gone home."

"No," she quickly interjected. "It's too dangerous." Rolfe's suspicions, she was sure, were thoroughly aroused. He would be watching her like a hawk watches an unwary wood pigeon. Her eyes locked on him. As he slowly advanced towards her, he was delayed as first one person then another stopped to exchange a few words with him.

"A week," she said, "in another week, everything will be arranged." She was thinking of the passports she had yet to procure from Charles Lagrange. "A week tonight, I shall meet you when everyone has retired for the night. Now go, please, before you are discovered!"

Without waiting for Leon's reply, she spun away from him. Intent on creating a diversion, she moved quickly to the piano. A moment later, a gong sounded, signaling that Zoë was ready to begin her recital. Her guests scarcely had time to make their way to their places before their hostess launched into a piece by her favourite composer.

Lounging with lazy grace against a plaster pillar, Rolfe listened absently to his wife's spirited rendition of Scarlatti. The young man with whom Zoë had been in heated conversation had melted into the throng. Without haste, Rolfe scanned the faces of his wife's rapt audience. At Zoë's salons, so he had been given to understand, there was always quite a following of the *jeunesse dorée*. With their uniforms of squared skirt coats, tight pantaloons, and braided hair, it was almost impossible to distinguish one from the other. But *he* was no longer there. Rolfe was almost sure of it. His wife's brow was too tranquil, her smile too radiant not to be genuine, and a far cry from the look of strain which had pinched her features when she was in conversation with the young *muscadin*. Rolfe's eyes were as gray as the North Sea when they finally came to rest on Zoë.

* * * *

One of Zoë's guests, known in *La Compagnie* only as *Le Patron,* surveyed the beautiful young woman who played the piano so passionately. But behind the absorbed stare, a mind was actively at work.

La Compagne had served its usefulness, *Le Patron* was thinking. The writing was on the wall. The White Terror, the failing health of the young Dauphin, the almost certain threat of Royalist invasion — these circumstances made the society's position precarious in the extreme. There was a new climate in France. *La Compangie* and all its members were doomed to be hounded down and ruthlessly exterminated.

There was another, more compelling reason to be troubled about *La Compagnie. Le Patron*'s eyes unerringly found the Swedish diplomat. The Englishman, *Le Patron* was thinking, was confident to a degree. His disguise was easily penetrated once one knew that he was not who he pretended to be.

The man was Zoë's divorced husband. He was also the man who had blown the operation in England sky-high. He'd been dealt with — or so *Le Patron* had thought at the time. And now the Englishman had turned up in Paris.

Once apprised of the man's identity, a number of things came sharply into focus, among them the failed attempt on Deputy Tallien's life. *Le Cache-Cache* was not having the success that he had once enjoyed, and *Le Patron* was coming to suspect that the society had been infiltrated. Of late, all its moves had been checked. In the interests of self-preservation it had become necessary to sacrifice *La Compagnie.*

Le Patron smiled, thinking that in a very short while

the authorities would be congratulating themselves on having completely routed the most dreaded secret society in existence. They would not be satisfied, of course, until they had tracked down the prime mover of the whole enterprise. *Le Patron* had no intention of being caught in their net. No. It was necessary to set things up in such a way that all suspicion was averted from the real leader of the society.

Already, things had been set in motion. In the next few days, the only members of the society who were in a position to point a finger at *Le Patron,* that is, the section heads, would be systematically eliminated. It was a ploy *Le Patron* had used in London with some success. Nothing was left to chance. No one must be able to tie *Le Patron* to the society.

With the demise of *La Compagnie,* a lucrative business would be shut down. Murder, *Le Patron* had discovered, was a paying proposition. And *La Compagnie* had made an excellent cover. Those who paid to have an "obstacle" removed from their path were assured that not a breath of suspicion would touch upon them. How should it? All the evidence was carefully laid out to point to *La Compagnie.*

Le Patron reflected that there was little regret in having to relinquish this lucrative trade. It was time and enough to retire with all the wealth which had accumulated. But before that day arrived, all the loose ends must be tied up. And this time, there must be no errors. *Le Patron,* personally, would see to it.

Before the week was out, all Paris was buzzing with the report that the Committee of Public Safety had flushed out those subversives who were members of *La Compagnie*. Those who did not die resisting arrest were quietly though quickly executed with no questions asked. Few escaped.

Rolfe's first thought was that Housard, before time, had deliberately passed on the information they had painstakingly garnered to Deputy Tallien.

"Why should I do that?" asked Housard.

"Wasn't that the plan? Once our work was done, you were going to turn informer?"

"Our work isn't done, leastways it wasn't until this happened. We are no nearer knowing who *Le Patron* is than ever we were."

"Then if you didn't inform against them, who did?"

They were resting their horses in the Bois de Boulogne at the top of a rise overlooking the river. Rolfe's mount was nervous, reflecting the tension which gripped his rider.

Housard's eyes squinted into the sun. He stood in his stirrups as if the view out over the Seine was of supreme interest. Without shifting his gaze, he said, "I don't know who the informer is, but I could hazard a guess."

"*Le Patron* himself," said Rolfe dryly.

A slow smile touched Housard's lips. "So," he said, "I'm to be let off the hook, am I?"

Almost reluctantly, Rolfe allowed, "On reflection, I admit I was too hasty in my judgment."

"I should say so." Housard turned in the saddle. His look was long and direct. "I gave you my word that I would do nothing until you had Zoë safely away."

"And her brother also," said Rolfe quickly.

"I'm sorry about the boy. His fate does not look

promising. My advice to you is to forget about him and leave France as soon as may be."

"That's all very well for you to say," answered Rolfe grimly. "You don't know my wife. Nothing will budge Zoë until she knows what has happened to her brother." He fell silent for a moment or two, then asked in a more normal one. "You've heard nothing of the boy?"

"Nothing. He seems to have vanished off the face of the earth."

"He's in hiding, then?"

"It would seem so."

"And desperately in need of friends." Abruptly, Rolfe asked, "What happens now? What are your plans?"

Housard took a moment before replying, *"La Compagnie* is finished. Out task is done. On the whole, we have accomplished what we set out to do."

For a long interval, there was a silence as both gentlemen reflected on their conversation. Finally, Rolfe said, "He's outwitted us. This is all his doing. We were closing in for the kill. He must have suspected as much."

"If so, he's got clean away just like the last time. Who is left to point a finger at him?"

Rolfe scanned his companion's expression. "Somehow, Monsieur Housard, I did not think that you would give up so easily."

"I haven't given up, or at least, only temporarily. One day, information will come my way, another piece of the puzzle will fall into place, and I'll have my man."

"Meanwhile, *Le Patron* gets off scot-free?"

"As I said before, who is left to identify him? Unless . . ."

"Yes?"

"I was thinking of *Le Cache-Cache,* but even if we find the boy first, it's not likely that he'll be able to help us. In all probability, he has no more idea of who *Le Patron* is than we do."

At the mention of Zoë's brother, a frown pleated Rolfe's brow. "She'll try and get to him, or he'll come to her. Nothing is more certain."

"Then get her away now, man, before that happens."

"It's not so easily done," said Rolfe. "Zoë would never agree to it, and if I tell her all I know, she might be panicked into doing something foolish."

"She already has," answered Housard dryly. "Haven't I already told you about the gold and the passports she has procured?"

At the mention of this sensitive subject, Rolfe's face darkened. "I'm indebted to Deputy Tallien for passing on that piece of information," he remarked formally.

"Yes, it pays to have friends in high places. Still, if he finds *Le Cache-Cache* before we do, nothing will save him. Since the assassination attempt, Tallien has been out for the boy's blood."

"You're sure that no one is watching the house?"

"Quite sure."

"Then it would seem that the authorities have no notion that *Le Cache-Cache* and Leon Devereux are one and the same person. That's something, at least."

"They are hunting for someone they know as Louis Reubell."

After a moment's consideration, Rolfe said, "Bear with me for a little while longer, Monsieur Housard.

I understand that our work here is virtually over. But I hope that I may call on your resources to help me solve the problem of my wife's brother."

"How much longer?"

"A week. No more."

Without prevarication, Housard answered, "You have it. But I warn you, to delay longer is to place your own life in jeopardy. I am not the only one who is remarkably well informed. *Le Patron* must also have his sources."

Darkness shrouded the house and gardens. An unnatural silence pressed heavily about. The night was humid. A storm was brewing. The sweet fragrance of herbs was distilled in the air.

Zoë hesitated, her back pressed against the door through which she had just exited. Gradually, her breathing evened; her eyes accustomed themselves to the velvety blackness. For a moment or two, a shaft of moonlight illumined the stand of beeches leading down to the boathouse before heavy cloud obscured the view.

Like a creature of the wild alert to every peril, she remained frozen, poised for flight, forcing herself to a calm she could scarcely sustain. Her fears were not easily quelled. This past week, she was reflecting, was one of the most harrowing she had ever endured in her entire life.

It had begun with the report which had swept through Paris. The Committee of Public Safety had smashed that most feared of all secret societies, *La Compagnie,* and its members were either dead or on the run. Rumor was rife. Some maintained that that glamorous figure, *Le Cache-Cache,* had already been executed but the authorities were keeping it quiet in the interests of public safety. Others confidently predicted that *Le Cache-Cache* was merely in hiding and would emerge to wreak a terrible vengeance on his persecutors. And though desperate to know more, Zoë had compelled herself to act the part of a disinterested observer, concealing her fears for Leon behind a mask of polite interest, and never more so than when Rolfe's eyes came to rest upon her.

He was watchful. More than once she had surprised a brooding look in his eyes before he had time to veil his expression. There was a new constraint between them. Conversation was difficult. His manner was unpredictable, veering from solicitous to downright dictatorial. And always, he was there, by her side, a stern and forbidding presence.

She shivered, feeling suddenly cold, and she drew her lightweight cloak more securely about her person. Nerves, she thought. As one day had slipped into the next and no sign or word from Leon, her nerves had been stretched taut. And the contretemps which had taken place that very evening at Madame Tallien's salon had almost shattered her fragile control.

A duel. There was to be a duel between Rolfe and Tresier, and Zoë could still not determine what had led to this new catastrophe.

Rolfe had taken her into supper and, as ill chance would have it, they were joined by Varlet and Tresier. All was politeness, as far as she was aware. And as the gentlemen had conversed, she had become absorbed in her own thoughts, toying with the delicacies on her plate.

Suddenly conscious that Rolfe was bristling, she raised her head. Tresier, it seemed, had made a remark to which Rolfe took exception. Tresier refused to apologize. Suddenly all three gentlemen were on their feet. Without warning, Tresier threw his glass of wine in Rolfe's face.

A petrifying silence seemed to grip the whole room. Rolfe's smile was unlike any Zoë had ever seen on him before. It chilled her bones to the very marrow. His voice, when he spoke, was equally terrifying. She didn't have to look into his eyes to know that they would have taken on a silver glitter.

"Name your seconds," said Rolfe, breaking that electrifying silence.

Something moved in Tresier's eyes, and Zoë knew that, for all his bravado, the young man was deathly afraid. So was she, for both of them.

Desperately, almost ill with fear, she tried to avert the catastrophe. But nothing she said made the least difference. Tresier had insulted her. And though she insisted that she had not taken offense, honor must be satisfied.

Later, both gentlemen denied that their little quarrel was of any significance. Everyone knew that dueling wasn't permitted. They had settled their differences amicably, they gave out. No one believed them, least of all Zoë. Paul Varlet's self-satisfied smile gave the game away. There was to be a duel, and Zoë had yet to think of a way to put a stop to it.

She could not think of that now. Leon, she hoped, would be waiting for her in the boathouse. It was the night they had arranged to meet during her salon. As she glided towards the path which led to the river, she tried to force from her mind the conviction that only injury or death would keep her brother from their rendezvous.

She felt for the key to the boathouse under a stone crock by the door. It was missing. "Leon?" she whispered, and pushed inside.

"Shut the door," came the terse reply, and Zoë made haste to do as she was bid.

Out of the darkness loomed a tall shadow. "When did you get to be so tall?" she asked, and sobbing with relief, she slipped her arms around her brother's waist, and rested her head against his chest.

"Careful," he said, wincing, "I took a fall. My shoulder has been acting up again."

"I did not know if you would be here," she whispered, her throat aching with tears. "I've suffered agonies."

"Forgive me, Zoë. I did not know where else to turn. This last week . . ." He faltered, shook his head and said, almost savagely, "God forgive me for involving you, but you are my last hope. Someone has betrayed me. They know all my usual haunts. Everywhere I go, they are waiting for me. Thank God they know me only as Louis Reubell, else they would be waiting for me here also."

"Darling, it's all right," she soothed. "It's all right. You are safe now."

He was *hors la loi,* an outlaw, and by helping him, that made her one too. She could find no justification for the path he had chosen. At the same time, he was her brother. The rights and wrongs of what she was doing might escape her. But Zoë knew her duty. It was more than duty. It was love that guided her. And where Zoë loved, she would brave the wrath of the gods if necessary. The laws of France seemed insignificant in comparison.

In a low tone, she embarked on an explanation of the steps she had taken in preparation for their flight to America. Everything had been arranged, she told him. She had procured false passports. They would have to book passage for America once they reached Bordeaux. There should be no difficulty there, since French ships regularly plied the ocean between Bordeaux and New Orleans and there were often American ships in the harbor. She had enough gold to pay for their passage and to take care of their needs for a long time to come.

When she came to the end of her recitation, Leon gave a disbelieving laugh. "Good God!" he exclaimed. "Is this the little Zoë who, last time I saw her, scarcely knew how to tie the bows of her bonnet under her chin? How did you get to be so grown up?"

She shrugged off the good-natured cajolery. "I grew up in haste when you and Claire were not there to look out for me," she answered.

"Poor Zoë," he said, and touched a hand to her cheek. "You've done well."

"Thank you."

"When do we leave?"

"Soon . . . very soon. There are still a few things I need to arrange. In a day or so, everything should be set."

Something in her voice alerted him. "You do intend to come with me?" he asked.

Her hesitation was barely noticeable. "Of course."

Leon noticed it. His voice expressionless, he said, "You're thinking of him, aren't you — your protector?"

"Yes." When Leon said nothing, she went on, "I

love him, you see. But you needn't think that I shall remain with him. It's better for everyone if I go with you." And very much afraid that she was on the point of losing her control altogether, she forced herself to turn to more prosaic matters.

Though Leon was against the suggestion, fearing that detection would lead to Zoë's certain arrest, he was finally persuaded to return to the house and hide himself in the attics. It wasn't Zoë's logic that decided him, but the thread of hysteria which underscored her words.

There was nothing more to say. Zoë was the first to leave the boathouse. Leon was only a step behind. The door creaked as it closed. Leon carefully locked the door and slipped the key into its hiding place. He straightened just as someone stepped out of the shadows.

Rolfe's voice came to them, chilled and rigid with anger. "You must be Zoë's brother. *Le Cache-Cache,* I presume?"

And before Zoë had gathered her wits, Leon had launched himself at the bigger man, his short leaded stick making a vicious arc in the air.

Zoë gasped as she heard the crack, then cried out in relief when she realized that Rolfe had brought up his walking cane to ward off the blow.

Panting, grunting, the two men went at each other like demons. Zoë circled them, crying out for them to stop. "Rolfe! Leon! For the love of God! Oh please! Don't do this!"

Neither man paid her the least heed. In desperation, with some obscure notion of protecting the one who lost the contest, she reached for one of the paddles which leaned against the side of the boathouse.

And then she heard it. The sickening thud against flesh and bone as a blow struck its mark, and almost immediately afterwards, the groan of someone in acute pain.

One man, obviously the victor, was crouched over his felled opponent. In the dim light, Zoë could not make out who was who.

Sobbing, she raised the paddle and brought it down smartly, meaning only to knock the wind out of the victor. Her aim went wild. It hit the man on the side of his head.

"Oh forgive me, forgive me," Zoë sobbed out, and dropped the paddle.

Her words were the last thing Rolfe heard before he slipped into darkness.

Rolfe moved ...... to converse with him, Zoë ...
miserable ...... silence. She gasped when h ...
...... great ... surprise, th ...

Chapter Twenty-two

Rolfe lost consciousness for only a few minutes. But it was time enough for Léon to slip away. As he shook his head to clear his dazed senses, Rolfe could hear Zoë above him, muttering to herself. It registered that she was bathing his face with a wet kerchief. Since the threatening storm had finally broken, and the rain was pelting down in buckets, soaking him, her attempts to relieve his distress were scarcely appreciated.

Batting her hand away, he let out a roar of rage. "You damn well tried to murder me!" If she had shot at him with a pistol, he could not have felt more betrayed.

Zoë sat back on her heels. "It was an accident," she said contritely. "The paddle slipped."

"He won't get away, you know," he said savagely, suddenly remembering his assailant. "I have men posted at every exit." And as if to add weight to his words, shouts and sounds of a struggle came from farther along the riverbank.

"Oh God!" wept Zoë. "What are you going to do with him?"

Rolfe sprang to his feet, looming over her like a great beast of prey. A man came running up and

Rolfe moved aside to converse with him. Zoë sat in miserable, sodden silence. She gasped when Rolfe reached down and swung her into his arms.

"What I'm going to do with your brother," said Rolfe sternly, "is take him back to England. It's yourself you should be afraid for, not that misguided boy!"

Forked lightning streaked across the sky, turning night into day. Rolfe's features, hard, forbidding, looked as if they might have been etched in stone. A peal of thunder directly overhead made the earth and air vibrate alarmingly. Zoë threw her arms around Rolfe's neck.

"I'm afraid of storms," she mewed in his ear, pressing herself into the shelter of his body.

Rolfe cursed and made rapidly for the house, hugging Zoë to him.

Once in her chamber, he threw her none too gently on the bed, then went to light a candle. They were both soaked to the skin.

"Strip out of those wet things," he snarled at her.

Zoë was not sure whether she was more afraid of the tempest which raged outside or the tempest which raged inside the quivering towering man who seemed to dwarf her chamber. Round eyed, she made haste to do his bidding.

Though she knew that it was not the time to argue with him, her fears for Leon could not be stayed. "I don't understand," she said. "What has my brother to do with you? Why should you wish to take him to England?"

She was down to her lacy underthings, and made no attempt to remove them. Rolfe had no hesitation in peeling out of his wet garments. With quick, angry movements he stripped to the skin. He found a towel and began to dry himself vigorously. All traces of the elderly Monsieur Ronsard seemed to vanish before Zoë's eyes.

As a specimen of the male animal, her former husband was splendid, Zoë acknowledged. That blond hair, those broad shoulders, sleek muscles, lithe movements—as her eyes devoured him, her breath quickened. So much masculine power, she hoped, would not be let loose against her own puny person.

"Didn't you hear me?" he barked, startling her. "I told you to get out of those wet things."

A flash of lightning, a clap of thunder coming almost simultaneously, acted on her like the lash of a whip. In a matter of seconds, she was naked and drying herself off with the towel Rolfe had thrown at her.

"You still haven't answered my question," she pointed out as inoffensively as she could make the rebuke.

Rolfe tied a fresh towel around his waist and turned to scowl at her. What he wanted to say was that he was taking her brother to England to hang him as a spy. But even though his temper was at boiling point and his wife deserved to suffer some of the agonies *he* had been made to suffer, he could not voice the lie. Strangely, his reluctance to hurt Zoë tested his temper to the limits.

"You need not fear for your brother's life," he snarled viciously. "And before you voice one more untruth let me tell you that I know everything there is to know about his involvement with *La Compagnie*.

In England, he'll be given sanctuary. I give you my word. But as for you, my girl . . ." He let the unsaid words hang threateningly on the air.

The threat did not register with Zoë. Leon would come to no harm. Rolfe had said so. She believed him. And suddenly, the weight of the whole world seemed to have lifted from her shoulders. Rolfe had taken command. And she could only wonder at herself for not confiding in him sooner.

Her thoughts brought a smile to her lips, and Rolfe, noting it, exploded into wrath. "Damn you, Zoë! Your blow might have killed me! But you knew that, didn't you?"

She could no longer doubt that Rolfe was in a towering temper. He had every right to be, she silently allowed. But that he should think that she had tried, deliberately, to do him an injury hurt her to the quick.

"The paddle slipped out of my hands," she said imploringly. And because his scowling face unnerved her, for something to do, she reached for her nightrail.

Rolfe snatched the filmy garment out of her reach. Slowly turning to face him, she tensed for what was to come.

Reading her wide-eyed look correctly, Rolfe smirked. "You're afraid of me," he said nastily, "and you damn well ought to be."

She tried reasoning with him. "Rolfe, remember that you are an English gentleman." There was no softening in that hard look. Desperate, Zoë fell back on flattery. "An English gentleman, Rolfe! There is no higher praise you can aspire to. Everyone knows that the English are kind to weaker creatures." And by her whole demeanor she tried to convey that she must surely be a prime candidate for that protected species.

One foot on the floor, one knee braced on the bed, he crouched over her. Zoë inched away. "And what word of wisdom do you have for a betrayed husband?" he demanded through set teeth.

"B—betrayed?"

"I know it all! Passports! Gold! America!" His voice increased in volume. "Damn you, Zoë! You were making plans to run away from me again."

Zoë had sometimes witnessed Rolfe in a temper. But never like this. He was shaking from the force of his emotions. She licked her dry lips. There was something primitive here that she had not quite grasped, something to do with the sexes. She did not think it was the moment to point out that she had divorced him and was therefore free to order her own life to suit herself.

As if responding to her unvoiced thoughts, Rolfe went on in the same implacable tone, "You are my woman, my wife, do you understand? That divorce of yours holds no brief in England. You still belong to me. And what belongs to me, I keep. I permit no one to come between us, not Tresier, not your brother, and least of all you, yourself."

There was a blooming of something deep inside her. For a moment, she forgot her fear. "Can it be true?" she whispered. "Are we still wed?"

Mistaking the meaning of her shocked stare, Rolfe became even more nettled. His look became fiercer, his voice more menacing. "I've been too lenient with

368

you," he raged. "I see that now. You have no respect for me, treating me as less than a pet dog. But no more. I tried to tame you with love, and failed. So be it. If you cannot love me, than you will learn to fear me. I admit I had hoped for so much more from you. But you're not willing to give an inch. To earn your trust and love a man would have to be a blessed saint."

She had hurt him. The thought was so fleeting that it was gone before she had time to examine it. "Rolfe, you are frightening me," she cried out, and gave him her most piteous look. She wasn't acting. She really was afraid of this stranger.

"Don't try that little-girl act with me," he snapped, and braced one arm on either side of her head. "Those tactics may have served you in the past. But I'm wise to you now. You're not going to get off scot-free this time."

Gingerly, Zoë touched her fingers to the bunched muscles of his arms, trying to restrain him. "Rolfe," she cried out, "don't hurt me!"

"Hurt you!" He pulled back to study her face. "When have I ever hurt you? Damn your eyes, Zoë, for saying such things to me!"

"Then . . . then if you are not going to beat me, what is the point of all this?"

"The point," said Rolfe viciously, "is that you will learn once and for all who is the master here! In the past, I've held back. God, can you believe that? Your scruples kept me at bay." He laughed unpleasantly. "I thought you were fragile. Fragile! You're as strong as tempered steel. But you'll learn to bend to me, my girl. You'll bend or I'll break you in the attempt."

369

Finally, everything was clear to Zoë. Malelike, Rolfe meant to demonstrate his power over her in that most intimate act of conjugal life. He had chosen the marriage bed as his battle ground.

"Rolfe," she said desperately, "you're not yourself."

"The hell I'm not! You brought this on yourself, Zoë. If you don't like the man I have become, you have only yourself to blame."

Rolfe bent to his task. Zoë moved to thwart him. As his lips brushed one hardening nipple, gasping, she threaded her fingers through his hair, and dragged his head back.

"Don't be stupid," he said roughly. "If you fight me you'll only get hurt."

"You fool!" she hissed. "What you are doing is hurting us both."

He wasn't in the humor to listen to her. He was too intent on teaching her a lesson. Every nerve in his body quivered in outraged masculine pride. She had betrayed his trust, and it would be a very long time indeed before he would forgive or forget her transgressions.

"I won't allow you to do this," said Zoë.

It was the wrong thing to say. In answer, Rolfe laughed and sprawled on top of her, holding her down with his weight. "Do your worst," he taunted, "and see where it gets you."

Anger flamed through Zoë. Bucking, twisting, rolling, heaving, she tried everything to dislodge him. Nothing worked. She was like a child in his grasp. He simply held her by the wrists, both arms over her head, until she was breathless with her struggles. When she quieted, he bent to her again.

He pressed his lips to hers and stifled her protests with fierce kisses. Again and again his tongue forged into her mouth, forcing her to accept his invasion of her body.

"Not like this," she whispered at one point.

"Then give in to me."

She glared up at him in silent defiance.

His smile was bitter. Slowly, deliberately, he brought his lips to the dark peak of one breast. "So sensitive," he said hoarsely. "Engorged. Wanting me. See?"

The touch of his tongue sent a jolt of sensual heat from her nipples to her loins. She bit back a moan. He closed his lips over one swelling crest, sucking gently, then hard. This time she could not choke back the little throbbing cry of pleasure. Slowly, surely, he edged her towards a delirium of desire. She was no longer fighting him. He freed her wrists.

He rained kisses from her throat, down, down, over the soft swell of her belly to the secret place between her thighs. "Open your legs for me, sweetheart," he said thickly.

"No!" panted Zoë. "No."

"Yes!" he contradicted. "I've held off before now because I thought you were too much the innocent! After tonight, we'll both know that every inch of you belongs to me." And he positioned her limbs just as he wanted. His head dipped, and his mouth and tongue touched the secret core of her femininity, moving delicately to claim her.

Every kiss, every caress, every movement was calculated to make her his slave, and he told her so. In that moment, Zoë did not care. She could barely

371

breathe. Her body was a mass of riotous sensation.

Restlessly, feverishly, she moved beneath him, crying out for the torment to end. Even then, when he brought himself fully into her, his control was ruthlessly maintained. He moved slowly, deliberately making her follow the rhythm he wanted, making her aware of his power over her. Words could not have told her more plainly that he was the master and would accept nothing less than her complete surrender. He was torturing her, refusing to give her the rhythm she needed to assuage the hollow ache deep inside. She clung to him, and let him have his way. Only when he felt her relinquish everything to him, did he give her what they both wanted. And the storm that he unleashed was scarcely eclipsed by the storm outside their window as it ferociously played itself out.

Afterwards, he lay in lazy contentment, his arm hooked loosely around Zoë's waist. It took some minutes before he realized that his wife was unnaturally quiet.

"Zoë?" he queried, his blue eyes gleaming his satisfaction. He had no idea that the smile which turned up his lips was blatantly smug, blatantly male.

Throwing his arm off, Zoë wrenched herself round, sitting at the edge of the bed with her back to him. His hands clamped on her shoulders, preventing her escape.

"Zoë!" he chided softly, and he pressed his lips to every vertebrae on her spine. "It was good. You know it was good. Tell me I did not shock you."

"You did not shock me. You shamed me."

He dragged her round to face him, one hand cupping her neck. Anxiously, his eyes scanned her face. "What nonsense is this?" he asked. "I did not shame you."

"You said that you would prove that you were the master, and you did."

"Oh that!" he said carelessly. He smiled and forced her back against the pillows, nuzzling her throat. "Sometimes, my little ignoramus, a man needs to prove himself to the woman he loves, do you see?"

"No," she said, and pursed her lips in that peculiar way which warned her intimates that little Zoë had turned mulish.

Rolfe kissed those pursed lips.

No response.

This was serious. "Zoë, sweetheart," he cajoled, "it happens sometimes that a man feels . . . well . . . less than a man when his woman thwarts him at every turn." His hands brushed over her bare arms, gentling her.

"And *that* made you feel more of a man?" demanded Zoë, half credulous, half querulous.

"Infinitely," averred Rolfe, and this time he was aware that the smile which turned up his lips was blatantly male. "You made me feel ten feet tall. Your response to me is what I mean. I touch you, and you go up in flames. You can deny me nothing. Bed is the one place where I feel absolutely sure of you. It's a heady feeling, kitten. So much of the time I feel like a doormat and that you are walking all over me."

Zoë sniffed derisively.

"What?" asked Rolfe.

"You were angry," she said. "You wanted to punish me."

"Punishment was the farthest thing from my mind," protested Rolfe.

"But you were angry."

"Only until you gave into me."

She pounced on that. "There! You see? 'Slave' you called me! 'Slave'!" And her face and voice registered her feminine outrage.

Inwardly, Rolfe groaned. "I said that in the heat of passion. It's a sort of . . . you know . . . masculine fantasy. It doesn't mean a thing."

"A masculine fantasy?" echoed Zoë, wrinkling her nose.

"Yes," said Rolfe, not quite meeting her eye.

"Mmmm."

There followed an interval of silence before Rolfe was moved to say, rather defensively, "I rarely indulge that particular fantasy, kitten—only when I'm at my wit's end and you are at your most truculent. You must own that this time you went your length. You are my wife. It would be nice to know that, even if you cannot give me your esteem, you will respect my wishes where they touch on your conduct, if only for your own safety."

She looked deep into his eyes, startled by his choice of words. "How can you possibly think that you do not have my esteem?"

His voice was tinder dry. "You deserted me. You divorced me. Need I say more?"

Zoë gave an impatient shake of her head. "You didn't want me, remember?"

"I have explained all that. I wanted you more than anything. I still do. Why won't you believe me?"

And suddenly, she did, though why this sum and

substance of a woman's fantasies should choose *her* when he might choose Roberta Ashton, or Rosamund, or Mimi and Fifi—women who were more than like to be the sum and substance of a man's fantasies—was more than she could fathom.

Her head came up off the pillows and her eyes shone with a new knowledge. "Rolfe!" she said. "Is that the only reason you came to Paris—to find me and take me back to England with you?"

It was the truth, more or less. His involvement with Housard was only of secondary importance, at least by his lights.

"Of course," he answered without equivocation.

"What about the peace talks?"

Smiling easily, he answered, "I made that up. I had to give you some reason for my presence here. I was playing for time, you see. I did not know how long it would take to persuade you to return to England with me." Or how long it would take to clear up this business of *La Compagnie*. That thought, however, Rolfe prudently kept to himself.

Dizzy with happiness, she fell back against the pillows. She could see it all now, and she felt weak with the knowledge of it. Rolfe had loved her so much that he had put himself in the gravest danger to come and fetch her. And her reception of him, to say the least, had been less than welcoming. Any other man would have simply walked away from her.

Rolfe must love her. He regarded her as his wife. And the pretense that she had accepted his *carte blanche* was no more than that—a pretense so that he could protect her in the only way that was open to him. How different, how generous did his actions

375

with respect to herself now appear. And how thankless, how churlish her own with respect to him. She was so ashamed.

He had trusted her with his very life. She might easily have denounced him. He had trusted her that much and, oh God, she had not trusted him. She had told him nothing of her brother. And the pity of it was that, had she done so, her anxieties these many weeks past would have been easier to bear.

"How did you find out about my brother?" she asked.

For the first time, Rolfe hedged. He had a very good idea of what was going through Zoë's mind. She was flattered to think that his only reason for coming to Paris was to find her. Evidently, his iniquities, one by one, were being exonerated. He was not so confident that he wished to disabuse his wife of this new softening towards himself. This was not the time to explain his involvement with Housard. Later, in England, when he had her safely under his hand would be time and enough to explain the whole. He wasn't about to deceive her. On the other hand, he would take whatever steps were necessary to tip the balance in his favor.

"What touches you, touches me," he said simply. "Naturally, I pursued every lead on your brother and sister that came my way. I am not without friends in France. With their help, I discovered what I wished to know. I set a watch on the house. The rest you know."

"But how did you know that my brother was *Le Cache-Cache?* How did you know about *La Compagnie?*"

Without blinking an eyelash, he answered, "I

heard it all when you were talking in the boathouse. You were not very discreet."

Zoë looked up at him, her eyes betraying the torment of her thoughts. She said one word, "Claire?" then faltered before continuing with a catch in her voice. "It's the not knowing that is so awful. Oh God, if only I knew, one way or another, whether she lived or died, I could bear it." Her eyes never leaving his, she swallowed and whispered, "If you know something, anything, Rolfe, you needn't be afraid to tell me. Nothing, oh God, nothing could be worse than this." She wanted to say more but she could not trust herself to speak.

Rolfe said her name on a sigh and wrapped his arms around her, as if he would absorb some of her pain. Measuring his words, he said, "I don't want to give you false hope."

Abruptly she pulled back. "You know something!"

Damning himself for doing the one thing he had promised himself he would not do, he said cautiously, "What little I know makes no appreciable difference."

"What do you know?" She could not know that her nails were digging into his shoulders.

It was too late to retract. "Your sister Claire was in Bordeaux in the Spring of '94."

Leon had told Zoë as much. "Go on," she said.

"At that time, there was a flotilla of American ships in the harbor. She may have booked passage for America under a false name. It's more than certain that she tried."

"Claire? In America?" Her voice had taken on a feverish quality. A light leapt to life in her eyes.

Rolfe shook his head, depressing her hopes. "If she

377

is in America, why has she not sent you word? That was more than a year ago. There's been more than enough time."

"I don't know. There could be a million reasons."

"There! You see? This information, if it is information, scarcely adds one jot to your peace of mind."

"Rolfe, tell me the truth! What do you think has happened to Claire?"

For a moment, he debated whether or not he should confide his misgivings. Not all of those ships had reached a safe harbor. It was entirely possible that Zoë's sister had found a watery grave in the middle of the Atlantic Ocean. He looked into those half-fearful, half-hopeful eyes and knew that he would do almost anything to keep them free of pain.

He swallowed his uncertainties and said, "What I think is that, for some reason, your sister does not wish to be found. Think carefully, Zoë. Do you want to find her in these circumstances?"

Into the aching stillness, she whispered, "Yes."

"Then we shall find her. Once we are safely in England, I shall put men onto it. If Claire is alive and in America, if it takes the rest of our lives, we shall find her."

She knew that the task must be monumental. "You would do that for Claire?" she asked.

"No, my darling. I shall do it for you."

The moment was too charged with emotion. Zoë knew that one more word in this vein, and she would shatter into a thousand pieces. There were questions that must be asked and answered. There were things that she must say to this proud, generous man whom she had wronged. She had misjudged him not once,

378

but twice. He was no hero, but he was no knave either. He was merely a man, with a man's share of flaws and absurdities — and oh, she loved every one of them.

She reached for him, her hands cupping his dear face. "You make me feel ten feet tall, do you know?" And she promised herself, silently, that from this moment on, she would do everything in her power to make him feel the same way.

A shudder passed over him. His voice rough with emotion, he said, "Does this mean that you forgive me?"

"No," she said, and lost her voice as she swallowed the ache of her tears. The light in his eyes dimmed, and she hastened to complete the sentence. "Not unless you forgive me, too."

Her answer brought a constriction to his chest. "I don't deserve . . ."

She practically flung herself at him and rolled him to his back, pressing her lips to his in a long silencing kiss. When she pulled back, she was panting. Breathless and menacing at the same time, she said, "What you deserve, my dear husband, is exactly what you are going to get."

"And what is that?" he asked, slanting her an unquiet look.

Her eyes were dancing. "I aim to play out a female's fantasy," she purred. "Do you think you are man enough to take your punishment?"

For a moment, bemused, he stared at her. There was no mistaking the gleam in her eye. Grinning, stretching, he linked his hands behind his head. "I'm man enough for you," he baited.

She crouched over him. Trying to bite back her laughter and failing miserably, she got out, "I hope I don't shock you, but even if I do, it won't do you a bit of good to beg for mercy."

His smile was brazen. "You won't shock me and I won't beg for mercy."

"No?"

"Emphatically not!"

In a very short while, his wife proved that his boasts were empty. Rolfe did not care.

Chapter Twenty-three

"For God's sake, don't keep after me! I'm doing it for you! Don't you understand? I'm doing it for you and our unborn child!"

Jean Tresier cursed vehemently as the tears started in her beautiful blue eyes. "Rose," he said, and though the anger was almost choking him, he gentled his voice. "After this is over, we'll go away somewhere. We shall make a fresh start. That's what you've always wanted, isn't it?"

She ignored the inducement, and asked tearfully, "Why are you so angry? Is it because I found out about the duel? You weren't going to tell me, were you? When was I supposed to find out—when they brought your corpse home for me to lay out?"

He pulled her onto his lap and cradled her gently in his arms, letting her sob out the fears and frustrations for both of them.

She was right about one thing. He was angry. But not with her—never with Rose. He was angry with the fates, those capricious deities which decreed that good fortune should smile on one man while another should be dogged by ill luck.

Helpless. He felt helpless to change his lot. But Paul Varlet had offered him a way out. A man would be a fool not to seize his chance when it was offered. A do-or-die chance. It was worth the risk.

By degrees, she quieted. Trying to lighten her mood, he said, "I'm not angry. I'm hungry — starving, in point of fact. Go on now. Put supper on the table while I wash up."

He watched her for some few minutes as she busied herself about the room. Rose, he was thinking, was not cut from the same cloth as any mistress he had ever known. When he thought of her at odd moments during the day, he did not often think of her in the boudoir. He thought of her as she was now, as she went about her domestic duties, doing the scores of inconsequential things that she deemed necessary to make a home for him. He smiled, thinking that he had only to picture her as she was now, totally absorbed in the task of slicing up a loaf of bread, and his whole body would go hard with wanting her. And since he had discovered that she was with his child, the wanting had increased to almost unmanageable proportions.

He went to her then, wordlessly taking the knife from her hand and setting it on the table beside the loaf of bread. "I've changed my mind," he said. "And the hour is late. You should not have waited up for me. But since you have . . ." and he drew her into their bedchamber, loosening her clothes as he urged her to the bed. In the sweet solace of her body, he found a momentary oblivion.

The following morning, when she tried to deflect him from his purpose, the anger returned.

"This duel is over *her*, Zoë Devereux, isn't it? You

still love her! Why do you deny it?"

"I love you," he soothed. "I'm doing it for you. I never loved Zoë. It was always you."

His soft words had no effect on her. She was jealous, and he could not blame her. For months, he had courted Zoë. He had offered her his hand in marriage. As is the way of things, Rose had come to hear of it. She could not understand that it was necessity that drove him. He must marry where there was a fortune. He had never had any intentions of setting aside Rose. She could not be persuaded of that truth.

"If what you say is true," she burst out, "if Varlet wants her, why must *you* fight the duel. Why not he?"

He could not tell her that in a duel fate played a part. It happened sometimes that the most skillful duelist fell to an inept opponent. There was no necessity for Varlet to put his own life at risk, not when he could pull the strings of his marionette and have him, Jean Tresier, take the risks for him. For a price.

He rolled from the bed and began to dress himself. "Look," he said, "we've been through all this. You know that Varlet holds my note. That debt will be wiped out. This time, I really will be free. We can start fresh."

Already, he had decided that he would marry Rose. He wished their marriage could take place before the duel—to protect their child from the taint of illegitimacy should anything happen to him. He dared not suggest such a thing in her present state of nerves. She would know, then, that he was not so confident about the outcome of the duel as he pretended.

But he had every reason to be confident. He was the younger man. And Ronsard had stipulated that the duel should be fought with pistols. Tresier was a crack shot. Everyone knew it.

"When does the duel take place?" she demanded.

He lied through his teeth. "Tomorrow," he said.

She was staring at him as if he were a stranger. "Rose, what is it?"

She looked away and shook her head.

"Rose?"

Her eyelashes lifted and the tears welled over. "Jean." She brushed at her wet cheeks with impatient fingers. "This is not like you. This is not honorable. You might as well be . . . a . . . a paid assassin."

His jaw clenched. His whole body went rigid with fury. Her accusations touched him on a raw nerve. Honor. His father had always boasted that the word *honor* and the Tresier name were synonymous. And his father had held to that view even on the scaffold, when his fortune had gone to support losing causes and his family had been decimated by the Revolution. What price honor when a man had to live like an animal simply to survive? What price honor when his wife and children went to the wall because the name they bore incited hatred in the mob? Honor had no place in his life. He could not afford it.

As the bitter words poured from his mouth, she flinched away. "Honor! How dare you fling that word in my teeth! Look at yourself! Whore! Where is *your* honor?" His fingers were digging into her arms.

Wrenching away from him, she covered her ears with her hands. Her shoulders shook as she choked back the anguished sobs.

"Oh God, Rose! Don't cry. I didn't mean it. I didn't mean it, love."

He dragged her into his arms and held her close to

384

his heart. His own tears fell unhindered and he could not say if it was for the past or for the future that he wept.

Like Rose, Zoë also tried to dissuade the man she loved from the forthcoming duel. Rolfe, however, displayed a far more casual attitude than his adversary.

"It's nothing but show—a mere matter of going through the motions," he explained dismissively.

The hour was early. The sun had yet to come up. Rolfe was dressing himself. He was eager to get to the Swedish Embassy, so he told Zoë, where Leon was being held.

"You must be tired," he said, flashing her a devilish grin, and added gratuitously, "after last night. Why don't you go back to sleep?"

Doggedly, she kept to the subject which interested her. "People have been known to get hurt when they duel."

"Nonsense. Tresier is not such a fool as to do a foreign diplomat an injury. Think of the scandal. And I am scarcely like to do anything to jeopardize our plans. If anything happens to Tresier, I'd have the Committee of Public Safety down on our heads."

Exasperated beyond reason, Zoë demanded, "Then what is the point of the duel?"

Grinning wickedly, Rolfe approached the bed. His lips brushed hers and he responded lightly, "Honor must be seen to be satisfied, kitten. Gentlemen expect it."

Zoë was not quite sure that she believed him. But since Rolfe had intimated that there was always a period of grace where the seconds tried to effect a

385

reconciliation before the duelists met on the field of honor, she deemed that she had some time in which to think of a way to prevent it. It could well be that they might leave France before Rolfe and Tresier could meet each other. That would be the best solution. Still, she wasn't going to take any chances.

Before Rolfe left for the Swedish Embassy, he tried to exact a promise from her that she would remain indoors.

"Why can't I come with you?" she wanted to know. "Leon is—"

"In good hands," responded Rolfe. "You're not thinking, Zoë. How would it look if you paid a morning call on Germaine de Staël at this unearthly hour?"

"We could go later."

But Rolfe could not be moved. No one would question his presence at the Swedish Embassy. He must be the one to go, if only to reassure Leon that he had nothing to fear.

"I would have gone last night," said Rolfe, "but you were as much in need of reassurance as he. I could not leave you, nor will I permit you to shelter your brother under the same roof. It's too risky," he said, cutting off the protest she was about to make. "He is a hunted man. I don't want him anywhere near you until we are actually on our way. Now will you give me your solemn promise not to leave the house while I'm gone?"

Only when she had given her word did he take his leave of her. Zoë rose and dressed herself. In the morning room, she lingered over breakfast, her thoughts drifting every which way. She was on the point of rising from the table to compose a note to

Charles Lagrange, asking his advice about the duel, when Samson entered and informed her that there was a young lady at the door wishing to speak to her.

"What name?" asked Zoë.

"Mademoiselle Lefebre."

The name meant nothing to Zoë. "Show her into the yellow *salle* and tell her that I shall be with her directly."

When Zoë entered the *salle,* a stranger, a young woman in a modest gray walking dress, turned to face her. It registered that the girl was as fair as she was dark. A pair of cerulean eyes dominated the small, heart-shaped face. Those beautiful eyes, Zoë noted, were red rimmed. The hands which clutched at her reticule were shaking.

Zoë's first impulse was to rush to the young woman's side and put her arms about her. But something in the girl's demeanor, something in her expression, made Zoë hesitate. Veiled hostility, thought Zoë, and waited quietly for the girl to explain herself.

"My name is Rose Lefebre," began the girl, "and I have come to beg you to put a stop to the duel." Her control gave way. She covered her face with her hands. "He's not a bad man, really," she choked out. "This isn't like him. He does not know what he is doing. He's doing it for me. I wish, oh God, I wish I were dead."

The two ladies had no way of knowing it, since the gentlemen had not taken them into their confidence, but at that very moment Rolfe and Tresier were turning to face each other at twenty paces with leveled pistols. A sweat had broken out on Tresier's brow.

His hand had developed a slight tremor.

Rolfe was the first to fire. No one was surprised when the shot went wide of its mark. As was to be expected, the diplomat, a foreigner, was not *au fait* with French modes. He did not take the duel seriously. His opponent was honor-bound to follow his example.

When Tresier, however, remained in position, his pistol still cocked, his finger curled around the trigger, a murmur of unease went around the few waiting gentlemen.

A mist seemed to form before his eyes. Tresier shook his head, trying to dispel it. One shot, he was telling himself, only one shot and he and Rose would be free to make a fresh start.

To remain in France, of course, would be out of the question. He would be regarded as a cold-blooded killer. His name would be infamous. They must go where no one would know him, if only for the sake of the child. No son or daughter of his would be made to bear the shame of a father's iniquities. His children would be proud of their name. He would teach them all the things that his father had passed on to him. Only one shot, he promised himself, only one shot and he need never again toady to the likes of a Paul Varlet. He would be his own master, the kind of man in whom his father, God rest his soul, would have confidence.

Tresier's eyes narrowed as his opponent turned to face him square on. Didn't the man know that he was giving him a better target to shoot at? Yes, Ronsard knew it. It told in every nonchalant line of his stance. Ronsard was a fool. He was also a man of honor. He expected his opponent to subscribe to the same code. Honor. Tresier hated that word and wondered if it would haunt him for the rest of his days.

A movement caught Tresier's eye at the same moment as someone shouted "Assassin!" He didn't take time to think of what he was doing. His arm moved automatically. He pulled the trigger.

Several things happened simultaneously. Tresier's shot hit the would-be assassin in the arm. His gun went off, kicking up the earth at Rolfe's feet. Men were running and shouting at the same time. The assassin took to his heels.

Only the duelists remained in position. For one long moment, across the twenty paces which separated them, they seemed to assess each other. At length, Rolfe smiled and shook his head. Tresier crossed the distance between them and offered the older man his hand. It was accepted.

Tresier had some difficulty in expressing himself. "I beg your pardon. I did not . . . I could not . . . forgive me if I gave you a few unquiet moments there."

"You did," said Rolfe, clapping the younger man on the shoulder. "But I *do* forgive you. You saved my life."

More shots were heard, and soon after, they were joined by their seconds.

"He got clean away," said Charles Lagrange.

Tresier gripped Rolfe's hand. "Why did you fire first?" he asked. "Why did you put yourself at my mercy?" It was plain that the answer to his question was of grave significance to the younger man.

Rolfe's stare was long and level. "I fired first," he said, "because the damn fool pistol went off in my hand. It was an accident. You may believe, Monsieur Tresier, that I would not have spared your life had our positions been reversed. When I raised that pistol, I aimed to shoot you straight between the eyes."

For an interval, Tresier looked to be stunned. A moment later, a deep-throated chuckle escaped him. Rolfe frowned, but soon after, he too let out a burst of suppressed mirth. Their seconds looked at them as if they had gone mad.

"Who was he? Did anyone recognize him?" asked someone, referring to Rolfe's assailant.

It was Tresier who put a name to him. "André Valazé," he said. "He hangs out with the *jeunesse dorée.*"

Rolfe wasn't thinking of the *jeunesse dorée.* He was remembering the young man whom he had met on the stairs when he had gone to Madame Montansier's Theatre to rescue Zoë. At that time, André Valazé had been Paul Varlet's companion.

Housard was known to have the patience of Job. He reminded himself of that fact as he felt his control slip away from him. He never lost his temper. In his field of work, he could not afford the luxury. Once, not so long ago, he had followed the profession of law. Logic, clarity, and an unshakable sang-froid— these were his hallmarks. To lose one's temper was to allow one's emotions to cloud one's judgment. An enemy could soon use that weakness to advantage.

But the Englishmen wasn't an enemy. He was a colleague. He was more. Housard genuinely liked the younger man. He wished him well. And now that his mission in France had been successfully concluded, by and large, the English aristocrat's first thought should be to remove himself from the danger zone.

And he, Housard, should be congratulating himself on a job well done.

Contrary to every expectation, the Englishman had embroiled himself in a boyish scrape—a duel, in the name of God! Housard suffered agonies when he lost an agent in the line of duty. That Rolfe should flirt with death for no good reason strained his patience to breaking point.

For a full five minutes, he gave vent to his spleen. The walls of his small office in the Swedish Embassy seemed to reverberate with the volume of his voice. When his harangue finally ran its course, Housard could tell at a glance that the object of his vituperation was in no way chastened.

Rolfe lounged in an oversized armchair, his booted feet propped negligently against the fender. In the chair on the other side of the empty grate, equally negligent, lounged his young brother-in-law, Leon Devereux. A long look passed between them before Rolfe half-turned and made to answer Housard's long litany of reproaches.

"Tush, man, I was never in any real danger. We were only going through the motions for form's sake. Tresier insulted my wife. I demanded satisfaction. Honor must be satisfied. What would you have had me do?"

Through set teeth, Housard grated, "What we agreed that you should do—take your wife and her brother and get the hell out of France."

"How could I? Until the other night, Leon was still a fugitive. But you may believe, now that I have him under my hand, that I shall follow your advice as soon as may be."

This reasonable answer, far from mollifying

Housard, only increased his ire. "Your cover is blown, man! Hasn't that fact penetrated whatever passes for brains inside your head?"

"My cover?"

"Valazé. He tried to assassinate you. You know as well as I do that *Le Patron* is still on the loose. This whole episode has shades of what happened to you in England after we smashed their network. Someone is out for your blood."

"I'm aware of that," said Rolfe, turning serious. "But I'm not convinced that Valazé is involved with *La Compagnie*. What do you think, Leon?" Rolfe's eyelids drooped lazily. "Do you know anything of André Valazé?"

Since Leon had been taken into custody by Housard, he had told them very little, though, by degrees, the hard edge of his hostility had softened. His captors knew who and what he was. He did not need to be told that he was not in the hands of the regular deputies of the Committee of Public Safety. His fate, in those circumstances, was a foregone conclusion—summary execution. Still, Leon was suspicious.

His expression was inscrutable as he returned Rolfe's stare. This man was not the older man he had once pretended to be. The limp was no longer in evidence. The old-fashioned wig had been thrown off and lay discarded on top of the desk. This was the man his sister vowed she loved. He claimed that he was Zoë's husband. It seemed entirely possible that he was the English husband she had divorced.

Ignoring Rolfe's question, Leon put one of his own. "Why did my sister divorce you?"

Rolfe straightened in his chair. Something very unpleasant moved at the back of his gray eyes. His nostrils flared. "I don't answer to anyone, least of all to a young cub like you, for what transpires between my wife and myself. Furthermore, you may discard the notion that your abominable sister obtained a divorce. In England, I take leave to tell you, that piece of paper would not hold up in a court of law."

"I would not be too sure of that," interjected Housard with something close to glee. When Rolfe emitted a rough expletive, Housard forgot about his anger and chuckled. At last, he was thinking, he had pierced the Englishmen's insufferable indifference. And to add insult to injury, he promptly needled, "If I were in your shoes, I would lose no time in making the lady my wife, else the children she bears you may find themselves bastards."

"The lady *is* my wife," said Rolfe with so much menace that the very air seemed to crackle with electricity.

Nothing daunted, Housard smoothly responded, "Of course. What I meant to say was the you should persuade her, if she can be persuaded, that is, to go through a second wedding ceremony, just to be on the safe side, you understand."

Belatedly conscious that Housard was deliberately baiting him, Rolfe modified his rigid posture. He inclined his head as though acknowledging a hit. "Zoë is stubborn," he admitted, "but not so stubborn that she will thwart me on so grave a matter. Your point is well taken, Monsieur Housard."

"Stubborn, is she?" mused Housard, enjoying himself immensely. "Yes, I think one may say that Zoë can claim that distinction and no one would dispute it. She has certainly led you on a merry chase since you first clapped eyes on her."

To keep a curb on his tongue, Rolfe snapped his teeth together.

Leon, who had been observing this curious byplay with growing interest, offered innocently, "My mother was used to say that Zoë had a will of iron. Once she made up her mind to a thing, nothing could sway her."

Rolfe scowled. Housard laughed. Leon cleared his throat.

"To get back to André Valazé," said Leon, and there was a slight softening around his unsmiling lips.

"What about him?" asked Rolfe. His mind was still occupied with the unpleasant problem Housard had raised.

"I shouldn't think that he was a member of *La Compagnie*. The members, at least the ones in my cell, were fanatics. Valazé took opium. He would do almost anything to lay his hands on that narcotic."

At the same moment, the two older men raised their heads like wolves sniffing a fresh scent. A quick look of comprehension was exchanged before their glances fell on the darkly handsome youth. In the space of a few minutes, it was evident that something — a stray look or word — had persuaded Leon Devereux to relax his guard. He had never yet volunteered any information.

"Good lad," said Rolfe.

The next several minutes were taken up in putting a series of questions to Leon. And though the boy's attitude had undergone a material change, the results were disappointing. He could add very little to their knowledge of *Le Patron*. One interesting fact, however, did emerge.

"The three section heads make up the fourth cell," he told them. "They are the only ones who report to *Le Patron.*"

"And are therefore the only ones who can identify *Le Patron?*" murmured Rolfe.

The boy nodded.

"And you say that your section head was one of the first to fall foul of the authorities?"

"He was the first of my cell to go," corrected Leon. "But if the authorities were involved, that is news to me. No. He and his mistress were found murdered in their beds. They had both been shot."

A look passed between Leon's companions. "It all fits," said Rolfe.

"What fits?" asked Leon.

"The fourth cell," answered Rolfe. "It would seem that as soon as *Le Patron* scents danger, he eliminates his lieutenants. That way, he is in the clear. We'll never discover his identity now."

When they met with Deputy Tallien some time later to make their final report, Rolfe diplomatically allowed Housard to voice that unwelcome fact.

"I am sorry to inform you, Deputy Tallien," intoned Housard gravely, "that our chances of ever discovering the identity of *Le Patron* are remote, to say the least. It seems that the only members of the sect who might have identified him were the first to be sacrificed. In short, my friend here and I agree that *Le Patron* made sure that the members of the fourth cell were eliminated before he passed information on to the authorities."

"It was to be expected," said Tallien in a not unkindly tone. "You have nothing with which to reproach yourselves. No, gentlemen, it is not *Le Patron* who interests me. His influence is finished. He must have known it before he betrayed his own people. But this *Cache-Cache* fellow, the one who tried to murder me—I shall not rest until that young terrorist is found and executed."

"That is only a matter of time," answered Housard, and changed the subject with a smoothness which Rolfe inwardly applauded. "I wish my young colleague here could remain to assist us, but as you know, he must leave France with all speed."

"I do know it," said Tallien, rising to his feet and coming from behind his desk to extend his hand to Rolfe. His eyes were twinkling. "A most unusual assignment for you, eh, Ronsard? And a most uncommon obligation for me—to thank an enemy for his aid to France. Theresia will miss Zoë. She's very fond of your . . . the girl. Please convey my compliments to her."

Rolfe murmured something suitable if vague, and Tallien continued in the same jocular tone, "It's as well that you did not kill young Tresier, else you would have placed me in a very awkward position." He laughed, and Rolfe managed to look shamefaced. "Oh yes, I know about the duel," he said. "Good God, man, you've quite restored my faith in the English character! I thought you were a cold-blooded race!"

Shaking his head, laughing softly to himself, he returned to his desk. "And now, gentlemen," he said, lacing his fingers and resting his hands on the flat of the desk, "time is short. Shall we get down to business?"

* * *

The other gentleman who was party to that duel was, at that very moment, taking the stairs which led to his rooms two at a time. He had spent hours looking all over the city for Paul Varlet. But that gentleman was nowhere to be found. And since it occurred to Tresier that Rose might have heard something of the duel and become anxious for him, he had given up the search.

Rose heard the click of the latch as he entered, and she sprang to her feet, spinning to face him.

"Jean," she said, "It's all right. You don't have to go through with the duel. You can snap your fingers at Paul Varlet. She's given me gold and passports. D'you see? We don't have to stay in Paris. We're free. We can go anywhere you want to go."

She knew that she was babbling and that she wasn't making sense, but she could not seem to stop herself. "We can go to America. New Orleans, perhaps. There are always merchant ships in the harbor at Bordeaux. Zoë said so. We should have no difficulty in booking—"

"Rose!" Tresier reached her in two swift strides. His eyes anxiously scanned her paper-white face. She was quivering like a wild thing caught in a trap. "Rose," he said again. "What is it, my love?"

"The duel," she whispered brokenly. "It isn't necessary for you to go through with it. Oh God, promise me you won't go through with it!"

"Too late," he said, smiling. "I already have."

Her eyelashes fluttered and she swayed against him. "No!" she sobbed. "No! Do not say so! Do not say you killed him!"

"What the devil . . . ?" Sweeping her up in his arms, he carried her to the small sofa beside the window. He sat down, cradling her against his chest.

"Look at me, Rose."

Her eyelashes were spiked with tears. Slowly, they lifted.

"Everything is all right. I could not go through with it. I might easily have killed him. I did not. I could not. I am more my father's son that I knew I was. And do you know — the most extraordinary thing — I've taken a liking to Ronsard? We parted the best of friends."

If he thought to win her to smiles, he was to be disappointed. A great shuddering sob wracked her shoulders, and, as if a dam had burst, the tears overflowed.

For several minutes, he did nothing but hold her and soothe her with soft words and gentle touches, stroking his hands through her hair and down her spine to her waist. When it was evident that the storm had run its course, he said in a matter-of-fact tone. "Now, what is all this about gold and passports and going to America? You are not making sense, Rose."

It took some time to get the story out of her. Haltingly at first, and then with growing confidence, she began to relate that morning's events.

On her own initiative, she had gone to see Zoë, she told him.

"For what purpose?" he asked.

"To try to stop the duel. How could we know that it was already in progress?"

"Go on."

Her eyes dropped to her clenched hands. Zoë Devereux, she was thinking, was not as she had imagined the girl would be. She was beautiful. She was wealthy. She moved in the highest reaches of Parisian society. She had refused two honorable offers of marriage and had taken an old man for her lover.

Such a woman, Rose was sure, must be voluptuous to the point of vulgarity and would be a calculating bitch. Zoë Devereux was none of those things. She was simply a warmhearted girl who had tactfully if determinedly elicited from Rose the whole story of her relationship with Tresier. And Rose had felt as if a burden had lifted from her shoulders.

"She's in love with Ronsard, you know," said Rose. "She was just as eager as I to find a way to stop the duel."

"And did you think of a way?" asked Tresier in some amusement.

"Zoë was going to approach Charles Lagrange to have him use his influence to stop the duel."

Tresier stifled a smile, but he could not prevent himself pointing out that Charles Lagrange had been one of Ronsard's seconds. "Go on with your story," he said.

Having some confidence that the duel would never take place, Zoë then turned to the problem of Rose's future with Tresier.

More sternly than he meant, Tresier said, "And I suppose you told Zoë that we had sometimes talked of going to America if only we have the funds to establish ourselves there?"

"No . . . yes." Her eyes slid away from his. "I didn't mean to. It just seemed to come out naturally in the course of the conversation. It was Zoë who introduced the subject of America."

"In what connection?"

"Something to do with her sister Claire. And that's

when I told her that we had talked of going to America to start a new life."

"And she promised to get hold of passports and gold to buy me off?"

"It was nothing like that! Zoë said that it was the hand of Fate."

"The hand of Fate? What was the hand of Fate?"

Wordlessly, she struggled free of his arms and moved to a commode against the window wall. She lifted the lid and looked back at him.

Tresier rose to his feet and obediently answered that silent invitation. "What's this?" he said, peering into the depths of the commode. He extracted two official-looking documents. Beneath them he found a small leather grip. It was so heavy, it took both hands to lift it out. Inside were hundreds of gold pieces.

"It's the loan she promised you," said Rose earnestly. "She was going to invest it elsewhere. But this very morning, she discovered that the opportunity for doing so was no longer there."

Bewildered, Tresier asked, "And the passports? Where did they come from?"

"She had them there with her. The people for whom they were meant no longer have need of them. She said so."

Passports and gold—there was an interesting story here, Tresier was thinking, if he cared to pursue it.

"She said it was the hand of Fate," said Rose, studying his closed expression.

For a long moment, they stared at each other. Rose's eyes were alight with hope. Her thoughts were transparent. The passports and the gold represented a solid foundation for their life together. They could marry. They could start afresh.

"We could stay in France," he said.

She shook her head. "No. Let's not tempt Fate. This was meant to be. Don't you see?"

She was so intense, so much on edge, as if her life was hanging in the balance. For a moment, he closed his eyes, searching for the words that would forever banish that uncertain look from her face. He had done this to her. She loved him and he had taken everything she had to offer. God, Rose deserved so much better than what he had given her.

A pain seemed to lodge itself in his chest. He had taken her love, her innocence, her honor, with callous indifference. He had made her his mistress. In return, he had given her nothing which was of any significance to her. She had no desire to move in his exalted circles. Fine gowns and baubles held little interest for her. Her ambitions were modest, and oh God—he could see it now—so much finer than his own.

He had to swallow before he could find his voice. Softly, as humble as she had ever seen him, he said, "I don't care about the gold. I don't care about the passports. If you want to keep them, fine, we'll go to America. If you want to give them back, fine, we shall remain in France. It's you I care about, Rose, you and our child.

"Just as soon as I can arrange it we are going to be married. No, don't say anything yet. Let me finish. I've been giving this a lot of thought. My father had very humble beginnings, did you know? He started off as a clerk. I've had things too easy. I see that now. But I swear to you, from this moment on, I am going to follow in the Tresier tradition. I don't care if I start off as a clerk, or a farmer, or whatever. I'm going to make my own way in the world. And one day I hope to make you proud of me."

Though her throat ached with tears, she managed to get out, "Oh my darling, I'm proud of you now. I'm proud to be carrying your child. I shall be proud to be your wife. And if you let me, I'll be proud to follow in the Tresier tradition."

She was in his arms and they were both laughing and crying at the same time. And then the laughter left them as they became lost in each other and the miracle of their love.

Much later, he asked softly, "What are you thinking about?"

"Fate," she whispered.

"Which means?"

"America."

He laughed. "So be it," he said. "America it is."

Chapter Twenty-four

The moment he entered the foyer, he sensed that something was very much amiss. It was not Samson who was on duty, but one of his underlings, a young footman who generally waited on table. The murmur of voices came to him from Zoë's yellow *salle*. Rolfe threw down his walking cane and strode purposefully toward the door.

At his entrance, three people turned to face him. Salome was wringing her hands. Samson hung his head. And Francoise, Zoë's friend, was dabbing at her eyes with a balled handkerchief. Three voices started to speak at once.

Rolfe cut them off with the wave of one hand. "Where is she?" he demanded.

There was a silence, then Francoise, with a look of acute trepidation, forced herself to her feet. "It's all my fault," she said, her voice low and scarcely audible. Her eyes dropped away from Rolfe's riveting gaze. She swallowed convulsively. "If I hadn't agreed to go with her, none of this would have happened."

"You know where she is?"

Her eyes were brimming with tears. "I do. And I have a message for your ears only."

Over Salome's protests, Rolfe ordered the servants to clear the room. Having closed the door firmly upon them, he moved to a small commode. From a

403

crystal decanter, he poured a generous splash of amber liquid into a glass and thrust it into Francoise's trembling fingers.

"Drink it," he said with so much sternness in his expression that Francoise took a long swallow in mute obedience before she realized the glass contained strong spirits.

It took some minutes before she could find her voice. "I don't know where to begin," she said and stared miserably at the liquid eddying in her glass.

In a tone of strained patience, Rolfe said, "You have a message for me?"

Francoise nodded. "From Paul Varlet. He has Zoë, you see. You are to go alone. He said that this was between the two of you and that if we involved others, you would never see Zoë again." She bit down on her lip and fresh tears started to her eyes. "Oh yes, and I was to tell you that you are to come unarmed, and that the house is being watched. He'll know if you try to trick him. Oh God, there isn't much time." She cast a despairing look at the clock on the mantel. "He gave me two hours to find you, and, oh God, there's barely an hour left. If I don't take you to him before sunset, something dreadful will happen to Zoë. Please . . ."

He silenced the spate of words with a look. "You have seen Varlet in the last two hours?"

She nodded, then sniffed. "If anything happens to Zoë, I shall never forgive myself."

"It's not your fault," he said grimly. "I should have expected that Varlet would try something like this. I did expect it. That is why I gave orders that Zoë was not to leave the house. You can fill me in on the details as we go."

He took the glass from her shaking fingers and set it aside. "What address?" he asked.

"That's just it. I don't remember. It was in the letter, and Zoë still has it in her possession. But I know the house. It's on the road to Picpus, in the St. Antoine district. The house stands in its own grounds. I shall recognize it once I see it again."

Rolfe strode to the door and summoned Samson. When he turned back, Francoise looked at him curiously.

"You look different," she said. "What happened to your cane?"

"I'm not Ronsard," he answered. "I'm Zoë's husband." He studied her carefully. "You don't seem surprised?"

"I was beginning to suspect as much."

"My disguise didn't fool you?"

"Not latterly, no. And I thought that your limp might be a relic from the injuries you sustained in that attack in London."

Samson entered at that moment and Rolfe gave orders for the carriage to be brought round.

Though she was trembling in her shoes, Francoise countermanded the order. "It won't do," she said. "You are to come in an open carriage, one that you can drive yourself. There must be no coachmen."

"It would seem that Varlet has thought of everything," observed Rolfe. "Very well, Samson. We shall take the curricle. You may follow in the carriage. But at a safe distance. I won't take chances on anything happening to Zoë. And Samson, once we find the house, you are to fetch help at once. Do you understand?"

"Aren't you going to at least alert the authorities

to what is going on?" asked Francoise in an agitated tone.

"To what purpose?" asked Rolfe. "If they rush in before I have a chance to speak to Varlet, anything might happen to Zoë."

"I suppose you know what you are about," she answered, though it was evident she was far from satisfied with the steps Rolfe was taking to protect her friend.

As the curricle pulled out of the courtyard, Francoise covertly studied her companion. His hands were steady on the reins. Not a flicker of emotion showed on his handsomely chiseled profile. She shook her head.

"You're very cool," she said, "and yet you must know that Paul Varlet hates you. You could be walking into a trap."

"What choice do I have? Besides, I shall tell Varlet at the outset that I have sent my man to fetch the authorities. He'd be a fool to try anything, and he knows it. No, it's not my own skin I am worried about. But, my God, if he has touched one hair of Zoë's head . . ."

Such a look blazed in his eyes that Francoise flinched involuntarily. At length, her confidence returned, and she said, "Nevertheless, you surely won't enter that house unarmed? If anything should happen to you . . ."

"You may be sure that I am not such a fool!" Rolfe patted his coat pocket with one hand. "And now, Francoise, I wish you would tell me how Paul Varlet got hold of my wife. I'm still very much in the dark."

It had all begun, so Francoise told him, when a

letter came by hand to Zoë's own door. No one knew who had delivered it. The letter purported to be from Zoë's sister, Claire.

"And you were with Zoë when the letter arrived?"

"I was."

"And was the letter from Claire?"

"Zoë seemed to think so. She recognized the writing."

"Go on."

Francoise continued with her story. The contents of the letter had upset Zoë greatly. Claire, it seemed, was an inmate of an asylum for the insane. The name she went by was not her own. She suffered from terrible fits of madness. At the moment, she was lucid. She had begged in vain to be released. No one would listen to her. Zoë was her last hope.

"None of this makes sense," cut in Rolfe, striving for patience. "How could Claire have known that Zoë had taken up residence in St. Germain? How did she know that Zoë was no longer in England? Surely you must have asked yourselves these questions? There are other things that must have made you wonder, if you had thought about it."

"That's just it," said Francoise, her voice and expression betraying her anguish. "We did not take time to think about it. We acted on impulse."

"I cannot understand why Zoë did not send someone to fetch me. I warned her, in no uncertain terms, that she was not to leave the house."

Francoise hung her head and said miserably, "That is something else that you may lay at my door. I told her about the duel, you see."

Rolfe uttered something very explicit and very

Anglo-Saxon. He flung questions at Francoise in quick succession. In very short order, he had a clear idea of the sequence of events.

With a verbosity which was most unbecoming in a gentleman, Charles Lagrange had spilled the whole story of the duel to his wife. She, in her turn, made postehaste for the house in St. Germain to relate the same story to her friend, Zoë.

Rolfe could well imagine Zoë's frame of mind. The fragile trust which he had taken such pains to establish had shattered. On top of this first shock, almost immediately, came the shock of the letter from her sister — an almost certain counterfeit, in Rolfe's opinion. But Zoë, he knew, would clutch at straws.

And while he had been closeted for hours with first Housard and then Tallien, tying up all the loose ends of the assignment he had just completed, Zoë had given her vigilant servants the slip. Oh yes, he could well imagine Zoë's frame of mind when she set off with Francoise to chase down this lead on Claire. His credibility must be nonexistent. She would be heedless with anger.

They edged into the Faubourge St. Antoine and Rolfe chanced a quick look over his shoulder to ensure that Samson was following in the carriage. That act cost him dearly. The reins slipped from his fingers. He made a grab for them. His team felt the sudden jolt on the bit and went plunging and snorting to the right, almost overturning the curricle into the ditch. Francoise was flung half out. Only Rolfe's quick thinking saved her. One hand closed around her arm, dragging her back. Somehow his action sent her reticule flying out of her hands.

408

"My reticule," Francoise cried out. "It's in the ditch somewhere."

She made to alight but Rolfe prevented her. "Hold the reins. I'll fetch it," he said.

This was soon done, and they were on their way again, as if nothing had happened.

"You have yet to finish your story," said Rolfe. "What happened when you arrived at the asylum?"

Francoise felt in her reticule and withdrew a handkerchief. She mopped her face. The sun was low in the sky. The houses on this lonely stretch of road were few and far between. She looked over her shoulder. Samson, she noted, was keeping the carriage at a respectable distance. She became conscious that her companion was waiting for her to reply to his question.

"There was no asylum," she said. "Just Paul Varlet and a couple of his cohorts. At first, we thought the house was deserted. They grabbed us in an upstairs chamber. Turn here."

Rolfe obediently turned into a lane. "But Varlet let you go," he said.

"Yes, so that I could carry a message back to you."

The carriage which was following stopped at the end of the lane.

"That's it," said Francoise, pointing.

The curricle rolled to a halt. Rolfe gave the reins into Francoise's hands. He jumped down. His eyes quickly scanned a house of recent Palladian vintage. One comprehensive glance told him that it was a rich man's house. A second glance informed him that the house was standing empty. The gardens had an air of neglect.

He waved to the carriage at the end of the lane, and Samson dutifully made a turn, directing his team towards the city.

"This is it, then, Francoise," said Rolfe. "Give me ten minutes. If I am not out by that time, I suggest that you get the hell out of here." And without subterfuge, he advanced toward the avenue of limes which led to the front entrance of the house.

Bracing herself against the elegant lady's escritoire, Zoë pulled herself to her knees. The dull ache in her head blazed to life and she let out a gasping cry. She waited a moment or two till the pain had dulled, then she pushed to her feet. Gingerly, she touched her hand to the back of her head. It came away sticky with blood.

Think. She must think. Her last recollection was of Paul Varlet's evil smile of triumph as he advanced upon her. And while she had stood there like a terrified rabbit, someone had struck her from behind with a fair force.

"Francoise!" she cried out, and looked around wildly, fearing the worst for her friend.

She was alone in an upstairs chamber. The first rush of relief subsided. Oh God, she thought, what had Varlet done to Francoise?

As she forced herself to take slow, careful steps toward the door, the pain came at her in waves. She had to fight back the nausea. For a moment, she rested her aching head against the cool, painted surface of the door. This was more than a hoax, she thought. This was a trap which had been set by Varlet. Rolfe had been right to warn her against him. The man was obsessed.

He had known exactly how to lure her from her safe lair. It had all sounded so reasonable. The note was in Claire's hand. But this was no asylum for the insane. This house was a showplace, some rich man's retreat. The elegance of the fine furnishings had astonished her from the moment she and Francoise had stepped over the threshold. Claire was not here, had never been here. Hadn't Rolfe told her that, in all probability, Claire was in America? But when had she ever listened to Rolfe?

"Rolfe," she sobbed. "Oh Rolfe."

He would not know where to begin to look for her. And it was her own fault. She'd left the house in a fit of temper after Francoise had told her about the duel. She had decided, then, that her husband was not to be trusted. He was a barefaced liar. Though not in so many words, he had given her the erroneous impression that she had hours in which to devise some means of putting a stop to the duel. And that both gentlemen had survived the ordeal without so much as a scratch did not mitigate her sense of ill usage one whit. As was his habit, her husband was treating her as the veriest child.

And like a sulky schoolgirl, she had taken matters into her own hands. Not that she had believed that there was any danger to herself. Claire needed her. Francoise was there to offer her support. And that she was acting against Rolfe's express wishes, in that moment of defiance, did not weigh with her. Rolfe was not there.

No, there could be no hope of rescue. She had deliberately tricked her servants. She had given no one her direction. No one would know what had

411

become of her. If there was to be a rescue, she must effect it herself.

"Oh Rolfe," she sobbed again. She did not know if she had the courage to brave what must be braved on the other side of the locked door. Only the certain knowledge that Paul Varlet would come for her sooner or later strengthened her resolve.

She tried the door, knowing before she did so that it must be locked. Sinking down to her knees, she peered through the keyhole. As luck would have it, the key was in the lock. It would be mere child's play to retrieve the key. It was a trick Leon had taught her years ago, when, as children, they had sometimes been locked into their respective chambers for some prank or other.

Having made her decision, Zoë soon assembled the necessary articles to achieve her object. With great concentration, she pushed the blotter she had removed from the escritoire under the door. This done, she inserted the thin blade of a letter opener in the keyhole. After a few jabs, she heard the soft thud as the key landed on the blotter on the other side of the door. Carefully, slowly, she pulled the blotter with the key upon it towards herself. She used her fingers to angle the key through the small gap under the door.

When she came out onto the landing, she paused. She did not know where to begin to look for Francoise. There was only one thing to do. She must make her escape and go for help.

With every instinct alive to her danger, she descended the wide sweep of the marble staircase. Again, she was struck with the unnatural silence of the place, as though the house were empty. But the house was not empty, she reminded herself. She had come upon Paul Varlet in one of the upstairs chambers, and someone had struck her from behind.

She was crossing the marble foyer toward the main entrance when something, some faint sound, some slight movement, arrested her attention. The door to her right, leading on to the bookroom, was ajar. She had an impression of papers on a desk fluttering in the draft of an open window.

The house was oppressive with silence. It was an uncanny moment. Almost against her will, Zoë was drawn to that open door. On the threshold, she halted. Slowly, she pushed the door wide. She had a clear view of a man. He appeared to have fallen asleep. His head was resting on the flat of the desk. She recognized the man as Paul Varlet.

She could hardly breathe. With halting steps, she advanced upon him. And then her eyes became riveted to the pool of red ink which had spilled onto the blotter beneath his bent arm. In horrified fascination, she extended her hand and touched the blotter.

This was how Rolfe found her a moment later when he entered the bookroom.

"He's dead," quavered Zoë. She held up one hand. "And this is not ink. It's blood."

Rolfe quickly crossed the distance between them. "Are you all right?" he asked.

She looked up at him with dazed eyes.

His hands clamped on her shoulders. His voice became rougher, more urgent. "Did he touch you? Did he harm you?"

Comprehension gradually dawned. She shook her

413

head, then winced. "Someone hit me on the head. No, really, I'm all right.

But she wasn't all right. She sagged against Rolfe, trying to get her bearings. "He's dead! Varlet is dead, isn't he?" she asked brokenly.

He left her then, and went to examine the man at the desk. "It's Varlet all right. And someone has blown a hole in his head." He picked up one of the papers on the desk, quickly scanned it, and replaced it before returning to Zoë.

She was close to panic. Rolfe could see it in her eyes. And there was not the time to reason with her.

"You're to leave here at once, do you understand?" There was a leashed violence about him that made her quail. "I want you out of here. *Now!* There's a lane. When you come to it, you are to hide yourself until Samson returns with the carriage. Have you got that, Zoë?" He was propelling her none too gently to the open window. "The closed carriage, Zoë, not my curricle. And whatever you do, keep clear of—"

Suddenly, she pulled out of his arms. Though she swayed alarmingly on her feet, she glared into his face. "I'm not going anywhere without Francoise," she said. "Oh God, Rolfe, I'm so afraid that something terrible has happened to her! And it's all my fault."

"Nothing has happened to Francoise."

"Then where is she?"

"I'm here, Zoë, right behind you."

With a start of surprise, Zoë turned toward the door. Her brows knit together. Francoise shut the door quietly and turned the key in the lock, all the

414

while pointing the muzzle of a wicked-looking pistol straight at Rolfe's broad chest.

"You are armed, I believe you told me," she said softly. "If you would be so kind, place your weapon on the floor and kick it toward me."

A pulse beat in Rolfe's cheek as he obeyed Francoise's command. "There is no necessity for this," he said. "What I did not tell you was that my pistol is not loaded. It's useless."

"We shall soon see," said Francoise, and picked it up with her left hand. "Sit down, Zoë, before you collapse," she went on in a voice so devoid of expression that Zoë scarcely recognized it. "Sit," she said again, and gestured with the pistol in her right hand.

"Do as she says, Zoë," said Rolfe quietly.

As if in a dream, Zoë obediently moved away from Rolfe and sank down into the leather armchair Francoise had indicated. "I don't understand," she said, looking imploringly from Rolfe to her friend and then back again.

"I don't suppose there is any point in asking you to let Zoë go?" drawled Rolfe.

"Hardly!"

Rolfe leaned one hip against the desk. He folded his arms. "There are two of us," he said. "And as I told you, my pistol is useless. It would be a grave mistake on your part to think that Zoë would succumb without a fight."

Zoë felt as if her brain was frozen. "Will somebody please tell me what is going on," she said plaintively.

Francoise addressed Zoë, but her eyes and the pistol never wavered from Rolfe. "I never wanted to hurt you, Zoë," she said. "In point of fact, though I used you as the bait for my trap, I made sure that you were safe. I locked you in that room upstairs. If you had only stayed there, it would not be necessary now to do what must be done."

Zoë closed her eyes momentarily, trying to make sense of what she was hearing. She could not believe that Francoise meant to do her harm. Francoise was her friend. And Rolfe was too much at his ease. It did not seem as if he was taking Francoise's threats seriously.

As though the same thought had occurred to her, Francoise said, addressing Rolfe, "No one is going to help you. I made sure that Samson followed your orders. By the time the authorities get here, it will be all over."

Without haste, she leveled the pistol at Rolfe's chest, and Zoë, half rising from her chair, cried out, "Francoise! This is madness! Rolfe has never done anything to hurt you."

"I think I must have done," said Rolfe. "Before you pull that trigger, since, as you say, there is time and enough, indulge me a little. Why have you singled me out for death? We weren't onto you, you know. You were quite safe from detection. You have put yourself at some risk in your determination to get at me. I think you owe me an explanation."

The pistol lowered imperceptibly. Francoise's lips twisted in a travesty of a smile. "By all means," she said. "Do you know, I am rarely given the opportunity to explain myself?"

"I should imagine," said Rolfe pleasantly, "that your position as head of *La Compagnie* is a singularly lonely one."

Francoise's eyes narrowed on Rolfe. "I am *Le Patron,* yes. You must have surmised as much when you walked in here and found Paul Varlet at his desk?"

"Is this Varlet's house?" asked Rolfe, looking around interestedly.

"No. The house belongs to me. Not that that is common knowledge, of course. Very soon, I shall be in a position to openly take up residence. For the moment, however, the records show that the house is let to Paul Varlet."

"I'll wager Varlet did not know it," said Rolfe dryly. "So, you lured him here with the promise that he could have Zoë. As a matter of interest, did you set this up before or after you knew the duel was to take place?"

"You are doing so well," said Francoise, employing the same conversational tone as Rolfe, "that I think I shall let *you* tell *me.*"

Zoë had to choke back a sob. If one did not hear the words, she was thinking, one would imagine that her companions were engaged in polite drawing-room conversation, so sanguine, so pleasant, so utterly civilized was their manner towards each other. She, on the other hand, was near to fainting with panic.

"Correct me if I am wrong," said Rolfe, "but I see it this way. You hoped that Varlet's scheme to get rid of me would save you the trouble?"

"You have it exactly," agreed Francoise.

"What scheme?" demanded Zoë.

"The duel," answered Rolfe shortly. His attention reverted to Francoise. "The assassin—was that your idea or Varlet's?"

"That was Varlet's doing. There is no place in *La Compagnie* for the likes of an Andre Valazé. He was one of Varlet's lovers. He's addicted to opium. I shouldn't think you were ever in any real danger from him."

"Your hopes were pinned on Tresier?"

She shrugged faintly. "He's known to be a crack shot. However, these things have a way of going awry."

Rolfe's brows rose fractionally. "And you were prepared for the worst?"

She laughed, very softly, and there was something in the sound that was more chilling than anything that had gone before. "Varlet's obsession for Zoë played right into my hands. It's common knowledge that you and he are rivals. When your bodies are found, it will be assumed that you killed each other over Zoë."

"Masterly!" said Rolfe, and his eyes gleamed with admiration.

"Thank you," said Francoise.

"But there is more, if I am not mistaken?"

"You're very astute," allowed Francoise.

"If I were astute," said Rolfe, with a small ironic smile, "I would not be here with you now."

There was a silence, then they both laughed softly, and Zoë pressed a hand to her eyes, wondering if her companions were truly demented.

"You've left evidence to implicate Varlet in *La Compagnie*," said Rolfe, turning sideways to glance over his shoulder at the papers which strewed the desk.

"More than enough," agreed Francoise. "When this is over, the authorities will have all the proof they need to convict Varlet twice over as the head of the society."

"But he never was involved, was he?"

"What do you think?" she returned provocatively.

"Do you know, I was coming to suspect your husband?"

"Charles?" Amusement laced her voice. "I will admit, it did occur to me to set him up as the scapegoat. But all things considered I think you will agree, Varlet is the more logical choice."

Zoë's shocked gasp turned the heads of her companions, "But Francoise! You *love* Charles!"

The mask of cool politeness slipped. Francoise's eyes flashed fire. "How could I possibly love that boring old fool? I married him because it was the expedient thing to do. Because of your husband, *La Compagnie* was crushed. We were being hounded like dogs. I had to return to France. Charles moved in the right circles. What choice did I have?"

"But . . ." Zoë shook her head as if to clear the confusion of her thoughts. Hoarsely, she whispered, "You were devoted to Charles."

Francoise made a small sound of derision. "In my whole life, I was devoted to only one man, and he was my brother, Betrand."

"Ah," breathed Rolfe theatrically. "So Betrand was your brother! Now I begin to understand."

He moved slightly, and the pistol jerked up. "It fits," said Rolfe.

"What fits?" asked Zoë.

"The attack on me in London which nearly cost me my life. All this . . ." He waved one hand vaguely.

Rolfe's words only added to Zoë's confusion.

419

Seeing her blank look he explained, "This is in the nature of a personal vendetta. Your friend, Francoise, holds me responsible for the death of her brother."

"You *were* responsible," cut in Francoise. "You and that little actress between you. I saw you with her outside the theatre." In an aside to Zoë, she said, "Do you remembet that night, Zoë? You saw them too. The spectacle was disgusting." Turning once more to Rolfe, she went on, "You and the girl were locked in a passionate embrace. I knew you were Zoë's husband. I knew that my brother had been seeing that actress before his death. I began to put two and two together. Within days, I discovered that you worked for British Intelligence. The last thing I did before I left England was order your execution."

"And the girl? Did you order her execution also?" For the first time, a trace of steel edged Rolfe's words.

Francoise's lip curled. "She deserved to die. She betrayed my brother."

Zoë's panic-stricken tones cut across the terse words. "I don't understand any of this. What has either of you to do with *La Compagnie?*" In point of fact, she was coming to have a fair idea. But her brain refused to accept it.

It was Francoise who answered her plea. "Your husband, as you must know, is with British Intelligence. Evidently, his assignment was to infiltrate and destroy *La Compagnie* in England. He succeeded."

Rolfe acknowledged her words with a slight inclination of his head. "And your friend, Francoise, as you must have gathered, is the prime mover in that secret society of which everyone goes in terror. In short, she is *Le Patron*."

The words seemed to hang on the air. Zoë had never heard of *Le Patron* and was still trying to make sense of what Rolfe said when Francoise began to speak again.

"Do you know I was never more shocked than when I finally realized that you and Ronsard were one and the same person? It struck me, then, that the spate of bad luck that had dogged *La Compagnie* in recent weeks was more than mere coincidence."

"No!" said Zoë faintly. "Rolfe came to Paris for one reason only and that was to persuade me to return to England with him. Tell her, Rolfe."

"I think not," said Francoise.

"So," said Rolfe, ignoring Zoë's imperative, "you penetrated my disguise. Why not simply denounce me? Why go to so much trouble to get rid of me?"

"Obviously," said Francoise, "you have friends in high places. I could not take the chance, you see, that they would not protect you. Was I wrong?"

"No. As it happens, you were right."

The amusement in Rolfe's tone only added to Zoë's sense of unreality. She had begun to grasp, however, something of what was going on. This was no misunderstanding, no hoax. All was in deadly earnest. Francoise was set on doing away with first Rolfe, then Zoë, just as soon as the conversation was exhausted.

But, as Rolfe had said, it was two against one. Surely Francoise could not suppose that she would sit tamely by and see her husband murdered before her eyes? Evidently, Francoise had put her, Zoë, down as little more than an annoying gadfly, and just as easily dealt with.

Belatedly, Zoë remembered the letter opener in the upstairs chamber, and she groaned. She had left it there, on the floor, after she had retrieved the key. She shut her eyes, thinking that she must be the stupidest woman in Christendom. The pair before her were made of much sterner stuff. They were evenly matched. That thought gave her hope. Perhaps all was not lost. Rolfe's confidence was something to behold.

Her eyes shifted to the threatening figure of her friend. It struck her, then, that Francoise was enjoying herself immensely. It was as though she was an actress, giving the performance of her life before an audience. All that was lacking was the applause.

The performance appeared to be coming to an end. Zoë made haste to keep it going.

"What about that note from Claire?" she asked.

"A forgery, my dear. But you must know that now."

"Claire never corresponded with you! How could you copy her handwriting?"

"Zoë, I had the run of your house. Think about it. It was no great feat to steal one of your sister's letters."

"That was not very nice," snapped Zoë. "I trusted you. I thought you were my friend. And now you tell me that you are going to murder me?"

The glitter in the overbright eyes became muted. "It was never part of my plan to hurt you." Her voice held a suggestion of regret. "You were always kind to me, Zoë. Against my will, I found myself liking you. I had hoped to keep you out of it. I locked you in that upstairs chamber. Sooner or later you would have been discovered. But now you are a witness, you see."

A thought struck Zoë. Rather indignantly, she demanded, "Was it you who hit me on the back of the head?" and she instantly cringed to think that out of everything that had happened or might soon occur, she had taken offense over something so trifling.

"It was necessary," said Francoise, "so that you would not hear the report of the shot when I dealt with Varlet. At that time, I was trying to protect you."

Francoise straightened. The performance was about over. Zoë could not think of a single thing to say to prolong it. The final act was beginning.

Very softly, Rolfe said, "This isn't going to work, you know."

The ensuing laugh chilled Zoë to the bone. "It will work," said Francoise. "Admit it. I've outwitted you."

"I'm afraid not," said Rolfe in a mock-sorrowful tone.

He was the picture of indolence, thought Zoë. And as though to emphasize that he had nothing to fear, he lazily crossed one booted foot over the other as he lounged against the desk.

"You see, Francoise," he said gently, "I was onto you before we left the house."

"I take leave to doubt that."

"You made a fatal blunder, my dear."

Her laugh sounded forced. "All right, I'll humor you. What blunder?"

"When you mentioned my limp. There is only one person in the whole of Paris who knows about

423

that attack on me in London. You gave yourself away with that careless slip."

"What attack?" asked Zoë. "That's the second time you've mentioned it."

Francoise inclined her head in acknowledgment of the hit. "Even so," she said, "I might have heard of it from Charles. He still corresponds with friends in England."

"There were other things."

"You're playing for time," she said, "and it won't do you a bit of good. Still, you have piqued my interest. Don't stop now."

"Thank you. Nothing glaring, you understand, just trifles that confirmed my suspicions. The address of this house for one thing. To execute your plan, it was necessary for you to come with me. What better way to ensure that I would not leave you behind than by pleading ignorance of the address but knowledge of the whereabouts of the house itself? And then there was your insistence that the authorities must be informed. That had me puzzled for a time."

"And what conclusion did you reach?" asked Francoise dryly.

"That your insistence was at best only halfhearted and a ploy to discover whether I really meant to come alone or whether I would bring reinforcements."

"And knowing all that, you still walked into my trap?" A muscle clenched in Rolfe's cheek, and Francoise laughed softly. "I think I understand. You said it yourself. You would not take the chance on anything happening to Zoë. You must have suffered agonies on the way here, not knowing whether she was alive or dead!"

"I could barely keep my hands from strangling you," agreed Rolfe amiably.

"Rolfe," cut in Zoë in a very subdued voice. "I don't think I've ever told you that I love you. I should like to say it once before I die. I love you, Rolfe."

In an amused tone, Rolfe said, "I'll remind you of those words, kitten, when this is all over."

"Rolfe!" shrilled Zoë. "I want the words!"

"Oh, very well, then," said Rolfe, not very graciously. "I love you, but you know that already."

The pistol was raised. Though Rolfe's expression remained unchanged, in that moment, Zoë knew the end had come. She edged forward in her chair.

"Easy, Zoë," said Rolfe. "I'm not Paul Varlet. Your friend won't get rid of me as easily as she got rid of him." His next words were addressed to Francoise. "I can scarcely credit that he just sat at this desk and allowed you to pull a gun on him. How did you do it?"

Francoise lowered the pistol fractionally. When she laughed, Zoë winced.

"My dear Rivard, you may believe that it was child's play. I promised to deliver Zoë for a rather substantial sum of money. Varlet sat down at the desk to write out the draft on his bank. Zoë was all he could thing about. The rest you may surmise."

The pistol jerked up. Zoë started to her feet. "No!" Zoë screamed as Francoise pulled the trigger. Nothing happened. Nor had Rolfe moved from his negligent pose.

"I disabled it," he drawled, "when the curricle went into the ditch. And you may take my word for

425

it, my pistol is useless. I never thought to reload it after the duel with Tresier, you see."

A look of awful comprehension crossed the woman's face. She flung both pistols at Rolfe's head. He ducked, then went to retrieve them. Francoise backed toward the locked door. A movement at the open window caught her eye. The bloodied figure of a young man climbed over the sill. Zoë recognized him as André Valazé. In his good hand he held a pistol.

"André. Thank God you are here!" Francoise cried out. "He murdered Paul. I couldn't stop him. They were quarreling over the girl. Kill him, André, kill him, and I'll take care of the girl."

There was a deafening roar as a pistol went off. Smoke filled the room. A blessed paralysis seized Zoë's brain as she waited for the end to come. The smoke cleared. She heard someone sobbing. It was the boy, André. He was bent over the crumpled body of Paul Varlet. Rolfe was crouched over Francoise's inert form.

The room was tilting crazily, but there was a question hammering inside Zoë's head that must be asked. "Rolfe!" Was that her voice, so thin and distant? She must concentrate. "Rolfe," she said again, "was your pistol loaded or was it empty?" She knew that her life depended on his answer.

"It was loaded, of course," he answered absently. "Oh God, she's dead! Francoise is dead!" He looked over at Zoë. "What the deuce . . . ?"

For the first time in her life, Zoë fainted.

Chapter Twenty-five

Zoë was to remember very little of the hours which followed. She was in shock. Her mind was numb. The horror of those last minutes with Francoise seemed unreal. She expected to wake and find that the whole thing had been nothing more than a bad dream.

By degrees, she began to get a grip on herself. Even so, again and again, she found herself reliving that awful scene in the bookroom. Snatches of conversation came back to her. There was so much to assimilate, so many unpalatable truths which must be faced. The girl whom she had regarded as her very best friend was a cold-blooded killer and the brain behind a fanatical secret society. Rolfe's presence in France was more devious than he had let on. He was an agent of some sort with the avowed purpose of destroying *La Compagnie*.

That truth was borne in on her when they returned to the house in St. Germain. The gentleman who met them in the foyer was vaguely familiar. Housard, Rolfe called him. The name jogged Zoë's memory. And then it all came back to her. Housard had posed as their coachman on the ride from Rouen to Coutances. She had not set eyes on him since the

427

night of the Devonshires' party.

She could sense his jubilation. Rolfe was jubilant also, though he was more restrained with it, and it came to Zoë that he wished to spare her feelings. But though the gentlemen spoke in low tones, they failed to disguise their sentiments—against every expectation, *Le Patron* had been unmasked and dealt with.

They moved to the yellow *salle*. Zoë tried to concentrate on the conversation which buzzed around her head, but she could not prevent her thoughts straying.

At one point, she struck in, "What about the boy, Andre Valazé? What is going to happen to him?"

"Samson is taking him to a safe house," answered Rolfe, addressing Housard rather than Zoë.

Zoë's head was reeling. "Is . . . is Samson in this too?" Her gaze flitted from Rolfe to Housard.

"Samson is my man," answered Housard shortly before asking Rolfe, "How much does Valazé know?"

"Very little, I should say, otherwise he would have stopped Francoise sooner than he did. No. It's my surmise that he arranged this rendezvous with Varlet to report on the duel. He must have come upon us in the bookroom in time to overhear Francoise boast that she had shot Varlet. The poor devil was crazy with grief."

Housard's next words electrified Zoë. "It makes no difference. By tomorrow, he will be a wanted man." He heard her sharp intake of breath and hastened to add, "Because of the duel, is all I meant. He was recognized. But you may believe that no one's interests will be served if the boy should be questioned by the authorities. We shall see that he gets safely away."

Zoë looked to be unconvinced, and Housard diplomatically interposed, "If we had wished Valazé ill, we had only to leave him in that house for the authorities to find. He's safe, Zoë. I give you my word."

After an interval, she nodded. Her eyes moved to Rolfe. "And Charles? Poor Charles! What is he going to think of . . ." She found it impossible to voice her thoughts and added lamely "all this?"

Rolfe made his tone as gentle as he could make it. "He must never know the whole truth, of course. Put it out of your mind, Zoë. Everything has been arranged."

"How has it been arranged?"

She recoiled at his next words. Francoise's body was to be conveyed to an alley off one of the streets close to the Palais Royal. Everything of any value had already been removed from her person. When she was found, it would appear that she had been waylaid by footpads.

"And . . . and Paul Varlet?" she asked.

"Everything has been left at the house exactly as we found it."

"I see," said Zoë, and lapsed into another reflective silence as the gentlemen took up where they had left off.

The days which followed were equally nightmarish for Zoë. Circumstances necessitated delaying their departure for England, and she must act as naturally as possible.

As was to be expected, Charles Lagrange was desolate when his wife's body was found. "I warned her about going about without an escort," he told Zoë brokenly. "Francoise was so headstrong! She would never listen to reason. I feared something like this would happen one day."

429

Zoë's distress was acute. She did not have the words to console him. Rolfe showed greater presence of mind. His glib explanations left Zoë feeling deeply perturbed.

"I blame myself for not seeing her to her door," he said. "As I told you, I took her for a spin in my curricle. But Francoise insisted that she had an errand to run. And I could not persuade her to go home for her maid."

Later, Zoë was to ask Rolfe, "Why did you say that? Why mention it at all?"

His tone was harsh when he answered, "I must say something. What if someone saw Francoise with me? She *was* in my curricle. How would it look if I tried to conceal it?"

It came as no surprise to anyone when the diplomat Ronsard gave out that he was removing Zoë from Paris in the interests of her health. The dark circles under her eyes, the wan cheeks, the absent-minded lapses when she was in conversation—all gave evidence of the depths of her grief for Madame Lagrange.

Rolfe's forethought was staggering. Nothing was left to chance. The way was being paved for their permanent removal from France. Zoë was instructed to write a letter to Theresia Tallien indicating that she had decided to return to her husband in England. The letter would be passed along in due course.

"And what about Ronsard?" Zoë asked. "What is going to happen to him?"

"It will be given out officially that he has been posted abroad." Something about Zoë's look compelled Rolfe to add, "The last thing we want is to

430

rouse suspicion. If we disappeared without a trace, how long do you think it would be before people began to ask questions about your friend's death? Trust me, Zoë. This way is best."

Even the house in St. Germain was not lost to Leon. With a thoroughness which Zoë was coming to expect in her husband, Rolfe made sure that Devereux's Bank held the deed in Leon's name.

"One day, when this is all over," said Rolfe vaguely, "Leon will be able to claim his birthright."

They were making their escape, only it did not seem like an escape to Zoë. Everything was aboveboard. Their papers were perfectly proper. The only odd note was that Salome was going with them, and the man who was posing as one of the coachmen was not Housard this time, but Leon.

On the journey, Zoë scarcely exchanged two words together with Rolfe. She was lost in her own thoughts. Even the hustle and bustle of each successive hostelry where they stopped for refreshments and to change horses could not jog her from her reveries. And each night, just as soon as she had partaken of the supper that was laid on, she retired to her chamber with a bare nod in Rolfe's direction. Nor did Rolfe make a move to join her.

Rolfe was not sure what to expect from Zoë when they reached the last station in their journey toward the coast. He had taken the liberty of arranging a little surprise for his wife in the house that had been rented for them.

"A priest? For what purpose?" she asked.

Rolfe was prepared to use force if need be. It wasn't necessary. They kneeled before the priest with Leon and Salome as their witnesses, and in a matter of minutes, the thing was done.

Afterwards, Zoë said, "This isn't legal in France, you know. Only civil marriages are legal nowadays."

"I care nothing for French law," he replied cuttingly. "In England, it will serve."

Rolfe watched her, trying to read her expression. But her face gave nothing away. As each day had slipped into the next she had withdrawn into herself, ignoring him as if he were a stranger, as if he meant nothing to her. He was furious with her, and furious with the turn of events that had forced him to reveal his role in crushing *La Compagnie*.

By her lights, he supposed that she had reason to be wary of him. He had deceived her into thinking that she was the only reason he had come into France. In point of fact, she *was* the only reason. His assignment with Housard was the price he had been forced to pay for her safe return. Not to put too fine a point on it, Housard had blackmailed him.

On the one occasion he had raised the subject, attempting to exonerate himself, Zoë had denied that there was anything wrong.

"You don't have to explain anything to me," she said. "I'm grateful to you. Don't you think I know that my brother stands in your debt? I'm no fool, Rolfe. Without your intervention, God knows what would have become of Leon or me, for that matter."

"Then what's wrong?" he demanded. "Why do you make strange with me? Is it the duel with Tresier? Is it because I didn't intervene when Valazé shot Francoise? There must be some reason for you setting me at a distance. You've turned against me, Zoë, and I want to know why."

It was evident that his words shocked her. "Don't

432

be absurd!" she said. "Of course I haven't turned against you! It's just that . . ." she faltered, then ended in a rush, "It's just that I thought I knew you, but I see now that I do not know you at all."

He thought he understood. In that final confrontation with Francoise, Zoë had witnessed a side of his character that he would have preferred her not to see. She was shocked, naturally. He had been cold-blooded and ruthless. For Francoise's fate, he had felt not one ripple of regret, nor would he pretend otherwise. Zoë must see him as some sort of monster. He was well aware that, formerly, she had looked upon him as something of a knight errant.

Tant pis, he thought viciously. Perhaps he wasn't the man she thought he was. But he was the only man for her. When they were back in England, he had every confidence that he could make Zoë see reason. He would break through that wall of remote politeness when she had no one to turn to but himself.

As things stood, Zoë's brother and maid were always within earshot. And Zoë was not above using Leon and Salome as a buffer between them. Rolfe was hedged about and knew it. Once in England, however, things would be very different. He would make sure of it.

The journey from the coast of Normandy to Jersey and thence on to Weymouth and London was made without a hitch. They arrived at Rolfe's house in St. James well before dark descended. As Zoë and Leon went off to their respective chambers to unpack their boxes and wash the dirt of their travels from their skin, Rolfe closeted himself with his steward. It was

433

some time before he got round to going through the considerable correspondence which had piled up in his absence, and longer yet before he came upon a letter addressed to Zoë.

Without compunction, he opened it. The letter was from her sister Claire. Rolfe lost no time in tracking down Zoë. On the stairs he met Leon.

Without stopping, he waved the one-page epistle in the air. "It's from your sister," he said. "Claire is alive and well. She's in Boston."

When Rolfe barged into his wife's chamber with Leon hard at his heels, he found Zoë in her wrapper, having stepped out of her bath moments before. Salome was brushing her hair.

Unable to contain himself, Leon burst out, "Claire is in Boston, Zoë! She's alive and well! God, can you believe it? We've found Claire!"

With trembling fingers, Zoë took the letter from Rolfe's hand.

"She sailed from Bordeaux on the *Diana*," said Rolfe, smiling into her eyes.

She quickly scanned the contents of the letter. Her face fell. The letter said very little more than Rolfe had told her except that Claire was well and that she was to give her letter into the safekeeping of a gentleman who was bound for England. Zoë looked at the date and her spirits sank even lower.

"The letter was written a year ago," she said faintly.

But nothing could dim Leon's exuberance. He grabbed for Salome and danced her round in a circle. "Claire is in America," he chanted. "We've found her. We've found her."

"Rolfe?" asked Zoë, her voice and expression half fearful, half hopeful.

Rolfe laid a reassuring hand on her shoulder. "We know that Claire sailed on the *Diana*. We know her direction. It's more than we hoped for. As soon as it may be arranged, I'll send someone to go and fetch her."

"I'll go," said Leon at once.

"Fine," said Rolfe. "Leon will track her down, kitten. And when he does, he'll bring her to you, I promise."

It was inevitable, from that moment on, that Zoë's reserve toward Rolfe would thaw, and just as inevitable that Rolfe would make capital of this chink in her armor as soon as possible.

He came to her chamber late of the same night. She was sitting on the edge of her bed, gazing into space.

"I've been patient with you," he said, and he drew her unresistingly into his arms.

"Yes."

With one hand, he tilted her chin up. Their eyes met and held, hers wide and enigmatic, his heavy lidded, smoldering. His head descended, and he captured her lips. He kissed her again and again, softly at first, and then with growing hunger. She stood passively in the shelter of his arms, following his lead, not trying to evade the response he so easily evoked. He wanted entrance to her mouth, and she obediently parted her lips for the rhythmic surge and thrust of his tongue.

He took her arms and draped them around his neck. "Zoë," he said, and the word was almost a plea. Her fingers splayed out, and she ran them across his hard muscular back and shoulders, the way he wanted her to, pressing herself against him, tempting

435

him with her softness.

He found the knot on the belt of her wrapper and quickly dispensed with it. The buttons on the front of her nightrail were similarly dealt with. His hand pushed inside her bodice and cupped her naked breast, his thumb tormenting the engorged nipple until Zoë whimpered with the pleasure of it.

That soft sound of arousal sent Rolfe's senses spinning. He crushed Zoë to him, stealing her breath, straining her against the hard length of him. Zoë didn't try to pull away. She arched into him, her soft cries of pleasure inviting more.

Rolfe went wild for her. He didn't take the time to remove her night clothes. His hands swept under her skirts, sliding over her bottom, hauling her hard against the cradle of his thighs.

It was too fast, and he could not seem to stop himself.

In a fever of impatience, he lowered her to the bed, thrusting her skirts to her waist. His hand was between her legs, stroking into her, arousing her to the same mindless pitch of wanting that fired his own blood.

Breathing harshly, he pulled back to tear out of his clothes. Zoë cried out, her arms reaching to pull him back to her. When he spread her legs wide, his features were taut with the violence of his passion. He felt a fierce surge of satisfaction when his eyes took in Zoë's dazed look. She wasn't submitting to him. She was shivering with desire, as eager for him as he was for her.

Then he was over her. "I love you," he said, the moment before he drove into her, blending their bodies as one.

Once was not enough for him. He could not get enough of her. He had smashed through her wall of reserve, not with words, but with something that went beyond words. He loved her. She loved him. Long, involved explanations of his past iniquities might prove disastrous. In that shattering act of love, everything else paled into insignificance.

Sated at last, he allowed her to drift into sleep. Even then, her capitulation was complete. She curled into him, accepting his cupped hand across her breast. With one powerful leg, Rolfe anchored Zoë more closely to his naked length. "I love you," he said. He had to nudge her before her voice gave him back the words.

Rolfe was more than content. He was basking in an unfamiliar haze of sensual satisfaction. Every man should be married, was his benevolent thought, so long as he chose for his wife a woman made in the image of Zoë. He could not get over how fortunate he had been to snatch her for himself.

She denied him nothing. Zoë's bed had become his bed. Morning, noon, and night, he took his fill of her. And if sometimes he found her regarding him with a strangely considering eye, he shrugged it off as of little consequence. In every way that counted, she belonged to him. Her reserve was natural to her. She loved him. Hadn't she said so? Zoë was not the sort of woman to hold grudges. And so she had proved to his complete satisfaction. There was no question that he must strive to earn his place in his wife's good graces. But that was Zoë. She had that happy knack of making a man feel ten feet tall.

Contrary to Rolfe speculations, Zoë did not dwell overlong on the deceptions he had practiced. The duel with Tresier, the fiction that her husband had come into France with the sole purpose of persuading her to return to England— these things were pushed to the periphery of her mind. Rolfe was right in this, however—it was the scene in the bookroom with Francoise that was responsible for Zoë's lingering reserve.

Zoë was thinking that it would take a lifetime to understand the man who was her husband. When they made love, all her misgivings melted away. He was only Rolfe to her Zoë, male to her female, and her perfect mate. But at other times, she would brood on that nightmarish scene in the bookroom when Rolfe and Francoise had played out their deadly game.

That Rolfe Zoë did not recognize. That man filled her with awe. In the face of overwhelming odds, he had conducted himself with a disregard which bordered on insanity. *That* Rolfe was more fearless than was wise. He had faced down his adversary knowing full well that she had the power to annihilate him. Hadn't he told Zoë that his pistol—the one he had kicked to Francoise on command—had been loaded? And hadn't Francoise had that very same pistol in her own hand?

Those two, decided Zoë, were cast in the heroic mold. They had been well matched. It was more than that. Like two seasoned Roman gladiators of old, they had gloried in every thrust and parry of their spine-chilling contest. While she—would she ever forget it?—had fainted clean away from sheer panic. Just to think of it made her blush in mortification.

Hero. Rolfe was a hero. And if Francoise had chosen a different course, she would have been mourned as a heroine. Of such were martyrs made. One must, of course, admire them in their different ways. They were above ordinary mortals such as herself. They were giants. When she measured herself against them, she felt like a veritable dwarf. She wondered how soon it would be before Rolfe took her measure and found her wanting.

Chapter Twenty-six

Toward the end of June, Leon embarked on the first leg of the long journey which would take him to find Claire. It was time, thought Rolfe, to set his house in order, time to make amends to Zoë for all the unpleasantness she had been made to endure in the past. In short, he proposed that they remove to his estate in Kent.

Zoë heard this suggestion with the deepest misgivings. She could not forget the humiliation she had suffered at the hands of Rolfe's mother, or the pain of Rolfe's rejection. He had, quite literally, deposited her at the Abbey like so much baggage and then he had returned to town to pursue his own pleasures.

Rolfe watched Zoë's expression with veiled interest. The closer their carriage drew to the Abbey, the more finely drawn her features became. Her flow of small-talk gradually dried up. He had a fair idea of what was going through her head.

"Things will be very different this time," he told her. "For one thing, I shall be there to lend my support."

She looked at him, then, with those huge eyes of hers. "Won't you have business to attend to in town?" She was remembering the last time when Rolfe's excuse for staying away was that the press of business necessitated his presence in London.

"That business is over," he said. "You must know that I was working with Housard even then to unmask the members of *La Compagnie*. Now that I've resigned from that side of things, I'm free to pursue the life I love. At heart, I'm a farmer, Zoë. You'll see."

For a moment her eyes warmed and a smile touched her lips, but only for a moment.

"What is it?" asked Rolfe.

"I was thinking of Francoise."

Rolfe captured Zoë's hands in a comforting clasp. Zoë's knowledge of Francoise was very sketchy and Rolfe was determined that it should remain so. She knew only that her friend had been *Le Patron,* the mastermind behind a society fanatical to Revolutionary principles. She knew nothing of Francoise's lust for wealth and how she had used *La Compagnie* to pursue her own ends.

Zoë also knew nothing of a communication from Housard which had reached Rolfe via the War Office. Housard had been making inquiries into Francoise's background. He was almost sure that *La Compagnie* was the conception of Francoise's father. When he had gone to guillotine, one of his sons had stepped into his shoes. How and when Francoise had taken over the reins of the society was a matter of speculation.

"Don't waste your sympathy on Francoise," said Rolfe quietly. "She was quite without scruples." He was remembering how Francoise intended to snuff out Zoë's life without batting an eyelash.

"I don't," said Zoë. She was remembering how Francoise had trained the pistol on Rolfe without a

441

tremor. After an interval, she observed faintly, "If Valazé had not appeared when he did . . . oh God . . . I can't be sorry that Francoise met with her just desserts. All the same, I am glad that you were not the one to mete out justice."

Rolfe patted Zoë consolingly. He chose not to reveal that if the boy had not killed Francoise he would have been compelled to do the deed with his own hand. When he and *Le Patron* had faced each other in that room, they had both known that no quarter would be asked or given.

Observing Zoë's pensive little face, Rolfe exerted himself to lead the conversation into more pleasant channels. He succeeded remarkably well. It was only as the coach began the descent toward the Abbey that she remembered the coming ordeal.

She approached the door to the drawing room with drooping shoulders and flagging steps. Rolfe's hand on her elbow allowed no delay. He swept her inside. The small buzz of conversation suddenly died. Then, as if on cue, in perfect unison, the cry arose.

"Welcome home, Zoë. Welcome home!"

Later that night, in the privacy of their chamber, Zoë said to her husband, "You arranged the whole thing!"

"I did," he admitted, meeting her eyes in the looking glass. His fingers deftly undid the row of tiny buttons at the back of his wife's gown.

The gown loosened and Zoë stepped out of it. She threw it on the back of a chair.

Rolfe moved to the bed where he stretched full length on top of the feather coverlet. Locking his hands behind his head, he watched Zoë as she began to disrobe, and reflected that she could not possibly know how each artless movement inflamed a man's senses to fever pitch.

In the act of stepping out of her petticoats, Zoë paused. "You came on ahead. You must have done."

Rolfe grinned. "Those two days I left you to attend to business? I came down here to set my house in order. As I told you, kitten, things are going to be very different this time around."

Zoë cocked her head and slanted him a frankly curious look. She still found it hard to take it all in. A team of craftsmen had descended on the old dower house where the dowager was to take up residence as soon as the work was completed. Charlotte, blooming, was engaged to be married to a gentleman whom she had met while he had been visiting friends in the neighborhood. Sir Reginald and she were to be wed within the month, so she shyly informed Zoë, when they would remove to his estate in Hampshire.

"I shall be lonely without you, Charlotte," Zoë had observed.

"Nonsense," cut in Rolfe. "I shall be here. And you will have your hands full refurbishing these old halls. I thought something in the style of your house in St. Germain. You know, elegant without sacrificing comfort. I shall miss that house."

The dowager could not restrain her protests. "But Rolfe, the Abbey has remained very much as it is for generations. I never saw fit to change—"

"Precisely," said Rolfe in that aloof way of his which disallowed argument. "It's time for a change. And I am giving Zoë *carte blanche* to arrange things to suit herself." And he launched into a description of Zoë's house in St. Germain which had Zoë pinkening with pleasure.

Rolfe, she was thinking, had made it perfectly clear that a wife took precedence over a mother. And if the dowager ever doubted it, she must have known it when they went in to dinner and Rolfe seated her, Zoë, at one end of the dining-room table, directly opposite his own place. It was, Zoë reflected, too much too soon for the dowager to accept with grace. She resolved, then, to find a way to soften what must seem to her mother-in-law a betrayal on her son's part.

"What are you thinking?" asked Rolfe, bringing Zoë back to the present.

"I was thinking that some things don't change."

Rolfe's eyebrows shot up, and Zoë explained, "Ladies Emily and Sara, and their poor, harassed governess, Miss Miekle."

"Oh, I don't know," said Rolfe, patting the empty space beside him on the bed. Zoë obediently padded over and climbed in beside him. "Evidently," drawled Rolfe, "you missed the girls' introduction to Salome."

"Salome?"

"They've met their match, and they know it. I warn you now—those fickle infants mean to desert you." Zoë's lips turned up as he went on, "As I overheard Emily knowledgeably tell Sara, and I quote, 'Everyone knows that black witches have stronger magic than white witches.' So you see, my dear, your reign is coming to an end."

"Rolfe," protested Zoë, laughing, "that's no way to raise children."

"True. But until Reggie carries the lot of them off to his estate in Hampshire, it will serve."

He found a tender spot on Zoë's nape and began to nuzzle. "Rolfe," said Zoë, and after a few false starts, she shyly managed to convey that she was in a delicate condition.

Rolfe cupped her face with both hands. He looked deep into her eyes. "You've made me the happiest man in the world," he said. A dazed look crept into his eyes. "A father! I shall be a father!"

"And I shall be a mother," said Zoë flippantly.

Her jest brought Rolfe down from the clouds. He scanned her face intensely. "You are so young. Oh God, kitten, what have I done to you?"

Zoë started to laugh. "Don't be absurd," she said. "I'm young, yes. But I'm healthy. Don't take on so. Everything will be fine."

It was a very difficult pregnancy. The debilitating nausea, the aching muscles, the false labor pains, the restless sleepless nights — Zoë hated to see Rolfe suffer so. There was no necessity for it. It was she who was having the baby. But it seemed that any small discomfort she must endure was taken up by her husband and magnified tenfold. It was a strange phenomenon, but not unheard of, so the physician told them.

When her time came, as ill luck would have it, a sudden snowstorm descended, completely cutting off the Abbey from the outside world. The roads were impassable. There would be no physician or midwife in attendance. Rolfe must deliver his own child.

Zoë had every confidence in Rolfe, and so she told him. For the first little while, he behaved heroically. Without warning, however, at a most inopportune moment, Rolfe fainted dead away. Two stalwart footmen were summoned and conveyed their master's inert form from Zoë's chamber. The dowager and Salome demonstrated that they were made of sterner stuff. It was they who delivered Rolfe's son.

Much later, when it was all over, and Rolfe, fully recovered, was allowed to return to his wife's room, like any new parents they gazed in rapt astonishment at the miracle they had created.

"He's perfect," breathed Rolfe.

"And as bald as an eagle," pointed out Zoë. She had expected a thatch of dark hair like her own. "And did you ever see eyes so blue?"

Rolfe grinned. "I'm afraid he's going to take after me. Shall you mind very much, my love?"

"I don't mind so long as the next one takes after *me*." She yawned hugely.

Rolfe's grin faded. "Zoë," he said, "you can't ask me to go through that again."

"Was it so very bad, my darling?" she asked solicitously, and brushed an errant lock of blond hair from his brow.

"I fainted!" He looked shamefaced. "I've never fainted in my life before."

"It can happen to the best of us," allowed Zoë generously.

"You must think I'm a veritable coward."

Zoë brought her head up from the pillows and kissed Rolfe lingeringly. "You're no hero," she agreed, her eyes soft with love, "but you are no coward either. You are simply a man, my darling, and in some things women are superior. You'll just have to accept it. Next time, you'll do better."

She drifted off to sleep with a secretive little smile

turning up her lips. She was pleased with him, and Rolfe could not understand the reason for it.

"There won't be a next time," Rolfe promised his sleeping wife with feeling. He meant it.

Time proved him a liar. Rolfe was to discover that he was not immune to his wife's persuasions.

Having babies, he told Zoë a year later, was the most harrowing experience of his whole life.

Exhausted from her labors, Zoë smiled languidly up at him and promised, "You'll do better the next time, dear."

Rolfe groaned. Salome laughed. The dowager gently rocked Rolfe's second son in her arms.

Embrace the Romances of
Shannon Drake